P9-AFZ-591

THE THINKING REED

"Man is but a reed, the most feeble thing in nature; but he is a thinking reed. The entire universe need not arm itself to crush him. A vapour, a drop of water, suffices to kill him. But if the universe were to crush him, man would still be more noble than that which killed him, because he knows that he dies and the advantage which the universe has over him; the universe knows nothing of this."

—PASCAL'S PENSÉES.

THE
THINKING REED

REBECCA WEST

THE WORLD PUBLISHING COMPANY

CLEVELAND AND NEW YORK

Published *by* THE WORLD PUBLISHING COMPANY

2231 WEST 110TH STREET · CLEVELAND 2 · OHIO

By arrangement with The Viking Press

FORUM BOOKS EDITION

First Printing February 1948

THE THINKING REED

I

T H E K N O C K I N G on the door did not wake Isabelle because she had started up from sleep very early that morning. This was a new thing. Until about a fortnight before, she had slept for nine hours every night, no matter when she might have gone to bed. She needed the rest, for she was still young, she was two years younger than the century, she was just twenty-six; and though her white skin never flushed, and her fine small features were as calmly gay as if she were a statue that had been carved looking like that, she was in motion all her waking hours. She was beautiful, she was nearly exceedingly rich, she had been tragically widowed, there was an exotic distinction about her descent from an Orleanist family which had never lost its French character, though it had been settled in St. Louis when that was a fur station in Louisiana. Therefore many people liked meeting her. All sorts of houses were open to her, from the kind where the dirt-dimmed chandeliers seem like snuff-droppings on the bosom of the ancient Faubourg Saint-Germain air, to the kind where the modernist furniture looks like the entrails ripped out of locomotives. Isabelle went to most of them; and in between her visits she rode horseback, hunted the wild boar down in

3

the Landes, sailed a boat at Cannes, played tennis with
the aces, and enjoyed the beating because there was
beauty in the inflicting of it. The game was too fast for
her body, but her mind could always follow it.

There were times, indeed, when she completely ab-
stained from doing any of these things. She would lie
for hours on a chaise-longue, so inert that the folds of
chiffon which dripped from her body to the floor hung
as steady as if they were stone, her clear face upturned
to the ceiling, still bright but not brilliant according to
its custom, like a star reflected in tranquil waters. But
even then her right hand moved ceaselessly, turning on
her wrist as though it were throwing a shuttle. There
was indeed a shuttle at work, but it was behind her
brows. Her competent, steely mind never rested. She had
not troubled with abstract thoughts since she had left the
Sorbonne, but she liked to bring everything that happened to her under the clarifying power of the intellect.
For she laboured under a fear that was an obsession. By
temperament she was cooler than others; if she had not
also been far quicker than others in her reactions, she
might have been called lymphatic. But just as it sometimes happens that the most temperate people, who have
never acquired the habit of drinking alcohol, or even a
taste for it, are tormented by the fear that somehow or
other they will one day find themselves drunk, so Isabelle perpetually feared that she might be betrayed into
an impulsive act that was destructive to such order as
reason had imposed on life. Therefore she was for ever
running her faculty of analysis over in her mind with
the preposterous zeal of an adolescent running a razor
over his beardless chin.

So, between sport and pedantry, she was busy enough, and on most nights her eyes closed the minute her head touched the pillow. But last night she had lain awake for quite a long time facing the fact, which seemed to be adhering to the ceiling just above her bed, that so long as she was linked with André de Verviers, she was the ally and the slave of everything she hated : impulse, destruction, unreason, even screaming hysteria. The accusation that posited a state of affairs shameful to herself, that was barbed with horrible circumstantial details for which there was not the smallest foundation in fact, that was suddenly supposed to have been annulled—and this she found most disagreeable of all—by a violent embrace which could have no logical bearing on it, and was loathsome to her because she wanted the accusation discussed on its own terms and withdrawn as untrue—this must be her daily bread, so long as she was with André de Verviers. This would have been abominable to her in any case, even had there not been so near at hand an embodiment and a promise of the kind of life she longed to live; even if Laurence Vernon had not come over from Virginia to see her.

She was miserable, but she was young. All that day she had ridden in the Forest of Compiègne. She rolled over, she murmured, "Ah, if only Uncle Honoré were here to tell me what to do!" and suddenly she slept. But after a few hours she was as suddenly awake again. She remembered how she had stood in André's room, shaking herself as if his arms had left bonds about her, wiping her mouth impatiently, and crying out, "Yes, that's all very well, but why did you say you were sure I was having an affair with Marc Sallafranque?"

André had not answered her but had shuffled barefoot past her to the table, poured out a glass of Evian, and sat back on the duchesse sofa, taking a long drink. "Oh, how beautiful you are!" he breathed over the rim of the glass, nodding his head in connoisseurship.

"But you must tell me why you said it!" she cried. "I have the right to know!"

He shrugged his shoulders, laughed, and went on sipping the water. The trees in the courtyard rustled, and a tram wailed outside in the Avenue Marceau; the quality of the sounds said, "You are alone with him late at night." The candles in the silver sconces were guttering; their reflection on the mother-of-pearl veneer of the Venetian furniture said, "Everything is romantic here." She knew pride and humility in acknowledging that as he sat here, his fine hand lifting the glass to his fine face, he was not less beautiful as a man than she was as a woman; and about his eyes and mouth there was the signature of wit. This should have been perfection. It was not.

She implored him, "Why won't you tell me? There must be something you've heard! You see it spoils everything! I can't understand how, if you think I've been unfaithful to you with Sallafranque, you can want to make love to me! It spoils everything."

He stretched out his hand to her, holding it as one does when one summons an animal, palm down, the thumb fluttering against the curved fingers. She perceived that her demands seemed like the begging of a pet dog at meals, to be soothed rather than granted by the wise master. It appeared to him that she was making an error in timing, probably due to her foreign taint, by arguing with him about his accusations. That had served its purpose in making trouble, delicious, exciting trouble, which had scourged the nerves to a climax. There was no need, therefore, to worry about its validity now. This principle, that any means was justified to whip up excitement, ran through his life. It explained his royalist politics. He and his friends knew perfectly well that nothing was less likely than that France should have a king; but royalism made for trouble, it provoked libels, face-slappings, duels, deaths, imprisonments, escapes from prison. Therefore they upheld it, they did not reason about it.

She found herself shuddering with disgust. Her knees gave way under her; she had to let herself fall on the sofa beside him.

He thought she had come to be nearer to him, and circled her body with a loving, turning snake of an arm. In a way he loved her. He had the extremest preference imaginable for her society and he evidently believed this to be eternal. Though he did not need her money, he was always asking her to marry him. It was extraordinary how little these considerations alleviated her distaste for the cruel, brawling quality of half his dealings with her.

As his lips touched her ear and found a patch of sensitiveness, her nerves made her break out in complaint, and into the wrong complaint, a lesser one than that which was making her feel clumsy with misery. "And you said it before we left the drawing-room," she mourned. "Madame Vuillaume must have heard."

"She is so stupid she would not have understood if she had," said André comfortably; and, seeing a loophole for his Parisian passion for anecdote, he continued, "Did I ever tell you how her husband made his money? It's rather a good story. When Ferdinand of Bulgaria came to Paris in 1912 . . ."

While he was telling the story, she kept her eyes on the parquet, and in its peat-coloured depths she saw the face of Laurence Vernon, and behind it the avenue of cypresses that led from the old post road to his quiet home, Mount Iris. As André finished, she said, "You do not understand, André. I want to leave you. I want all this to stop."

"Oh, my little one!" he exclaimed. He was really alarmed. She must be quite upset not to laugh at a really funny story like that. "You mustn't say such things to your André. I haven't done anything to make you unhappy, have I?"

She cried out, "Of course you have! Again and again! I tell you I loathe all these scenes and accusations and rages. I want this to come to an end. I don't love you."

"Oh, my little one, how can you say such things? Think what wonderful lovers we are! You are too young," he said, a pedagogic tone coming into his voice, "to realize how exceptionally fortunate we are in that respect."

"But that isn't enough. It doesn't make up for the abuse, the excitement, the hatefulness." To her own surprise she began to weep. "I tell you I can't bear it any longer. I can't go on."

"My poor child," he said remorsefully, taking her in his arms. "Stop trembling like that, you're safe with your André. Ah, I see what the matter is." He assumed an air of solemn authority over physiological mysteries.

"I have been too much for you, I am afraid. My little darling, I am wicked, I should have been more careful of you——"

"You haven't been too much for me," she said, with some indignation. "When I tell you that I am sick to death of the cruel, lying things you say to me and the tempers you fly into, why should you assume that it's something else that's the matter with me? Particularly when the things I'm complaining about nobody could help hating, whereas what you're talking about nobody would mind very much"——she broke off, and he released her with a pat of the hand.

"When a woman is very tired," he said with a return of midwifely sententiousness, "she does not know what is the matter with her. It is then that a man who loves her understands her far better than she does herself. Come, darling, put on your things, I am going to send you home now."

"Yes," she said, "I am going home. And I will never come here again."

"Ah, my darling," he said, down on the floor, where he was looking for his shoes, "when you wake up to-morrow after a good long sleep, you will have forgotten that you ever said or thought these words."

She sighed in despair and stood looking down on him, full of foreboding at his physical power and distinction. He was so finely made, so well dowered with the dignity of grace, that on all fours he was as little at a disadvantage as a tiger. He was an idiot, but his body did not know it. Resting her chin on her clasped hands, she turned and went slowly to the other end of the room. She took her powder-puff out of the bag she had left on the mantelpiece and passed it over her face, peering into the mirror, for here the sconces were not lit, and her reflection swam white in brown darkness shaken by ruddy firelight. With an exclamation of dismay she pressed still closer to the mirror, unable to believe her own expression. She was young enough not to have outgrown the persuasion adults plant in children, that their emotions are trivial and cannot carry the full freight of human joy or woe, so she was surprised to see on her face the mark of utter weariness, of deep suffering.

André's voice called to her from the distance, "Hurry up, darling. You'll be getting cold." At its charm she shuddered: His good looks, his adroitness, his amiability, had lost all power to affect her. They were admirable of their kind, but they were so inextricably entangled with elements she detested that for her they might never have existed. But he had a hold on her for the simple reason that, when he and she were linked by passion, they formed a pattern which was not only æsthetically pleasing but was approved, and indeed almost enjoined, by everything in civilization that was not priggish. When, an hour or so before, he suddenly paused in the denunciations he was hissing into her face, swayed for a minute and grew paler, and then drew his arms softly yet closer and closer round her body and pressed his mouth gently yet heavily on hers, she would have felt stiff-necked and ridiculous if she had resisted, like a republican who refuses to stand up in a London theatre when "God Save the King" is played. She felt herself the victim of some form of public opinion, which was so firmly based on primitive physical considerations that

the mind could not argue with it, and it operated power-
fully even in the extremest privacy.

She felt that again in the little hall, when he opened
the front door, looked back at her, and shut it again.
Looking down on her tenderly, he murmured, "You
have given me more pleasure than any other woman."
She said sharply, "Ha! King Lear!" and wanted to explain that at last she understood how Cordelia had been
cloyed by her sisters' excessive protestations of affection, but she could not prevent her body yielding, not to
the spirit but to the shape of his embrace, as water fol-
lows the contour of a river-bed.

When they were out in the courtyard, with the spring
sky curdled by starlight above them, and the wind swinging in the tree-tops, Isabelle felt relieved. The stars were
very high, and the wind was fresh as if it had come from
woods and fields a long way off to visit these imprisoned
branches. A vast universe stretched away in all direc-
tions from this house; and she would be a fool if she
could not find some path of escape through it. In the
street outside, her long, low, speed-shaped car made her
exultant. Of space there was plenty, and she had the
means to cover it. She called out to wake her chauffeur,
softly but sharply, desperately, as if some danger had
overtaken them while he slept, and they had just time
to fly.

But once she was in the car and André was bending
over her, tucking her rug about her, her sense of freedom left her. Behind his subtle, changing expressions
there was a deadly composure, sign of a settled calm
which would always leave him in a position to seek what

he wanted in the most workmanlike style. She remembered that she had come to his house that night only because at a certain time at Madame Vuillaume's party,
when the Princesse de Cortignac and Monsieur de Gazière
were coming towards the alcove where they sat, he had
gripped her wrist. In another moment that couple of
mauvaises langues would have had something to wag
about, so she had to whisper, "Yes, I will go back with
you now." She had meant to shut the door on him as
soon as she had got into her car, but he had managed to
delay her passage across the pavement until some other
people had come out of the house behind them. Turning
on him to say, "I only told you that because you forced
me, you can't come with me," she looked past him at
the faintly smiling, inquisitive faces of men and women
older than herself, natives of the country where she was
a stranger, compatriots and therefore partisans of André,
watching to see if her movement changed into some
dramatic and betraying gesture. There is nothing more
frightening than the faces of people whom one does not
know but who seem to know one, and be amused by
one. So she had smiled up at André and settled back on
her cushions while he took his seat beside her. That was
why she was still with him, hours later, and entangled
still further with the trivial and the time-devouring. And
it would always be so. Any night that he wanted this
pleasure, so much sillier than drunkenness, of screaming, shaking hate, that dared to change at its ugliest
climax into the likeness of love, his tactical genius would
force her to procure it for him.

    She cried out desperately, "I want to leave you!"

    He gazed on her thoughtfully, like a cook who has

been brought an unfamiliar kind of game and wonders
if she ought to prepare it like quail or like plover. "My
dear," he said gently, "I thought I had made you too
tired. Now I begin to doubt whether I have made you
tired enough. Come back and stay a little longer with
me."

"Oh, don't be such a complacent idiot!" she exclaimed. "Will you stop regarding me as a technical
problem in appeasement? I'm just a woman who intensely dislikes you. Can't you grasp that?"

He bent his face closer to hers. It was like a young
moon in its pale, calm radiance, its remoteness from any
human appeal that might be raised to it. Isabelle flung
herself forward and rapped on the glass, calling to the
chauffeur, "*Allez! Continuez! Vite!*"

Then she sat back and shut her eyes, and thought of
Laurence Vernon and his home. Her husband had taken
her to Mount Iris two or three times in the last few
months before he was killed. One morning when they
were staying in Washington, Roy had found on tho
breakfast table a letter from Laurence, whom he had
come to know through some reunion at Princeton, saying he had read in the papers where they were, and asking them to come and stay with him as soon as possible,
that very day if they could. Roy had said laconically
that Laurence was fine, that they must go and start at
once, since they must be back at the Aerodrome in a
week's time; and she had been put at the telephone forth-
with to call up various people and say that they would
not be able to come to the party after all. She remembered well how she had sat at the window while she
made these calls, rejoicing in the warmth the sunshine

sent through her silk morning-gown, and smiling up at
the high blue sky between the roofs, because the answering voices were always so exactly what the outer world
would have derisively expected from them. They were
at first surprised, not conceiving what alternative could
possibly tempt anybody from a good Washington party;
then they were clouded by the suspicion that the only
conceivable alternative to a good Washington party was
another and better Washington party, and that there
had happened some monstrous overlapping of dates, in
which they had been worsted. But she soothed them, saying that it was because of Roy's next big flight that they
had to leave.

They left the hotel an hour later and motored south
through the warm fall day. Many miles lay before
them, they stopped only once for a stand-up lunch outside a road-house. To the end of her life she would remember again the taste of the fried egg sandwich on
her tongue, could bite again into the stored coolness of
the apple she picked up from the red heap on a trestle
table. Looking back on her marriage, she saw it always as
a time when tastes were more pungent, colours brighter,
sounds clearer and more intelligible than they had ever
been before or since. She would never again see the
country round Laurence Vernon's home as she saw it
the first time with Roy. They had been travelling long
hours when the automobile climbed the height of the
pass; through air soft with evening, soft with autumn,
they looked down on the inspissated fires of the woods
that tumbled up and over half a dozen ranges which
met here and pooled their rivulets in one deep, sinuous,
richly growing valley. This had been a battle-field, Roy

told her. Boys had drunk like beasts from those rivulets, and had given back blood for water as they drank. As she sighed, Roy pointed out a line of cypresses that had found a level plane running through the contours of hills and dales and marched on in a straight black column. That, he said, was the avenue that led to Laurence Vernon's home, which would make her forget that there had ever been war in these parts. Every white pillar of the colonnade was intact, though if one looked closely, it could be seen that each and all were pock-marked with bullets. The Gothic chapel by its side was still as it was when the first Vernon in those parts had built it to relieve his nostalgia. Indoors the china and silver shone on the polished table with a lustre that had not been dimmed by the months they had spent buried in the earth while the looting Yankees searched in vain; and as one sat there one could not believe that both Laurence's grandfathers had been killed in Pickett's Charge in their early twenties, and that even Laurence's father and mother had never seen them, for it seemed impossible that this household was not ordered by someone who had at least been in contact all his youth with someone of the old unshattered South.

Isabelle believed what he had told her when, just as they had turned into the avenue, Laurence Vernon stepped forward out of the cypress shadows and stopped the automobile. He climbed in, was introduced to her, told her in precise words how glad he was to welcome her, and settled down beside her, making civil inquiries. The letters on a book that he laid on his lap spelled Plato. Always, every time they visited him, he strolled down the avenue to meet them, an open book in his hand, and always the letters on the cover spelled an ancient name, Plato, or Lucretius, or Plotinus. Those books had made her wonder if she might not work out some spiritual equivalent of the Einstein theory regarding the re-entrant nature of time, for it was plainly through reading these writers of the remote past that Laurence owed his serene command over the present. Perhaps we are all of us born with one foot on the present, and can grip it with the other only if we swing it far enough back into the past. Her husband, dear Roy, had never made the experiment, and he seemed as if he had to hop about, whirling his arms and legs, to keep his balance on the moment. There was always a fine, fairish glaze on his skin, a dampness about his red-gold curls, as if the sweat of effort had no chance to dry on him. But Laurence, with his fine short pointed brown beard, which he never fingered, his clear brown eyes, which never sparkled, his trim body in his formal and unnoticeable clothes, seemed to rest as comfortably in the hour as if it were a library chair: so comfortably that he could think with a coolness and detachment that she knew to be rare triumphs over the modern world. During that and other visits she learned that he had thought himself right out of the illusions common to the Old South. He preferred the classical to the picturesque any day; he knew that any tradition festered which did not in every generation take fresh vows of service to the timeless gods of justice and reason. But he had not made the error that others who have performed that feat of divestment have fallen into, by adopting the illusions of the New North. He was full of schemes for bringing money down to the South, for developing the resources of his country and making her nobody's old downtrodden mammy; but he was fighting—if one could use that word of an activity in which there was no passion—every attempt to enslave the people by the same conscienceless industrialism as has made the Yankees the drab men-machines they were. When he told her what he was doing, she felt, not only in the interest of the first hearing, but all the many times after, "Laurence is what I would have been if I had been a man. He is living the life I would have liked to live."

They had always known they were the same sort of people, she believed. There had been a moment once, when his recognition of that had struck her mind as clearly as if he had spoken it aloud, in the dining-room, when his neighbour Mrs. Bellamy had come in to take port. It had been a recognition without the smallest practical consequences, it had even been without any emotional effects. For across the table had sat Roy, who had a power over her that made mere community of tastes seem a good that was indisputable but no occasion for enthusiasm, like a plate of cereal; and as for Laurence, everybody knew that he would marry Nancy as soon as her invalid husband was dead. But that arrangement obviously might leave some of his mind free for other imaginings. When Southerners said, "Why, Mrs. George Fox Bellamy, she was Nancy Rivers Taylor," it sounded glamorous, because of the southern habit of speaking the maiden style of every matron as if it had been the name of a beauty, but this woman's thirties were certifying her as insipid, and the trailing cut of her chiffon dress hinted that she had a silly conception of romance. Still, the Bellamy place was but a bare five miles from Mount Iris, and Laurence was much too busy to go far afield seeking for a woman; and there was just enough there, in a water-colour way, to make a man who needed to fall in love able to find his need in her. There could be no question but that vows had been exchanged. If they had not, Laurence would not have risen suddenly from table and closed the French window, for no one of the party was cold, and his acute perceptions must have known it. She had known from his face that that had been a symbolic gesture by which he reminded himself where his obligations lay, by which he shut up the wild thing that had threatened to come out of the unfettered darkness and break up the order he had imposed on his emotions. Isabelle had remembered that when she had come to life after the disaster and realized that no amount of grieving can put together a crashed aeroplane or anything that was in it. It had seemed sensible to come to Europe and treat her life as a room that had to be completely refurnished.

It was her fault for not having attributed due importance to the chiffon dress. It should have told her that Nancy was wholly given to the trailing and the asymmetrical, and when it came to the point, would commit any folly to escape being incorporated in the formal design made by Laurence and Mount Iris. There, Isabelle was conscious, she had for a moment stopped thinking. She should have foreseen that, when the invalid husband died, Nancy would be dismayed by a situation no longer irregular; that she would fling herself into a marriage with a stranger that, for no reason that the character of the involved persons could suggest, gave the disorderly impression of an elopement; and that Laurence would come over to Europe. She should have foreseen that one day Laurence would be shown into her drawing-room and that she would know, as she smiled rather blankly into his more ardent eyes, how justly she had read the meaning of that moment in his dining-room. Now he and Mount Iris were hers for the taking. The thought made her breathe slowly for a minute. It was not greed that she was feeling, for she could have acquired as good a home as Mount Iris by purchase, and several better ones by marriage. It was the most naïvely good part of her that was pleased. She wanted Mount Iris for the life that Laurence lived there, because it seemed to exclude all the heated sort of wrong she feared more than anything else in life. She could imagine herself sitting at dusk, in the hall, looking out at the white afterglow that was divided by the dark pillars of the colonnade, while Laurence walked up and down, passing as a black silhouette across the strips of light, as an ordinary clothes-coloured figure across the strips of darkness, his head down, his step regular and slow. He would be thinking over the material the day had brought him; he would be weaving an intellectual protection for him, for her, for their children, from the arrows that the passion-governed world without shot so recklessly. She trembled in an ecstasy of gratitude; and then was still, as she remembered that at the moment Mount Iris was wholly inaccessible to her.

She had treated her life as a room that had to be completely refurnished. A week after she had landed in Europe, she went to a ball in one of those houses which are in the heart of Paris yet have an ivied cryptic woodland looking in at all the windows that do not give on the streets. She had thought as she went through the shabby-gorgeous rooms, among the plain and unperturbed people, "This is utterly unlike America." America then seemed to her a lying continent that by a gloss of comfort and luxury disguised itself from what it was, a desert stretching fifteen hundred miles to the field where Roy lay among the ashes of his plane, and fifteen hundred useless miles beyond. "This was the place where my forebears lived; it is more truly my country than America. Perhaps it will be kinder to me." It was then that for the first time she caught sight of André de Verviers. He would have been easy to see in any case. His square but not broad shoulders, his long waist and narrow hips, gave him the tense, shaped appearance of a figure on a mediæval church carving, and his head, though decently and masculinely moderate in its beauty, was so definitely cut that it at once impressed the mind as deeply as if long years had made it familiar. But he was specially easy for her to see because he had already turned on her a look of brilliant and candid interest. It had the same meaning as the first look Roy had ever given her. It said, "You are beautiful. Your beauty is so far over the boundary line of argument that I am sure I do not need any more time for deliberation before I commit myself to that opinion. So here and now I claim that you and I are the same sort of person, and that we could be happy companions." A storm of grief ran through her because for nearly a year now Roy had been unable to prove that claim. She preferred him to everyone else, alive or dead. Then she swung about, feeling dogged about this unknown man, bobbing her head up and down under the tide of an adjacent bore's conversation, saying, "Yes, yes." "Yes, yes," waiting till she should find him at her elbow with an introducing friend.

It had seemed certain that their meeting was fortunate. Isabelle had felt no misgiving that day when they were riding in the forest, under the fine black bones of the winter trees, and there suddenly fell from the dark purple sky raindrops like spinning pennies. She and André both transferred to the rainstorm the excitement they felt about the storm of feeling that was gathering within them, and while she exclaimed in fear, he cried out that they must hurry, they must gallop, to come in time to a hunting-box he knew near by. The trees grew thinner before them; they found themselves crossing a tongue of open country, which now looked livid and fantastic because it was suffused by a peculiar grey-green light like the colour of water in a chalk-pit. The dull emerald of the winter grass had become sharp and acid, the few houses looked like painted paper; and on the white road a black string of orphans, and the two bunchy nuns at their tail, seemed stricken with madness as they bent and gesticulated under the invisible missiles of the rain. "Oh, it all looks so strange," she gasped. "It looks as if the end of the world was happening. I want to see this," and she tried to stop her horse. But André was beside her, his hand on her reins. "Hurry, hurry!" he cried. "We must make haste!" They were over the road, they were thundering up a hill, they passed through iron gates and were in a wide avenue in the forest, the smell of a wood fire came to their nostrils. They were in front of an old grey house, soft with the stone embroideries of the Renaissance, which were softer here with moss and fern, flanked on each side by new stables and cottages. When they jumped down from their horses, they were both pale and were breathing deeply, as if they had escaped some real danger.

An old groom came out of one of the cottages, and André hailed him by his name, but Isabelle turned aside abruptly, because she could not bear to feel anybody's eyes on hers. In the centre of the courtyard was the statue of a lion, and though the rain was still falling, she went to stand in front of it. A few dead leaves were rustling in the trap of its open jaws. Presently she heard André's step on the gravel and felt his hand on her arm. He told her that he had telephoned for his car and his groom and that, though the lodge was closed and fireless, they could take shelter in the groom's cottage while they were waiting. She murmured acquiescently, and then he said, in a lower tone, and with some stumbling, "There is a woman watching us from behind the curtains in one of those upper windows. You cannot think how shy that makes me feel. I am young and awkward again, as if I were a boy. But I must say what that woman guesses I am saying, even though the thought of her guessing makes me want to die of confusion. I love you, I love you, I love you." She went on smiling at the dry leaves that turned about in the vault of the beast's jaws. A little rivulet ran down from the brim of her hat to her shoulder. After a silence he told her, "But you must say you love me. Say it, say it. You do not understand how naked and unarmed I shall feel until I hear you say it." She tried to say it, but no sound came. Then she forced her voice, and only achieved a cracked whisper that she stopped out of shame. He laughed, saying,

"My little one, my dear one, you need not tell me any more, now I know that you are feeling helpless and childish as I am."

Yet their meeting had not been fortunate. Worse than that, it had confused Isabelle's ideas of what might be reckoned as good fortune. She had been stunned at finding that a passionate love-affair was not, as her marriage had led her to believe, a prescription for general happiness. It was an indisputable fact that both André and herself found a great joy in each other's company, that as soon as the one came into the room the other felt an electric invigoration of the whole body, a saturation of every movement of the mind by pleasure. It was an indisputable fact that when André took her in his arms, there began for both of them a period of intense delight which softened and broadened down into contentment. To her the logical consequence of these facts was a pervasive mutual kindness, which would give them an armour against the world, so that they could go about calmly, laying out their lives to the best advantage. Hurry and panic, it seemed to her, should have been eliminated from their experience as soon as they recognized the nature of their feelings. And for about a week after they had been like children dazed by sudden passage to fairyland, he had been simple and kind, they had lunched at little places in the country, they had lunched at big places in town and felt invisible, they had met at night at parties where everybody else was invisible. Then life had unfolded in exquisite order, though following no plan. But suddenly he became no longer at all simple, and often not kind, and their life was full of plans but empty of order.

First Isabelle began to notice that whatever they arranged André wished to alter so soon as she had fallen in
with it. If she told him that one day soon she must go
and spend a day with Blanche Yates at her château in the
valley of the Chevreuse, and it was agreed that Thursday was the day they best could spare, the memory of
the agreement went from him before their next meeting. By that time Thursday had come to mean to him
the one possible day for taking her to see his cousin
Berthe, who had such a charming house near Meaux. To
begin with, she dealt with such situations by reminding
him of their agreement, and then, when he denied it on
one ground or another, by trying to find out what these
powerful reasons were which made it imperative they
should go to Meaux on that particular day and made
him ready to put her to the vexation of writing apologetic letters. There were always none; but at that she
only fell silent. If he had this queer streak of eccentricity in him, to suffer it was a small price to pay for
the exorcism he had performed over her loneliness and
despair. She wrote to Blanche, she went to Meaux. But
that did not give them peace. She had said to herself,
when she had first made these concessions, "I shall hate
it if I see that because I am giving in to him he feels
triumphant," but she hated it still worse when she saw
that what he was feeling was disappointment. After a
time she had to admit that he had made his unreasonable demands only in the hope that she would resist them,
and that hope made him screw up his demands to a
higher and higher pitch of unreason, with the horrid
furtive avidity of a drug addict who manœuvres towards
the gratification that he dare not name. She had told

herself again, but a little wearily, that this was not too great a price to pay. But she was relieved when, very soon, the amount of change and whim he was imposing on their common affairs became so great that it began to make his own life quite uncomfortable. In shifting backwards and forwards the date of a visit to a village on the Seine, which was said to be very beautiful in the springtime, he forgot an engagement to dine with a Bourbon duke, which greatly upset him. At once he abandoned that form of sport with her.

But still that did not mean peace. For it was then that André began not to feel but to make use of jealousy. One afternoon, when she went to visit him, he greeted her with bitter reproaches about certain men whom she liked and who liked her. Smiling, she offered him her promise never to see any of them alone again. She had every sympathy with the jealous. To lose her lover to another woman would, she knew, cover her with shame. If in a contest where she had wanted to be first she came in second, she knew that her flayed pride would turn round and round trying to argue away the fact of her defeat, and that her mind would flay it again by coldly asserting the flaws in all such arguments. Of course she would not expose André to the fear of such a hurt. Nor was the sacrifice entailed anything but trivial, since none of these men gave her anything like the happiness she received from André. The cry of exultation with which André heard her promise and caught her in his arms shocked her by its excessiveness. She felt an uneasy suspicion that she had been given a part to act in a play which had seemed innocent only because she had seen just her own lines and cues, but which offended all her sense of values once she heard the other actor's words. That suspicion vexed her again when during the next week or so he made some sudden raids on her hotel sitting-room. She saw that when he always found her alone or in the company of women, he was pleased, and even touched, to a degree that struck her as false in taste. An expression of almost maudlin pity used to pass over his face, as if he were a gambler who, in passing through the heated rooms of a gaming-house, had found the strayed child of some officer of the place quietly playing marbles in a corner. She wished he would take it more simply, as her performance of a sensible and not very difficult promise. But she liked even that expression better than the one she saw on his face when he rose to go. He looked wistfully round the room as if to visualize a delight he had hoped it might have offered him, and she knew that he would have liked to find her with a lover, so that he could make a scene. Or, rather, his desire took a form less brutal and perverse, more purely silly. What he really wanted was to find her with a friend whom he could have pretended to believe her lover, so that he could make a scene.

Nevertheless she had kept to her cloistral ways, though she was conscious that there had crept into her attitude more of the ramrod stiffness of a sentinel rather than the shy recession of a votary of love taking the veil. She would not let this brawl enter her gates, and that was all. But she was to lose her resolute calm, and the force that sustained it, during the time he led her to think he was deceiving her with Princess Natalie Avitzkin. He said he had not done this, that it was she who had misread inevitable movements, which meant no more than that he was doing his social duty, and built fantastic dreams on them; but she knew he spoke falsely. It could not be by accident that he had so perfectly forged the appearance of surfeited ardour hankering after change. Perhaps they might speak of Natalie and how she had looked at the Opera, her fairness giving out rays as she sat in front of the blackness of a box, though Isabelle would not say that it had struck her that he had bowed a little too long and too low before that box. A little later he would talk of the paramount beauty of golden hair, and then would break off in embarrassment, and lay a kind hand on her dark hair, as if he were caressing a child about whose future he knew a sad story. At meals he would become absent-minded and stare into the distance, and then come to himself with a start and be uneasily cheerful and affectionate. He became hesitant and distracted about appointments, and at last presented himself with a melancholy air of bearing up nobly under his own penitence. That evening she dismissed him quickly and coldly, contriving that they should be interrupted, and telephoned to the American Express Company to reserve a compartment for herself and her maid Adrienne on the train for Berlin the next night. She had read that her old Professor of Archæology was staying there till he went on an expedition to Siberia, and she knew that he would probably be glad of her as a bottlewasher and a financial aid.

When André rang up the next morning, Isabelle would not speak to him; and she heard a sound as if her coldness had been so pleasing that the air had been forced out of his lungs in a spasm of delight. She turned away from the telephone, foolish with misery. It appeared to her proven that he had divined her plan of

departure and was so eager to be rid of her that he re-
joiced. To be able to answer any of the other people who
rang her up that day, she had to affect an air of mænad
joy, as if it were with an impulse to hysterical laughter
that she was struggling. "Yes, I am going to Berlin, and
then to Russia!" she cried, as if she were going there to
be whirled up in the vortex of some orgy so riotous that
already it was pulling her off her balance. She never
knew who among them told him; but an hour before
she had to leave the hotel for the station there was a
knock on the door. Her maid opened and then turned
round to her, silently asking what she was to do. André
leaned against the doorpost, so white that she forgot the
trouble that was between them, and asked herself what
frightful physical cause, what sudden malady or over-
dose of drug, could have changed him to this. But in a
croaking cry he asked, "You are going to Russia?" and
she remembered everything, and stiffened. "Of course,"
she said. Adrienne went. He flung himself forward on Isabelle; they collapsed together in trembling entangle-
ment on the top of a shoe box. "But—but—" he stammered, and had to begin again in French, for he had
forgotten all his English, though normally he spoke it
almost as fluently as his own tongue. "You were really
going to Russia?" She whispered, "Yes." He took possession of her again in a long kiss, which was honest, which
gave himself to her, so that she was not ashamed of her
return. From this embrace he broke away to gloat on the
look of her and cry out, "You were going to Russia!
You were going to leave me, just because I made you
jealous!" He was trembling and running with sweat, he
looked like a man who has escaped by a hairbreadth

from a great danger, who has stepped aside just as the propeller begins to whirl and has felt its breath on his brow, who has arrived so late that the gates of the elevator are clanged in his face and he sees it drop like a stone down the shaft. "You were going to do that to me! But I tell you we belong to each other!"

There had followed a whole month of peace, during which they had progressed with their love and had done much towards changing it into permanent kindness. But even then she had been disquieted, and had sometimes raised her fingers between his lips and hers, and shuddered with a lightning flash of enmity as she lay in his arms. For he had cried out, "You were going to leave me, just because I made you jealous!" although she had never told him that he had made her jealous. She felt it as their common misfortune that a sentence which was wrung from him in what was perhaps the sincerest moment of his life should be damnable and unforgettable evidence of his insincerity. She felt the sham hope, the real despair, of a woman whose husband has just come out of a clinic after the last of a series of cures for morphinism, and is doing very well, just as he always has done during the first few weeks after treatment. Not in the slightest degree was she surprised when he began to wriggle through the one loophole she had left him. She had dismissed all her admirers, except Marc Sallafranque. Marc had to stay. He had to stay, for one thing, because to dismiss him would have conceded that André and she were two insane persons gibbering at one another, since it was perfectly obvious that she could not possibly entertain Marc as a husband or a lover. He was too grossly, too comically successful as an industrialist,

his very name had passed from him to the article he
manufactured. A Sallafranque was no longer a man, but
a cheap car. A woman might as well ally herself with
Monsieur Eau de Cologne or Monsieur Pâté de Foie
Gras. Moreover, though he was not unlovable, he was
grotesque. He was tall enough but he looked short, because his body was overweighted with the cylindrical
fatness of a robust little boy, and his square jaw went
straight down into a bull neck almost the same size
round as his head, so that he seemed made all of one
thick, rubbery piece. In the midst of this podginess his
melting brown eyes, his snub, dilating nostrils, and his
wide mouth made a muzzle like a terrier's, expressing a
purely sensuous gaiety and melancholy so candidly that
one would no more deal with him by cold reason than if
he were a terrier, and one felt at no time that one was
dealing with a man. It was a terrier that did funny
tricks, too. He was comically violent; when he wanted
to go upstairs in a hurry, he would put his feet together
and hop up several steps at a time, with great springs of
his strong legs, and once, when he had grown impatient
in a restaurant, he had rushed on a waiter carrying in a
pile of plates and had dealt them like cards on the floor
around him. It was impossible to think of him without
laughing, but the laughter was always kind, for he was
so good, so generous, so guileless, so bravely humble in
his subservience. It would have been as absurd and in-
sulting and heartless to count him among the admirers
who must be dismissed as if he had been a trusty footman. But not doing so had given André his chance. They
happened almost every third day now, these revolting
scenes, when he pretended to believe her capable of be-

ing unfaithful to him with this grotesque, when his voice pattered out accusations against her on one persistent note till she swayed and had to clap her hands over her ears, when his arms would sweep out in menace, not against her, but against the order of the room, so that a vase would be hurled from the mantelpiece and crash on the hearth, until he drew her to him in a reconciliation which would have been shameful to both of them if he had believed half of what he had been saying, which was an irrelevant climax to an evening of slapstick idiocy if he had not.

And she could not get rid of him. It had earlier been the intention of both of them to be married in June, and that was still his intention. She was grimly conscious of his power to carry it into effect. He would see to it, by such technical devices as he had employed that very evening at Madame Vuillaume's party, that they should constantly be alone together, and that the generic woman in her who loved the generic man in him should have endless opportunities to botray the individual woman in her who loathed the individual man in him. He might even draw so much public attention to their continuing relationship, that she would find it socially necessary to marry him. What he would make of marriage she would not let her mind run forward to discover fully; if she had been threatened with cancer, she would shrink from precise foreknowledge of her ultimate torture. Marriage with André would not be torture, but it would be tomfoolery. In spite of herself, infuriating visions passed before her. At the very best, he would practise private fidelity to her and public flirtation with innumerable conspicuous women, so that she would be ridiculed by the world as a complaisant wife, and yet would have no reason to complain. Nothing sane could proceed out of their marriage, because it would have to be based on André's assumptions about love, which had the madhouse trick of cutting up the mind into inconsistent parts. He was himself two people in his attitude to passion. When he was her lover, he was grave and reverent, but too often there was afterwards this solemn clowning about sex, this midwife chatter about the bringing to birth of pleasure. Don Juan, it seemed, was a case of split personality; his other half was Mr. Gamp. And he did what he could to draw her with him into the madhouse, for he tried to split her personality into two. It was suggested to her that her beauty and her capacity for passion were a separate entity, a kind of queen within her, and that it was to this that his loyalty was given, and that the rest of her was a humbler being, who ought to feel grateful that this superior part had caused her to be associated with such a grand gesture of chivalry. She, Isabelle, was supposed to be possessed by *la femme* as by a devil. Such an hypothesis made her feel as if she had been plucked back to the dark ages, to find her way among the cobwebby delusions of alchemists.

But in Laurence Vernon's mind she would find unity. He would have but one image of her there and that distinct as the figure on a Greek coin. He would have but one clean-cut image of their marriage, as simple as the year in the mind of a farmer. In the spring he would lay the foundation of his plans for public things and she would have her children, in the summer they would admire to see how their work fared in the heat of the day, in the autumn there would be harvest, and since the days grow shorter and they would have so much to talk over, no doubt winter also would not hang on their hands. Men grow weary of many things, but not of the seasons of the year. The thought of how she was being cheated of a profitable simplicity for a complexity that was sheer loss made her have tears to wipe from her face as her automobile stopped at her hotel. It made her mutter miserably as she fell asleep. It had made dawn look colder than its own greyness when she woke, as it looks to those who have been roused by recollection of their bankruptcy. It made her sit up in bed and stare when there came a knock on the door, as if that must mean sudden danger, and pull on her dressing-gown and rush to turn the key as if the world were so full of such dangers that precaution was worn out, and there was nothing to do but put down the head and charge them.

There stood in the corridor outside nothing more terrible than two women, their arms full of flowers; but at that their arms were full of importunities, of threats to her peace. For even if some of the flowers they carried were from Laurence, the others must come from undesired intruders. Crossly she told them, "You have knocked at the wrong door, you will find my maid in the salon along to the left," but they bowed their heads before her sharp tone so meekly that she repented. She was always susceptible to the pathos of the army of plain women in drab gowns who moved about Paris, carrying to their more fortunate sisters their flowers and dresses and hats, serving the central purpose of the place but not partaking of its full glory, like lay sisters in a sternly governed convent. She ran back to the table by her bed, found a few francs for them, and came back, holding out her arms for their flowers.

"Ah!" she sighed, as she took the first sheaf, and knew it was from André, since it was made of the red and white roses which he always sent her, as symbols of something or other. "These I don't want, not at all. Will you not take them away with you, Madame, to use in your own home?"

The women exchanged glances of embarrassment. It was as if a visitor to the convent should from kindly ignorance propose to a lay sister that she should avail herself of some privilege strictly reserved for the nuns.

"But no, Madame," one of them murmured hesitantly, "that's not really possible. Why, Monsieur de Verviers might get to hear of it, and he's one of our best customers. It would never do to annoy him."

"Life is difficult," said Isabelle, and they agreed, pleased as French people always are when they are offered an established truth to rest on, as it were, in the course of their day's work among unresolved experience; and she said good-bye and shut the door. First she put André's flowers in the waste-paper basket, and then looked at the card to be quite sure they had come from him. "Darling, last night you were more wonderful than ever," he had written, and she groaned aloud. It was evident that, early though it was, he had already been out and about for some time, feeling marvellously well. She saw herself successfully pursued by him through life, as one is by the income-tax authorities.

Shuddering, she turned to the other flowers. She knew at once that Sallafranque had sent the immense and aerie sheaf of cattleyas, so fragile that they seemed not like flowers at all but like assemblies of tiny winged creatures which might decide at any moment to swarm in other shapes, or to disperse into a rising cloud. It was odd that this human barrel should choose always the most delicate and exotic flowers as the ambassadors of his so simple feelings. Since his puberty, gardens the size of a department must have lost their blossoms in the service of his desires. His card was sealed in its envelope, and was scrawled with yet another request that she should marry him at once, so honestly and humbly put that tears came to her eyes, and she put it by to slip into a pocket of her dressing-case, where she kept valuable papers. There remained the pale gold roses, which she hoped Laurence had sent her. He had indeed, and on his card he reminded her that she had promised to lunch with him that day at Laurent's, and begged her not to fail him, since he wanted to discuss what he thought the most important matter in the whole world.

Her heart beat so strongly that, had she not preferred restraint to all things, she would have run about the room, crying aloud, so nearly all was well. Being as she was, she lay down on the bed and kept quite still. She looked at the flowers to quieten herself with their beauty, and her thoughts went to the two plain women in their drab gowns who had so gently borne with her harshness in the corridor. Her conscience smote her that she should have so much and they should have so little. But her feeling of remorse was lessened by the suspicion that the difference in their states was in its practical effects not altogether to their disadvantage. If she had been poor like them, she would have had to eat her heart out in

widowhood among her familiar and vigilant surroundings until the proper and valid distraction was offered;
she would not have been able to run about the world
making experiments in oblivion, and she would not have
experimented so rashly. The high degree of security she
enjoyed thanks to her money had persuaded her that
practically nothing she could do could bring her into
serious difficulties.

André, too, she thought, would have been in some
ways the better without his wealth. Had he been a poor
man, he would not have been free to spend his whole
life proving a silly point about his power by leaving
women who wanted him to stay with them and staying
with women who wanted him to leave them. Really, she
reflected, he was not a fool, for he knew that perfectly
well. In realizing exactly what he owed to the *status
quo* he was cleverer than the more intellectually active
Laurence or the more practically effective Marc Sallafranque, who both regarded their lives as purely individual achievements, which they could have made the same
in any world. André was well aware that anything
that threatened the existing conditions of society threatened him with extinction. He spoke with equally personal dread of the growth of Communism, of the rearm-
ing of Germany, of the imprudence of anyone belonging
to his own class who, by adoption of an extreme religious
or political faith, or by a gratuitous divorce, or by cla-
mant bad manners, became the subject of adverse public
comment. The structure must not even be shaken.

At that Isabelle sat up in bed and stared at the opposite wall. That, of course, was the secret of her attrac-
tion for André. He had recognized her fundamental tem-

perance, her inaptitude for any kind of violence; he knew
that in her company he could play with danger to his
heart's content, that no matter how he challenged her to
misbehaviour, she would perpetually be moderate. He
loved what he feared, as spirits sapped with luxury always do. The thought of screaming and shouting men
made his heart stop with terror; it gave him therefore an
immense pleasure to raise his voice and hear what a
scream and a shout sounded like; and he knew that in
the stillness of her atmosphere all such violent noises
were at once annulled. Suddenly she realized the true
nature of the problem before her. All she had to do was
to convince him that his impression of her character was
false: that she had within her a mænad, who might some
day break loose, answer his raised voice by her own
screams and shouts, and invoke the forces of disorder.
A single uncontrolled gesture would bring about this
change of view, for the first hint of this hidden self of
hers would make him so nervous that he would lose his
usual critical faculty. But control was obstinately a part
of all her nature, even including her imagination. She
murmured, "But what can I do, what can I do?" and
slid her feet out of bed, feeling for her slippers, as if
moving her body would make her mind move too. She
rose and pulled on her peignoir, and then became suddenly motionless, staring again at the wall; and indeed
she saw what she had to do as if it were written there.
Shuddering with distaste, she said, "That would do! Yes,
that would do!" and went to the waste-paper basket and
took out André's flowers.

II

S H E L I K E D so little what she had to do, and knew
so well what happiness lay on the other side of doing it,
that all the morning she was trembling with nervousness. Her hands shook, her mind shook; she was a trifle
stupid. When Sallafranque rang her up and asked her at
what time he might see her, a rush of tenderness for his
affectionate simplicity made her desire that he might
know about Laurence and herself sooner than anybody
else and count as her first friend to be adopted as their
friend; so she told him that she was lunching with a
friend at Laurent's and that, if he called for her at half-
past two, he might hear great news. He answered with a
bubble of joy which she took as proof of his good nature,
his readiness to rejoice in the pleasures of a friend as if
they were his own, until he had rung off. Then she
realized that he had thought she meant she was going to
promise to marry him. She sat and stared at the telephone aghast. She would not have exposed him to such
humiliation for anything in the world. But she did not
see how she could ring him up and make the matter plain
without a degree of indelicacy which, in this already sul-
lied day, she felt reluctant to undertake. Besides, the
morning was getting on, and she had arranged to have

a manicure and a face massage, as an anticipatory rite
of purification for the disorderly act she was to commit
later in the day.

At half-past twelve she took André's roses in her hand
and looked at herself in her long mirror, not that she
needed reassurance of her beauty, which had ceased to
be relevant to any serious purpose of her life, since by
now Laurence must have received some final impression
of her appearance. What she needed was to recognize
herself as the person she knew, who she had been all her
life, who was incapable of being forced to make a scene
by the pressure of passion. She waited till it was nearly
twenty-five to one, to make quite certain that André
would be out, for though he ought to allow a full half-
hour to get to Versailles for that lunch, he would perhaps
not hurry, since his hosts were not French. Then she
went down to her automobile, and told the chauffeur to
drive to André's house. As the car travelled up the
Champs-Élysées she looked ahead at the Arc de Triomphe, raising against the whitish spring sky a shape
appropriate less to architecture than to furniture, as if it
were a wardrobe storing the idea of French military
grandeur, and she childishly attributed her troubles to
her residence in a country where life stamped itself in
such spectacular forms. Then she knew the vertiginous
pain of a patient who is going to a nursing-home for an
operation which is not strictly necessary, which is under-
gone solely as a precaution against future crises; she
wanted to stop the automobile, jump out, to take the
chance that some other way of ridding herself of André
would present itself. Perhaps her Uncle Honoré would
come to France this summer, and would be able to sug-

gest something. It was well known that that old man
understood everything. But when the automobile slewed
off the Champs-Élysées into the avenue whose trees
marched down to the Seine, she remembered how often,
and with what feelings of humiliation, she had forced
herself against her will to make this journey during the
last few weeks. She picked up the roses she had let fall
on her lap, and held them tightly.

"When will Madame want me again?" asked the
chauffeur.

"Oh, at once, at once!" she said gaily, and went forward to her deed.

Decidedly, part of her trouble had been merely that
she was in France, for nowhere else in the whole world
would there have been this courtyard. She had liked
coming here, and since it had an air of liking to be
visited by happy lovers, she had humoured it. Yes, that
accounted for at least part of the trouble. She passed
through the archway, and sniffed as always the antique
pungency of the concierge's meal, seething in a pot that
had no doubt never been emptied and filled afresh since
Paris was Lutetia, that might have begun its simmering
in even earlier and sterner times, so that the basic flavour
still carried a trace of tender prehistoric child. She was
peered at as always by the concierge's wife, pressing
against the dimness of her window her drooping bosom
and features congested by malevolence; how realist are
the French to keep at their doorways a perpetual reminder that the body of man is corruptible and his nature
fundamentally evil. Then she entered into the courtyard itself, into the tender evidence that the French are
romantics; that though civilization constrains them to

live in great cities, they remain provincials at heart, and when they have to build high walls, knock them down again with their minds. This place was like a square in a little town, not the square where the market is, but the smaller one where the women sit and gossip over their sewing in the evening. There were cobblestones underfoot, clean as they are in the country, and trees tall as they are by village fountains. It was quiet with more than absence of noise, it seemed to be manufacturing quietness, in which the toot of a motor-horn in the street outside sounded as feebly as if a tiny child had set its lips to a toy trumpet. In the very middle of the square an old dog lay asleep under its flies. To the left was a tall cliff of dwellings determined wholly by necessity, its windows placed at ugly intervals, its dark stone scored with pipes. It was entered by a double door of glass and yellow-painted iron, such as might have admitted to a lycée. One knew nothing about it except that there existed behind one of its windows a human being who knew the emotions of fatherhood, for near the entrance was propped up a child's bicycle that some adult had been painting green. One knew also that behind another of its windows was a woman who had once been young, who had learned nothing since, for she was singing an air from *Thaïs* by propulsion of the breath from a bosom choked with syrup, in a manner that one had thought long universally discredited. In fact, there were in that building souls whom metropolitan influences had tried in vain to ravish from their simplicity.

To the right was the house, much lower, only three stories high, where all the shutters were always closed because the banker's widow was still dying at Nice. She had been ill so long that her residence had fallen into some disrepair. The creepers had not been cut back, and tendrils grew about the faded green slats of the shutters. But it was one of those houses which, in emptiness, are fragrant as an empty scent-bottle. One saw the darkness of the rooms peopled with ghosts of women belonging to the eighties, with frizzed light auburn hair set forward on their heads, fawn-dark, faintly Mongolian eyes, long slender waists rising from a fluff of frills like silk-cased spiral springs, and vitally important explanations, long withheld from the noblest reasons, turning to red phthisis between lip and tiny scrap of handkerchief. Beside the lachrymose charm of this home of spectres most other houses would have looked gross and bourgeois, but not this house of André's, which some nobleman had built during the Second Empire as a replica of a Renaissance pavilion in his country park. It was looking its best at this moment, for the grey stone, marked with purplish shadows where the rains had dripped from the rich mouldings, was wreathed with the languid green leaves of wistaria, and its mauve flowers, which, in spite of their fragility, hung with the weightiness of fruit. But it owed little to the benevolence of the seasons; it could depend on its own style, the magnificence that had here curbed itself and been for a moment light, that had with perfect justice scaled down its method of elaboration from pomp and castle-size to the moderate measure of a man living alone except for love. She had cried out when she first saw it, it had seemed so beautiful. It was small blame to her that she had entered it! It would be beautiful again when André was a ghost like the women in the house next door, and was visible only to such

lovers of the past as had a special feeling for this age.
Then he would be seen looking out under the broad
brows of the mansarded windows purged of his trivial-
ity and restlessness by the censorship of man's romanti-
cizing memory, dark and beautiful and grave with consideration of private delights, like a young man painted
by Giorgione. It was only in the present that he and his
house were intolerable; and that present she was now
going to shatter and elude.

She went up the flight of four curved steps that led to
his door, rang the bell, and went down the steps again.

In time old Michel hobbled out, his greenish-black
trousers concertinaing round his legs. André would not
dress his maître d'hôtel properly because his aristocratic
relatives were very poor and never renewed their servants' liveries. At this reminder of the complete factitious-
ness of André's existence she was swept by a wave of
irritation, and she began to get the roses into the right
position, their flowers in one hand, their stalks in the
other.

"Ah, Madame!" Michel called down to her. "Monsieur André did not expect you, he's gone to Versailles
for luncheon. But won't you come in and write a note?"

She tried to answer him in the words that she had
been rehearsing since the morning; but her lips were
dry, her mouth opened and shut but emitted no sound.
She could, however, perform her planned action. She
broke the flowers in two across the middle of the stalks;
she did that easily enough, because she had prepared
them with scissors at home. Her pleasure at finding that
she could execute at least part of her programme, and
that it succeeded so far as to make Michel's eyes pop out

of his head and bring him down to the second step, gave her back her breath.

Isabelle cried out, quite loud, "Tell your master that I want neither him nor his flowers!" And she began to tear off the petals from the flowers, the leaves from the stalks, and scatter them on the ground.

"But, Madame!" said Michel. "But, Madame!"

He came down another step, but no further. Horror, even fear, was on his face. She did not wonder. She wished she could stop at once, having made her point. The air from *Thaïs* had stopped, and in the stillness she heard above her a métallic clash, as if someone had very sharply thrown open a window high up in the flats. Perhaps she was being watched. She longed to turn round and run out of the courtyard, but a peculiar motion which Michel had made with his right hand, and a canny narrowing of his eyes, had filled her with alarm. It was as if he were promising himself that when she had gone he would sweep up all this detritus of blossoms, and would spare himself the embarrassment of telling André. She looked down and saw, between the cobblestones and the slab of pavement at the foot of the steps down from the house, a narrow section of earth still wet from the early morning showers. Down on this she cast the most complete red and white roses she had left, and with her heel she ground them into the mud. She knew that Michel, who was clean as a cat, would not dabble in the dirt to retrieve them. André would see them as he came in and would inquire what had happened, and Michel, she knew from the gape of his old jaw, would tell everything; for the savagery she had put into the grinding of her heel on the roses had made him feel concern for the

safety of his adored master. Yes, late that afternoon the
two men would bend over the muddied petals, and
Michel would quaver, "Like a madwoman, I tell you,
Monsieur André, like a madwoman!" and André would
grow pale with apprehension of hitherto undivined resources of recalcitrant womanhood. He would fling back
to the house and spend the evening smoking very quietly
in his library; and when her engagement was announced,
he would do nothing, absolutely nothing.

She took one last look at the pavilion and its wistaria,
and went out of the courtyard, saying to herself, "This
is good-bye to all the French thing. It's lovely but it is
not really a part of me. Our family's emphasis on its
French origin is a piece of snobbery like André's refusal
to buy Michel a new livery. By this time our blood has
become wholly American. Now I am going back to my
own people."

She felt so light-hearted, so freed from the past, that
she walked past her own car, and her chauffeur had to
call her back. When she got to Laurent's, she wished she
had walked, for she was too early. There was no Laurence
waiting in the lobby, and she was sorry, for she wanted
someone to greet her at once, so that she could release
the happy laughter that was welling up in her. She
chose a table on the terrace, for she knew he would want
to eat out there where the trellis wall shut out all the
urban lower part of the landscape, with its babies and
nurses and seats and gravel walks, and admitted only the
full-foliaged tree-tops and the bright crest of the fountain spray. She ordered some tomato juice, for she would
never again need a cocktail to pick her up, since she was
never going to be down, and sat at her ease and sipped it,

looking at a group of trees, a chestnut and two planes, that were swaying rhythmically together, like gods wrestling together and coming to no falls because their forces, being divine, are equal. But presently she looked at her watch. At first she had been alone because she was too early; now she was alone because Laurence was late. Yet he was never late. Surely he had said Laurent's? She leant back on her chair, and was able to look into the lobby, and there he was, standing quite still with his back to the terrace, his arms crossed on his chest, his head bowed, as if he were pondering something of a desperate nature.

She called to her waiter. "Tell Monsieur Vernon that Madame Tarry is here."

"But I have already told him," he answered.

They both stared at the long, rather stiff, narrow-waisted back. "Perhaps Monsieur is expecting another guest?" suggested the waiter.

"I don't think so," said Isabelle, and smiled to herself. It was touching that even Laurence, the most polished and self-possessed of human beings, should be timid before this moment and should try to stave it off as long as possible. At that instant Laurence chose to swing round, and though he lifted a hand in gay greeting, he showed by a lifting of the shoulders, a compression of the lips, that he found their scrutiny embarrassing. The waiter pivoted on his heel and became part of another group, and Isabelle smiled up into Laurence's face as he bent over her hand. "Had you forgotten you had asked me?"

"No, I certainly hadn't," said Laurence, and sat down

opposite her. His body slumped into his seat heavily and clumsily for him. "What's that you're drinking?"

"Tomato juice," she said. She could have wished that he was not taking the approaching moment quite so seriously, for his voice was harsh, his pallor was ghastly.

"I'll not have that," he said. "Waiter, waiter, what have you got that's nearly all gin? A dry Martini, I suppose, is the nearest thing. Well, make it strong." He looked after the waiter with an intensity of gaze that served no purpose, and drummed on the table with his finger-tips. He did it so silently that she could make no complaint on the score of her nerves, but she found it odd that he should do it at all. It was incredible that he should be so schoolboyish, so uninitiate. After all, Nancy must at some time or other have received some sort of attacking proposition.

She said lightly, "Well, what have you been doing this morning?"

"Paying a visit," he answered, and added in a tone that was level yet gave the effect of a rebuke, "a visit that would not have interested you. It was far too placid. To Madame Dupont-Gaillard." He fixed her suddenly with eyes full of vehement emotion, that were at once hard and imploring. "You know that name, don't you?"

"I've heard it somewhere," she reflected.

"Heard it? Haven't you seen it?" he insisted precisely.

She shook her head.

"Ah, you don't remember," he continued. "She's a teacher of languages, of one language only, really. Her own. She takes in young men who are getting up their

French for the diplomatic service; she helps foreign students who are struggling with their University courses. I lodged with her the two years I was at the Sorbonne." He broke his bread and angrily swallowed a crumb or two. "I don't know why, we all got very fond of her. She's a stupid old woman, really, but she's got an absurd bronze wig, and she quotes La Fontaine, and if anyone got sick or homesick she was extraordinarily kind. We all go up and see her quite often when we happen to be in Paris. I went up and called on her this morning. Waiter, waiter, where's that dry Martini?"

"Coming, coming, Monsieur."

"Why, you've just ordered it," Isabelle chided him. He was really very nervous. For the last few minutes he had been talking of Madame Dupont-Gaillard as if he were reproachfully confronting her with an exemplar, though she felt she could hardly be blamed for not wearing a bronze wig, or not quoting La Fontaine, and she knew that he was in no position to judge how she behaved to the sick and the homesick. "Well, what's the matter?"

His gaze, that had been fever-bright, went leaden. "Oh, nothing," he said courteously. "But that's where I was, and I'm sorry I was late and kept you waiting. Nothing's the matter, really . . ." His voice trailed away, he became still paler, he raked the terrace with his leaden gaze, and suddenly galvanized himself into a show of exclaiming interest. "Why, surely that's Michael Baker over there."

"So it is," said Isabelle.

"And that's his new wife, that used to be Claudia Greenway Green, of Nashville, Tennessee." He stood up and looked across the terrace at his friends with an expression oddly fatigued and calculating; and then he looked down at Isabelle's uplifted face. "Shall I ask them to come over and have lunch with us?" he said, very slowly, as if he wanted to show that he understood fully all the implications of what he was saying.

She smiled. At least she could do this sort of thing quite well. Her smile was probably quite convincing. "Why not?"

"Yes," he agreed, "why not?" He held her eyes with his, he would not let them go. "We had nothing we wanted to talk about alone, had we?"

She shook her head. "Nothing. Nothing at all."

He bowed gravely and turned his back on her to go to his friends. The tears rushed into her eyes; his tall stiff back, the white cloths on the tables, the striped black and yellow awning, the gay blue dress of a woman lunching happily with her lover, and the green hedge ran into shining confusion like molten glass. She remembered the infamies she had heard of that men practised on the dignity of women, and with a shout of surprise from her nerves realized for the first time that they might be practised on her. A story came back to her which she had been told by an indignant Frenchwoman, a young widow, whom she had met on board ship during her last voyage. This girl had been a vendeuse with a great French couturier, who had lent her for six months to a Fifth Avenue store; and while she was there she had excited the admiration of a Jewish broker, who whirling her round in night-clubs, holding her hand at the Opera, had told her that he was just crazy about her, and could hardly wait to take her down

to City Hall. He was repulsively fat and ugly, but he
was kind, and she longed for a home and children; so
one night she had told him that she was willing to go
down with him to City Hall any morning that he chose.
At that his jaw had dropped, and he had stammered that
he hadn't thought she was a girl to misunderstand a
fellow that was just giving her a rush and take it that he
was playing the heavy lover. The girl's pride had been
broken, and at some loss she had thrown up her post,
terrified of staying longer in a country where the code
of manners did not preserve the decencies between the
sexes. Isabelle had listened to her story sympathetically,
but had privately felt that the girl must have been guilty
of some indiscretion, even of vulgarity, which had invited this humiliation. Well, she had been wrong. For
this same humiliation had befallen herself to the fullest
extent. She realized that the tone of every word she had
addressed to Laurence since he had arrived in Europe,
the quality of every movement she had made in his presence, had been determined by the silent assurances he
had given her regarding his intention of asking her to
marry him; and that now that he had sharply withdrawn these assurances, there was not one of those words
and movements but was ridiculous and shameful.

Now the Bakers were standing over her, offering
handshakes, exploding amiably in greetings and profes-
sions of surprise. She found herself thinking grimly that
Michael's face had grown looser with happiness, that he
had been a great deal handsomer when he was married
to the first, the notoriously scourge-like Mrs. Baker.
Then her heart sank. So it was thus that life forced on
one unawares the characteristics that earlier had seemed

most pernicious and most easily avoidable. Till then she
had thought of the hatred felt by the unhappy for the
happy as sheer gratuitous vice. The thing that Laurence
was doing to her. She would never, she saw, feel free to
be honestly friendly with any man again or, as it appeared, with any woman either. She was aware that
thousands of women, when asked what they wished to
order for a meal, thought fit to announce with a little
laugh that they were dieting. It was nothing to their dis-
credit, they might be as useful and agreeable as the
many women who wore corsets or sang to their friends
after dinner, or did any of those things which, though
they were not illegal, she would not do herself. Yet she
found herself counting this heavily to Mrs. Baker's dis-
credit, and doubting the debit when, after all, she ordered a rich and schoolgirlish repast; and the reason for
this injustice was simply that the little bride's face, which
was round and wholesome as a cup custard, had plainly
never been flushed by any sort of shameful withdrawal
of the conventional value attached to her sex. Isabelle
understood at last why women are supposed to hate each
other. Such an experience as hers was bound to engender
a hundred kinds of enmity. Henceforward she would feel
abashed before any woman who had not been rejected
like herself; she would be cagy in her dealings with any
woman who, having suffered such a rejection, would be
likely to guess her own disgrace. This was a poisoning
of the very springs of sincerity. Even now she was grinning too much, prolonging throughout the meal an affec-
tation of palpitating interest in the honeymooning couple
which it would have been natural to have dropped after
the first five minutes. But at least Laurence was doing

that too. For whatever reason he had decided to hurt her, he was hurting himself too. She was not too sorry about that. So she had grown cruel too.

But suddenly she found herself sincere again. "What, must you really go?" she exclaimed when Michael rose at an incredibly early moment, when some compote had just been put down before her, and said that he and his wife must return to their hotel to be picked up by some friends who were making an early start for the country. Nothing indeed could have been more real than her distress, for it meant that, unless the honeymooners were to suspect how things were, she must stay and finish her meal alone with Laurence. Fortunately he went right out to the pavement with them, and by the time he got back she had only a greengage or two to swallow. But when he was sitting opposite her again, the fineness of his hands, which were all of him her downcast eyes could see, as they lay folded in front of him on the tablecloth, brought a lump to her throat because they were so typical of his general fineness, such evidence that he had been really what she wanted.

"Well, Laurence, this has been very nice," she said, as she put down her spoon and prepared to pick up her bag and gloves. Her dislike of soiled things was so strong that even at this moment, even after there had opened this breach between them, she had to cry out, "Why, what has happened to my gloves! I thought they were clean, and look at all those little brown marks."

"That is blood," said Laurence; "there must have been sharp thorns on those roses."

He raised a half-finished glass of wine to his lips,

though a smear of rouge on the rim showed that the little bride had drunk from it.

She looked past him into the distance, at the emerald-green chestnut, the gold-green planes, tossing and writhing together. She felt herself back in the courtyard, her body forcing itself into the unfamiliar and detestable hieroglyphic of rage; she saw Michel's old eyes sagging forward in astonishment; she heard, high up in the sunlit air above her, a metallic clash. She said, "So it was you who threw open the window?"

"Yes," he answered. "That's where Madame Dupont-Gaillard lives, in one of those flats."

She found herself resorting to the pitiful expedient of a little laugh. "Did I look very dreadful?"

"Well, I gathered you were not feeling very pleased with Monsieur de Verviers," he said, resorting to the same expedient. He drank some more of the little bride's wine. "I had no idea," he told her as he set down the glass, "that you were such a mænad."

"I am not," she told him.

He gave a good-humoured smile, as if to tell her she need not keep up pretences with him any longer and could be assured that, now he knew her temperamental peculiarities, he would watch her career with amused and not unkindly interest.

"I have never done such a thing before in my life," she insisted. But he continued to smile, and she became aware that she had raised her voice a tone higher than she had meant. Biting her lips, she began to pull on her gloves, making every movement as calm as she could.

Laurence gesticulated to the waiter for the bill, sat

back in his chair, and passed his handkerchief over his lips. Impulsively, as if he were so sorry for having mismanaged their scene together that he must apologize even if this destroyed the pretence that they had had no scene, he said, "I thought you would understand when I told you that I had been calling on Madame Dupont-Gaillard. She has a plate up in the hallway."

"Yes," said Isabelle, "but it is very old, the letters are quite level with the brass, you cannot see what they are."

For now she had remembered how it was that she had heard the name, though she had never seen it. She and André had come in very late, and while he fumbled for his keys under a light, she had stopped by the plate and run her fingers over the hardly perceptible ups and downs of the vanishing letters. "Tell me whose name has time licked off, like a cat cleaning a saucer?" she had whispered, and André had whispered back, "It is an institutrice, Madame Dupont-Gaillard, who like Château Gaillard is in ruins." His whisper had ended on her lips, his arm had clasped her waist more tightly, and they had moved, mouth to mouth, towards his home. With quiet fierceness, with an assumed smile, she turned to Laurence, meaning to tell him of that midnight conversation so that he would guess the parts she would be mum about, meaning to hurt him. Jealousy she knew not to be so strong in his sex as it was in hers; women objected to marrying widowers far more than men objected to marrying widows. But in its lesser quantity it was there, and could be roused and tortured; and if it were tortured enough, her mind sprang on to say, it would go mad and try to prove itself as good as the other male, claiming its own. She had only to speak her story in the right way,

with certain hesitancies, and she would end that afternoon in Laurence's arms, and she knew well that, if he
were once her lover, she would never lose him.

She shuddered with distaste. She was being swept
away into the horrible world of violence that she feared,
where one soul delighted in inflicting pain on another,
where force and fraud were used to compel victories
which were valueless unless they were ceded freely to
an honest victor. It would be far better to resign herself
to losing all she wanted. She looked across at him as a
farewell to what she had wanted, and at the sight of his
fine, grave face, on which even this crisis had failed to
mark the lines of any expression that was not noble and
reasonable, a storm of refusal raged in her. Why should
she lose him? And had she tried all ways of keeping him?
She had rejected dishonesty, but she had not made full
trial of honesty. It was a difficult thing for a woman to
be honest; it required from her the full organization of
courage. She found that as she coughed to clear her dry
throat and leaned forward to make the attempt.

"Laurence," she said, "I want to tell you why I threw
down those roses outside André de Verviers's door."

With that detestably distant smile he answered, "I am
sure it is a most romantic story."

Lowering her eyelids she spoke it out. "No, not romantic! One would have to be starved of all pleasantness, a
tired, homely stenographer or an old hospital nurse, to
think it romantic. It is a very silly story, Laurence. When
I came over here after Roy's death, I was desperately unhappy and lonely. I wanted a companion with whom I
could build up a new life; I have no family to fall
back on."

"You are very young," he said reflectively. "One forgets how young you are."

"Oh, not so young," said Isabelle. "No younger than most of the women in the world who have had to make great decisions. That is the special handicap of our sex, the important part of our lives comes before we have acquired any experience. And in my ignorance I thought there was nothing very difficult about the decision that was before me. I merely had to choose a partner, and I looked round and chose André de Verviers."

Laurence made the faintest moan of disapprobation.

"Men do not look the same to women as they do to other men," she reminded him, "and I had no superior tie. I knew of nobody whom I could have loved, who was free to love me. And André is a superb human being, just as Roy was. I thought I could have had some of the same sort of happiness with André I had with Roy. So we were to be married this summer." She pondered for an instant whether she ought to be more precise about her relationship, and decided that she need not. Though men were not very jealous, they thought they were under an obligation to be extremely so, and it would relieve Laurence of this tiresome necessity if she were to leave him the possibility of thinking that André and she had not been lovers. "But, Laurence!" She looked into his eyes. "André isn't any good."

"I can believe it," he nodded.

"It was not so terribly foolish of me to think that he might have been," she defended herself. "What else had Roy got to start with except just that physical faculty, that trick of accomplishment, that André has? Only something hidden, that turned everything he did to gaiety and happiness. Well, it was hidden too, the thing that governed André, and turned everything to fever and violence and disorder."

He murmured sympathetically, "Yes. Yes. I know. One doesn't see it, the thing that governs people . . ."

"And I had, you know, other ideas. I wanted to make something decent of my life. I wanted to marry a man who was devoting himself to some work that mattered, I wanted to help him and have his children, and bring them up well. I wanted to live at the centre of a focus of pleasantness, and harmony, and things coming right. And instead I was tossing about in a whirlpool of useless passion and frenzy and jealousy, that wasn't even real, that was all put on to whip up sensation. I didn't want that, I didn't want it any more than I wanted to marry a drug-taker and be forced by him to take drugs. And I couldn't get rid of him. That was the frightening thing. He wouldn't take any notice when I asked him to go away."

"A man who will not take his dismissal," said Laurence, sounding more southern than was his habit, "is a scoundrel."

"Nothing I could say made any impression. So, at last, I thought of this way." She swallowed the bitterness in her mouth. "This hateful way that you saw."

He raised his eyebrows as if to assure her that she was wrong, that he had not thought it hateful at all.

"You see, André loves violence because his life is utterly peaceful," she explained. "He has a large income, he has an unassailable position, nothing can happen to him, so he likes a little fictitious excitement. But only so long as it doesn't threaten his security. That's why he liked me. He knew I was calm, he knew I could be trusted never to lose my self-control and cause a scandal, however much he stormed. So I set out to pretend that that wasn't true, that I could be dangerous. I took those roses and threw them all over the courtyard so that his servant would tell him, and he would think that he had driven me beyond the limits of self-control, and let me go." She lived through the moment in the courtyard all over again, and cried out, "Oh, I hated it all so, I hated acting like a madwoman!"

While the blackness was before her eyes, she heard his soothing murmur; but when his face was clear again, it was not wholly kind. She could not quite believe that; she stared. His eyes were kind, but they immediately slid away from hers, and his mouth was pursed, his nostrils dilated. He began to tidy the crumbs by his plate into a little heap, and he seemed wholly absorbed in this task, though his eyes stole back to hers once and he gave her a guilty, insincere smile before he looked back at the tablecloth.

The blood beat in her ears. After all, he was not quite what she wanted. He had understood and accepted all she had told him; he knew that she was the same sort of person as himself, that she had fallen into the hands of the enemy and had suffered outrageously and had taken what means she could to free herself. But he was not going to tell her that he loved her and wished to marry her because he belonged to the vast order of human beings who cannot be loyal to their beloved if a stranger jeers. There had been reason in what she did in front of André's house, but someone who knew nothing of the circumstances, who had merely looked down on her from a window, could not have known that reason, and would have censured her. Perhaps that had happened, perhaps Madame Dupont-Gaillard had leaned against his shoulder as he watched her grind her heel on the roses and had said, cruel as people are when they speak of those they do not know, "Look, she must be mad!" And his fear of what a stranger might say, of what had been said by an old woman who had forgotten how life sometimes drives the poor dog mad, had outweighed all the promise of sweetness there had been between them. Well, it was not the kind of fault that men outgrew.

She fastened the studs at the wrist of her gauntlets, looking at the distance, where the chestnut and the planes rocked together as if they were rooted in a painful place and longed for freedom. She felt a little less humiliated now she knew his disloyalty than she had when she had thought his rejection of her a causeless caprice, but she was far more apprehensive. For she knew that his mind would be ashamed of deserting her, and would try to justify itself by looking on her with a jaundiced eye and imagining in her a thousand defects which would make the desertion seem a necessity. Everything about their intercourse would be vilified. As she thought how her candid unveiling of her plight would then be regarded, she shuddered and looked at her wrist-watch, to find a pretext for an early departure. She saw that it was half-past two, and remembered something that had slipped her mind.

Lifting her eyes to Laurence's, she said gaily, "You understand why I was specially anxious to get rid of André de Verviers at this particular moment, don't you?"

As she had feared, he flushed and looked embarrassed.

He might as well have said aloud, "Why, of course I understand. You hoped to marry me. But how can you be so indecent as to talk about it?"

This, she found, she could not endure. To have him thinking of her like that was more disagreeable than any price she would have to pay for putting an end to it.

"How odd it is," she said, taking care not to laugh too extravagantly, "that my excitement over the hateful thing I had to do this morning should have put out of my head what is far more important! Have you noticed nothing about me lately?"

He shook his head, a little stiffly.

"I've sometimes wondered if I haven't seemed a little too frank and free with you, if you might not have thought I had 'gone gay,' considering our friendship was so far from intimate. I would have kept my distance and my party manners properly if there had been only André. But when one is in love, you know, one becomes extraordinarily indiscreet, one treats all other men in a way that must be rather puzzling to them if they haven't got the key."

His eyes had become glassy, he was leaning forward to listen to her.

"Yes, I'm in love!" she told him gaily. "And if I've been successful in ridding myself of André, I shall marry quite soon. And if I've been boring you with an explanation of all the whys and wherefores of this morning's scene with the roses, it's because I've wanted to appear to you with a clean sheet, since I'm a little shy about telling one of Roy's friends about my new choice."

The waiter had laid down a plate of change at Laurence's elbow, and Laurence swept it back to him with a gesture full of hate.

"You see, Roy was perfect." He was, he was, her heart said. He would have sent any stranger to hell rather than think disloyally of me. "And my second husband hasn't, poor dear, anything of Roy's outward perfection."

"Who is it?" asked Laurence. "But who is it?"

"Why, Marc Sallafranque."

"Marc Sallafranque," repeated Laurence. He sat for a second in silence, then exclaimed, "But I thought you didn't like Sallafranque?"

"Ah, you've evidently seen some gestures that were meant for André," she laughed. "But do say you'll approve, and not cast me off. I know he looks the funniest thing in the world, but inside he has a lot of the goodness and sweetness of Roy." She paused, because she had suddenly felt a click in her brain, as if these words which she had spoken for a false purpose had coincided with the truth. "Take that on my word," she said, "and say you'll be my friend." She stood up, but he did not say the word, or do anything but regard her with the queer mask, as of a stricken hyena, that people wear who are making haste laughing at themselves before other people can start laughing at them. Her plan had evidently succeeded perfectly. Its only defect was that it left her in possession of Sallafranque, which was a responsibility that she might as well assume fully at once.

"Marc will be waiting in the hall now, I expect," she said. "I told him to come here at half-past two so that you could congratulate us. I'll go and fetch him."

"What, is he here?" said Laurence in tones which betrayed that he had been nourishing even to the end a hope that her story was not really true. "Oh, yes, I'd love to see him."

Isabelle went from the terrace into the hall, leaving him sitting in his chair with far less than his usual elegance, and was in time to see Marc Sallafranque jumping out of his cream-coloured car, which was indeed a Sallafranque, but had a special body put to it, lustrous and inclining to the baroque. He began to hurry towards the door, but turned back to caress the two wire-haired terriers that stood on the seat beside the Negro chauffeur, lifting up muzzles sharp as cut tin and howling because they were not to go with their master. Then he continued towards the restaurant, not seeing her within the darkness of the porch because of the bright sunshine. His lower lip pouted forward, he stared at his feet and from time to time sadly shook his head; he looked like a child going to an interview which might mean a beating.

When he found her waiting for him, he came to a standstill. He took his hat in both hands and held it in front of him and said, "Oh, Isabelle, my little one, my little cabbage, my little angel, I am very stupid, nearly everybody is cleverer than I am, I often do not understand things properly. But say I was not wrong about what I thought you meant on the telephone this morning?"

She nodded and smiled. "You were right."

He continued to stand quite still, and twirled his hat round and round and round, his face growing very red. "Isabelle," he said, "my Isabelle."

She remembered the click her brain had given when she had spoken of his goodness, telling her that the statement she had meant to be false was in fact true; and it shamed her that she was making him so solemnly happy by what she had coldly conceived as a ruse to protect her pride. Penitently she murmured, "I will try to be good to you, Marc."

Tears stood in his rich animal eyes, he ceased to twirl his hat, he crumpled it in his fist. "It is I who must try to be good," he growled. He took her hand and crushed it against his warm, throbbing, rubbery side.

The tears stood in her eyes also, in another moment they would roll down her cheeks. She said, "My dear, I have been lunching here with Laurence Vernon. He is out there on the terrace. You cannot think how much I like him, you must be friends. Come out and meet him."

"Ah yes," said Marc. "I must be very polite to your friends. It will be my only way of winning them, they will be all so much cleverer than I am." But as they went he slipped his arm through hers and tugged her back. "And our marriage," he begged like a dog. "When can it be?"

"As soon as you like."

"Ha, ha! Next week?"

"Next week, if you will."

"But it can't be," he cried, "that I am going to be married to you next week? My God, I am going to be married to you next week?"

A waiter passed them, carrying two glasses of brandy on a tray. Marc's left foot clothed in a yellow shoe shot out and caught him on the behind. The tray clattered on

the floor underneath the caisse, a wall was streaked by
two brown stains and shivers of glass, the waiter howled,
the caissière bent forward a Roman eyebrow and a
fortress bosom, the vestiaire ran out holding one grey
and two brown hats, chasseurs swarmed, glad that this
time nobody could say it was their fault, the maîtres
d'hôtel of the inside and outside restaurants ran in and
stood like stars in conjunction.

"Ah, mesdames, messieurs," said Marc, "it's only
me."

"Ah, good day, Monsieur Sallafranque," said the
maîtres d'hôtel, laughing.

"Forgive me, Gustave," said Marc, bringing out his
wallet. "I had need of a behind just then, for purposes
of celebration, and yours was the only one that was
handy. But here's something!" He flipped a thousand-
franc note on to the man's palm. "And here's another,
Madame, for the damage and the nerves of the person-
nel." It drifted on to the mahogany of the caisse.

The waiter grinned, the Roman eyebrow abated and
the fortress became more like a pleasure palace, the vestiaire, the chasseurs, the maîtres d'hôtel flowed backwards like an ebbing tide, in a rhythmic series of obei-
sances.

"But, Marc," breathed Isabelle, "but, Marc!"

"Ah, little one, don't bother about that!" said Marc.
"I am very impulsive, and sometimes I like to do silly
things *pour rigolo*, but it doesn't matter. They all know
me here; Maman used to bring me here for treats when
I was a tiny boy. They all adore me really. Come, darling, where is your friend?"

She had contrived that violence should not make her

life a tragedy. It might yet make her life a farce, which she would find hardly more tolerable. They went out on the terrace, Marc's fingers opening and closing on her wrist, to the man who had brought this on her.

III

ISABELLE HAD been right in her supposition that André de Verviers would be too alarmed by her vehement rejection of his roses to take any steps to interfere with her engagement. But she was wholly prevented from exulting in her success by the circumstance that the engagement thus preserved intact was not the one she had had in mind when she formed the plan. She was, however, too busy for melancholy to master her days as it did her nights, for without pause her unpremeditated marriage thrust unforeseen experiences on her. Very soon she was made aware that there was some truth in the rumour that a Jewish strain accounted for Marc's close black curls and his rubber-ball vitality; for nothing else, she realized, could account for the emphasis which his family laid on the necessity for perfect Catholic orthodoxy in the conduct of the marriage, not only at the first meeting with her, but almost in the first moment of that meeting. Hardly had she been freed from the embrace of Madame Sallafranque, a small and smart woman whose gleaming Schiaparelli clips gave her the air of a competent vivandière, when she was introduced to two priests, who were sitting back on the lambskin and aluminium sofa, with finger-tips pressed to finger-tips,

66

looking self-consciously shrewd. They regarded her with
an eye at once solemn, negotiating, and bland, as if she
were a coffin that had presently to be carried down a
winding staircase, and they could promise her that she
would suffer no rude concussion during this progress,
since they were neat-handed men of infinite experience
in these matters. It appeared immediately that they were
there to instruct her on the steps that would have to be
taken for the nullification of her first marriage, in order
that, as a good son of the Church, Marc should not err
by marrying a woman who had divorced her husband.
When Isabelle explained that she had lost Roy not by
divorce but by death, they were at first incredulous, as
if they had believed till then that natural widowhood
was impossible in the United States, but on learning that
he had been killed in an aeroplane they nodded and said
several times, *"Ah, mais parfaitment, mais naturelle-
ment!"* and addressed themselves to the subject of her
conversion. Isabelle felt obliged, though she knew she
was offending against the social spirit of the occasion, to
tell them that her family had never lapsed from the faith
and that she had been baptized into the Church in in-
fancy.

It was as great a contretemps as she had feared. The
priests showed the coldness natural in undertakers who
had been summoned to a house where there was nobody
even ill; and Madame Sallafranque overwhelmed them
with profuse apologies that were at once domineering
and abjectly mendicant. This was very different from
the attitude to which Isabelle had become accustomed in
her own home, where the priest took his place with the
family doctor and solicitor as an expert in a defined

sphere, whom prudent men consulted and obeyed when they were vexed by certain problems, and where he was treated, in consequence, with the unemotional respect due to one who fulfilled a useful function. Here, she saw, ecclesiastical approval was being snatched at as if it were a material object conferring a benefit, say a card of admission to a gala fête from which one would otherwise be excluded with some implication of contempt. But there was something not petty in the appeal; it might have been admission to a fortress that had been sought by those who had fared ill under the hail of arrows outside. There was even something profound too. Perhaps there still existed people who had not intellectualized their relations with their medicine man out of all recognition. She was not at all distressed to find herself among men and women who were simpler, more unashamed, more acquainted with humiliation, and more primitive than those she had known before.

But it would have been foolish if she had felt it was condescension for her to mingle with the Sallafranques. Marc's father and grandfather had been great industrialists, who had called into being a small township within the shadow of Lille, who had been formidable as ironmasters were in the days when ironmasters were formidable. But the Germans had occupied that township for four years, and in the third year Marc's father had a stroke. It was easy to believe that, by these vehement little people, prolonged disappointment and heartbreak might be dramatized as a suspension of all bodily faculties, though their vitality would dispute death inch by inch. When the Germans went, they left the works a heap of old iron on ravaged ground; and Marc, who was

twenty-four when he came back from the war, showed a
curious reluctance to build them up again. With no
counsel to guide him but a few croaks from a sick-bed,
he began to badger the Government for permission to
spend only a driblet of the reparations money due to his
firm at Lille, and to devote the mass to the factory for
making cheap automobiles which his father had started
as a side line ten miles outside Paris. He had got that
permission by jumping up round ministers like a big
eager puppy, by being a pest like a puppy; and for the
next ten years he had worked so hard that midnight often
found him laying his head on his desk and blubbering
with fatigue. At the end of that time the factory had
grown into a town larger than the one the Germans had
destroyed.

Its size appalled her when Marc drove her there
for the first time. Like most Americans, she felt
that great industrial undertakings were proper only in
the United States. It was in the first place upsetting to
all preconceived notions that Europeans should have
sufficient energy for them; and in the proofs they fur-
nished that they had there was something specially stark
and alarming. The town was sallow with cement, which
had been hacked up into little cubes as separate dwellings
and vast cubes as apartment houses, lavishly dour with
the meaningless tension, the scowling balconies, the grim
uncorniced walls, of modernist architecture; and around
them stretched gardens lusciously rank with the product
of dogged labour. There was no hint of poverty here,
but nothing communally owned or public was handsome.
The principal square was a waste of ragged grass, which
supported nakedly the plate glass and chromium band-

stand Marc had built as a memorial to his father. The shops were not very different from village shops, with just space enough for tradesman and housewife to wage a bargaining battle, and the cafés were gaunt resorts with round tin tables. There was no place of amusement at all except a shooting-gallery and the cinema palace which Marc had financed; and the population, the strong men who seemed to be slouching along in maillots and trousers not so much out of slovenliness as out of insolence, and the many-chinned women, who trundled their immense corpulencies in front of them with the confidence of beauties, did not look as if they would be easily distracted by any form of entertainment from their gloating contemplation of the inexorable practical demands of life, its harshness, and its willingness to be placated by the performance of certain harsh rituals. Nothing could be less like the reassuring appearance of an American industrial town, with its evidences of the existence of a new race which can find absolute contentment in the consumption of sweet foods and drinks, the possession of radios, and the contemplation of films. She looked at Marc with a new respect as she realized what terrifying material he worked on, and, as the car slid into a courtyard huge as the approach to some Egyptian palace, and as they walked later through hall after hall, where the whirling driving-belts lifted the eye from the innumerable squat machines with the soaring and admonitory effect of pillars in a cathedral, how tremendous was his creation. And when she told him this he said, "Well, darling, perhaps it's not so bad. For a factory, it's a factory."

Yes, Marc was a great man or, at least, a great industrialist. But he was a child, too. Social fictions deceived him completely. He placed complete credence in everything that anyone said to him, whether it was a servant telling him that his master was out, or a woman saying she had not been able to attend his mother's reception because she had had a headache. One serious consequence of this was that, when people said that they were pleased to see him, he really believed that at the sight of him they had been transfixed by an actual *frisson* of pleasure. As he had been in childhood the son of a rich man and all his adult life had been himself a rich and spectacularly successful man, people had always been declaring that they were pleased to see him, and had put considerable emphasis to their declarations; and he had deduced from this that he was universally popular. This was not due to immodesty on his part, for if he had set himself to analyse the situation, he would have without hesitation pronounced the operative factor to be not his own charm, but other people's generous readiness to give affection. It was not even due to insensitiveness. Isabelle knew that she was free from any such delusion only because she had been warned from childhood that a great part of the homage she would receive would be caused by public knowledge of her family's wealth. First her parents, and after their death Uncle Honoré, had gone to great pains to give her this instruction in a vein of cynical but happy humour which would prevent her feeling either arrogant or aggrieved over the situation; and later this instruction had been confirmed by literature. But the Sallafranques had not been able to bring so much subtlety to the education of their son. They had done their best, and it was far from being a mean best, to train Marc never to imagine that money gave its possessor real consequence, and they were unable to go further, because they had no humour except good humour and were wholly deficient in irony; and Marc's natural sweetness had led him to accept this imperfect teaching absolutely, and to assume that everybody else in the world was of the same high-minded opinion. Literature had no chance to correct him, for since he had left school he had never read a book.

So entirely creditable to Marc was this delusion, so purely the product of his candour and humility, that Isabelle felt ashamed of suffering embarrassment at it, and she set about disciplining herself not to notice it. But that she could not do during this visit to the factory. For there it continually appeared, from minute to minute, that just as his enormous vitality had transformed his father's plaything into an industrial masterpiece, so it had developed this charming error into a fantasy which departed so monstrously from reality that it was dangerous. As they drove into the courtyard they passed a crowd of workmen standing round the door of one of the workshops, and Marc lifted his arm and saluted them with a panache which Isabelle had thought fallen into desuetude among all persons of authority save princes in musical comedy. They answered with a roar of greeting that was partly spontaneous, a response to the spontaneity of his own gesture, but which was in the main raucous and unloving. Some genuine affection there must have been, for he was a fair though an exacting employer, and a fountain of kindness for hard cases. And it was true that there was a ring of gross good comradeship about the cheer, but that was because the sight of the boss made

them visualize and taste in their imagination the pleasures he enjoyed as a very rich man, the food, the drink,
the women, the right to sail in white boats on blue seas,
the right to hit and not be hit back. Perhaps, too, some of
them had won money backing his horses or his racing
automobiles. But a sense that it was only in imagination
that they could enjoy these pleasures, and that, though
they may have won their bets, the horses and the automobiles remained their master's, was making the faces
they turned towards him wolfish behind their smiles. So
it seemed to her eyes, and the history of Europe during
the last fifty years or so gave her no hope that she was
seriously mistaken. Yet Marc turned to her and beamed,
"You will see, they all adore me here."

It was the same when they sat in his office, a stupen-
dous apartment designed in that modernist style which
represents the last attempt of bad taste to escape the
criticisms of good taste. Having been reproached so often
for excessive and ill-conceived and ill-executed ornamentation and poor design, it has set about getting rid
of all ornamentation, and as much design as possible.
Here onyx mantelpieces set flat in the wall stared out
with the nakedness of a shaved cat; and tables that were
plain circles of glass on glass rods, and chairs that were
not even cubes but mere outlines of cubes in aluminium
and canvas, seemed to grudge being three-dimensional.
Isabelle had observed, in the houses of such of her
friends as had followed this fashion, that such featureless
settings threw into unnatural relief the characteristics of
everything introduced into them and made it seem in-
trusive. A red book left on one of these glass tables
looked scarlet and untidy; a woman sitting on one of

these chairs looked highly coloured, her attitude asymmetrical, her dress a trailing extravagance. This effect of the style made it peculiarly unsuitable for an office. The neat piles of paper look litter, the desk a pretentious indoor form of rubbish heap; the file of people called into the room to meet the future Madame Sallafranque showed against the plain background not as employees, but as human beings, diversified in type, active of soul. Marc, however, sat swinging from side to side on his aluminium and rubber revolving chair, with his strong hands patting his sinewy yet plump thighs, turning on all these people an invariable smile which implied that they were all alike, and in nothing more alike than this passionate loyalty to him.

There was, indeed, some truth in his theory; for certainly there were some who loved him. There was an old bearded man, with a proud carriage of the head and humble eyes, who plainly felt for the Sallafranques as a shepherd feels for the just master that protects him and for the sheep that he must protect. There was a man with a cock's wattle of chins and a chest like an air cushion, who introduced several abstract nouns such as "*la civilisation*" and "*l'humanité*" into his greeting to Isabelle, which took the form of congratulations on her good fortune in marrying into such a great industrial family. It was evident that he had made some identification between the Sallafranque business and "*la civilisation*" and "*l'humanité*"; and there was no limit to the sacrifices he would have made for any one of the trinity. There were one or two spectacled, high-shouldered intellectuals, whose genuinely amused yet tender smiles showed that they had perfectly grasped Marc's farcical

and noble character, but unfortunately they represented
a type of which Marc was always afraid, which he constantly suspected of laughing at him. And there were
several younger men who idolized him, but that was only
because they thought he was sly, hard, and greedy, as
he was not. Their admiration would have been tinged
with contempt if they had ever realized that he was candid and diffident, and would give up any advantage
rather than use it to another's hurt. She saw that contempt in the eyes of some of the middle-aged men, and
with a thrill of pleasure and surprise realized that she
resented that look almost as much as she had resented it
once on the flying-ground when she heard two envious
pilots speaking maliciously of Roy's aviation; she must
be nearly in love with Marc.

Yet she knew she was falsifying the situation if she
saw nothing happening save the spurning of Marc's virtues by little-minded subordinates. They had their case
against him. She had already guessed, from the hours he
kept, that he overworked all the employees whose ranks
brought them into personal contact with him; and now,
from the harassed, almost exasperated manner in which
many of these men came into his room, as if they could
not trust him on any occasion whatsoever to refrain from
laying an excessive burden on them, she knew that he
was a worse slave-driver than she had feared. It was a
matter, again, of over-simplified instruction. To guard
him from laziness he had been taught to work every
drop of strength out of his body, and to guard him from
conceit he had never been allowed to suspect that he was
stronger than other people. So from youth he had strode
through the twenty-four hours at the pace of a Marathon

race, dragging with him in increasing numbers human beings who had not his bull neck, his thick veins, his ropy sinews. And none of them could leave him, being manacled to him by the fact that he was their employer and they were his employees, and the same fact was a gag which prevented them from crying out and indicting him for lack of consideration. She saw, she did indeed, that there was a case against him, which was not less formidable because all his crimes were rooted in his innocence.

She saw it presented in terms of pageantry as they left the office just at noon, when the air was full of the stretched sound of siren-bleats, and all the workers were tumbling out of the shop doors to their midday meals. Out of one door tumbled a rainbow stream, the upholstresses in the blue and green and rose overalls Marc let them wear according to their taste. They were all springing and bounding with life, and some among them were beautiful, particularly certain exquisite blondes of the type the French working-classes occasionally produce, colourless but perfect creatures, in whom all the enticing qualities of youth are exhibited as in a transparent medium. When they saw Isabelle with Marc, they knew who she was, and they surged across the road and closed in on the automobile; they blotted out the sober day and the factory chimneys by a sudden flaring out of carnival laughter and the waving of handkerchiefs; they addressed Marc with hoarse cries as if they were rallying him on this new triumph of his potency, as if they were challenging him to turn this triumph into an orgy and embrace them all, and were threatening a jeering resistance so that he could thresh it all down,

all in the sphere of fantasy but with the plangency of the
intensest sort of day-dream. Marc grinned and roared
back at them like a bull, and from the workmen, who
were standing in dark, steady masses round the leaping,
dancing, multi-coloured women, came an answering
roar, harsh, wistful, mocking, stoical, full of what would
declare itself, if it were ever profitable to do so, as
definitely hatred. Isabelle smiled at them all, brilliantly
and rigidly, but she found herself clutching Marc's arm
defiantly, as if he were a child who was behaving intolerably before a crowd of censorious adults, but who
would have been faultless if only the whole world had
not conspired to spoil him.

"Tell me," she said, when they were on the road
again, "do you ever have strikes in your factories?"

He was driving, and he used it as an excuse not to
answer her for a moment, and then in a single word,
"Sometimes." Then, after a hundred yards, he went on,
as if he were nerving himself to speak of something infinitely tedious, perhaps a little shameful. "Yes, we have
strikes. Sometimes very bad ones. There was one terrible
one two years ago. As you see, they all adore me, down
there. But agitators sneak their way in and persuade
them to do what they don't intend, *les pauvres gosses.*"

"There may be more than that in it," she said.

"Perhaps, perhaps," he agreed, "but there's that in it,
too. And it's serious. You see, the factories have to be left
running like clockwork. When those silly fellows beyond
the Rhine attack us again, we've got to make big guns
and so on. The wheels must go on turning. Ah, but it's
difficult to talk about such things. Let's talk of something
else, my darling."

It was indeed very difficult to talk to him about these things, for he knew nothing about principles or the past, but everything about the facts brought before him by his vast business. It was impossible to carry on any truly contrapuntal conversation with him, in which theory and practice, or his particular experience and the general experience of all other beings, could be harmonized. Whoever his adversary might be, their dialogue was certain to stagger him by its alternate revelations of Marc's ignorance and his own. But Isabelle felt less and less acutely any pressing need to remedy this state of intellectual inchoateness, for she was growing more and more content with Marc as he was. The one embarrassment that vexed their intercourse was her inability to share fully with him her satisfaction at the progress of her emotions. But there was no help for that, since a woman cannot tell a man whom she is about to marry how pleased and amazed she is to find herself daily coming nearer to loving him, though in the circumstances he could not possibly hear better news. This discomfited her by its suggestion that the world in which human beings lived was not the same as the world of which they spoke and thought. But she forgot her discomfiture in the amusement of preparing for her marriage, of choosing her trousseau and her house, in the relieved knowledge that, though she had jumped a long way to escape from Laurence's humiliations, she had landed on her feet, and in this gratifying and convenient growth of her affection for Marc.

About five nights before the wedding Isabelle found herself in a mood which she could surely take as a certificate that all was well. She dined with Marc at Larue,

and was so happy with him that they both found it intolerable that they had to go on to a ball given by a
certain minister, and grumbled about it comfortably in
the automobile all the way to the Avenue Henri Martin,
but did not mind it in the least when they got there, because they were still together. They walked through the
rooms smiling up at the pictures, though these were
Boldinis and de la Gandaras and Carolus Durans, awful
exhibitions of that facility with paint which has nothing
to do with painting, which is closely akin to the Italian art
of winding macaroni round the fork; and they greeted all
their fellow-guests with acclamation, though these
were for the most part of spurious distinction, pompous old men who seemed to believe in the importance of
the orders they wore, and women whose pretentious conduct of huge hips and bosoms showed that they had misinterpreted the homage that had been offered to their
fortune and their early beauty as evoked by some real
and permanent value in themselves. Marc came on one
of these last who had been a friend of his mother many
years before; and such was his mood of melting benevolence that he greeted her with civilities which might
have been mistaken for the first frolics of an infatuation.
Why had they not met since his childhood, he inquired,
though the answer was obvious to anyone who had
known him in his manhood, and would she not dance
with him? He cast round an eye to see if he could leave
Isabelle in pleasant company meanwhile, and at the sight
of a tall figure leaning against the wall near by, he
clapped his hands, as if this was an encounter which
was something more than convenient, something really
opportune.

"Ah, but Isabelle, this is most fortunate! Here's Monsieur Campofiore! How are you, my friend? Now, you two must meet! Isabelle, this is one of my closest friends, one of my co-workers whom I really couldn't do without, who has done I can't tell how much for my silly little affairs. Though, mind you, Papa sometimes puts his little boy across his knee and gives him what for!" He smacked his friend hard on the back, and flung back his head, roaring with the laughter which means comradeship rather than that anything funny has happened. His friend smiled. "And this, old boy, I'm telling you, is Madame Tarry, to whom I'm going to be married at the beginning of next week. Isn't that a piece of news? Well, I'll leave you two together to conspire over what you're going to do to keep your foolish child in order! And now, Madame!"

Isabelle kept her eyes on him as he whirled the elderly lady round and round the room, watching him with tender amusement, for though he danced quite neatly, he infected every dance with the bounce and hop of the polka. But she was not unmindful to bow her head and murmur acknowledgments as the tall stranger beside her uttered certain formal sentences of felicitation, for she had a notion that he might be an odd and touchy kind of person. There was something old-fashioned about his aspect, reminiscent of the elegant gentlemen in the illustrations scattered through the text in the old editions of Maupassant and the Goncourts, for he had a silky, pointed beard and an air of self-contained gravity, and his clothes had a touch of fantasy and abundance about their cut, unusual in modern tailoring, which so envies the clinging economy of the human skin. He was per-

haps one of those misfitting people, more commonly female than male, who find no way of getting on terms
with their own age but are ambitious, and so go about
cutting a figure in the manner of those who struck them
as glorious when they were children. She was at pains
to make herself agreeable when he came to a pause by
saying, "You speak French as if you were French,
Monsieur. As a foreigner I am jealous."

"Madame," he answered, "I am French."

"I beg your pardon! I was misled by your name."

"I owe my name, which no doubt seems to you ridiculous——"

"Not at all," said Isabelle warmly, "it is far from being ridiculous, it is beautiful. What could be ridiculous
about a field of flowers?"

"I am not simple enough to think that most people
are of your mind," said Monsieur Campofiore. "But such
as my name is, I owe it to the circumstance that I come
from a little town called Origno, in the Alpes Maritimes,
behind Nice, very near the Italian frontier."

"Ah, in the mountains! That must be charming."

"It is not charming at all," said Monsieur Campofiore, in such a manner that she was obliged to believe
him. "The mountains there are without beauty or dignity. They are heaps of rubble overgrown with scrub.
In summer the country is excessively hot, in winter there
is flood and avalanche." After a moment's pause he
added, with no increase in cheerfulness, "My father was
the tax-collector there."

"That must have been interesting," said Isabelle.

"He did not find it so," replied Monsieur Campofiore.
There seemed to be no fruitful way of continuing this

line of conversation. Isabelle looked round the room to find a happier topic, and said, "I wonder who those two very beautiful girls are, who have just come in. They are the best-looking women here, don't you think?"

"My opinion would be valueless if I gave it," replied Monsieur Campofiore. "I regret that I am forced to regard the ladies of your world as failures, since they do not succeed in excelling the women of the people in beauty to any extent that would justify the greater amount of care and money that they lavish on themselves."

"I am sure you are right," said Isabelle.

A silence fell, which was broken only when Monsieur Campofiore said coldly, "I take no pleasure in such occasions as these, none at all. I am forced to attend them by my official position. But I cannot express how tedious, how insipid I find them."

"I can understand that very well," said Isabelle, "but all the world has not the same tastes. Lots of people here imagine that they are having a most wonderful time." Just then she caught sight of Marc, his face shining with absent-minded happiness, while he spun his gratified old lady round and round and round. "Why, look at Marc!" she said, laughing confidently, since this was his friend. "He seems to be enjoying himself quite a lot."

"Ah," said Monsieur Campofiore, "Marc Sallafranque would enjoy himself on the edge of the pit."

It was the pure voice of hatred that spoke. He hoped that Marc would fall into the pit, he hoped that the pit would be deep. Isabelle continued to smile at the dancers, but a shudder ran over her scalp.

Presently she saw old Sam Soutar from the Embassy and beckoned him to her. As he obeyed, the man by her side muttered his respects, bowed, and retired.

"Sam, you know everybody," she said, "who is that terrible man I've been talking to? His name is Campofiore."

"Why, what's Campofiore been doing? He's usually a quiet chap."

"But what is he? What does he do?"

"He's a bottle-washer in one of the Ministries, either Finance or Commerce, I can't remember which at the moment."

"But is he very important, has he much power?"

"No, I should think he was quite insignificant. He's got no family connexions, he's got no political backing, nobody seems to take much notice of him."

"You're sure?" asked Isabelle. But just then Marc came to a standstill in front of them, beaming with satisfaction at the treat he had given his partner, though it was apparent from her dishevelment that what pleasure she had felt at his attentions had for some time been obliterated by sheer physical pain. Isabelle could not bear to tell him that somebody he had claimed as a playmate was an enemy, that there was hateful stuff in human beings which was incensed by his simplicity; and if Campofiore was unimportant, she need not speak of the incident. It would do later on, say if there was any question of inviting him to their house. She held out her arms to Marc, and he drew her into the dance. She bobbed like a cork on the choppy motion of his steps, and was quite happy, for though this was not in any strict sense of the word dancing, it was dancing with him. But again a shudder ran over her scalp when a vista opened among the dancers and showed her Campofiore, back in his place against the wall, his lips moving and his head jerking, as if he were repeating over to himself a conversation in which he had had very much the best of it.

The incident came back to her during an hour of panic on the night before her wedding eve, which did not affect her very deeply because she had known that it was bound to come. To help herself through it, she had kept unopened till then a thick envelope imprinted with her Uncle Honoré's Californian address, which she imagined would contain an amplification of the affectionate but brief cable he had sent in reply to her announcement of her engagement. But its thickness proved to be due to the presence of several legal documents which required her signature immediately after her marriage, for Uncle Honoré had contented himself with an expression of his love and his readiness to give her the benefit of his sixty-five years' store of wisdom whenever she should need it. At this she felt curiously desolate, and sat for a long time by her window, staring at the moon, wishing that she knew more of the fixed principles by which life was determined, and regretting that she had never had a prolonged private conversation with Uncle Honoré. She had really not the faintest idea what he believed. All she knew was the easy attitude of tolerance, stiffening only when the distaste for violence was aroused, which his beliefs had led him to adopt. That she had imitated as far as possible, and it had helped her; but she was aware that in her own case it was a façade without foundations which, well as it had sheltered her from bad weather, might be blown down by any worse weather. She shivered as if the moonbeams falling on her breast were cold, though the night was warm.

But the morning after her wedding she woke up enjoying renewed confidence in Uncle Honoré's wisdom. He must have divined, from what she had told him about Marc, that for the moment she would be in no need of his counsel. On waking she found herself alone, and leant from the window sill for a minute, humming, before she began to dress. They had started so late from Paris on their journey to the South that they had arrived at this little inn long after nightfall; and she found herself in a part of France that was quite new to her. It was the France one sees in tapestries. Over rolling country, very cool in colour, were scattered pastures and cornfields and tall woods standing on higher ground. A grey village lay like its own map on the side of a hill, and the flat square summit was a great church, visible far away not only as a building, but as a symbol of the faith in the land. Everywhere there was a spreading beneficence of mild light. At the end of the inn garden, which was so neatly cultivated that the hoe marks between the cabbages showed like fine stitching, was a stream that gave back some of this light, sliding quickly yet glassily by the willow trees. On the brink of it stood the innkeeper and Marc, looking into the water and wagging their heads, plainly exchanging platitudes, as Frenchmen do, for the pleasure of feeling their mouths full of the good meat of common sense. She turned away with tears in her eyes, remembering how the night before, in his arms, she had found herself in a country quite new to her, more full of gentleness and tenderness than any other she had known.

They lingered five days in Yonne; but after that they were obliged to make their way down to the villa at Cap d'Antibes, which was being lent them by Marc's grandaunt Berenice, because the offer of it had been an olive-branch. For the last two years, it seemed, Grandaunt Berenice had been very much displeased with Marc, for some reason or other, and this was the first movement she had made towards a reconciliation. There was really no hardship in accepting the offer, for the house was a kind of Moorish palace, full of hoarded coolness which the summer could not dissipate, and round it was a walled and terraced garden watered by its own springs, which slid perpetually along broad marble conduits. Marc and Isabelle used to sit there when they got up, looking across the milky bay of Cannes and the dark islands that seemed to be floating sometimes on the water and sometimes on the air, at the Esterel mountains, which were so like the morning mists in their ragged majesty that it was always surprising when the full light confirmed their fantasy and showed them solid rock. As the sea turned blue, they went down and swam or sailed their boat, and they lunched on a wire-screened veranda with half a dozen tropical birds making bright streaks under the shadowed eaves. In the afternoon they rested in a vast bedroom, where the darkness was reflected in old mirrors as amber and much lighter than it was, and in the evening they played tennis, or swam again, or walked up through the pines to the lighthouse and sat by the chapel, with the sun setting behind the Esterel

on their right hand and on the left the Bay of Angels
growing inky with night, though the pillars of rock
behind Monte Carlo and the Italian mountains beyond
still flushed like stone roses. They dined at home or at
a little restaurant in the old port of Antibes, where an
arch in the high wall showed masts black against blue
and rigging with stars caught in it. At no time in such
days was Isabelle not amazed by the infiniteness of
Marc's good will. Though all his ties were with the
strong and not with the weak, he would not have had a
sparrow fall, anywhere in the world.

But people began to find them out. When they dined
by the port, the great cream-coloured automobile waited
for them in the square at Antibes, and it was excessively
recognizable. From that time their gardens might as
well not have been walled. Their early mornings were
still free, and they padlocked behind them the road down
to the private beach, but when they came back for
lunch, there were people all over the gardens, and sitting on the veranda, dressed like the Russian ballet and
often beautiful in themselves, but not what they wanted.
These people had to be given cocktails, they often had
to be asked to stay to lunch, and though they left in the
afternoon about three, they were back again in the early
evening, not so different as they should have been considering that this time they were not the same people.
Gladys and Nikolai had gone over to dine with Daisy at
Monte Carlo, but they had been replaced in all essentials
and in most superficialities by Iris and Serge. As Isabelle
extended her hand to the apparent third and fourth of
this actual pair, and realized that she and Marc would
not be able to go up to the lighthouse this evening be-

cause their dusk was going to be overpopulated by Dop-
pelgängers of the crowd that had camped all over their
noon, she saw that her married life was going to be made
as difficult by Marc's wealth and position as if his work
had compelled them to live in an unhealthy climate. She
had thought that she had many friends, but hers were
a handful compared with the army that insisted on its
vague ties with Marc. Her friends represented the cast
of a legitimate play, which hardly ever exceeds a moderate number, since a theme cannot be crisply expounded
by too many mouths, but his friends represented the cast
of a Follies show, which, debating no particular point,
but stirring certain large loose fantasies of delight in the
lower levels of the mind, can be as numerous as the hosts
of a dream. The fault in the situation was that he, like
her, had his true place in the legitimate drama. He was,
as his mother had often told her, serious. His heart
wanted to work out one simple theme, and his naïve and
powerful mind was eager to grapple with ideas in its
Douanier Rousseau way. He was in this world not because of anything in himself, but because he had become
associated in its eyes with the most erethic of all its
fantasies, wealth. Once there, he was not altogether unhappy, for he loved to play for recreation as these people
loved to play out of idleness, and his good tough stretchable
body gave him a pleasant pre-eminence among them.
But he and she made the same effect here as actors from
the legitimate drama when they are called upon to play
specially exacting parts in a revue or a musical comedy;
they might stand out for their competence and their
subtlety, but they lacked the bloom, undisturbed by the

touch of thought, which made others round them delec-
table as peaches.

Isabelle found her visitors not unlikeable people. It
was true that they were catarrhal with affection; whether
they were French, Russian, English, or American, en-
dearments flowed from them as freely as rheum from an
irritated mucous membrane. This was only in part due
to mercenary motives, for a considerable proportion of
them were so rich that they had no need to curry favour
with their friends. It came rather from their intention,
never formulated but governing all their actions, to treat
life so that it would never form any pattern, to rub down
each phenomenon till it became indistinguishable from
all others of its kind. They hampered friendship by taking its special vocabulary and distributing it as largesse
among all human beings, so that it could not perform its
function of building up strong preferences. They themselves paid a price for this, for all their relationships
were in a constant state of flux; inseparables of a fort-·
night ago would today speak only about and not to each
other. But this they did not mind, for they were dedicated people who, the better to serve this intention, had
taken vows of wealth, unchastity, and disobedience to all
standards. No vows are easy to keep, since they demand
a quality of persistence which the human race does not
possess, and these votaries failed as frequently as any
others. They all carried on so far as they were able a
machine-gun-like succession of disbursements for goods
which did not endure, such as food and drink and hotel
accommodation and the attendance of world-famous and
epicene hairdressers, or some hours at the baccara table,

and thus did their part in reducing the monetary system
to sheer nonsense; but a considerable proportion fell by
the wayside, and found themselves in an impoverished
condition that any Franciscan might have envied. These
lapsed cases excited just such censoriousness among some
of their fellow-votaries, and in others just such a kindly
determination to lift them up and restore them to the
right path, as they would have found had they committed
their faults as members of an ascetic organization.

They were perhaps happier in their campaign
against chastity. It seemed to be much more successfully
conducted. Isabelle was startled to find how many of
the women had had Marc as a lover. He always betrayed
it when he introduced them to her by the pensiveness of
his terrier eyes, a penitent protrusion of His lower lip,
and a disposition to smack them on the behind, a part of
the body which, in the female, he regarded as symbolical
of that which was urgent yet not important. But she was
still more startled to find that, although all these people
knew that she and Marc had been married only a few
weeks, several of the women showed signs of desiring to
renew or initiate relations with Marc, and several of the
men offered to seduce her. This was not because they
were wickedly perverse, but because they lived in a sexual universe in which all frontiers had been broken
down, including those of time, and it was not less likely
that people would commit adultery on their honeymoon
than at any other time.

But here, too, there were lapses. Outbreaks of love
paralysed free sexual exchange, and both satiety and age
inexorably worked for abstinence. But there could be no
question but that unchastity was a far easier discipline to

follow than disobedience to all standards. That meant waging a constant battle with the flesh and the spirit, for man is an inveterately theorizing animal, who cannot look out of his eyes without basing opinions on what he sees, and basing on those opinions preferences and parties and flaming loyalties and steely repudiations, and, in fact, the formation of standards and obedience to them. These votaries did what they could to stop the trouble at the source by softening what their eyes showed them, through the constant self-administration of small doses of alcohol. Many of them never became actually drunk, and those that did were usually sober enough until evening, but nearly all made a practice of sitting down the minute they had finished their swimming or their motor-boat racing, or their surf-riding, and drinking enough cocktails to dilute the universe round them, to rob it of its power, and to prevent it taking advantage of their momentary disengagement from physical preoccupations. They practised, too, a resolute canalization towards personal ends of all their emotions, even of tho sorts that one had thought inextricably associated with the intellect. The passion which men bring to debates regarding free will and determinism, or capitalism and communism, which never wearies of the controversy and longs to burn its opponents at the stake, was here directed to interminable arguments as to whether Gordon Lloyd had a right to do what he did on Ferdy Monck's yacht at Saint-Tropez last week, and whether Laura had really said what Annette said she had at the bridge-party at Super-Cannes just afterwards. To restrain their force within these channels they barred all others. Marc never read a book, but these people went further. They had no dealings with printed matter at all except in the morning when they looked at the headlines of the newspapers, and on journeys, when they read illustrated papers and detective stories.

It was there that the main difficulty in their lives began, that the problem arose which made them, on the whole, noticeably more driven and irritable than the people in the world outside. They had refused all succour offered to them by the mind, and there is simply not enough for the body to do unassisted during the whole twenty-four hours. They could sleep, but not for very many hours; they could not sit longer than a certain limited time over their meals; if they filled up one day with love-making to any considerable extent, they only had all the more time on their hands for the next day or so; and if they gossiped for more than a certain time, they felt either a kind of uncomfortable vacancy, like a neurotic who has been gulping air, or became involved in acrimony. There was always physical exercise, but that had a fatal way of coming after a time to raise more problems than it solved. What one does too well becomes not worth doing, unless in rivalry with equals—and it becomes a matter of increasing difficulty to find them— or with some honour or wager depending on the issue. It was then that they turned to number, and let it into their lives, keeping it abstract, dissociating it from any computation affecting human interests, at the bridge table or the backgammon board. But numbers, however they are treated, make the head spin after an hour or two. There was dinner, of course, and they could eat and drink a great deal then, and there were the hours afterwards. Of course there might be a party, which

gave an opportunity for public submission to the vows,
for further disbursements, and fresh sexual transposi-
tions. But sometimes there was not, and then they had
to have careful recourse to number again, as it was presented in the Casino, with due regard for post-prandial
conditions, with croupiers doing most of the work, and
plenty of gold and cocottes about to give the right lick-
erish atmosphere. However, the result of saying "Banco!"
at the wrong time might be one of those painful involuntary lapses into Franciscan poverty, and the stale heat distressed the lungs which the physical exercise necessary to
fill in other hours had made exigent of fresh air. They
went to bed, most nights, feeling miserable. The invisible
scourgings in this convent without walls had power to
draw blood.

Marc and Isabelle found themselves constantly attacked by this world, and they fell under its total domination the day they spent with Gustave Bourges and his
American wife at their villa on Cap Ferrat. They went
over before lunch, taking their evening clothes, because
they had all been invited to a party in Monte Carlo. The
day began well, with a walk along a cypress avenue that
ran its dark cool vista to a round swimming-pool lined
with blue tiles, where they bathed in fresh water and
looked as they swam at the salty blue glint of the sea a
hundred feet below, and the far range, vague now with
distance but still sharply fantastic, of the Esterel mountains. Afterwards they lay on mattresses on a marble
bench, a little Capuchin monkey skipping backwards
and forwards over their bodies. They patted it tenderly,
feeling pity for its animal folly. But it began to seem a
very long time until lunch, and after they had discussed

for some time whether Gordon Lloyd had had a right to do what he did on Ferdy Monck's yacht at Saint-Tropez last week, and were unable to follow through by discussing whether Laura had said what Annette said she did at Super-Cannes, because Laura herself was present, the backgammon boards were brought out. Then the menservants came up with cocktails, which recalled a children's party by their light and creamy appearance and sweetish taste, but which acted like a powerful brake on all discontented and aggressive movements of the mind. The party moved with calmer spirits through a vaguer world down to the house, where they dressed again, and sat down to lunch, and ate and drank. as happy as if they were in Eden.

But the afternoon was endless. Marc and Isabelle played bridge and backgammon until their eyes ached, and then they revolted, though Laura grew waspish, since she could gamble for ever. Then they went out to the tennis-courts but there they had to choose their partners from Madame Bourges, who was unalterably a rabbit, and the professional, whose play with his employer's guests was panderish, and young Dan Creed, who was six foot six, and Mrs. Postleham, whose game was said, by those who ought to have known, to represent the excess of an insatiable temperament. Later they went to the sea and tried surf-riding with the Bourges' new motor boat. But Marc and Isabelle had long mastered that art, which is exciting only so long as one is a novice and uncertain of one's balance; once it becomes a matter of standing upright on a board till muscular fatigue makes one drop off, it ceases to be a sport and resolves into its component parts, of which the last two, the im-

pact with the sea at a high speed and immersion until
people in a boat choose to pick one up, are not in themselves attractive. Later they went back to the swimming-
pool and drank more cocktails, the Capuchin monkey
skipping backwards and forwards over their bodies. They
patted it tenderly, envying its animal wisdom. Then
they went back to the house to dress. Isabelle flung herself down on the bed, and Marc came and lay beside her,
nuzzling his face against the curve of her waist and
grumbling, "I'm bored! I'm bored!" To him boredom
was a tragedy, for he had no more realization than if
he had been an animal that any state he was in would
ever come to an end. She murmured comfort to him and
stroked his hair, which was strong and wiry like a dog's
coat, and presently rose and began to put on her evening
garments. She walked up and down the room, brushing
her hair, in a white satin slip that made astonishing the
gold of her sunburned arms and legs. Marc rolled over
on the bed and grunted wistfully, "Ah, if we hadn't
had this dreary day, I could have done something about
that!"

It was difficult to get him up and make him dress, because he had gone back to being a little boy, and his
starched shirt affected him as if he were five instead of
thirty-two. But downstairs, when they were all gathered
together, their sunburn glistening like grease paint and
giving their evening clothes a look of theatrical costume,
and had drunk some more cocktails, the feeling that at
some point during this expedition they were going to
have a good time regained the ground it had lost during
the day. They found further exhilaration in the speed
of the great automobiles, and the brilliance of their

swoops round the darkening curves of the Corniche, and they dismounted laughing at the Duchess's villa. They cried out with admiration when they passed through the house and were greeted by her and the other guests beside the lily pool, for by some device of lamps set on the ground the whole air was flooded with gentle, diffused beams, and the terraced gardens marched down the hill to the sea like a staircase of starlight. Men and women alike turned to each other faces shining with magic, romantically hawklike with deep shadows, and distant groups either floated in silver or were silhouetted black and leaner than they were, like gay and fluid skeletons. Presently they all sat down at a long table, the length of the terrace, and shadows filled their glasses with the muted sharpness of champagne and covered their plates with food that was either burning hot or icy cold. A flower of good cheer ought to have burst into bloom, were it not that there is a special foe of dedicated persons known as accidia. It descends on them suddenly and is not to be repelled by argument. They are living their customary life, they are performing the exercises they have found most suitable for the promotion of their faith, but the wells of the spirit run dry. The purpose to which they have vowed their souls stares at them like a senseless monster, not worth nursing. The support of grace is withdrawn from them, melancholy flows in their veins. This disorder has most often been noticed in monasteries and convents, but no votaries are exempt from it, whatever their vows.

It was here in the villa gardens, triumphant as the plague, before the dinner was eaten. As the diners sat over their coffee, the window of the music-room above

them was thrown open, and the voice of a famous Polish
tenor strode out and was suspended in the night. But it
would not serve; the auditors sat glum. When there was
silence again, they scattered miserably among the flowers and fountains, murmuring that they had never
known a lousier party. Later the gardens suddenly became dark around them, and there was a moment's hush,
when only the sea spoke on the rocks below. Then there
began the hissing, tearing, knocking sounds of fireworks,
which touch and lacerate because we remember them
from our earliest childhood, and the soft curtain of
night was riven by showers of golden rain, by burning
Catherine-wheels, by emerald flowers wider than a con-
stellation, and a peacock that for a minute blotted out
half the universe with its more brilliant fires. Those who
sat and watched in the darkness did not find the darkness
in their souls dispersed by these simple but supreme
achievements of light. Even as anchorites in their cells
are at times tormented by voluptuous visions, so these
people, who had come together with the intention of
breaking down their experience to elementary sensa-
tions of pleasure, were distraught by a momentary dis-
ability to find anything whatsoever agreeable. When the
peacock had furled its tail and was itself furled into the
night, and the blackness closed in on them again, they
turned to each other, muttering plans for immediate
flight, and when the lamps were switched on again, the
white beams disclosed most of them already on their
feet, in fugitive attitudes. It seemed to Isabelle as they
went out that the Duchess was near to tears; she was
growing old. But Isabelle could do nothing, she and
Marc had been brought by the Bourges, who were now

murmuring frenetically that they would feel better at
the Sporting Club. In the great automobiles the whole
party sat huddled up, saying over and over again, "Say,
wasn't that terrible? Wasn't it perfectly terrible?"

The Sporting Club was shut, because it was summer.
They had to go to the Casino, at which some of them
exclaimed in distress, though they did not abandon their
intention of gambling, just as good Church people will
grumble if they have to attend a place of worship higher
or lower than their habit, but will not contemplate miss-
ing a service. When Marc and Isabelle were sitting on
opposite sides of the roulette table in the Casino, they exchanged sickly smiles, and she perceived from a shadow
of concern in his eyes that she was looking ghastly. She
was indeed aching with that depression, which oddly
takes the form of a sense of guilt, that comes to those
who find themselves alone in sobriety among the al-
coholized; but he was looking ghastly too. Through boredom he had accepted most of the drinks that had been
offered him during the last twelve hours, and though he
was not drunk, since the resilient composition of which
his nerves were made was almost impermeable to alcohol,
he was suffering from indigestion, just as if he had
stuffed himself with a like quantity of cakes or fruit.
His pallor was blue in the shadows, and he kept on yawning, to his own great distress, for he had had perfect
manners drilled into him in his children's party days,
and he felt he was being rude to the two women on each
side of him. When he yawned, it filled her with panic
lest she should go to sleep, and she began to talk with
a drowning grip on animation to the man next to her.
The only subject she could think of was the mural

decorations, feeble and yet robust in their presentation of
their feebleness, decadent and yet strong as any pioneer
in their confident assault on their audience, the pictorial
equivalent of the ballet *Coppélia*. When they were finished laughing at a panel depicting some girls in that kind
of peasant costume which involves wearing their corsets
outside instead of inside their clothes, she looked across
the table and saw that Marc had left his place. She
thought that he must have gone out because he was ill,
and she was much relieved when he came back with a
handful of chips.

"Ah!" she said to her neighbour, "I'm so glad. I
thought my husband had gone out because he was ill,
but he only went to change some money." "Ah, did he
now!" answered her neighbour, in such a peculiar tone,
amused and cynical, and something even more malicious
than this, that she stared first at him and then at Marc.
But she could see no reason for the amusement or the
malice. Marc had bought chips for ten thousand francs
or so, and he was putting them out in fairly substantial
piles; the amount was no larger than what was being
risked by at least two others of their party, and his pro-
cedure differed not at all from anybody else's at the
table. It was true that his expression was sulky and
desperate, and fitted grotesquely on a face that had been
designed for good humour, and she suspected that perhaps her neighbour had been misled by this into thinking
him a little drunk. But then, had that been so, there
would have been nothing specially noteworthy about it,
for both Gustave Bourges and Prince Ostrogin were in a
state of being moonishly amused at anything that passed
before their glassy eyes. She passed her hand over her

forehead, and was about to dismiss the matter as a fantasy born from the toxins of her fatigue and the hot stagnant air, when she looked across the table and recognized on Sarah Bourges's face an envenomed version of the expression she had suspected in her neighbour. It was impossible to mistake its meaning. It betrayed the glee felt by the mean-spirited when they see people who do not deserve humiliation forced to suffer it through some accidental contact, of which they themselves are unaware. So do they look when a wife finds herself in the presence of a woman who is or has been her husband's most beloved mistress, but, knowing nothing of it, sits unperturbed. It suddenly seemed to Isabelle that there was something ashamed and voluptuous about the heavy mask Marc was bending over his counters, and she had to exercise the sternest self-control to prevent herself staring round the room to see if it contained any specially desirable woman. It was a great relief that Marc lost his money in a very few turns of the wheel, shrugged his shoulders, and rose in an almost churlish insistence on departure.

IV

NEXT MORNING Isabelle woke up in Marc's arms, muttering, "It was horrid last night in the Casino."

He looked past her with the grave eyes of a beaten dog. "It is funny that once I quite liked roulette," he said.

"We'll never, never, never do that again," she yawned, rubbing her face against his chest.

"Never again," he said.

They purged themselves by leaving the house as soon as they had breakfasted, and spending the whole day on the hills between Grasse and Draguignan. The amber walls and rusty roofs of Fayence, the pure blue flowers that showed on the grass as fine as spiders, the steep town of Callas, set on a hill like a dunce's cap, a cistern glowing like an emerald at the bottom of a valley of olive-terraces, these gave them the cleansing and remorseful pleasure felt at the first natural objects seen outside the sickroom by an invalid whose prolonged illness has been in part his own fault. They came back at dusk, and dined at the little place by the port, and went to bed early, having seen none of their friends all day, and therefore feeling reconciled to mankind.

When she woke up on the following day, she felt magnificent in health, and very playful, even a little cruel, and she stretched out her arms towards Marc, to embrace him, to torment him. But he was not there. He had risen, in a hurry, it appeared, for he had left the sheets thrown back, and had not tucked them in again, as he had always done before when he had got up while she was still sleeping. She sat up in bed rubbing her eyes and trying to exorcise her feeling of alarm. The bathroom door was closed and from behind it was a sound of running water. Marc was having his bath, the morning was going on its normal course; there was nothing extraordinary about it except the earliness of the hour. She could see, from the angle at which the sunshine lay on the balcony, that it was long before their usual time for rising; and as her eye dwelt anxiously on this differently shaped patch of brightness, it was drawn, and forgot its anxiety, to the view palely painted above the balustrades.

Today the milk-white sea was divided by glassy waterways into crinkled continents, and was divided from a sky almost as colourless as itself by a broad blurred line of indigo blue. All the landscape was tenderer than she had ever seen it. The rising sun discovered rosy sands under the dark trees on the edge of the islands, and picked out the houses on the high land about the bays and made them almost as warm as flesh. The Esterel mountains no longer showed as a rugged and continuous range, blue and fantastic, but disclosed themselves as a multitude of gentler hills, of mild hues which claimed that here also was the soil, which men live by, which being watered gives grass and flowers. There was a plenitude of light, as much as the space between earth and sky could hold;

but there was nothing to tell the eye of heat; and when she went to the window, a cool wind blew on to her bare body, as if there were a mystic essence in the morning which would preserve its freshness however the sun might assault it, for so long as the season decreed for its existence. It was inviolable though doomed. To enjoy its brief perfection, to feel all around her this magically renewed air that would in an hour be as used as if time had never known morning but had always stood at noon, she put on pajamas and ran barefoot out of the room and downstairs. The salon felt dead as living-rooms do before the household has arisen; but in the garden the air was like the breath of life.

The wind of the morning was light as yet, a mere wandering freshness; within the netted loggia the tropical birds flashed brightly back and forth, more silently than later in the day, as if the light had not yet made its full call to them. There was such a stillness among the trees as there is after dawn. The green fireworks of the four palm trees that stood at each cornor of the walled garden dripped gently rigid from their proud, gnarled rocket-sticks; the gold-powdered mimosa branches waited delicately, ready to bend beneath the weight of an air, but no air leaned on them; the fig tree bore up under the pervading corpulence that plumped its stocky trunk, its sleek leaves, and its fleshy fruit. Each presented to the eye, whole and observable, a form utterly undisturbed by movement. The flowers, too, the high hedges of oleander with their clear and vivid yet somehow impure range of reds and pinks, like fruit juice stained with cream, and in the beds the fawny-orange gladioli and the dahlias that were made sombre by their velvety surface even when they were white, were more themselves than they would be later in the day. There was a fineness of colour there now which the noontide sun would take by its heat, as it would take by its light the power from the eye of the beholder to see delicately the residue. All brightness of leaf and flower looked cool as if the day were damped with mist, only there was no mist, but an extreme clearness. She walked slowly through the garden, liking the cold shock of the tiles under her feet, lifting her arms above her head and drawing the freshness deep down into her lungs.

Suddenly she dropped her arms by her side. A man was sitting on the marble edge of the conduit on her left, only a few yards ahead of her. She had not seen him before because he was wearing a white linen suit that at even a little distance made him invisible against the marble and, furthermore, he was perfectly still. He held on his knees a folded newspaper, but he was not reading it. He was staring up at her so intently that when at last she saw him he could not alter his pose for a minute to rise and greet her. Plainly he expected her to know him, and, indeed, after a second, she did. It was the old-fashioned pointed beard that first reminded her, but confirmation came from the cut of his suit, which was very different from the austere and elastic attire that Isabelle's contemporaries wore in the south; it recalled rather one of Pierre Loti's colonial heroes.

"Ah, Monsieur Campofiore!" she exclaimed. "How do you do?"

"You are wonderful," he said, "but of course all

ladies in your position are trained to recognize the obscure."

"Not the obscure but the energetic," she replied gaily.
"We have few such early visitors as you!"

"Well, as I do not have to remind you," he said, "I
come from a level of society that is too busy earning its
bread to lie in bed late in the morning. And today I had
need to see your husband immediately, so I came down
at the first possible moment and paid no regard to cere-
mony."

"You have not just come off the train?" asked Isabelle
anxiously, thinking she would offer him coffee.

"Oh, no," said Monsieur Campofiore. "I am staying
in the neighbourhood."

She remembered the transparent amber Italian mountains she had seen from the lighthouse. "Ah, at Origno!"

"No, not at Origno!" exclaimed Monsieur Campofiore,
with the appearance of fury. "I am staying at Cannes!
At the Miramar! I have a bedroom, a sitting-room, a
bathroom!" On the last word he choked and grew scarlet, as if he felt that he had been guilty of an absurdity.
"I mean I have a suite!" But that statement, too, af-
flicted him with a sense of gaucherie, and he continued
to be scarlet and to stammer.

"Ah, you are very wise," said Isabelle. "Everyone
says it is a very comfortable hotel."

She was annoyed by the destruction of her cool, still
morning by the intrusion of this hot misery, which she
could not remedy, which she did not believe she would
respect if she knew its cause. For a minute she stood,
smiling vaguely up at the light, trying to find something

more to say; then to recover the freshness the hour had lost, she went over to the conduit and thrust her hands into the stream, then raised them, dripping, to sluice her face.

She raised her head and stood with her wet hands in front of her, staring at Monsieur Campofiore; for she had heard him utter a cry of rage and atrocious suffering. He looked, indeed, as if her action had convulsed him with pain. He had crushed his newspaper against his chest in a dented cylinder, and his face was contorted with what was very like a sexual grimace, though utterly gleeless. Her eye caught the dark core of this grimace, and she shuddered in her understanding of it. In a desire to depreciate everything belonging to Marc, his ox, his ass, and his wife, Monsieur Campofiore had told himself that her beauty was artificial, her perfect skin a matter of paint and powder; and when she had sluiced her face with water, she had not only deprived his hatred of its food, she had also made him discontented with some faded woman that he had taken because there were great names in her past. She had made Monsieur Campofiore feel that, try as he could, it was his lot to enjoy only the second-rate, and leave the best to his masters.

Resolutely she smiled, though she was trembling. She wished her jacket was not lifted by her breasts, she wished that more than thin silk covered her nakedness. "Well, I will go in now," she said, speaking very slowly, "and I will tell my husband that he must not keep you waiting any longer." From his bow, which was deep and too humble, she knew that he was ashamed of his out-

burst, and that his shame would make him still more full
of hate. It was hard not to hurry, and not to look back
at him as she walked to the house.

In the salon she met Marc, and she threw herself into
his arms.

"My poor little one, what is the matter?" he said, and
though he spoke tenderly, Isabelle could see that she was
only adding one more to worries that had found him
earlier in the morning.

She pulled herself together, but she said, "Marc, need
you go out and see that man? He hates us so."

"My darling," he answered mildly, "you exaggerate.
I don't think that he hates us. I have always found him
very friendly. He is only doing his duty."

"I can't think what his duty can be," she said impatiently, "but don't see him."

He lifted her hands from his shoulders, kissed them,
and put them down at her sides. "That, however," he
said with a sigh, "is just what I must do."

She watched him go from her with alarm, and a sort
of aggrieved indignation because he would not take her
warning that immediately struck her as absurd. "After
all, he is not going to fight a duel!" she reminded herself. "This man Campofiore is not going to take out a
pistol and shoot at him!" Very quickly she ran upstairs
and rang for her maid, and began to take her bath and
dress. When she was sitting before her mirror and the
maid was brushing her hair, she suddenly cried, "Stop!"
and rose, and went into one of the bedrooms that over-
looked the gardens. Marc and Campofiore were now
side by side on a bench that faced the window, and the

newspaper now lay on Marc's knees. He sat looking down
at it, while the other leaned towards him and sometimes
tapped on it to emphasize a climax in his argument, a
denunciation, or whatever it might be. From the unnecessary thrust of his beard, from something at once
cowering and aggressive in his attitude, which made her
think of a shabby menagerie wolf that through an accident has its keeper at its mercy and tries to revive its
long beaten and suppressed ferocity, she knew that he
was speaking to Marc with intolerable insolence. But
what horrified her in the scene was that Marc made not
one movement of protest against the steady rain of insult. Sometimes he put his elbows on his knees and rested
his head in his hands, but that was plainly in order to
gain self-control. It could not be doubted that he felt
himself entirely in the power of this twisted and malig-
nant man, even to such an extent that his impulsiveness,
his manliness, his dignity, were for the moment wholly
paralysed.

"Why," thought Isabelle, "it must be that he's being
blackmailed." There crept over her skin like vermin the
realization that she was no more exempt than any other
human being from being touched by squalor. But she
reflected that, if this affair were bad for her, it must be
far worse for Marc. She went back to her bedroom and
finished dressing herself, taking a long time over it,
partly because she was sure that the interview would go
on for some time, and partly because she wished to appear before Marc as aware of his plight and completely
unshaken by it. Then she went and saw the chef, who
was just back from market, and told him how many

there would be for meals, and praised his way of cooking aubergines. The old man was not very pleased. He said that when he was a boy and had started cooking in the kitchens of the Countess Greffuhle, the fine world had liked to eat delicately, but now all that was changed; one got no praise unless one served food that might have come out of a peasant's pot, and if it reeked of saffron or garlic, so much the better. Isabelle smiled and made apologies for her grossness, but her mind flashed back to the scene in the garden and its threat, and she thought, "You are right, people of our sort are different now, they are not delicate creatures set apart, vulnerable as we used not to be." She shuddered and left the kitchen, and cautiously peered round a column of the loggia to see if the detestable interview had come to an end. It had indeed. Marc was sitting alone on the bench, drumming with his hands on his knees, the newspaper lying between his feet.

She hurried out and sat down beside him. There was a gardener working in a flower-bed a few yards away, so she could not throw her arms round him, but she took his right hand and held it to her breast.

"My dear," she said, "has he been very horrible to you?"

Marc nodded. "Pretty horrible. I think now that you are right. That man hates me." He took his hand away, from her breast, and stroked her fingers tenderly, looking down into her palm. Then, when his breath had grown calmer, he said mildly, "But, my dear, I must be fair. Considering what he was here for, he was not so horrible."

She said fiercely, "But he can't do anything to you! Why do you see him, why do you bother to talk to him? Why do you not hand him over to the police?"

"My darling," asked Marc, "who do you think Monsieur Campofiore is?"

Isabelle looked straight into his eyes and flung back her head, to show she did not care. "A blackmailer," she said.

"Ah, my darling," he said, "who could blackmail me? I have never done anything to be ashamed of. I have never been able to understand how people put themselves within range of this blackmailing business. If a thing is so disgraceful that one would not like it published, one simply does not do it, that is all. With people who have special morals, poor things, that is different, of course. But you ought to know that I am not among them. Monsieur Campofiore is something quite different. He is a government official, my dear. He is the head of the state department that deals with such matters as my factory."

"He is a government official?" she repeated stupidly.

"Yes, my darling."

"Of course, so he is!" she exclaimed. "Sam Soutar told me so." It was an even greater shock to her to remember that this disordered and passionate creature was a government official than it had been to fancy him a blackmailer preying on her husband. She had always thought of the state as manned by people eternally equable in their good sense and patience, and she felt now as if she had found herself a passenger on a ship where one of the chief officers was

blatantly lunatic. But her mind quickly recapitulated all
her past relations with the state, and assured her that,
though as a tax-collector it certainly suffered from an
exorbitant greed for her money, it showed no other ill-
will. It seemed, indeed, to exist for her protection. Monsieur Campofiore must be a rebel in his own camp. Again
flinging her head back, she said, "But what can a government official do against you?"

"Ah, it is such a long story," said Marc, "but the long
and short of it is that he can do almost anything to me."

Her knowledge that she was shrewder and quicker
than he was about to make her say, "Nonsense! What
can he possibly do to you!" But she realized that they
were treading now on his territory and not on hers; it
had not seemed extraordinary to him that this demented
being should belong to the government. "Please tell me
all about it," she asked.

"I suppose you might as well hear all about it now,"
Marc said. "I had hoped you need never know anything
about it, and I am glad that it is not quite my fault that
I must tell you. You see, my dear, I am not quite a free
agent. I think I told you once that at the end of the war
I did not ask the Reparations Fund to rebuild my father's
iron works. I had a kind of a notion that those silly fellows across the Rhine had done worse than most people
imagined at the time, and that maybe the old key industries were not going to be the source of unending
wealth they used to be. But toys, that is different. When
men are fearful about the future, they will not put their
pennies together to build railways and bridges; they will
keep their pennies for themselves and buy toys. That is

what the little automobiles my father had been trying
to make before the war were, the best toys you can
imagine for a mechanically minded age.

"So I got them to give the money I might have had to
rebuild my father's works and I put it all into the place
you saw at Lorinet. I wanted it very soon, so that nobody
else would get in first. And I got all the money I needed,
and I got it almost immediately. But I had to pay
through the nose; in the way of terms I had, of course,
to make my factory capable of being put at the service
of the state. We would need only a week to switch over
to the manufacture of guns and ambulances, you know."

"What nonsense that all is!" exclaimed Isabelle.

"How innocent all you Americans and English are
about war!" said Marc gently. "You are like little children, who think it cannot rain tomorrow because you
are going to the Zoo with your papa. And there were
other strings to the money, too. I must be a good little
boy. The factory must go on and on, so that Frenchmen
shall buy only French cars, and people abroad do that
too. If I am incompetent, I have to go. That is as it
should be. If I am not good enough, it is only right that
I should be kicked out. I thought that might happen
quite soon, since I am not clever. But somehow I got on
all right so far as ability went."

"But of course you are wonderful!" Isabelle said.
"Everybody says so. And what right has the government
to demand anything more?"

"The government has a right to ask anything of anybody," he told her mildly, "and here they are reasonable
in exercising their rights. We must not have strikes, you

know. There is no sense in strikes at all. They destroy the business, they cause discontent everywhere, and if the Germans attacked us while there were big strikes going on, there would be great disorder, and anyway the poor workmen do not want them. It is only because agitators get among them and talk them over that they ever come out."

"Perhaps there is more to it than that," said Isabelle.

"Ah, no, my love, you do not understand. The people are so happy in my factories, they are just like my children, and they are quite grateful. You saw for yourself how they all adored me. But about four years ago it began to be very unpleasant. There was a lot of money going about then, from Moscow. They came out again and again, on one pretext after another. And two years ago, there was a very grave strike, very long and very bitter. I have not liked to talk to you about it, though it meant so much in my life, because it was so painful. Just think of it, they had to bring down soldiers to fire on my poor deluded children. It was terrible."

"It may have been terrible, but all the other employers have strikes in their factories too. It's part of the system, it's bound to happen. How absurd of them to blame you for it. They must be very unfair."

"Nobody has been unfair to me at all," said Marc. "Not even Campofiore. I am sorry if I gave you a wrong impression when I said that now I knew he hated me. I did not mean that I had found him out doing anything malicious. I only meant that as he spoke I could see that he felt ill-will against me. And heaven knows why I should complain of that, there is no law forcing people

to love me. Neither he, nor anybody else in his department, has ever been anything but just to me. For, you
see, I was very foolish."

"We have all been that in our time," said Isabelle,
thinking of André de Verviers.

"You will never believe it because I have never said
one word about it—not out of any desire to deceive you,
my love, but out of sickness and weariness at the whole
thing. I was for a short time very fond of gambling. I
liked roulette, I liked baccara."

"But you don't seem to like them now!" she exclaimed. "There isn't a trace of it, you can't have been
so very bad."

"Well, I never cared for the game in itself very
much," he said. "It was all part of the life I was leading
at the time. You see, I had had no time to take a holiday
and kick up my heels when I came back from the war, I
got right down to work. Then suddenly, just about five
years ago, I found I could afford to slack off for a little,
and that I had loads of money to throw about, more
money than I had ever dreamed about. So I ran about
with some people that were very gay and very chic, and
it was wonderful to find that they did not mind me being
with them, and they all gambled. You have seen how it
is, my dear, here. The day is planned so that one must
end up in the Casino." He sighed. "Well, I was not very
discreet, that is all." His lower lip protruded piteously.

"When you had just been let loose from all those
cares, who could blame you? And what did it matter to
the government? It can't have affected your work at the
factory."

"Ah, but it did. You see, I was about with a great

many people, particularly women, who were not at all
serious. They were people the whole of France knows
about; they are written about in all the papers. I felt
very fortunate that these people who were so bright and
amusing would go about with a dull fellow like myself,
who hadn't put his nose outside his factory for years,
and was so funny to look at, and I got into the way of
acting like a clown and throwing my money about, because it made them laugh, and I felt I was giving them
some return. And, you know, I had a prodigious lot of
money. I found I could throw it away in handfuls if I
wanted to, and I did. I did it in all sorts of ways, and
often in the baccara-room, or at the roulette table, if I
was at Monte Carlo, and because I was with these people
I was under the limelight. Why, you are laughing at
me? Oh, yes, I know I was very stupid."

"I was not thinking you were stupid at all," said
Isabelle. "I was thinking how humble you were, and
how charming it was."

"You think only nice things about me, I have noticed," he said. "I feel that in future, whenever I make
a fool of myself, I will only have to think, 'Ah, I will
go home and tell Isabelle about it, and she will prove to
me I am quite wrong, and that I have shown myself a
very fine fellow.' " He circled her waist with his arm
and dropped his lips gravely to her shoulder. "I like my
marriage," he said, and went on. "Well, my darling,
the news of all this got back to the factory, and the agitators made use of it in the strikes. I can tell you, it was
not very agreeable."

Isabelle had begun to understand that there was no
part of this story that she would enjoy, but she was aware

that she had to know more of it. "How did they make use of it?"

"Oh, they kept on saying that they ought to get more than a thousand francs a week if I could take enough money out of the business to lose fifty thousand francs in a single night at a Casino. It's nonsense, of course. A thousand francs is an enormous wage, far bigger than they ever had before, and a master must take more than his men, otherwise there wouldn't be any masters, and the industries would never get anywhere. But it was so cleverly cooked up by the agitators that my poor children took it seriously, and we had a lot of trouble getting them to see reason. Then, two years ago, there was this strike I told you about, this very bad one. And then they made terrific play with an incident that had happened just before at Deauville." He looked straight at her, blinked, and then looked away at the horizon. If he had been a dog, he would have put his head down on his paws and pretended to go to sleep.

"What was that?"

"Well, there was a lady I was quite intimate with at that time, who is very well known."

"Who was it?"

"Ah, my dear, if I do not tell you, lots of other people will," he sighed. "It was Tourangelle."

"Tourangelle!" exclaimed Isabelle. "But is she not very old?"

"Well, the town of Cannes has been there for quite a time, and yet people still visit it," said Marc.

"Ah, yes," replied Isabelle, "and I suppose that if it lost all its attractions, people would still go on visiting it, because of the wonderful time that the earlier visitors used to have."

"I am glad, my dear, that you are still human," said Marc. "Well, I went with her one evening to the Casino at Deauville, and I lost rather a lot of money. Oh, an absurd amount. I know you will be cross with me when I tell you how much. It was that which made Grandaunt Berenice so furious with me. Good women don't like one to throw away money, that's why one has to go to the other sort when one feels the need to behave like a clown."

"How much was it?"

"Four million francs," Marc said, and in the silence that followed he began to whistle unhappily.

"Well, it all happened long ago," she murmured at last, reminding herself again that nothing in all this story was more foolish than her life with André de Verviers.

"It was a lot, I know," admitted Marc, "but I didn't kill myself losing it. I don't remember having had to go without anything to make up, the money kept on pouring in, and as you know, lots of people lose more. But it went very badly at the factory. For one thing, the papers exaggerated it wildly. Why, they said I'd lost five million francs."

"Which is quite a different thing from four million francs," said Isabelle.

"Different by a whole twenty-five per cent more," Marc told her seriously, "but you are a woman, figures mean nothing to you. And some of the papers exaggerated still more and said I had lost ten million. That

I wouldn't have done, I can assure you, that I see would
have been really foolish. But that's beside the point.
The important thing is that all these exaggerated reports
got back to the factory, and these agitators made my
poor people take it in the most extraordinary way.
Why, do you know they talked as if it were not my
money but theirs that I had spent? There was one young
fellow that they had got hold of, a very sad case because
four generations of his family had worked for us—who
got specially enraged about it. I sneaked in with glasses
on and a false beard to one of his meetings—it was quite
fun—and I tell you I never heard anything more im-
pressive. The poor lad's face was quite white, he shook
all over as he said that it destroyed all the dignity of a
workman's life if all his labour did was to pile up funds
for a libertine to dissipate. Poor lad, he meant so well."

"What happened to him?"

"Alas, the part he played in this strike drew the
police's attention to him, and they found he was in correspondence with Moscow, so he was tried and sent to
Guiana. Ah, my dear, there are tears in your eyes, you
are not listening to what I say. I know, you are worrying
about Tourangelle! Ah, my dear, I never see her now,
and anyhow she was just a good old sergeant-major."

"You are wrong, I am not thinking of Tourangelle at
this moment. I am listening to what you say," said Isabelle. "Please go on. What happened next?"

"What happened was that they got very cross with me
up at Paris, and they told me that it was all my own
fault, and that I was a perfect nuisance to them. It was
just then that Campofiore, who had long been second

man on the permanent staff of that section in the Ministry, was made head man. He came down and gave me a tremendous talking to. But I did not then see that he hated me, for I was feeling so guilty that I thought the best I deserved was to be sworn at like a trooper. Then I had to go up to the Ministry and I saw the minister himself, and they told me that if I went on behaving in a way that gave the union men a handle, I'd be thrown out, and they made most fuss about the gambling. They said that I must never play high again, and so I promised them—I signed things, I wrote it down—that I would never lose more than thirty thousand francs. That is what all the trouble is about now."

"How? What do you mean? Oh, Marc!" She put her hands to her mouth and spoke through her stiff fingers. "It's nothing to do with that idiotic night at Monte Carlo?"

He nodded.

"But you surely did not break your promise for the sake of those imbecile hours at the table?"

"No, I did not. I lost just nine thousand francs and not a sou more," he said. "I would never make a promise if I did not know I could keep it. I tell you, there is just a little of the child in me that likes to see the ball dancing on the wheel, and to watch for the card in the shoe to turn up, knowing that tremendous things hang on it. But I would be nothing at all without my factory. Think of me, darling, what could I do if I were cut off from my work? They could not take away all my money, but that would not help me much, I would soon be like all the men here."

She shuddered. He spoke solemnly, like one who knows his doom. "But go on, go on," she said. "If you have kept your promise, what have they got against you?"

Marc stopped and picked up the crumpled newspaper. "Why, they have not yet learned to speak the truth about me, the gentlemen of the press," he said, and showed her for a minute the headlines. "You see, they are not very polite to me; all the South is very Red, you know. And they are quite sure it was a hundred thousand francs. Ah, you need not read any more, dear. It will only worry you." He gently twitched the paper away from her, and folded it up and laid it on the bench beside him. "But it is unfortunate, is it not, that Campofiore should have been staying at Cannes just now and should have seen this rag?"

Isabelle took his hand and held it for a minute, then asked, "Did you tell him that you had lost only nine thousand?" But before he had answered, she made a grimace which Marc understood.

"Yes, my dear, you guess right," he said. "I told him, and he informed me that he did not believe me. And I have such a bad temper, you cannot think. It has been a difficult morning, this. However, I was able to point to a witness, for it happened that when I was buying the chips, Florentin, who is the Minister of the Marine, came up to me and said, 'What, Sallafranque, you're off again?' and I said, 'No, not really. Look, I've only bought twenty thousand worth.' I told him I knew Florentin would be pleased to come forward and bear my story out. But that didn't settle the business."

"Why? What are they going to do?"

"Nothing so dreadful," he answered, but broke off his

explanation to ask, "Why did you suddenly smile just
then? You looked so concerned—and then, all at once,
a lovely smile."

She had smiled with joy because she had realized that
she could not possibly feel more concerned for him than
she did, and that her progress to perfect satisfaction with
him was now complete. "I will tell you some other day,"
she said, nodding and smiling to tell him that what she
had felt was nothing disagreeable to him. "But now I
want to hear what that hateful man has done."

"All he has done is to treat me like a naughty baby,"
said Marc. "He has been on the telephone to the minister, and they have agreed that I must promise never to
sit down at any public gambling-table. Oh, I can go into
a Casino, I can have my dinner there, I can stroll with
my friends in the baccara-room and wait till midnight
to see the Tiller girls. But I mustn't risk fifty francs at
boule. It will be a little humiliating. But I have signed.
He brought the typewritten form."

Isabelle drew a deep breath and leaned back, looking
up at the pale and dazzling meridian. There was now
nothing virginal left in the day, and its excess of light
was well away with its murderous assault on form and
colour. The flowers on the oleanders were crumpled
coloured rosettes; the gladioli were pale brownish rags
gummed on their stems, with a threat of slime; and
though the dahlias were still fiery, they made no more
impression on the eye than the spurt of a match in sunshine. But the light was giving more than it had taken
away, for it was travelling down through this air that
was saturated with salt and the breath of pines, and
reaching earth as a fierce and vital Promethean benef-

icence. She shook back her loose sleeve and pulled down the opening in her blouse, so that her flesh, which was now like bronze satin, should be further burnished by this blessing.

"How strange you are," said Marc after a time. "A minute ago I thought you were so painfully concerned about this business that I blamed myself for not having hidden the whole thing from you. But now that is all over, you seem calm and happy as you are any morning when we sit in the sun. Are you sure you are not being uncomfortably brave and pretending?"

"Of course I am not," replied Isabelle. "I am really quite happy. Indeed, at the very moment you spoke, I was thinking how fortunate we would be if we never had any worse troubles than this."

"It is charming of you to take it all so lightly," said Marc. "But I know I have made a fool of myself in a very dangerous way, and I deserve to eat humble pie."

"Yes, but the wonderful thing is that it is all over, that plainly it is the grand folly of your life and yet it need have no consequences," she proclaimed lightly. "Gambling is so unnatural and artificial that it will cost us nothing to root it out of our lives." She laughed aloud. "Now, if our future depended on your never kissing me except on quarter days, I should feel much more doubtful."

He picked up her hand and kissed the palm. "We should be doomed all right then."

"Think," she mused, "if anybody from another planet should have seen Adam and Eve, and been told that hosts of their descendants would stake all their happiness on the number of marks on a card, or the place

where a ball fell on a wheel, he would not have believed it! It is a habit that we will be able to throw off
without an effort, just as I shall stop painting my toe-
nails scarlet when I leave here."

"Of course I will," said Marc. "You know, when I
have thought of gambling, it has always seemed something dark and powerful in my mind, a nightmare presence that could bide its time and then jump out on you
when you were least expecting it, as if it wasn't something I did, but something outside myself that could take
control of me and make me do things I didn't want to.
But you make life seem so simple. One just does what is
most reasonable, and everything is bound to go all right."

"Yes, of course it is," said Isabelle. "The world would
be a terrible place if that were not so. Look, there are
those doves again. The one is really quite a bright red,
isn't it? I never saw a dove that colour before."

They sat, hand in hand, watching the flight.

"We must hurry if we are to get in a bathe before
lunch," she said, but she was too contented to make a
move.

"Let us wait a little," murmured Marc. "See, François is coming out of the house with the letters. We might
as well have a look at them before we go down."

"And there is somebody with him. It is Luba. Look,
she has caught her sleeve in the door. I suppose she wants
to bathe with us."

"Ah, poor Luba," said Marc. "We must be nice to
her. I think she is going through a very bad time just
now. Leclerc is obviously tired of her. She is not so beautiful as she used to be, and it is no longer very chic to
have a Russian émigrée mistress."

"Poor dear," said Isabelle. "I like her so much." She waved her hand in welcome. "Good morning, Luba!"

"Good morning, dear people!" called Luba. "I come to see if you go swimming?"

"In a minute," cried Isabelle. "And we were only saying we hoped you would look in and come too. But just let's look at our mail."

Marc went and took the letters from the butler, then slipped his arm through Luba's and brought her along to the bench. She pecked in greeting over Isabelle, but was a little inaccurate in her aim, and then stood laughing and swaying between them, in pleasure at their company. Some other factor than nearsightedness made her move vaguely and turn her face about from speaker to speaker like a nearsighted person. There was a strange combination of opulence and indeterminateness about her appearance; her skin was so burned that it matched her tawny hair and eyes, and she was like a statue worked in golden haze; her pajamas were beautiful and costly, but they had been caught in so many doors that it was difficult to say if she were well or ill dressed; and Isabelle noted that it had lately begun to be impossible to tell if she were young or old.

"There is nothing here for me but a letter from Maman," said Marc, "and it will be all about finding her that Louis Treize armoire we've heard of so much already. Shall we go?"

"Wait a minute, I have a letter from Uncle Honoré I should like to look at," said Isabelle. "Sit down, Luba."

But there was nothing really important in Uncle Honoré's letter, though in his postscript he offered once more to lay at her disposal the store of wisdom he had collected during his long life whenever she should need it. The events of the morning made her feel grateful that she had this resource to fall back on, though she had complete confidence that they would lead to nothing disagreeable. She was replacing the letter in its envelope with a smile of satisfaction when Luba picked up the folded newspaper from the bench beside her, looked at it, uttered a cry, and dropped it.

"Ah," she said, turning dim yet shining eyes from one to the other, "you wonder why I cry out! It is because I see the date. Today used to be a great feast in Russia. You cannot think what fun we had with our friends; we used to go out and kiss each other on both cheeks, and give each other presents of little round flat cakes fried in goosefat. It was all so nice!"

"That is yesterday's paper," said Isabelle. "Let us go and bathe."

V

BY OCTOBER Isabelle was settled in the house where, she intended, she would live until she died. It was not one that she would have expected to choose. She had hoped to live in one of those high houses which make the Ile Saint-Louis look like a tall grey barge moored on the Seine, or in a discreet little villa in Passy which would have sent up prodigious thickets of lilac above its trellis-work palings in springtime, or in one of the blackened palaces of the Rue de l'Université, that long alley street full of amber antiquity and little shops which have stewed in their stuffiness for centuries, so that it seems kitchen-warm on the coldest day. She had hoped, in-deed, to live in some quarter where Paris made no at-tempt to disguise that it is an overgrown provincial town. But the house she chose was in the dreariest part of the Haussmannized boulevards, among over-handsome man-sions like heavy-bosomed dowagers, decked with dark stone garlands of swollen flowers so pompous and nine-teenth century that they could please no one save as il-lustrations to Proust. Marc and Isabelle had gone to look it over only because it belonged to a family friend who was eager to disembarrass himself of it, since he had in-herited it without the fortune to maintain it. Yet once

126

they had been inside the drawing-room, Isabelle was firm
that they must live there. It was not, indeed, that she felt
charmed by the sight of the vast chandeliers, which even
through their linen bags betrayed a vulgar turbulence
of curves like the cavortings of ill-painted nymphs in
the Salon, or anything else in the stupidly magnificent
room. It was that Marc had taken her to the window,
and led her out on to the balcony, to show her an oblique
view of one of the entrances into the Parc Monceau. He
had stood, for a longer time than he was accustomed to
spend on occupations unconnected with business or love
or sport, looking down on the nurses and governesses
stalking hip or shoulder deep in a bubbling tide of children through the gateway into the glades and vistas
which the incredible colours of autumn, added to the
fantasy inherent in the design, made exactly resemble a
setting for a fairy play. "Upon my word I wish I was
with them," said Marc. "When my sisters and I were
little, we used to play there every afternoon. We had
tremendous fun. There's lots of things in there, you
know. There is a grotto, and a colonnade, and a sham
tomb, and crowds of monuments. One to Maupassant,
particularly, which we used to pretend was really to
somebody else, a hero in a story we made up. I must ask
the girls if they can remember anything about it." It
appeared to her that, if her children played every afternoon in the park where their father had played when he
was a child, there would be restored to her life something that she had lacked till then, being an only child,
early orphaned, and early widowed.

She had no trouble in furnishing the house. A year
before, one of Marc's grandaunts had died and left him

her house in La Rochelle with all its contents; and when
they went down to see it, they found its creaking darkness peopled with the best kind of Empire furniture. The
first rays of light from the opened salon door showed
four golden eaglets, small and of a composed flight,
springing away to the four quarters of the globe, but
restrained by stiff yet gracious gold bands joining them
to the justly proportioned circle of a candelabrum. When
the caretaker threw back the shutters, she saw that in
the vast room there were three others of these arrested
flights, simple as diagrams, complete demonstrations of
a theorem of beauty. She would be able to use them to
replace those riotous chandeliers in her Paris drawing-
room; and everywhere she found things that would free
her home from its stupid metropolitan magnificence,
being themselves magnificent and provincial. There were
chairs that had a care for pomp and wore their stars and
swans with an air, but acknowledged the contours of
the human hindquarters, and stuffs on which time had
been able to work sunset wonders in the way of faded
colours, since they had been made to last and the design
was seemly; and upstairs there were beds that were fan-
tastically nursed between two walnut cornucopias and
shadowed by torrents of brocade falling from the rings
in an eaglet's mouth, yet were solid enough to hold one
safely while one was being embraced, or giving birth to
a child, or dying.

There were no marks of later taste anywhere in the
house, and all had been conserved by the most faultless
housewifery; this, she learned, was a consequence of
the condition of various married pairs. A well-dowered
bride and bridegroom of the days of Napoleon had been

contented with their home till they died, and their son and his wife had been too poor to alter it. Then Marc's grandaunt had brought their son a fortune, but an instant coldness between the two had made them reluctant to spend it on the house, as if both hoped that something might happen which would make all such expenditure waste money. In the meantime local scandal must be allayed, so the house was kept dusted and waxed as if it was beloved like other houses : and by the time the husband died, its care had become a habit with the wife. "It is a long story, I will tell you it some time," said Marc. "Anyway, she went often to Spa and Baden, but she always came back here, and it had always to be in perfect order for her." Isabelle was moved by the idea that happiness and unhappiness had worked together to deliver to her precisely what she wanted as the background of her life; and she felt gratified that she was about to restore these stable, solid things to just such a serene home as that in which they had begun.

When Isabelle explained to Madame Sallafranque, who, owing to some other node in family life, had never visited La Rochelle, how beautiful and useful the inheritance had proved to be, she was amused because her mother-in-law expressed gratification not at its beauty nor its usefulness, but at the amount of money it would save Marc and herself. Isabelle accounted for this thriftiness by recalling that, though Madame Sallafranque had forced herself into a contemporary mould by her clothes and her postures, she in fact belonged to an older generation. But to her surprise not only Marc's uncles and aunts, but his two sisters, Natalie and Yolande, whom she had regarded as bestriding the moment with a circus-

rider's ease, expressed just the same satisfaction at the
francs that had been conserved. With a start Isabelle
began to query the attitude in which she had been
brought up, which would have regarded it as unreasonable and even ungallant for her to consider any proposed
expenditure save from the point of view that she was
wealthy and that whatever money she laid out would be
replaced by next year's income. This attitude was perhaps not universal. It was perhaps peculiar to the United
States. It was perhaps not so sensible, nor even so entertaining, as the attitude of the Sallafranques. Once she
began to root out her early prejudice, she could see
plainly that it was really both more reasonable and more
gallant not to waste money but to use it to build up a
barricade between poverty and one's children.

"I like doing the things French people do,"
she told herself with the deepest satisfaction. "But
of course I am really French. I do not really belong to the United States." She remembered jests she
had heard made by Americans about the meanness of
the French; and though when she heard them those
who had uttered them had been her friends, she now
thought of them as her enemies. As she calmly scruti-
nized her household books, she recalled the uncompre-
hending frenzy that filled English and American house-
wives keeping house in France, when they performed the
same task, because they could not reconcile themselves to
the custom by which the chef collected commission on
foodstuffs, the chambermaid on the laundry, the butler
on the fuel for the furnace and on the wines. It was
surely something not easily distinguishable from meanness which made them unable to appreciate these charges

as a wise permanent tax, designed to stabilize the social structure by making employees benefit directly by their employers' high standard of living. She enjoyed her own calm acceptance of this institution, as she enjoyed fulfilling the obligation laid down on her of seeing that none of her servants threatened its foundation by exorbitance. There was nothing casual about life in France, it demanded perpetually that one should hit the note in the middle.

There was only one flaw in her new existence. She was friendless. That occurred to her one late afternoon in November, when she was walking along one of the avenues that lead from the Seine to the direction of the Arc de Triomphe, with an air, at such an hour, in such a season of the year, of passing somewhere on their route a woman weeping gently by an urn. A light mist hung about the trees and made the distance mournful; and the dead leaves which eddied slowly down through the windless calm, being the last, were so desiccated that they lay pallid and crepitant on the dark ground. The hurrying passers-by, bending their heads under the cold airs and the gathering dusk, seemed a different race from the people who swept by in shining automobiles, more pitiful, humble, innocent, and oppressed. One man, not ill-dressed or unhandsome, turned about after he had looked into Isabelle's face, walked at her heels for a time, and then addressed her gallantly; but his voice betrayed that he was quite old and there was no urgency in his gesture. This too was a dead leaf, a last witness to a bygone abundance. Everything in the scene spoke of dissolution, of a past that had taken everything with it, of a present that held nothing but regret and nostalgia. As the lights

went up one by one along the vistas that were as poignant
as if seen through tears, Isabelle found her own heart
aching, although she knew quite well that this melancholy was an illusion born of the time and place. She
asked herself, as she had often done before, how it was
that Paris should evoke as no other city a delicate
misery over the irrecoverable past, when it had been
built and was lived in by people who were exceptional in
their stoical, even brutal acceptance of the past as spilt
milk. But she supposed that in this respect Paris was like
all masterpieces, which produce in the spectators emotions which have never passed through their creators'
minds.

She reflected, as she drew near the warm glow of the
Champs-Élysées, that nobody had less reason than herself to feel discontented with the present, or anxious to
alter the past. There was Roy, of course. As she thought
of his destruction, the melancholic mood of the avenues
seemed only the bare truth. If she could have gone back
and haled him out of death, where he did not belong,
she would have done so at any cost. But she had Marc.
The only thing the past had ever given her which she
lacked now was friends, of the sort she had had at
school, like Eugenie Gray or Olive Mather, or Hilda
Chalk. The only one of the group who was like herself
transplanted to Europe, Blanche Yates, she scarcely ever
saw, except at parties where there were lots of other
people and they could not talk. She had no time left for
such things. By the time she had ordered the meals and
gone over the books, visited her hairdresser and her
dressmaker and her milliner, entertained at luncheon and
dinner the people whom she was obliged to entertain be-

cause of Marc's social and business connexions, and had
kept up her ties with Marc's mother and sisters, she
needed to spend any leisure that was left on being alone,
so that the springs of her vitality could renew themselves. There was a definite process by which one made
people into friends, and it involved talking to them and
listening to them for hours at a time. She walked along
for some time, wondering how her daily programme
could be changed so that she was freer for this process;
but it occurred to her that this press of business which
ousted friendship was not a peculiarity of her life with
Marc. She had made no friends when she was married
to Roy, because of the rush from aerodrome to aerodrome, the machine-gun rattle of receptions, confer-
ences, banquets. She had made no friends when André
de Verviers was her lover, because of the insatiable demands on her life of his jealousy and his caprice. Perhaps men, and the social structure which men have made,
saw to it that women were worked till they dropped, so
that there should be no force in them that was not ex-
pended in the service of their men.

But if that were so, and women must always be friendless, they were sentenced to a privacy of fate which
made a living woman not so alive as a living man, a dead
woman deader than her dead man. Nobody knows the
whole truth about one except one's friends. From husbands and lovers one must keep many things to oneself,
one must be silent about one's troubles, particularly
those that follow from one's choice of these beloveds,
since one dare not spoil their courage. She could not have
risked sapping the strength of Roy's nerves by telling
him that sometimes when she was watching his plane

fear rose in her breast as the plane rose from the ground, and circled and stunted round her heart and bowels as the plane played in the air, and was not quiet till the plane had landed. But she had still friends then, she had sat down and written to Eugenie and Olive, and when some day they saw the news of her death in the papers they would remember what she had told them, they would speak of the mixture of anguish and rapture that her first marriage had been, it would live again on their lips, maybe someone would hear them and repeat it again through the years. But what was happening to her now would go unrecorded, it would be shut up with her in her grave and would be dust when she was dust.

Well, if it was so it must be so. "But surely," she thought, "there is something extraordinary, something abnormal about women's lives." But how could women's lives be extraordinary or abnormal since there are more women than men and they have always led the same sort of lives? They are in the majority, time has approved, why should there be this feeling of oddness, of incongruity? It was perhaps because every inch of a woman's life as she lived it struck her as astonishing, either because nothing like what she was experiencing had ever been recorded, or because it had been recorded only falsely and superficially, with a lacuna where the real poignancy lay. She murmured, "Roy! André! Marc!" and at the sound of each name she felt bewildered as if she had been the first woman ever born, as if when she died she would go out uncomprehended from solitude to solitude. She was in front of her own house now, she drew to a standstill, astonished by intimations of strangeness as if she had been walking on an Italian

hillside in the dusk and had come on an Etruscan tomb.
The lit windows were not less mysterious than those
which were still dark.

But her key fitted the lock. The house was hers, everything she saw was familiar, her feeling of isolation was
simply a malaise that meant nothing, like giddiness. She
was Isabelle Sallafranque, she was wealthy, she had kin
and friends all over the world, the lamp at her desk in
the little library showed a pile of letters from them,
waiting on the Canton enamel dish. The American mail
had come in, and had brought a letter from Uncle
Honoré, which, since it was thick, probably contained
some business communication; but she dropped that as
she saw underneath an envelope addressed in Laurence's
agreeable angular writing. She stood with it in her hand
for a minute, staring into the shadows of the room,
wondering why she felt disturbed. She was certainly
not still in love with him. Though she would have stuck
to her guns if her first interpretation of his character
had been disputed, she knew now that his virtues were
of as little interest to her as the finest possible vegetarian
regime would be to a meat-eater. She shook her head
and smiled as she slit open the envelope: then bit her
lip, because he wrote that he was about to be married.

Behind her the door opened, all the lights were
switched on, she felt Marc's hands on her waist, his lips
on her nape. "Ah, leave me alone for a minute, darling,"
she cried impatiently. "I am reading such an interesting letter. Laurence Vernon has written to say he has
become engaged."

"Well, you will not like that too well," said Marc,
letting her go.

"What do you mean?" she asked, feeling alarmed.
"Why should it matter to me?"

"I always feel that every attractive woman I have
ever met should withdraw herself from the society of all
others of my sex," said Marc, "and shut herself up in a
sealed paddock till I get round to her. Mind you, I do
not mean to get round to her. I am serious, myself. But
I feel that it would be only nice of her if she took our
meeting that way. All men have that attitude, I think;
and it is only when one is being disagreeable that one
pretends women are not exactly like men in their attitude to these things. So of course you will not like Laurence getting married."

"How absurd you are," said Isabelle. "I mean that you
are perfectly right, of course." The young woman involved was a Southerner whom Laurence had met on the
steamer going back to America.

"Moreover," said Marc, as he read the letter over her
shoulder, "I think there was a little between you two
that you have not told me about. I do not think Laurence
was under the impression that you were an elderly gentleman, bald-headed, and employed in the Ministry of
Commerce."

"Why do you think that?" said Isabelle.

"Because he looked at me and was too fair-minded to
think anything spiteful about me," answered Marc, "but
I saw him examining my physique several times and telling himself that, though he was anxious that his dear
friend Isabelle should be happy, he thought it a pity she
should have chosen anybody so short and fat." He broke
off, moved back to the door, and turned out the switches
that he had lit when he came in, so that the room was

in shadow save for the little lamp that shed a circle of light on the letter in Isabelle's hand. "Laurence thought, probably," he went on, "that you, being beautiful, should marry some miracle of good looks like André de Verviers. Not understanding—for you Americans have so little experience about certain things—that there may be in such splendid beings whom one would think formed for the relationship between the sexes, something that prevents them from ever being serious, from being any good at the hearth, though one would never blame any woman for wishing that it might be otherwise."

A silence fell and Isabelle, still bending over the illumined letter, realized it to be Marc's belief that she had, like so many women in Paris during the last ten years, suffered an unrequited infatuation for de Verviers, that she had either wished to marry him, or had been left by him after she had become his mistress. Her first impulse was to throw back her head in laughter and tell Marc how much energy she had put into the business of getting rid of André. But in her, every impulse was followed by one forbidding her to act until she had deliberated; and the briefest moment of thought suggested that she had no right to betray André, since at times he had made her very happy. Besides, if she explained to Marc that he had mistaken the roles of the personages in her drama, that it had been Laurence whom she loved and André who was the superfluous suitor, it would have upset Marc's theory of values and left him puzzled and self-distrustful. He could understand and approve André's charm for women, because it was the result of physical vitality such as he himself possessed; and since he hardly knew André and underestimated his own

other qualities, he was able to imagine that the only difference between them was that in André this vitality
had found a beautiful envelope. To him, therefore, a
woman who loved André was demonstrating the possession of a taste which ultimately he himself might satisfy.
But he would find it totally incomprehensible that any
woman should love Laurence, and if he knew that she
had ever done so, it would set up in his humble mind a
dread that there existed some precious human quality
which he did not possess, and that for lack of this he
would never really please her nor deserve to do so. She
would not have had him think that for the world. The
longer she deliberated on it the more it appeared not
worth while correcting his misapprehension. He had the
elements in her story right, and if she had pedantically
insisted on further corrections, she would have placed
herself among those wives who interrupt their husband's
stories by crying out, "Now, darling, why do you say
we had three valises and four trunks? We had four
valises and three trunks."

As she stood in thought a blush covered her face and
ran down her whole body. The elements in her story
included her own humiliation and misery, and Marc
knew of them. Just such an exposure as she had feared,
and tried to avoid for ever by marrying Marc, had at
last befallen her. Then a kind of counter-blush, a wave
of relief and pleasure, broke over her face and body.
What one fears from the blow that leaves one exposed
and unarmed is what the world will do to one when it
finds one in such a case. Evidence piling up since childhood suggested that it would mock and chastise one. But
in the case of Marc the evidence lied. He, if he found a

human being delivered into his power, would clothe and comfort him. He knew that she had been despised and rejected by some man, and this knowledge was exciting in him no trace of harsh sadistic triumph, but only tenderness and pity. It came to her that he had spoken of André only from an exceptional delicacy, because she now recalled that yesterday at dinner somebody had asked her if she knew André de Verviers and, when she had replied, she had stuttered a little, which Marc knew to be her habit when she was embarrassed. He was saying to her, "Do not be afraid lest I should come to know anything about you. I know it already, and there is no part of your destiny which I do not accept." She contemplated Marc's attitude to her in this matter in ecstasy, as one listens in a concert-hall to a phrase of music by a master played by a master, feeling that the whole world is but a wall built round this performance, the sky the roof that covers it, that here is the centre of life.

She regretted that her controlled and secretive temperament had made her rest immobile, still bending over the letter which she held in the circle of light under the lamp. She turned slowly towards Marc, who was still leaning against the lintel of the door, and tried for a word, for a gesture, that would candidly avow her love of him, her gratitude for his love. But she found herself smiling mysteriously at him, not as if she were surrendering all her secrets, but as if she were withholding from him many more than she really had; as if she were saying to him, "Ah, you think you are clever, you think you know all about me, but you know nothing, though I like you so well that perhaps I might tell you everything if you went the right way about persuading me. But you must find out for yourself what that right way might be. . . ." It was as if an older woman of the coquettish type, full of factitious crises which she particularly disliked, had taken control of her body for a minute. But before she could correct the effect she was giving, Marc had come towards her and had taken her in his arms, and she was puzzled to see that he seemed to be ravished by her look. She would have been irritated had he not been so warm and tender that she wished for nothing better than to rest in his arms, her eyes shut, while his lips travelled along the line of her jaw.

"Tell me, darling," said Marc, "who is coming to dinner tonight?"

"Eighteen people," she answered, not opening her eyes. "To meet the Ortegas."

"Oh, my God," said Marc. "South Americans. They will never go home. I shall be so tired when they have gone. Darling, will you not go upstairs and rest a little?"

"Ah, no!" she said. "No!"

"But I think you will," he said, and drew her by the waist, out of the room, up the staircase. She made little murmurs of protest, and as she passed the door of the salon, she clutched at the handle.

"No, my darling," said Marc. "No."

"Ah, but I must!" she cried. "I will not be happy upstairs unless I know that they have done what I told them with the flowers."

"Very good," said Marc, "and I am glad to see that you admit that you will be happy upstairs, once you have learned that they have done what they should with the flowers."

He flung open the door and turned on the switches.

"Look," he said, "but quickly, look quickly. We mustn't waste time."

She looked round the great, brilliant room, and saw that her servants had set where she had directed the great vases full of Michaelmas daisies she had bought at the market that morning. Their lovely pale colours keyed down the brilliance of the room, and diluted as with moonlight the flood of yellow brightness from the candelabra, exactly as she had intended.

"Hurry, hurry," said Marc.

"Ah, Marc," she protested.

His mouth came down on hers, his hand that was not on her waist reached out and turned down the lights. "Ah, Marc," she protested again, "I wanted to see the room . . ." She pushed his shoulders away with the palms of her hands, and, partly to tease him, partly because she would have liked to make sure that they had set the little occasional tables as she had directed, and partly out of that virginal shyness which renews itself a thousand times if love is present, she delayed peering back into the darkness of the room.

"Come," said Marc.

"No, wait a minute! There is something I have always wanted to know, and I always forget to ask. Tell me, what is the French for Michaelmas daisies?"

"We call them *les vendangeuses.*"

"Ah, how pretty! But I wonder why?"

"Just look at them!" He switched on the lights; the pale clots of blossom stared at them again. "They stand almost as high as women, you know, and they never have the look of being originally the colours they are, pink and blue and mauve, but only of being white that

has been stained. They are like women that have been
to the vineyard and got stained with the grapejuice. Also
something might have happened to them there that is
apt to happen round the vineyards at vintage time. They
are not quite tidy like other flowers, they are wide-eyed
as if they had seen something surprising, they are very
still. Ah, the poor little things!"

His hand put out the lights and pulled ajar the door,
and his mouth pressed down on hers again, but she continued to look reluctantly into the darkness of the salon.
The ray of light from the landing showed her nothing
but the four eaglets on one of the ormolu candelabra she
had brought from La Rochelle, winging their way to
the four quarters of the globe, but held back by stiff yet
gracious bands. It was so in marriage, when one loved
one's husband. Wild things that would have flown away
and been lost in the violent airs above the edges of the
earth were restrained within four walls, to be perpetual
in their beauty. She turned to face her husband and her
body became fluid in his arms, her head fell forward on
his chest. She saw the melancholy evening slinking away
like a beaten dog from her warm and happy home.

The sole anxiety which troubled Isabelle in these days
was fear lest she might not have any children. Her marriage with Roy had been sterile through no design of
theirs. But that, she reflected, was hardly evidence. It
would have been almost as supernatural for her to have
had a child during that time when she was almost perpetually being propelled by combustion engines through
cold airs of transcontinental, transmontane routes, or
through still colder airs across the skies, as it would have
been for one of the automobiles and aeroplanes that bore

her on these flights to produce a litter of shining and
steely young. But now her life, though as busy or even
busier, was calmer and more deeply rooted; the times
were more propitious; and indeed by Christmas she had
reason for hope. But she was not convinced, since she
had often heard how resolute women could forge the
symptoms of maternity, until after the New Year, when
she and Marc had gone for a fortnight to St. Moritz.

It was on one of the horse-racing days. They had left
the stand because Marc had wished to see a new camera
that one of the newspaper photographers was using,
which appeared to be simply a glass box; and while he
examined it and talked with its owner, Isabelle strolled
away with Luba. Since their arrival Luba had constantly
been in their society, for though she attached little importance to the circumstance that Monsieur Leclerc, who
was in America, had not written to her for three months,
mentioning it with tender laughter as a proof that
though he was French by birth he was Russian in many
of his characteristics, they found it ominous Isabelle
felt her apprehension for her friend increase as they
walked through the crowd and it was herself, not Luba,
at whom the people stared in admiration. Public acclaim
had never meant much to her, since she saw no useful
end which it might serve; and now she was happily married she would have been quite content if custom had
ordained that she must wear a yashmak when she walked
abroad. But this withholding of admiration from Luba
annoyed her because it was unjust, since Luba had not
lost her beauty. As yet her only fault was that she had
been beautiful too long. It was a cruel injustice, for such
admiration was necessary to Luba since she was one of

those women who, if they are not chosen as queen at the
tourney, will never be chosen at all. Her splendid appearance could make claims upon the world, which all
the vague and apologetic rest of her would either never
make, or would relinquish without an effort. Isabelle
found her eyes blurred by her sense of the difference
between her own settled happiness and Luba's destiny;
and she turned her away from the crowd and brought
her to a halt beside the rails of the track.

There the genius of the place restored her to serenity.
They were looking across the lake at the dark theatre of
pinewoods on the farther shore, which man had hardly
marked, and at the superior and dazzling theatre of
white peaks, which man had not marked at all. She was
not ordinarily an enthusiast of the Swiss landscape, for
it seemed to her that if snow mountains were beautiful,
then vanilla ices and meringues also must be conceded
beauty. But she was exalted by the thin and glittering
air; its quality suggested that water might become intoxicating not only when certain substances are added to
it, but when others are taken away from it. All recol-
lected climates seemed by comparison stained and clod-
dish. Actually she did not doubt that too long a sojourn
there would be as perilous as residence in the tropics,
that it would stimulate to a perpetual physical activity as
destructive in the long run as languor to the balanced
life of body and mind. But that did not prevent her from
being transported into delight by the breath she drew
into her nostrils from this glorious atmosphere, brilliant as a diamond, which lay under the pure, purged
blue sky.

A pistol-shot rang out. This did not rend the nerves,

for it was a sound in harmony with the countryside;
such noises are heard on the glaciers when the ice cliffs
split, on the mountain-slopes when an avalanche breaks
away. In a world where the snow crackles under foot,
where the air itself crackles in the ear, a louder crack
than usual made no matter. Isabelle was almost surprised
that it had a meaning, that it was the signal for the
starting of the race. Smiling, she leant forward on the
rail as the horses came round the bend in the track, each
tailed like a comet with its cloud of sparkling, scatter-
ing snow. As they came nearer, she bent even lower and
her smile became ecstatic.

"Isabelle! Isabelle!" cried Luba suddenly, so emphatically that the people near by swung round to look at
her.

"What is it?" asked Isabelle. "Is somebody down?"

"No, no," said Luba, turning her back on the race.
"It is that I have just remembered that it is the fifteenth.
The fifteenth!" she repeated rapturously, though her
neighbours were throwing her unfriendly looks and giv
ing their attention back to the race. "Today it used to be
a great feast in Russia. You cannot think what fun we
had with our friends. We used to go out and kiss each
other on both cheeks, and give each other presents of
little wooden dolls painted in bright colours. It was all
so nice."

"It is, however," said Isabelle faintly, "it is, however . . ." For her world had gathered itself into a Cath-
erine-wheel of very pure colours. She had been listening
to the sound of the horses' hooves hammering on the
snow-covered ice, and as they travelled nearer she had
felt the hammered rhythm in the soles of her feet, her

spine, her temples. She had enjoyed participating in the
rhythm of the rushing brutes, knowing a pleasure she
had not known since as a child she had galloped about
her nursery, pretending to be a lion or a tiger. But then
suddenly from within herself had come a counter-motion
so potent that it nearly brought her to her knees. It was
brief, it was the feeblest possible flutter. But it brought
a new rhythm down like a hammer on the other rhythm
that was hammering on the ice, making her heart stop,
revealing to her that she possessed lengths of intestines
of which her mind had not taken an inventory, convincing her that nothing could possibly happen outside
her nearly so extraordinary as what was happening
inside her. The white peaks spun together, the pinewoods swam up to the pure sky, but she brought them
back to order by her deep, quiet breathing. "It is, however," she continued firmly, "not the fifteenth until tomorrow," and she gave all her attention to the horses,
which were now passing them. Proximity showed that
they were animals which would have been allowed to
race only in a thoroughly democratic country; but as
they passed, they crossed the light at an angle which
turned the spray of snow behind them to blown rain-
bows. It gave her an excuse to cry out as if in admiration.

"Ah, so you really are amusing yourself, darling,"
Marc exclaimed at her elbow.

"You cannot think how much," she said.

The place was intoxicating. It was her friend; when
she stood at her window in the morning and looked out
to the bronze woods, the white hills, the bright air, she
felt as if she would never grow old, as if no pain could

etch into the healthy hardness of her nerves. Yet there was an enemy here also. It was the mode of life she had encountered at Cannes, the rules of the lay brotherhood that had taken vows of wealth, unchastity, and disobedience to all standards. Suddenly she found herself in the midst of it, like one of those abducted heroines in old-fashioned Protestant tracts, who wake and distastefully find themselves immured in a convent. Beings richly endowed by nature and good fortune raced out in the morning on the ice-rink and the ski-slopes and the toboggan-track, and diverted their vitality away from their brains to their muscles. In this superbly invigorating air they were able to spend hour after hour in conditions precluding all danger that they might possibly lapse into thought. But when exhaustion and the failure of the day drove them indoors, they were faced with their dread again. Sound blood was coursing through their veins, astringent air was scouring their lungs, they were better animals for the day's exercise; and it is the inveterate habit of the human animal when it feels well to think, to speculate, to evolve standards. So, as on the Riviera, they called in alcohol as a prophylactic; they sat in the bar diluting the universe, and began to discuss whether Ferdy Monck had had a right to say what he had said to Gordon Lloyd at the ice-hockey match the other day, and whether Annette had really spoken to Laura as people said she had in the *patisserie* on Saturday morning. All possibility of friendship was undermined by their promiscuous amities and sudden enmities. They disciplined the flesh, which is by nature apt to pick and choose, until it became as hardy an acceptor of traffic as a railway junction; and they had as little to do as possible with that not inconsiderable human invention, the word, using as small a vocabulary as possible in their talk, avoiding it altogether when written, and substituting so far as possible for the use of it at the bridge-table and backgammon board the contemplation of numbers.

They were doing here in the winter, in fact, everything that they had done in the Riviera in the summer. These vows were for life. In this war there was no discharge. Isabelle felt herself as much alarmed by this demonstration of the tenacity of the system as the devout are before witness to the prevalence of the Freemasons, or Protestants when faced with the power of the Jesuits. She found, too, the demonstrators themselves much more alarming than they had been in the South. There the strong sunlight dimmed their quality, and the warm air, dense with salt, muffled their stridencies. Here, flushed with exercise and excited by the altitude, they disclosed how beautiful most of them were, how strong nearly all of them were. Whirling with the freedom of birds on the dark ice-rink, they were more graceful than any birds, with their flourished hands, their spinning heels. Coming in at the end of the day to sit round the bar, the hard brilliance the cold air had veneered on them melting with the warmth and what they drank, they shone like liquefying jewels. This way of living was not the resort of defectives, it was the deliberate choice of human beings who, judged by physiological standards, must be counted high types.

The perversity of this choice appeared more clearly here in Switzerland than on the Riviera, for here there was possible no nocturnal dispersions in gardens and on the borders of the sea, or to adjacent

towns or friends' villas. The icy night barricaded the
visitors in the village; they could be seen concentrated in a few hotels. The over-heated, over-crowded
rooms and corridors where they sat were filled with a
continual clatter, as if they were continually taking up
the substance of life and throwing it away from them
with easy, powerful gestures, so that it broke into pieces
on the floor. There were other people there, of course,
not of their kind, busy men snatching a holiday with
their wives and families, who had probably no sympathy
with ruin, who would be moderate and sensible in all
their ways. But it was disquieting that these seemed to
concede the importance of the votaries of incoherence,
to admit that they possessed a glamour and a force which
they themselves lacked. They were always staring at
them, stuttering if they had to speak to them, becoming
clumsy when they came too close to them. Isabelle, looking into her own mind, recognized with a shudder that
she herself would have been resentful if the glorious
Daisy had not accepted her as an equal, that she was able
to despise the votaries only because she was freely admitted to their company.

Towards the end of their stay she was happy only out
of doors in the morning, before most people were about.
Indoors, or out of doors at any later hour, the question
came to her too often, "Why do we need to know these
people?" and had always to be answered that it was quite
inevitable. She and Marc could exclude them for the
most part from their home; she was beginning to see
some sense in the reluctance with which the French ask
any but a small circle of intimate friends to sit at their
hearths. But all the same she and Marc were bound to

meet these unwanted companions whenever they tried
to take advantage of their wealth. Whenever they decided to play golf on the finest course, or go for a holiday in any specially beautiful place, they always found
the course and the place in the hands of these people.
They were the most prodigal spenders of their time, and
they could command the best all over the world. There
was, of course, a great deal of beauty too remote and too
untamed for their domination, but Marc and Isabelle
were too busy to seek them out; it troubled Marc if he
were not in touch with his factory by telephone at least
once a day.

A sojourn at a less fashionable hotel was as impossible, for there they would have been awkwardly
marked out from their fellow-guests as strays from
another world. The very name of Sallafranque spoke
of great, even gross wealth; and their legitimate taste
for beautiful things, combined with less worthy allies,
with their human inability to break away from the
standards of the groups surrounding them, and the
resolution of tradesmen, had supplied them with clothes
and accessories which made poorer people feel ill provided and resentful. Moreover, to keep in order these
clothes and accessories, they had to take with them a
valet and a maid; and in any smaller hotel these would
complain of bad accommodation and lack of company,
and spoil their employers' holiday with their ill humour.
So, though it would not have been impossible for Marc
and Isabelle to dissever themselves from this world, they
would have had to pay a price for the severance that
would have struck everybody they knew as absurd. She

therefore felt her desire to pay it to be as worthy of suppression as those desires some people have to run out of a room in panic as soon as the doors are closed, or to throw themselves from heights. Nobody likes feeling shut in or dizzy; but all the same one need not lose one's self-control in such states. Nobody, it seemed to her, could possibly like sharing the existence of Gladys and Serge, Iris and Nikolai, Gordon Lloyd and Ferdy Monck, Annette and Laura, Gustave and Sarah Bourges, Dan Creed or Mrs. Postleham, or Prince Ostrogin. But one must exercise self-control.

Isabelle was therefore greatly pleased when it came to the last morning of their visit; and she felt even more so when Luba said to her on the last morning, as they followed Marc and Ferdy out of the hotel towards the ice-rink, "Did you not see that funny-looking man who was standing in the lounge? He was staring at you and Marc so very hard, such a funny-looking man. There was something odd about his clothes, they made one think of that old book one used to read with one's governess, *Tartarin in the Alps*. Not so bad as that, of course, but they made one think of it."

"Had he a beard?" asked Isabelle, but she hardly needed to wait for the answer. She shuddered. She did not imagine that Monsieur Campofiore had looked at them any more pleasantly because Marc's conduct had been faultless, for in her school and college days she had noticed that those who rebuked her for a fault with more than a certain degree of intensity grew to like her still less if she failed to repeat it.

So it was truthfully that she said, "I am so glad to be

home again," the evening they came back to the house
by the Parc Monceau. Not all the lights were on, but
some; it was the family coming home, not a party. The
butler and footman looked glad to see them, and when
she inquired why the house was flooded with fragrance,
she was told it proceeded from a crateful of mimosa,
sent by Madame Sallafranque from Cannes. While Marc
was speaking to his secretary, she went into the little
library and turned over the pile of letters which were
lying in the Canton enamel dish on her desk, in the small
circle of light cast by her neat lamp. There was a thick
letter from Uncle Honoré, which she laid aside; it was
a pity that he was always offering her the use of his
wisdom only at some future date, that in the present he
gave her nothing but these impersonal communications
regarding steel, oil, and public utilities. She saw a letter
lower in the pile which bore an English stamp and drew
it out, hoping that it might be from Blanche Yates, who
was staying with her husband's family in London. It
came, however, from a press agency, enclosing a photograph of herself taken at St. Moritz and published in an
illustrated weekly, and offering to send her any similar
cuttings that might appear, for a small charge. The
photographer had caught her as she leaned on the rails
of the race-track. She seemed to be smiling rather foolishly. Her first desire was to call Marc with a loud cry
and weep on his breast. But it was surely impossible that
anything which worked through the acknowledged
mechanism of ordinary life, and that at its most trivial,
should be sinister enough to justify such distress. She
reproached herself for having allowed fatigue to affect

her judgment, and tore the letter and photograph into small pieces, resolving to think no more about them. But she could not rid herself for some days of the feeling that something extraordinarily disgusting had happened to her.

VI

ISABELLE FOUND the next few months of
her life much more delightful than she had been led to
expect. She always felt well, but now she found her own
good health a conscious exhilaration; her complexion
became more brilliant than it had ever been, so that she
was almost too theatrically beautiful; and she was amused
and entertained by the company of her unborn child.
She was able to claim indulgence to entertain no more
than she enjoyed, she spent a good part of her day
walking, and from Friday morning to Monday afternoon she stayed at the old mill that Marc had bought for
her in the valley of the Chevreuse, close to the château
where his sister Yolande lived. The winter countryside
enchanted her. The soot-black coppices, the delicate
monotones of the stubble and ploughed fields, the muted
green of the pastures, the morning skies, which in their
sunny emptiness were high as the crisp starry nights,
surprised her daily as if they were uncommon things;
and during this time she developed new and intense and
innocent gourmandises. The taste of milk was more delicious to her than any wine, and she became infatuated
with the smell of wood fires as she never had been with
any perfume, drawing the smoke into her nostrils till

she felt ashamed and apprehensive, as if drunkenness must necessarily follow such gluttonous indulgence of the senses. She liked arranging with Yolande which of them was to put up Madame Sallafranque or Natalie and her husband for the week-end and who was to come over to dine with whom during the visit; and she liked entertaining Yolande's Marcel and Madeleine, and Natalie's François and Nicole and baby Jacques, who had the serenity that French children seem to derive from the lack of surprise or resentment with which their parents regard their existence. She took great pleasure in her happy relations with Marc's family, because she had hardly anything in common with them. If she had resembled these impulsive and expansive people, it would have been natural enough that they should get on well together; but as she was fundamentally different from them in almost every way, it seemed to her of the best possible augur for society that the practical considerations which make the family hold together should furnish as a by-product this pleasant comradeship.

Towards Easter, however, Isabelle felt less exhilarated than before. There had been a season of warm and foggy weather, of heat without light, which had overpowered her spirits. At night she dreamed of the sharper airs of America, of great waves dashing on the coast of Maine, of a lake, clear as air, which she had once swum across in New Hampshire. She told Marc, who said, "Of course you need some sea air. You have been living either here or in Paris since Christmas, and it is time you had a change. We will go to Le Touquet for Easter."

"Am I fit to be seen?" asked Isabelle.

"I have seen mediæval figures that stood as you stand

now," said Marc, "and I have always been told that the
reason for it was that they were carved out of a tusk,
and the carver had to follow the curve of the ivory. I
will make the same excuse for you if anybody should
make a comment. But nobody will. Your body is showing
itself as discreet as your mind."

They wired that day for rooms to the Hotel Guillaume-
le-Conquérant, and told the family of it that night over
dinner at Yolande's. Madame Sallafranque's eyes turned
brilliantly in her head, and she remarked that nothing
could be better since young Philippe Renart and his
English wife were coming over from London to Le
Touquet, and Madame Renart had been telling her how
much she wished that there was someone there who
could introduce them to French people, since Philippe
had lost touch with his own country owing to the years
he had spent in South America, and she herself was too
much occupied with the care of her husband, who was
too delicate to attend to anything but his business, to
undertake her son's social re-education. Madame Sallafranque reported the conversation in a sad and dignified
tone, a little nobler than life, as if it had taken place
between two matrons in a drama by Corneille, and the
satisfaction she expressed at the prospect of Marc and
Isabelle taking care of the young Renarts was such as a
spectator of such a drama might feel at some turn in the
action which lifted the destinies of these matrons to
security, though it did not thereby take away their
solemnity. To Isabelle, however, it appeared that the
conversation might be related to a more contemporary
drama; and she inquired, rather in the spirit of a white
person trying to penetrate into the subtleties of the na-

tive mind, whether there was not some business connexion between the Renarts and the Sallafranques. It
was odd that Madame Sallafranque should answer her
rather in the manner of a white person who at last finds
a native displaying signs of intelligence, as she replied
that Madame Renart was the sister of Natalie's husband's uncle by marriage, and that since young Philippe
Renart showed neither ambition nor competence to succeed his father, preferring to live abroad in agreeable
countries but in subordinate positions, it was a matter of
some importance that Monsieur Renart had expressed
himself willing to take Natalie's François into the firm.

As François was not yet ten years old, Isabelle wished
to laugh, but she reflected how delightful it would be
for the child to feel that from his earliest youth his
family had done their best to make him honoured and
secure, and how natural he would find it to do the same
for his children. She answered therefore that she would
be delighted to be of service to Philippe Renart and his
English wife, though, she added, Englishwomen too
often did not appear to wish to be served. Madame Sallafranque shrugged her shoulders and made a sympathetic
grimace and gave a disgusted description of mint sauce,
which she had met with during a visit to the Grand
National with Marc's father about thirty years before.
But she admitted that the lamb it had accompanied had
been excellent and went on to say that she had never
seen a finer young man than the Duke of Westminster.
Some of the women, too, were not so bad, in their way.
This time she seemed to be speaking as one white person
conversing with another on the subject of the natives,
and trying to lay down the proper imperialist attitude

towards them by conceding their good points while keeping a crisp air of firmness.

When Easter drew near, Isabelle felt a lazy disinclina-
tion for the trip; but it was amusing to find herself fit
to go about like other women, at a time when she had
imagined she would be sick and miserable. The balance
was weighed down on the side of Le Touquet by remem-
brance of this conversation with Madame Sallafranque,
with its overtones which were calls to battle on behalf of
the family, on behalf of sensible bourgeois France, and,
later on, by another mission. They had decided to make
a long week-end of it and go down to the Guillaume-
le-Conquérant on the Wednesday before Easter, and two
days before that Marc came home with a face grave
almost to blubbering point. After he had greeted her,
he went over to the fire in her boudoir and rubbed his
hands as if they were freezing, though it was not very
cold.

"All women should be married," he said, "and happily married too."

"You are perfectly right," Isabelle answered. "There
is no other way of living for a woman. But what has just
brought this truth to your mind?"

"On my way home I went into the Ritz bar with
Raoul Moring for a cocktail," said Marc, "and I met
Luba."

"Ah, poor Luba!" cried Isabelle. "Heaven forgive me,
I have been too happy to think about her. I asked her
once or twice, and she did not come, and then she slipped
out of my mind. It is too bad of me!"

"No, my darling, it is not too bad of you," said Marc,
"you have had other things to think of these months.

And if people keep on blowing away like waste paper, one cannot run after them. Luba is very tiresome. But she is pathetic. Oh, my God, how pathetic she is."

"What has happened to her?" asked Isabelle. "Is it all over with Leclerc?"

"Yes, all," said Marc. "Mind you, he has not behaved badly. He has given her quite a fair sum on which she would be able to live if she were not agitated by the knowledge that she owes the couturiers three times her future annual income."

"But how did she find that out?" asked Isabelle. "She would never have noticed the bills if someone had not told her. Really, people are very malicious."

"Alas, she noticed because the couturiers will give her no more credit. They know what to think because Leclerc is bringing them another little friend to dress. All that is what is so very disagreeable. You see, Luba is a great lady and she has put herself in the position of a *fille*, and now she realizes it. And it is very painful to her."

Isabelle shuddered. "You mean she has taken the world's view of what has happened to her. I suppose she would, now she is alone. Yet, of course, her own view of what had happened was just as valid."

"What was that view?" asked Marc. "A man never knows."

"Well, she was not in love with Leclerc, of course," explained Isabelle; "she was in love with her husband, who was killed by the Bolsheviks. But Leclerc was somebody to cling to, and she liked doing little services for him, singing Russian songs to him in the evening after dinner at that dreary place near Provins. If he had been destitute and she had had money she would have given him all he wanted; so of course she took money from him. She was completely destitute—she had tried to work, you know, she was at Chanel's for three months but she drove everybody mad—and he was grossly rich. She really had no reason to feel ashamed."

"But now she feels ashamed," said Marc.

"Nobody ought to feel ashamed about Luba's situation," Isabelle told him, "except perhaps the generals who lost the war for Russia. It isn't fair to create a system in which a woman's virtue hangs on a hair, and then go round cutting the hairs."

"When one really talks to a woman, one always finds she believes in nothing," said Marc, "provided she is the kind of woman who has faith in life. If she has no faith, she will tell you she believes in everything. I have noticed it in Maman. She has infinite faith, and she does not really believe in anything. It is very puzzling."

"I am talking too much, perhaps," said Isabelle, "but you must forgive me. All the time I am a little drunk these days. I am so well. But go on telling me about Luba."

"There is nothing much to tell you except that she is miserably lonely and hurt, and when I asked her why she had not been to see us, her lip stuck out like a child's and she said she did not think we would want her, because she was *déclassée*. She talked to me like a whipped child."

"Oh, nonsense," said Isabelle, "let us take her with us to Le Touquet and she will feel better in no time, and forget all about it."

"Darling, that would be very kind of you!" Marc exclaimed. "Could you really bear to do that? For we must not forget, Luba is really very tiresome."

"Darling," replied Isabelle, "the question is not whether I can bear her, but if you can. As I tell you, I am always a little drunk now and amiably so. I will sit with her while you golf, if you can stand her at meals and in the evening."

"Oh, I can do that quite well. At night she really looks very pretty, it is a pleasure to have her about."

"Very well. Did she tell you where she is living?"

"Oh, at the old address. It seems that has been arranged. The little house belongs to her."

Isabelle picked up the telephone and, as she waited for the number, put her hand over the mouthpiece. "Is Luba still keeping up with people?" she asked. "What was she doing in the Ritz bar?"

"She had come to meet the Marquise de Trayas, but she was half an hour too early. I met her just coming in as I was going out."

"Ah, is that you, Luba?" asked Isabelle, and cut through the little blurred barkings of affectionate greeting with her invitation. "But of course we really want you," she said presently. "We insist that you come. It is no use your refusing, we shall fetch you in the automobile on Wednesday just after lunch."

"But, Isabelle!" broke in Marc. Isabelle, however, silenced him with her hand, and when she put down the telephone she said, "I know, Marc. You cannot get away till four. But I will send the automobile to her at a quarter to two, and with her servant and the chauffeur work-

ing at her all the time she will be ready by three and
then the automobile will bring her back here, and we
shall have some tea, and be off by four."

"I need never teach you how to arrange things," Marc
observed comfortably.

"But you must go on telling me about poor Luba,"
said Isabelle. "Did you say that the Marquise de Trayas
was concerning herself with her? I wonder if she sees
any possibilities in her future. Claire is always very
practical."

"Well, as a matter of fact, she did say something
about having hopes for Luba," Marc recalled. "It seems
that she had Luba to meet some people at lunch a day or
two ago, and that one of the men was immensely taken
by her and has been with her constantly ever since. In
fact, it was because the three were going to meet her
that she had asked Luba to meet her at the Ritz bar. But
the man was one of your compatriots, my darling, and
suffered thereby from the need to use modern methods
of transport practically incessantly. He had flown to
Brussels, and should have flown back today, but was
fogbound."

"Claire is serious," meditated Isabelle, "she is almost
never vulgar. She would not have tried to foster this
inclination had there not been the promise of some dignified future for Luba. I suppose she did not tell you the
man's name?"

"She did, but I have forgotten," said Marc, "it is
very stupid of me."

"How funny," said Isabelle, "you never forget anything as a rule." She picked up the telephone again and

called a number. "Ah, is that you, Claire?" she asked
presently. "How are you? Well, I hope. But I won't pretend this is a mere social call, I am not feeling frivolous. I
want to know about our dear Luba—Marc has said . . ."
After she had listened for a few minutes her eyes began
to sparkle, and she uttered little pleased exclamations. At
the conversation's end she turned to Marc and said,
"Why, it is more fortunate than I could have hoped!
Bizarre, of course, but then that brings it into line with
the rest of her destiny. The man is Alexander Pillans.
You have heard of him?"

"Weighing machines and scales, isn't it?"

"Yes, and marriages. He has been married three
times. He lives in St. Louis, but he is very rich and as
well known a figure all over the United States as if he
lived in New York, and the story has amused people.
You see, his first wife was just a plain little woman,
whom his dreadful old Scotch father who made all the
money forced on him when he was twenty-one. Then
she died, and he started marrying famous beauties. He
married Liane Mardi, first."

"She was a dreadful woman," said Marc, "very beautiful, but till I saw her at the Folies I did not know that
a pair of legs could look as mercenary as a face."

"Well, of course that did not last. She amused herself
spending his money for a time, but there is one thing
he insists on, that he must go on living in the dreadful
Pillans home that his father built, a replica of the Château of Chambord, in a flat park a mile outside St.
Louis. He is a poor little thing really, very short and
shrunken, with enormous ears and eyes. I do not expect

he feels safe anywhere except in the house where he was brought up. So she left him and he married Margherita Stravazzi."

"She is a splendid creature," said Marc, "but dreadful too. She is one of those women who have as deep and irresistible an impulse to offer herself up to disgrace as the martyrs have to go to the stake. If her whole material future depended on her being faithful to you, she still couldn't help deceiving you with the valet de chambre."

"There are very few valets de chambre in St. Louis," said Isabelle; "she did not stay long. But do you not think it sounds very hopeful for Luba? Obviously he longs for the glittering unchaste women that his father denied him in his youth, but he would never part with them if he could help it. Well, Luba is still glittering, and though she is not young, I suppose she is no older than Liane Mardi or Stravazzi, and she will give him everything that his plain and devoted wife gave him. She will notice nothing about the house, she will find something about it that reminds her of Russia. Claire says she will see that he comes to Le Touquet for Easter, and I see no reason why anything should go wrong. Yes," she sighed happily, lying back on her cushions, "I have arranged the whole business."

Marc burst out laughing, and she lifted her head sharply, crying, "Why, you're only pretending to be amused! What is it that displeases you in all this? You would not be hard on Luba because she is not a young girl in a white muslin frock, or on Mr. Pillans because he was born without dignity? We were born into this world, we must make the best of it."

"No," answered Marc, "I was thinking nothing unkind of Luba. I never would. And I am never contemp-
tuous of those among your compatriots who seem not to
have been taught by their surroundings how to live. It
is a form of poverty, one doesn't mock at it. It was
only . . ."

"Tell me, tell me," said Isabelle. "I cannot bear sus-
pecting that you disapprove of me."

"It is only that I am a little startled at the way you
propose to cure Luba's malady so simply by finding her
a suitable man," Marc smiled. "I am a man, and I feel
that when men break women's hearts it is only nice of
the women to let it appear as if the men had done them
irreparable damage. Luba should mourn a little longer,
I feel. Just out of compliment to my sex. It is quite silly
of me. It is only that . . ."

His voice died away. The flames of the log fire flick-
ered and seemed to shake the walls; it was as if the existence they had been leading in the room had sustained a
shock disturbing enough to quicken its pulse. Isabelle
turned her face away from him and rolled over on the
cushions, saying through laughter that he was a Turk,
a Pasha, but she was troubled by the sense of insecurity
which always filled her when she realized that the world
in which human beings lived was not the same as the
world of which they spoke and thought. Surely in each
human being there is both a hungry, naked outcast and a
Sister of Charity, desolate without those whom she can
feed and clothe and shelter; and these cannot minister to
each other. That is the rule which has been put in to
make it more difficult. They must find a stranger outside the skin to whose Sister of Charity the outcast can

offer his sores, to whose outcast their Sister of Charity can offer her pity. She had learned that by being an orphan, by being a widow, not during the days of weeping, for she kept on record nothing that she thought or felt under the stress of violent emotion, but in the empty later days; and she had learned it again by watching the conduct of several people, which, without this hypothesis, would have been inexplicable. But there was this other phantom world, to which Marc had alluded, where human beings were regarded not as dual but chaotic by nature, where human relationships were as arbitrary as dance steps, where sex appeared as a flight and pursuit instead of a collaboration to a mutually desired end, and men were supposed to have scored a point if they bungled a passage, and women were required to maintain their dignity by stiffening into rigid attitudes of suffering when they might still freely move their limbs, and no heed was paid to the real urgencies of life. When she heard people speak calmly on the assumption that they were living in such a world as that, and had accepted it, and were perpetuating it by their acceptance, there flashed before her a vision of humanity as a faintly smiling madman stepping out of a high window, of a coquettish madwoman holding a lit taper to her muslin gown, and she felt alarmed not only by what she feared of her fellows, but also by her solitariness in fearing it. But the moment passed, the flames fell and the shadows were steady. She continued to laugh, and presently there was no part of her mind that was not amused.

Their expedition was entertaining from its beginning, when the car brought round Luba on Wednesday afternoon. She was touching and delightful when she started on a journey, because the stated fact that she was going to a certain place for a certain time failed to make any real impression on her; she had found the world full of fictions, and she saw no reason why this should not be one of them. She waved good-bye to the Sacré Cœur where it shone white on the Butte of Montmartre at the left of the Beauvais road, owning that, though she had been very miserable in Paris, she had been very happy there too, just as though she were never to see these parts again. As they drew nearer to Le Touquet through the night, she peered smiling from the dark windows, as if to see the details of the home where she was to live in contentment, and for ever. Marc and Isabelle had been afraid she might want to stay up very late, but she was as tired out by her extreme imaginative abandonment to the idea of travel as most people are during their first day out on a transatlantic liner, and she could hardly stay awake to eat any dinner, though Marc had it brought up to their salon.

The next morning Marc and Isabelle slept very late, and woke up very good-humoured and lazy and gossiping, so that it was a long time before they were dressed. Marc kept on coming out of the bathroom, it might be to ask her if she had ever noticed some particular trait in his mother's character, or to tell her of how he had bicycled here from his father's place at Lille when he was fourteen; and she did not go to have her bath when he had finished, because greediness overcame her, and she took a brioche, clotting the fine yellow sponge with a thick layer of bland yellow butter. He stood beside her laughing, his hand on her waist, while she ate with the special innocent sensuality of her state, pressing the mingled substances against her palate, crushing out the flavour with her teeth. When at length they were ready to go out, they suddenly remembered Luba, whom till then they had entirely forgotten. They went into her room and found her still asleep and translating, as dogs do, all her dreams into little cries and movements. She laughed several times while they watched her, but then rolled over and seemed about to cry, so they woke her. She went into the bathroom to dress, but she kept on losing things, and would never have arrived at being fully clothed if Isabelle had not rung for her maid and told her to take the business in hand.

They stepped out at last into a day that was grey but not cold, and exclaimed at the flowers in the hotel parterres, the rigid imperial hyacinths, the mobile daffodils. Then they turned and looked back at the hotel and laughed at the forest of rounded turrets that rose from the precipice of windowed walls; for though the Guillaume-le-Conquérant might have been a legitimate version of a Norman château so far as forms went, it had been rendered not more imposing but comically raffish by being made so much over its accustomed size, just as cinema organs are. Isabelle and Luba were enchanted by the delicate birch woods all round, which were still black and bare except for a few witty little green leaves here and there; but they were drawn, as if they were children, as if they were poor folk who rarely had a holiday and must snatch the essentials, towards the wonder of the sea. They were pleased at the way that the town became more tawdry and homely as they went, and they found a long street lined with shops full of rubbish, where Marc bought brooches made of shells for his women, and a big rubber ball painted with a sprig of white heather. Then they made their way to the sands and walked for a little till they found a stretch where there were not so many people, and then Isabelle sat down and rested while Marc and Luba played ball. A black dog that had followed them joined in the game, but although its antics were amusing, Isabelle's eyes turned to the grey sea. She looked out over the face of the waves, and her mind followed her gaze, exulting in its power to realize space, swinging backwards and forwards like an eagle between the white surf and the dark bar of the horizon. She felt sure that she would not die when her child was born, and that she had strength enough to answer all demands it might make on her.

Presently Marc felt that Isabelle's attention had gone from him, and he stopped playing and ran back to her, and sat down beside her on the sand. He asked her if she was all right, and she answered that she was, and let him take her hand. They watched Luba as she ran about throwing sticks for the dog to fetch, and noted that she was looking rested and beautiful, and perhaps a little younger, and, as always in the open air, indistinct; for her yellow hair matched the sands, which under the grey sky and in front of the grey sea looked more yellow than usual, and for lack of sunlight her white woollen dress looked a beige shadow. Though she was older than either of them, they bracketed her and their child in their talk, as young things in their charge.

"When is this fellow Pillans coming down?" asked Marc.

"Tomorrow morning, she says," answered Isabelle.

"That's good," said Marc. "One thing at a time, and we have to make the acquaintance of young Renart and his wife tonight at dinner."

"Ah, yes, we shan't be alone much longer," said Isabelle. "I wish we could have gone to some little place in Brittany."

"But, my darling," said Marc, putting his hand to his head, "we hadn't time. I have only barely time to make this trip. As it is we shall have to leave on Monday afternoon. And I don't know anywhere in Brittany really comfortable that wouldn't have been crowded, and we never have time to run about looking for places. Besides, I hadn't time to get up a party, and here I can get someone to give me a round of golf if I just sit about in the lounge and wait. But I know what you mean, my dear. I wish we could have been more alone."

"I believe you are very tired," said Isabelle.

"I am tired as a dog," Marc owned, and for a little time he lay back and rested, his head partly on the sand, partly on the hem of her dress.

Sleep was another of Isabelle's gourmandises at this time. Every time she lay down on her bed the world around her became warm and very soft, like one of the more delicate furs, and she stayed lapped in its softness hour after hour, deliberately returning there every time she came up to the surface of consciousness, till she was aroused by some other person. That afternoon she sat with Luba in the sunshine till the last possible moment, and went to lie down about four, and slept until her maid came to dress her for dinner. She turned from side to side, with her eyes shut, pleading, half in jest and half in earnest, for just five minutes more, and telling the maid to go and dress the Princess first and then come back to her. But she was told that the Princess had been dressed for some time, that indeed she and Marc had already gone downstairs to wait in the lounge in case the Philippe Renarts were early for their dinner engagement. It was necessary that she should rise at once, and so she did, though her lids were still closed as she stood up and let the maid splash alcohol on her bare body, though she was rubbing her eyes when the maid sat her down in front of the mirror and brushed her hair. She opened them for assurance that she was not yet too ugly when the maid was slipping on her so unnaturally loose gown, and at the sight of herself, still seemly and looking not so much unlike any other beautiful woman dressed to dine, her splendid greed became excited by the thought of dinner. She hurried out of her room, hardly letting the maid smooth the great powder puff over her arms and shoulders, and put herself in the lift, smiling benevolently at the attendant.

But Marc and Luba were sitting by themselves in the bar.

"Not a sign of the Renarts," Marc said irritably, as he settled Isabelle in her chair. "My God, what I would have given to dine early and simply tonight. A plate of onion soup, a steak with some morels, and some apple fritters. And then to bed at ten."

"Are they happily married?" asked Luba. "Sometimes people are late for dinner because they have suddenly noticed something wrong about their relationship, and they sit down and talk it out."

"Talk it out when the dinner is on the table!" exclaimed Marc, really shocked. "No, Philippe Renart is

not that sort of man. He is not very brilliant, but he is
sensible enough. Waiter, another Martini." He pulled
out his watch again. "Even if the trouble was that they
were too newly or too happily married, they still ought
to consider that other people are waiting for their dinner."

"Oh, I am so hungry!" sighed Isabelle.

"My poor child, can't you possibly take a cocktail just
to keep you going?"

She shook her head and pursed her lips. In these days the
mere mention of alcohol made her mouth feel fouled.
"But I will eat some potato chips," she said, constrained
by her immense hunger, though she knew they were too
salt for her.

"They are showing themselves extraordinarily ill
bred," said Marc, pushing the dish towards her. "I never
care when I dine, me. But it is the bad manners of it
that disgusts me."

"What a pretty woman that is, sitting on the high
stool by the bar," said Isabelle, looking round for something to distract his attention.

"It is Suzette Lefèvre, and she is not pretty at all,"
said Marc, "she has pop eyes and she is too thin, you can
see all her vertebræ. In fact, she is like something you
find at the bottom of your plate when you eat bouilla-
baisse. Ah, why did I remind myself of food! It is not,
mind you, that I am hungry. But I dislike rudeness. Particularly to you, my dear, and I feel it is to you the
Renarts are being rude."

"But do you not like her dress?" asked Isabelle.

"No, I hate these queer materials that you women

think it smart to wear nowadays. Think of getting into an auto with a woman after having longed to be alone with her all evening and then finding that she is dressed in stuff like a fisherman's oilskins and that you might as well both be characters in *Les Travailleurs de la Mer*. This is abominable. Waiter, I will have another Martini."

"It was far worse in the Revolution," said Luba. "Then we waited and waited, and nearly always there was no dinner."

"But why should it be like a revolution at all?" asked Marc. "I have come to the Guillaume-le-Conquérant at Le Touquet for Easter. I do not see why things should be in the least like Moscow under the Bolsheviks. My dear, we will not wait any longer. I will just take this cocktail, and then we will go in to dinner. God knows, no man cares less than I do what he eats and when he eats, but to discourtesy I decidedly object. Ah, there is Philippe! The poor fellow, perhaps there has been some accident for which he has to make excuses! Ohé, Philippe!"

Isabelle was always delighted by the speed with which Marc's anger went from him. He stood up and waved to Philippe, a slight, apologetically built young man who was seeking them not by standing still and looking round the bar, but by threading his way quickly between the tables and chairs, dropping oblique glances on those whom he passed. His mild and furtive gait suggested that he was in the habit of purchasing his friends' liking by the performance of commissions that they themselves found too trivial or too embarrassing. Marc stood up and gesticulated to him, with wide, handsome, approving gestures. It was as if he were saying that, though his old schoolfellow did nothing but fetch and carry, he fetched and carried very faithfully and meant no harm.

"Well, here you are, you blackguard!" he shouted, clapping Philippe on the shoulders. "It's not us that kept you waiting now, is it? Isabelle, my dear, this is Philippe Renart, of whom you have heard me speak so often. And Madame la Princesse Couranoff, may I present to you Monsieur Renart. But, for God's sake, Philippe, what has been the matter?"

Lifting his face from the women's hands, Philippe began to explain in English, which was to him plainly not merely a foreign language which he had mastered, but a form of chic, "My wife has sent me down to cover myself with excuses and to promise that she will be down in a minute. It is entirely our fault that we are late."

"Well, of course it is," said Marc. "Who did you think we would blame for it?"

Philippe paused a minute and contemplated the interruption without humour, but without irritation. Isabelle suspected that he was recalling to himself that his old schoolfellow had always been naïve. He continued. "You see, as it happens, my wife has several relatives staying in a villa here, and they have a cocktail party this evening, and there were many important people there, so she found it difficult to get away. You see"—he paused and drew in a breath—"Poots was a Lauriston on her mother's side."

"But what does it mean this word Poots?" exclaimed Marc, who did not appear to be satisfied with the explanation.

"That is what my wife's friends call her," answered Philippe, outstaring him; and he repeated it firmly, "Poots."

"Well, sit down and have a drink," said Marc. "A Manhattan? Very well. But tell me more about this name. I have never heard it before, though it is charming, of course. Do you," he asked, turning to Isabelle, "have such a name in your country?"

"It is perhaps a nickname?" she suggested. "I have always heard that the English are very fond of nicknames."

"Yes, Madame," said Philippe, bowing as if to mark her recognition of the finer shades of living, "it is a nickname. My wife was Lady Virginia Sandways. But she is known by everyone as Poots."

"Poots," repeated Marc. "Ah! I see! It has something to do with Pussy, it is like *mon petit chat?*"

"No," answered Philippe doggedly. "It hasn't anything to do with that."

"It's just a nickname," explained Isabelle. "It doesn't mean anything at all. I've noticed that about English nicknames. Unlike most French ones, they often don't mean anything at all."

"So it is just Poots?"

"Yes," replied Philippe.

"Poots? Like boots, only it doesn't mean anything?"

"Yes," replied Philippe.

"*Tiens,*" said Marc. "Well, here's your Manhattan. Waiter, I'll have another Martini. There's nothing to do but kill the worm." He was now talking such rough grumbling French as one of his own workmen might have used. He looked round yawning, and indeed the

bar was nearly empty. It was after nine, and almost
everybody had gone in to dinner. Isabelle had emptied
a plate of potato chips. She found it difficult to focus her
attention when Philippe turned to her and courteously
said, "My wife was hoping that you and Marc and Madame la Princesse might honour us by coming to dine
with her aunt, the Countess of Barnaclouth, tomorrow.
She is a very celebrated figure in English life, you know."

"Yes, she once wrote to ask us to give her an automobile for nothing, because she said it would be such a
good advertisement," said Marc.

"I am sure we shall be delighted," said Isabelle. She
knew Marc would be sorry in the morning. He would
grieve over his unkindness to Philippe, whom he had
known all his life.

"At half-past eight, then, at the Villa Sans Souci.
It is in the woods not far away. That will be charming,"
said Philippe, a little soothed. "My wife will be so
pleased. There are several of her relatives staying there
just now. Lady Barnaclouth has her elder two sisters
there, Lady McKentrie and Lady Barron. They were all
painted by Sargent, you know. It is a very famous picture."

"Ah!" said Luba suddenly. "It was like that in Russia
before the Revolution. All the great families sent their
beautiful women to Paris to be painted by Boldini and
de la Gandara, and even before the war it was found
that they were worth nothing. Nothing at all." She
smiled at Philippe with a tender pity which he did not
appreciate.

"But Sargent is still a very famous artist. It is not like
that at all, is it?" he appealed to the other two.

"Yes," said Marc.

"Of course not," said Isabelle. But she could hardly keep her attention on what she said, she was thinking so intensely of soup.

"Of course it is not so," Philippe said. "It still hangs in the place of honour at Barron Hall. Lady Barron's son, the great sporting Lord Barron, owns it."

"I have met him at Washington," said Isabelle, feeling a little guilty. For if this little man had known that his wife's famous cousin knew her very well and had even asked her to marry him, he would have known the desolation of a small boy showing off his stamp collection to a schoolfellow and finding that the other possessed a duplicate of the parcel of his collection.

"Ah, you know him, our dear Sangaree," smiled Philippe.

"Sangaree?" snapped Marc. "Is that an English name?"

"No," said Philippe tensely. "It is a nickname. It is really the name of a West Indian drink, but he is called that because it was the name of a racehorse that won the Derby for his father the year he was born."

"My God, my God!" said Marc.

But Philippe had leapt to his feet. "Ah, here is Poots."

Isabelle felt it extremely annoying that they had had to wait so long for somebody so little individual as Poots. They surely could have gone in to dinner with any of those replicas of her which had surrounded them when they first sat down in the bar. For Poots had the face which had been fashionable among Englishwomen for some years; her complexion and her hair were lustrous as growing flowers, but her eyes were pulled wide open and her upper lip lifted by an expression of fastidiousness in which delicacy had no part. She might have been a horrid little girl at a children's party, staring at some unfortunate child who was being sick. And she had the voice which had been fashionable among Englishwomen for some years, a tired and timbreless gabble which made a curious claim to sense, which pretended that though the speaker was late, or in debt, or taken in adultery, it was the very contrary of her fault, since she had been besieged by people inferior to herself in sagacity, who had urged on her a delay so great, a financial policy so extravagant, a sexual habit so profuse, that the lesser degree of her actual fault made it appear by contrast a virtue, or at least an unusually practical and restrained way of dealing with the situation. She spoke as if, till only a few minutes before, she had been forcibly detained at her aunt's cocktail party by a guerrilla army of people who had not her sense of the obligation of punctuality, and as if a person without her own strength of character would still be there, would still be keeping the Sallafranques waiting. Several times she repeated, "So at last I simply said to them, 'Well, I can't help it, I've got to be going,'" raising her eyebrows and pulling down her mouth in an expression of weary common sense.

But although Isabelle was familiar with Poots's type, she recognized in it a certain mystery. Poots was a fool. Her activities and her affections were on the nursery level. Yet she was not without shrewdness. It could be seen from her manner that she had listened to all her husband had said about the wealth and importance of the Sallafranques; she made all her apologies several

times over, she took the trouble to uncover her teeth in
a smile when she caught their eyes. But it was also apparent that immediately she had set eyes on the party
she had divined that Luba's empire had passed from her,
that she was unhappy and down on her luck. Poots
bowed to her only a very little from the shoulders, her
eyes and mouth remaining sullen. She had seen it as
beyond all possibility that Luba would ever own a house
in which she would find it convenient to stay. That was
clever of her, considering that Luba was still beautiful,
and grandly dressed. But again it was stupid of her, for
she might have guessed that, if Luba was a friend of the
Sallafranques, they would prefer people to be polite to
her.

That shrewdness and stupidity should exist side by
side in Poots was, however, thoroughly characteristic of
her type, which, so far as it was ruled by anything, was
ruled by a preference for disorder. When they had sat
down to dinner, she destroyed the ritual of the meal by
saying petulantly to her husband, "Darling, I've got
such a pain." Isabelle reflected in wonder that she had
never known an Englishwoman of this sort who was not
constantly making this complaint, but she civilly asked
what special dishes Poots would like in these circumstances and saw that Marc ordered them. It seemed to
her that these dishes were not particularly suitable for
indigestion, but she was relieved from any apprehension
on this score, since Poots only pecked at them with a
fork and then thrust the plate away from her, so near
the centre of the table that it lost its look of order. She
destroyed the conversation, too, for though it was her
almost too obvious intention to listen respectfully to the

Sallafranques and regard them amiably over the rim
of her champagne glass, her gaze kept sliding past them
to explore the vistas of the restaurant, and she made to
her husband some such remark as, "Darling, Juliet's
sitting over there. Isn't she exquisite!" or "Who's that
with Ferdy Monck? Hattie'll be furious." In this way
she informed them that they were not to be alone for
Easter, that there were also present at Le Touquet
Gladys and Serge, Iris and Nikolai, Gordon Lloyd, Annette and Laura, Gustave and Sarah Bourges, Dan
Creed, Mrs. Postleham, and Prince Ostrogin. The manner in which she conveyed the information usually
obliged Marc and Isabelle to look round and scrutinize
the room when they would rather have kept their attention fixed on their plates, to make gestures of recognition
which they would rather have withheld. It frustrated
any possibility that at the end of this dinner party the
five people at table might have found some common
ground on which they might get to know each other better. This of course was part performance of the intention
to which Poots's world was dedicated. Life was again
prevented from becoming coherent.

Poots ran a hat shop, her husband proudly told them,
in partnership with the Duke of Norwich's eldest girl.
In the course of Isabelle's visits to London she had
learned what such hat shops are like. One was forced to
go there by an aunt of one of the noble milliners, met
at lunch, who insisted on taking one with a pertinacity
which would have seemed vulgar, had one not reflected
that in her youth there must have seemed so little need
for her to push and cadge that her preceptors might well
have omitted to warn her against such practices. There

were usually good models lying about on the shelves,
one was taken by the pretty skins, the victorious health,
the completely unchastened youth and vigour of the
saleswomen. One ordered a hat or two, but though one
made a definite appointment for the fitting, one had to
go back several times, because no note had been taken of
it, and then the hats were never delivered when they had
been promised. One went down on a Saturday morning
to see what had happened, because foolishly one had
wanted to wear them during the week-end, and was
faced peevishly by the noble milliner who had served
one, as if one were being unsporting in taking the business so literally as actually to expect to have the hats.
The beautiful child's face would go white with sullenness, her eyes would go blank as Poots's eyes did when
she looked at Luba, she would say obstinately, insolently,
absurdly, "I really can't tell you why they aren't ready";
and the interview would be made difficult to prosecute
because another beautiful child, partner or assistant in
the business, dressed in entrancing sports clothes for the
week end, was looking for something all over the shop,
tumbling a mess of patterns out of a desk, running into
an inner room and out again, repeating in that curious
gabbling head-voice, "But, darling, someone must have
taken them, I can't find them, I know I left them here,"
while outside someone waiting in an automobile hit the
hooter again and again.

It was a fatuous world to which Poots belonged. Perhaps it was worse. Benny d'Alperoussa paused by Marc's
chair and greeted him. Marc forced his head up, forced
a smile. There was no sense in making an enemy of a
man who, if he got far enough from the base of civiliza-

tion, would flay one before he murdered one. When
he had gone, Poots asked huskily, "Isn't that Benny
d'Alperoussa?" Marc nodded. "Isn't he one of the richest men in Europe?" she pursued. "One of the richest
in the world," answered Marc. "He got his business
training fighting with pariah dogs for food round the
garbage heaps of Constantinople." Poots laughed out of
politeness, but her eyes followed the old man as he
walked away among the tables. Isabelle realized that she
was avid as well as fatuous, and that she had married
Philippe for some insufficient reason, to get away from
home or to gratify some taste not more urgent than one
might feel for chocolate fudge, which, if it had ever had
the power to deflect her avidity from its normal course,
had already lost it. That certain women were ready to
sell themselves caused no excessive disgust in Isabelle.
It was inevitable that a number of both men and women
should compromise the institution of marriage by marrying for money, and once that happened there could
be no question of impressing on the toughly logical female mind the unique vileness of prostitution. She had
sometimes wondered, too, whether the contempt men felt
for women who market their favours did not in part
proceed from the sense of grievance eternally felt by
buyers against vendors. But however natural and ex-
plicable Poots's proceedings were, Isabelle could not see
that they constituted any reason why she herself should
spend any of her limited lifetime with her. When they
rose from dinner and went into the lounge, and were
surrounded by the people who had interrupted their
honeymoon at Antibes and accompanied them on their
holiday to St. Moritz, Isabelle had the same guilty sense

of frittering away mortality that they had previously provoked. But she had been into that before, there was nothing to be done.

They went to their room early, tired with their first day of sea air; and though Luba's Russian form of conscience made her try to rebut it when they told her she was yawning because she wanted to go to bed, she left them early. With their arms about each other's shoulders they sat side by side on the sofa, too lazy to undress.

"I arranged to golf with Philippe tomorrow morning," said Marc. "Dear Philippe. It is a pity he has tied himself up with that slut of a wife."

"She has a pretty figure," said Isabelle.

"Nonsense, lots of girls with just as pretty figures have to earn their livings doing acrobatics with sergeants de ville," said Marc. A grimace brought down the corners of his mouth, he began to rub his stomach. "Oh, my God, my God, waiting for that hen I drank too many cocktails, and that champagne on top of it has given me indigestion. I shall not sleep as I would have done if she hadn't been there, that hen, that crane."

VII

T H O U G H I N the early part of the night Isabelle
had woken up several times to find Marc threshing about
and grumbling, he was so strong that when the morning
came he felt very well. He jumped out of bed and
bounded to the window, and put his head out to snuff
the air, and when he found it almost as warm as summer, and full of the smells of the sea and the reviving
earth, he cried out in pleasure and called her to join
him. But she shook her head and pressed her face into
the pillow, feeling less healthy, more jangled in nerves,
than she had done since she had begun to have a child,
though that was not to say that she felt really ill. Marc
tenderly exclaimed in pity and came back to stroke her
cheek, and tell her that she would be better when she
had had her coffee, that it was all the fault of that Poots
for keeping them up so late, and that they would not
let the little ordure spoil another day of their holiday.
When their breakfast had come and he had buttered her
brioche for her, he went over to the window and stood
there reporting on what was happening below. He was
amused by the brisk cosmetic preparation to which a
pleasure resort is subjected before its patrons have risen:
the pulling down of coloured awnings, the sprinkling of

184

the roads with a hose pipe, the work in the garden that was not so much gardening as maquillage of the flower-beds, performed by men in sacking aprons whose appearance was more rudely suggestive of labour than any figures which would be seen about the town in half an hour's time.

"How artificial it all is," said Marc, "really too artificial! Now, that shocks me! Will you believe it, my dear, those hyacinths we liked so much are not growing in the earth at all! They are all in little pots. A boy has brought along a wheelbarrow full of them, and an old man is on his knees adding them one by one to make another row in the flower-bed and banking up the earth so that one does not see the pots. Now that I really think is going too far."

"I thought it might be so," said Isabelle. "Gardeners always want to do that, it helps them to make a good show. I have constant trouble in stopping them from doing it at home. But I do not know whether one is right in one's objection to it. Probably the gardeners are not shocked by the artificiality of the idea because, living a more simple life than we do, they realize how artificial it is to have a garden at all."

"You are perfectly right," said Marc. "But how difficult it is for us human beings to make up our minds whether we want to be natural or not! While I have been standing here, I have been watching the ladies' maids bringing down their mistresses' pets for their morning excursions. What repressed lives we insist on those poor women leading! They must wear black, they must be neat and nimble, they must never notice their employers' indiscretions, they must never have any of their own.

How human beings must love order and discipline, one would think, to have such mercilessly ordered and disciplined creatures around them! Yet, look, they carry in their arms those who are far dearer to their employers than themselves, and see how these little creatures behave when they are set down on the earth! It is plainly the charm of their disorder and indiscipline which makes such little dogs precious to their owners—I am watching one little Pekinese now who is scratching on the ground with such spirit, such bravura in the abandon of her white tail, as she behaves in a way no ladies' maid would dream of behaving in public. There is a human preference for the natural too."

"But is not some gardener making it plain that on the whole the human preference for the artificial is stronger?" asked Isabelle.

"You are right," said Marc. "A gardener is hurrying to her this very moment, to tell her to take the little beast away. Ah—but the natural is winning again. The maid is quite a pretty girl, a smile is coming over the gardener's face, they are beginning a pleasant conversation, the dog is going on doing just what it pleases. What a lot one loses by being artificial! How delightful are these sudden encounters, almost as simple and sudden as that the Pekinese will have with that pug-dog if its guardians are not more observant——"

"I had no idea that the life we lead was so artificial that you and your friends no longer had sudden encounters with the opposite sex," said Isabelle.

"Well, perhaps the men of my kind have not sacrificed that," owned Marc, "but, believe me, we have made our sacrifices. Why, I can see an example before me now, for, do you know, this landscape is covered with Cupids shooting their bows, just as if it were a Boucher wall-painting. The man spraying the road with a hose pipe has just seen a female friend approaching him, a female friend who is sufficiently pleasing. He has taken off his cap, he has uttered a polite cry, but he wishes to do something more, she is so very pleasing. So he is waving his hose pipe towards her, carefully, so that the water does not reach her, in a cross between a courtly flourish and what would be considered in our world an obscene gesture. But he is doing it very nicely, it is well over the borderline towards the courtly flourish, though its other aspect is quite apparent. And his friend is responding so nicely, too, she is quickening her step and wrapping her shawl tighter round her and casting her eyes down so modestly, and smiling so prettily. Ah, why cannot we make such gestures in our world? For example, as a man I find Madame Ortega immensely attractive, but I have no way of showing her that it is so. If I were to use words, I might find myself drifting into a declaration, which would be awkward, for she would either have to rebuff me or encourage me, neither of which do I want. But what a charming, warm friendliness there would be established between us if I could make some public, playful, yet fully masculine gesture like this."

"Darling, you do very well with the resources that you have," said Isabelle, "and there is something I must tell you. The little friend on the sidewalk when she quickens her step and draws her shawl round her and smiles downwards, is not obeying her own impulse, she is simply doing it because she knows it is a pattern that pleases men. Within herself she feels contempt for the

man because, when he is watering the road, he is thinking of something else than watering the road. Women
hate people to do more than one thing at a time."

"Yes, there is in women an extraordinary lack of
poetry," said Marc. "They dislike the uncontrollable excess in us, which produces the incalculable in life, which
strikes out its pattern. But I cannot go into that now, I
must have my bath. I promised to meet Philippe and his
wife at the Golf House for a round at half-past eleven.
But that camel Poots is certain to be unpunctual."

"Yes, but she is so perverse that that will make her
certain to be on time once one has adjusted oneself to her
habits," said Isabelle.

But because of one thing and another that passed
beneath the window, Marc stayed where he was, and
they talked very comfortably until Luba came in, holding a telegram which announced that Mr. Pillans was
arriving that morning at one o'clock and hoped that she
and the Sallafranques would lunch with him. They
greeted the announcement with pleasure, which they
were careful not to make too emphatic, lest they should
betray to her how desperate they thought her need for
help, or rather suggest it to her, for in so far as her
plight resulted from the heartlessness of human beings,
and the freedom of destiny from any bias towards harmony, her nature had as yet remained half incredulous
of it. She was already dressed, but her suit was on awry
and her hair looked like a clumsy yellow cap. Isabelle
rang for her maid and told her to straighten Luba's
dress and brush out her hair; and Luba was so purely
amiable that there was no need to soften this indictment
of her feminine competence by rallying her about it. She

took her seat at the window and let the maid unpin her braids with the meekness of a little girl who accepts absolutely that her elders know better and mean well. But Isabelle, watching her from amongst the pillows, was sad to see that her vagueness no longer gave the impression of drifting serenity. Across her face there was passing a constant stream of infinitesimally delicate changes of expression, the most minute possible contraction of the brows or pursing of the lips, which gave an indication of restlessness that, if at any moment these movements became more marked, would shift into a complete picture of misery.

Isabelle realized that she was watching something like the aimless twitchings of the hands of an enthusiastic knitter, who finds herself, by accident and not by design, without her accustomed work. Luba had had the habit of thinking lovingly of her lover all the time, even when she was talking and listening to the people about her with quite lively interest. Now she could not think of him with pleasure, or even with regret, for Tecloro had conveyed to her that he found it embarrassing to feel that she was suffering on his account; and she had accepted this final and supreme ejaculation of his egotism as a demand that he had no doubt some right to make, and she was acceding as far as she could. Except under the irresistible compulsion to suffering which is exercised by the night, she tried not to think of him; she averted her mind from him, as a dog averts his head from the master who has beaten it. But this prohibited her from exercising the tenderness which was her most essential function; it was thus an interference with the process of her nature that must in the end be fatal. Sit-

ting there at the window, with her head bowed before
the sunshine, she had something of the immobile and
submissive air of a woman in whom one of the vital
organs has begun to wither. "Oh, if only Alexander
Pillans will marry her!" Isabelle exclaimed to herself.
She reflected with surprise that innumerable people
would fail to see that poor Luba, the lover who was
denied the opportunity to love, was as dignified in her
piteousness as a nun who, after spending her whole life
performing pious offices in her convent, is suddenly flung
out into the world by an abrupt dissolution of the order,
and wanders lost and helpless, unless some devout household opens its door to her and permits her to remain within
it, following the rule which is the only way of living that
she knows. She shuddered in apprehension regarding the
quality of life, an apprehension which was for some
reason not allayed by the robust sound of Marc singing
in the bathroom, by the spectacle of Luba sitting in the
sunlight, her flesh glowing, yet still as alabaster.

At last they were all ready; but though they had taken
their own time, and were indeed some twenty minutes
late for their appointment at the Golf House, Philippe
and Poots were not there. This immediately put Marc
out of his good humour, and Isabelle too was vexed,
since it meant that, instead of leaving him to take a walk
with Luba, she had to sit down beside him on the veranda, where she immediately found herself to be surrounded by those who were inevitably her friends and
naturally her enemies. But if she did not relish being
told again and again that she was looking marvellous,
and having to tell people again and again that they were
looking marvellous, Marc was sociable by instinct and

enjoyed meeting his kind just for the sake of meeting
them, as dogs do, and the day placated her. It is as impossible for land on which there is a golf-course to be
beautiful as it is for a woman who wears spectacles and
has gold-crowned teeth, but the colours of the indefinite
long grasses and the definite close-cropped greens, the
frivolous larches and the graver pines, only temperately
gay with spring, and the more interesting superior countryside of high-sailing clouds, were scoured to a crystal
purity of tone by the salt air. Ferdy Monck was sitting
beside them, reading the *Continental Daily Mail,* and
sometimes calling out an item of news that he thought
might interest Marc; and he paused, after telling them
what amazing things were happening to aviation stock
in the United States, to say in his thick, wine-tasting
voice, "Your wife's looking very pretty today, Sallafranque." She was pleased at that, with the nervous
humility of a pregnant woman, and anyway Ferdy always amused her by the contrast between his loose spirit
and the physical envelope It had inherited from a great
English family of the governing classes. The deep lines
on his face had in fact been engraved by nothing whatsoever but his ability to satisfy women and his inability to
satisfy creditors, but the family habit of his flesh organized these lines into the heavy mask of a statesman
who has spent years pondering on the laws his firm hand
must impose on his people. His appearance lent to their
hour of idling on the veranda the spaciousness and moral
dignity of leisure enjoyed between sessions of Parlia-
ment. She closed her eyes and drowsed, sometimes smiling to herself.

Suddenly Renart and Poots were with them. They

were exactly seventy minutes late for the appointment. Renart was apologetic but not really perturbed. It was as if he had taken a job with some organization such as a circus, which was bound to cause a great deal of traffic disorganization, and while his natural politeness always made him apologize to the people who were thereby inconvenienced, he wore the steady serenity of one who knows that nothing is happening which is not inevitable and provided against by plan. Poots, however, was wholly without serenity as in her timbreless, worried gabble she said things which either meant that since early that morning a vast concourse of persons had surrounded the hotel while a horde of other individuals rang her up on the telephone, in a fatuous and malicious attempt to prevent her from keeping the appointment, or meant nothing at all except that she knew she was late. Marc briskly set about shepherding Philippe towards the game which they had so nearly missed, and Isabelle realized that Poots had not arranged for a partner and intended not to play golf but to pass the morning in her company. But as the girl still showed no disposition to be civil to Luba, and as she seemed even more objectionable by day than by night, since she looked even more healthy and likely to survive to old age, Isabelle backed away from her, borrowing her own technique, gabbling that a vast concourse of persons were even now waiting for her at the hotel, that a horde of individuals intended to ring her up there during the morning. Since this manner of speaking was so little Poots's invention, so much the fashion of her group, it did not strike her that Isabelle was being malicious in using it. But Isabelle laughed as she met Marc's eyes, and she laughed more loudly be-

cause just then an Englishman, strolling by with his
clubs, had looked up and seen Ferdy Monck reading the
paper, and had called out, "What, not golfin' today,
Ferdy?" at which Ferdy had shaken his head and answered, "No, not golfin' today." There was in the in-
quirer's tone such solemnity, such innocence of any
scale of values by which it could be a matter of unim-
portance whether Ferdy golfed or not; there was in
Ferdy's tone so rich a sense of judicial deliberation in a
high court dealing with cases of luxury, the unhurried
exercise of a sage preference among pleasures by an
epicurean so complacent and pompous that it might well
have assumed wig and gown. It was odd that she and
Marc should find themselves among such ridiculous
people.

She and Luba walked for a time among the woods and
avenues, which were still parti-coloured, the tall trees
being black as a funeral, and the bushes and the slighter,
more precocious kinds of tree as gay as a wedding with
sticky silver buds and new green leaves bright like wet
paint. Rain had fallen during the night and in the road
there were pools full of blue sky and white clouds, dispersed every now and then by the bathing of draggled
little birds; and a rich yet light and clean smell rose
from the earth. But the gross unpunctuality of Poots had
left them only a short space for their promenade, since
they had to be back at the hotel to lunch with Mr.
Pillans. Isabelle took Luba upstairs and bade the maid
carefully repowder her and recoiffe her hair, and then
went down alone so that she could have a few words with
Mr. Pillans by herself and decide in what direction she
should most profitably steer the conversation during

lunch. When the page pointed him out, he was using one of the most common expedients of the shy man left in a public place: he was patting a dog while having himself the air of a dog who would like to be patted. There was, Isabelle suspected, further evidence of a profound lack of self-confidence in the unsuitably thick and rustic suit he was wearing. He was probably one of those, men and women, who outwit the most careful personal servants by going into a tantrum of disgust when they see themselves finally dressed in the mirror, and insisting at the last minute on changing into other clothes, any other clothes. Beyond these he offered few hints of salient characteristics. His Scotch father had given him sandy hair and restrained lips. He greeted her with an agreeable voice, though with a Middle West accent much stronger than one would expect in the son of a very rich man; he looked younger than his forty-one years, and he was one of those men who, though not much under average height, would always be called little men, because of some patent but indefinable deficiency. When first he stood up, his face was stiff with shyness, and she noted that very deep lines, lines as deep as any on Ferdy's mask, could be graved on a man's face by his inability to satisfy women and his ability to satisfy creditors.

"He has suffered enormously," she thought to herself, "and Luba will be able to comfort him. She has probably never grasped what the physical act of passion is about, I am almost sure that the only satisfaction she really requires is permission to love someone. And she will annul his wealth, not by the amount of it she will spend, but by the way she will spend it, as if dollars were the chestnut conkers children use in their games, and by the way it will never cross her mind that people will ever alter their attitude to her just because she is rich. She is like Marc in that. Ah, Marc, Marc." For a second she was transfixed by the thought of his extraordinary candour and simplicity, of her amazing good fortune in marrying him; then went on aloud, "We are so pleased that you have come here, because you are a friend of Luba, and we adore Luba. As, of course, everybody does."

"I should think everybody would," said Mr. Pillans, " the Princess is so very, very beautiful."

"Ah, isn't she!" exclaimed Isabelle. She was aware that he would place her own good looks far below beauty, that her regularity and pallor must fail to please one whose simplicity demanded a golden, Eve-like abundance, so she went on confidentially, "You know, it is almost embarrassing to go about with someone who attracts such attention. Wherever we go, people stare at her."

"I would think folks would stare at you, too, Madame Sallafranque," he said, politely. "But yes, I know that's true. I stared at her pretty hard myself once, in a theatre in Paris three years ago. I thought then I'd be mighty pleased to meet her, but I was kind of busy." He sighed. "I dare say you know I've been married three times before," he said, and Isabelle did not find it indecent of him to mention it so soon. He spoke with the innocent wonder of a farmer in whose byre a two-headed cow has been born. In any case, had his manner been far less innocent, Isabelle would have forgiven him, so pleased was she at the implications contained in his use of the word "before." She murmured sympathetically, and he went

on, crinkling up his eyes in pleased reminiscence, "She
was with a big, tall chap they said was a very rich man
who was crazy about her."

"Ah, there have been many such," smiled Isabelle.

"I expect the Princess wouldn't even remember his
name if you told it to her," said Mr. Pillans, with the
air of one turning over an enjoyable thought on his
palate. "Beautiful women are very cruel. But here she
is." He rose to his feet, but did not go forward to meet
Luba as she walked down the hall to them. Instead he
stood still, watching her and nodding his head as if in
appreciation of a performance. Isabelle realized that she
had grounds for her hopes, that there was a constant
force in this man which would make him marry Luba as
it had made him marry Liane Mardi and Margherita
Stravazzi. It had been his unhappy lot to be born with a
craving for the picturesque into a community and a
countryside the least in the world capable of gratifying
it. If he had wanted beauty, the Middle West might
have given it to him with its prairies and its strong people; but he wanted crowned kings, cardinals in their
purple, Venetian courtesans, and a whole rich phase of
life that had long disappeared from almost every part of
the globe where his nervousness would trust itself. When
he had first seen stage women descending painted wooden
staircases in spectacular nudity topped to twice its height
with plumes, while cuirassed Negroes blew on trumpets,
he must have come nearer his dream than ever before.
But his dream had been better than that. He had a gentle
kind of taste. He had taken the counterfeit only because
he could not find the real; when a fragment of reality

was presented to him, he recognized it and stretched towards it a reverent hand. The stateliness which Luba had derived from her education for the Imperial Court had for long not been properly seen by those who saw it, because it was associated in their minds with the impossible task of trying to find work for émigrées who could not work; but Mr. Pillans was seeing it as the superb achievement that it was.

"I hope," he murmured anxiously, "that they have given us a really good table in the restaurant."

It was a pity, Isabelle thought, that when the head waiter confessed that the table he had reserved for them had been pirated by an American oil-magnate, who could not be crossed, Luba should have said so happily, "Ah, well, let us sit at the little table behind the pillar. What does it matter? We are friends, we want to talk, we want to eat, the table cannot be of importance!" She crossed the room without picking up the eyes of any of her important friends, smiling vaguely at the sunshine, and at waiters whom she probably quite wrongly believed to have waited on her at other hotels, and to have then shown her exceptional kindness. "I do not believe this affair will go, not at all," fretted Isabelle, and she became more doubtful still when Mr. Pillans bent deferentially towards Luba, asking what she had done the day before, and plainly expecting an answer like a crowded paragraph in the social column of the Paris *New York Herald*, for Luba replied that Marc had bought them a rubber ball painted with flowers and they had played with it on the sands. But as she remembered how pleasant that morning had been, her face became filled with visionary power, and she described just how pleasant it had been for the three of them who liked each other, down there on the clean yellow sands, with the grey sea swinging down its gentle, steady blows of tonic coolness and the ball bouncing from hand to hand, and presently Mr. Pillans began to nod his head and say, "It must have been fine. I'd have liked to be there." Of course he would like to have been there, thought Isabelle; he is one of us who prefer the occasions where human beings lay down their arms, who find battle disgusting. She knew then that all must go well. He could not fail to notice that it was Luba's distinguishing characteristic to have thrown away all arms, to be defenceless because she had so absolutely renounced battle. She smiled benevolently when Luba cried, "And I had forgotten! Down on the sands there was a dog! Such a beautiful dog, I cannot think how the people who owned him could let him run loose!" This caused Mr. Pillans to remember a dog he had owned when he was a boy back in St. Louis, that had long since fallen off a footbridge over a river and got swept away by the current, and another dog that he had seen in Brussels when he was there between trains, and had nearly bought, it was so cute, though goodness knows what he would have done with it if he had. Isabelle felt placidly that she need no longer listen, and retired into comfortable speculations as to what her child would be like.

As soon as decently might be after lunch, she left them and went upstairs to sleep and awoke late in the afternoon. Through her lashes she saw that Marc was sitting in an arm-chair not far from her bed, and she sighed and smiled in her contentment that she was married to him, that they had come to Le Touquet, which was such a pleasant place in springtime, and that everything seemed to be going so well for everybody.

"Darling," she murmured, keeping her eyes shut, but turning over towards him and smiling.

"My little cat," he answered. But he spoke so dryly and abruptly that she knew something was wrong, and instantly sat up.

"Marc, what has happened?"

"Ah, what a fool I am! I did not mean to let you know, because you have such a loving heart and you want your friends to be happy. But I always give things away. Well, the fact is that that affair we'd such hopes of doesn't seem to be going at all."

"What affair?"

"Luba and Alexander Pillans, of course."

"But it is going perfectly! You should have seen them at lunch. He is all that we hoped. He likes her splendid pictorial beauty, but what he really wants is affection. I tell you it could not be better."

"Ah," said Marc, "that was when you were there. You can always make things happen the way you want." A curious vestigial bitterness swept over her, and she found herself recalling the lunch with Laurence a year before, which had so signally proved the untruth of what Marc was saying. But she realized that this was probably the last time she would ever feel anything at all about that. "Go on, go on," she said, for Marc had stopped to sigh, and rub his forehead with his knuckles, and stare at his boots, as he did in moments of self-dislike. "I am so different," he grumbled, "if I had taken after Maman it would have been better, but the truth is father's family can't stop being peasants, and I can't handle people. I couldn't do a thing with the situation."

"But what has happened?" cried Isabelle. "What can have happened?"

"Poots has happened," said Marc. "To Pillans. He is mad about her at first sight."

Isabelle started up, and then fell back on the pillows. "Ah, but that we could not have foreseen!" she complained.

"I should have foreseen it," said Marc, "for, fool that I was, I told Poots that Pillans was many times a millionaire."

"Ah, darling, darling," said Isabelle.

"I tell you, I am a fool. I am half-peasant, I am without delicacy," said Marc. "I do not know why you have ever had anything to do with me. But I told her without meaning any harm, because it never occurs to me people are more interested in those that have money than in those that haven't."

"I know, dear," said Isabelle.

"I told her simply so that we could get away. It was intolerable. I thought we were going to be there the whole afternoon. You know how late we were in starting, naturally it was past lunchtime when we finished. It had not been a pleasant game, we had a difference with the foursome ahead of us, which would have been nothing if Poots had not been very rude. And she was not playing, mind you, she was only walking round. I was eager to get back here, I wanted to be with you, and this place makes me as hungry as a wolf. But then Poots began to gabble that she must see somebody called Bonzo."

"Did she say why?"

"Ah, no. She just kept on saying, 'You know, darling, I've got to see Bonzo,' and went about asking everybody where Bonzo was, and telephoning all over the place while I sat in the bar eating those abominable potato chips and drinking cocktails. Then somebody came in with the news that Bonzo was in fact at Frinton-on-Sea. The camel, the crane, the stone-worker of a Poots!"

"But couldn't you get away then?"

"It appeared so for a moment, but then she realized that if she couldn't see Bonzo she must see someone else. But the name of this person she had unfortunately forgotten. However, she went about describing his personal appearance to everybody she could find, saying, 'You know who I mean, oh God, you know who I mean, tall man with grey eyes, terribly good shoulders, won the Calcutta Sweep one year.' She went and had a long conversation about him with the bartender, she is one of those women who become very easily intimate with bartenders, and then I really could not stand it another moment. I got up and said that you were waiting for me with an American friend of Luba's to whom I particularly did not wish to be impolite. And idiot that I am, I mentioned his name. Then at once she said, 'Haven't I heard that name before? Who is he?' "

"She would have said that of any name," said Isabelle.

"Yes, I know, I know, but I did not think, I am a clown," said Marc. "I said he is many times a millionaire, and the trick was done. Her face went like a ferret's, and before I knew where we were, we were on our way together back to the hotel. Of course luck would have it Luba and this Pillans were sitting out at a table on the terrace, and before I knew what we were doing we were beside them, and she was arranging that we should all lunch out there off beer and sandwiches, so that she need not leave them. And, I tell you, he was like a rabbit that has seen a snake. He never looked at Luba again."

"But how is it possible?" asked Isabelle. "I have never heard of anything so extraordinary. Because he is a nice man, this Mr. Pillans. He is exactly the kind of man we imagined from his story; he needs tenderness, he could really appreciate Luba. How can he be attracted by that horrible little creature?"

"Lots of people like the smell of drains," said Marc. "It's understood that one shouldn't and nobody would really argue that it's healthy to live over a drain, but all the same you'll see a certain number of people throwing back their heads and sniffing in the air with ecstasy when they've passed a particularly pheasanty bit of Marseilles. The most respectable people have this weakness. And, mind you, this Poots is ambitious about being a drain. She has the eyes a fish would have if it were thinking lecherously about the things which I believe fish can't do."

"But what does this mean?" asked Isabelle. "Do the Renarts give the young people no money; are they very poor?"

"I do not suppose the Renarts give them very much, for I know they think their son is not serious," said Marc, "but that is beside the point. What this little creature wants is not so much the rewards of the prostitute's life as its excitements and disorders. Ah, when she was circulating about the golf club inquiring for Bonzo, how she reminded me of the little drabs that come into

low cafés about one or two in the morning and ask the
waiters if they have seen Jean-le-Bossu, or, if they
haven't seen him, the friend he goes about with, the
Pole with the squint. I tell you, she is an infection. There
is no way of making her behave."

Isabelle sat silent for a minute, then put forward her
chin. "I will not let her take Mr. Pillans from Luba,"
she said. "I will not let her spoil both their lives."

"You have a lot to fight," said Marc. "He sat and
worshipped her while she put a wall of scarlet paint on
her lips, not making any real attempt at maquillage,
just putting up an advertisement of whorishness. Well,
if he married the Stravazzi and the Mardi, I suppose it
was an ill omen."

"There is more in him than that," said Isabelle. "I
will not let this thing happen."

The telephone rang and Marc grasped it savagely,
shouting, "Allo! Allo! Allo!"

"Gently!" bade Isabelle, but he threw the instrument
down on the bed beside her, crying, "It is the ordure's
aunt, it's Lady Barnaclouth."

Isabelle picked it up and said, "Yes . . . yes . . . how
do you do . . . yes, we are dining with you tonight.
Philippe told us you had very kindly asked us . . . at
half-past eight, that will be very nice . . . Yes? Yes?
You want to know if we are Americans?"

"Impertinence," said Marc.

"Yes, I am, but my husband is not. . . . I don't think
you understood me. I said my husband was not. . . . I
beg your pardon? I beg your pardon?"

"What is she asking that surprises you so?" said
Marc. "Is she an ordure also, the aunt?"

"Be quiet," said Isabelle. "If we divorce some day, it will be because you do things like this." She continued down the telephone, "No . . . that is to say, not much . . . I mean, my husband can shoot, he shoots sometimes, but he has so little time. He is very busy. . . ." She looked at the instrument in perplexity, and then replaced it on the rack. "She has rung off," she said, and put her hand to her forehead.

"What in the name of God was that?"

"I could not quite follow the conversation," said Isabelle. "She suddenly asked if we were Americans, and simply would not listen when I told her you were not, and then she asked if you were fond of shooting."

"Fond of shooting?" asked Marc. They regarded each other for a moment. "Name of God, what can she want me to shoot after sundown in Le Touquet at Easter?"

"There must be an explanation," said Isabelle, "though I cannot think what it can be."

"The explanation is that the niece is an ordure and the aunt a lunatic," said Marc. "What a family! Never will I forgive the Renarts for bringing all this upon us. Waiting for dinner last night, hour after hour. My stomach with all those cocktails in it. This Poots. I will write to Maman tonight and say that Natalie's François will have to be a fireman after all."

"Would you like to ring up Lady Barnaclouth in half an hour, and say I have been taken ill, and that you must stay at home with me?" said Isabelle. "As you very well know, I do not do this sort of thing as a rule, but these people appear to be barbarians. I had meant to ring up and say that Luba could not come, so that she could dine quietly with Mr. Pillans."

"How naïve you are," said Marc. "Poots had not been talking to Pillans for half an hour before she drooped her eyelids and put on an expression that made her face look like an unmade bed and asked him to join the party this evening."

"Ah, well, then we must go," said Isabelle. "I tell you I will not have this thing happen."

"My dear," said Marc, "you are quite calm, but I believe you are near to crying."

"I cannot expect to have as much self-control now as I would at any ordinary time," replied Isabelle.

She was again aware of her special state when they were all in the automobile that evening, on their way to the Villa Sans Souci. It seemed to her that she was more conscious than she would usually have been that Marc was sulky, and would probably be rude to someone before the night was over. She was conscious, too, that even Luba's qualities had their defects, that her extreme beauty and its timeless, hieratic quality, made her less like a woman who could be fitted into other human beings' lives than an image whose place was among the candles on an altar, or on the shoulders of acolytes in procession during the feasts of the church. Her sweetness proceeded from her as solidly, as conspicuously, as invariably, as the stiff tiara of golden rays that such images wear. It was perhaps natural that Mr. Pillans, though his jaw dropped at each new revelation of her beauty, should want a companion nearer common earthly form. Isabelle's supersensitiveness made of the small, drooping shape on the strapontin opposite her a hieroglyphic, standing for all sorts of childish, enthusiastic, confiding qualities, which would have made him a perfect husband for Luba, which made it hideously probable that he would be seduced away from her. It seemed beyond doubt that they were not the best chosen automobile load in the world, and that this expedition could end in nothing good.

When they walked into the hall of the Villa Sans Souci, Marc came to a halt, thinking they must have come to the wrong house, since he recognized the footman as the servant of Madame Coulevois, a friend of theirs who had, he knew, a villa somewhere in the woods at Le Touquet. But the man assured him that there was no mistake, explaining with the air of sour despondency affected by French servants when they speak of any act of liberality committed by their employers, that though this was Madame Coulevois's villa, she had lent it to Lady Barnaclouth. They followed him through double doors directly into the sort of trouble which Isabelle had anticipated, for two plain and elderly women, very ill dressed, advanced to greet them, explaining with gusts of laughter which were purely social and had no relation whatsoever to anything at all amusing, that neither of them was their hostess, that they were her sisters, Lady Barron and Lady McKentrie. It appeared that Lady Barnaclouth had been obliged to go out and dine with some Americans who were anxious to take her shooting in Scotland for the season, and wanted to settle everything at once; and that she had been desolated by this obligation, and had left all manner of apologetic messages. Isabelle received this announcement with amiable murmurs, reflecting that one laid oneself open to this sort of thing if one accepted invitations from people one did not know, and that anyway nothing could be of less

importance. But Marc's voice boomed out, as loud as if
he were addressing a meeting, expressing profound rhe-
torical condolences with Lady Barnaclouth. He could
imagine nothing, he said, more painful to a woman of
good breeding than that she should have to go out when
she had invited guests. She must at this moment be en-
during agonies, he hazarded.

Isabelle remained quite still, practising that rigidity
of spine and smile which is the sign of conjugal loyalty
strained to its limits; for she did not think they ought
to quarrel with these people so long as there was a chance
of extricating Mr. Pillans from their clutches. But she
was able to relax in a minute, for it appeared that Marc's
outburst had made no impression on the two elderly
ladies, who merely expressed cheerful agreement with
his sentiments and began to introduce them to all their
fellow-guests, explaining complacently that they themselves were two of the famous Lauriston sisters, and that
nearly everybody there was either a Lauriston or of
Lauriston blood. It did not appear to have been a good
recipe for a party. Poots was sitting on a sofa with two
girls like herself, Bridget and Lettice Someone, all with
their eyebrows lifted, their mouths dragged down, with
this idiot expression of objectless sagacity, of imaginary
prudence; and Ferdy Monck was standing by them, still
handling his private preoccupations with his superb public air. He was looking down the bosom of Bridget's
gown as if he were thinking of India. On the other side
of the room Philippe, in a tremor of hero-worship, was
pressing more cocktails on two blank-looking and beauti-
fully made Englishmen, whose coats fitted exquisitely
over their sculptured shoulders. At the sight of them lit-

tle Marc began to try to stretch up his neck and straighten
his spine, and Isabelle was for the thousandth time surprised to realize how much she loved him. Then there was
a handsome dark man of about thirty, standing alone,
rather smaller and more carelessly dressed than the other
two Englishmen. He was there, Lady Barron explained,
because, though he was not a Lauriston, he had painted
a Lauriston: he was an artist called Alan Fielding, who
had done a portrait of Lettice. The entrance of the new-
comers seemed to have pleased him, and he gave them a
quick, glowing smile; and Isabelle reflected that, had she
not been married, this was a man whose friendship
might have given her pleasure. But that was a purely
technical judgment, untinged by regret. "But these are
true Lauristons," said Lady Barron, her voice swelling
again, as she came to an elderly man with silver hair, as
handsome and as without conversational promise as a
prize dog, and a plain woman of his own type.

There was a moment's silence, and Isabelle turned a
brilliant smile on the whole room, because her resentment that she was here and not eating bread-and-milk
in bed at home became suddenly so strong that she felt
it must be visible. Her smile vanished, as the tail of her
eye showed her that Poots and Bridget and Lettice were
all staring in a disagreeable way at Luba, who was standing incandescent with her own beauty. They were using
their queer trick of seeming to have authority to impose
their own meagre and garish looks as a standard, and
were condemning her as large and clumsy and unac-
cented. Poots put up her blood-tipped forefinger and
beckoned to Mr. Pillans with an insincere, tooth-baring
smile. He obeyed nimbly, and Luba was left alone until

Isabelle went to her. But almost immediately they went
in to dinner, and Mr. Pillans was put between Poots and
Lady Barron, where he sat looking pleased, and Luba
was put between Philippe, who gazed like a devoted terrier at his wife and his English relatives all the time, and
one of the young Englishmen, who apparently felt that
he had contributed sufficiently to life without making
conversation. Isabelle sighed, and the painter, who was
sitting on her right, asked her the reason, and she was
faintly exasperated because she had to answer him so
evasively that there arose opportunities for coquetry,
which he did not neglect. She could not turn away from
him, as the silver-haired man, Sir John Lauriston, was
sitting on her left and proved to be suffering from some
kind of mental disorder which compelled him to say
everything three times. So she talked to the painter with
amiable indifference till suddenly she found herself staring silently into his face, her mouth a little open, because she had overheard a passage between Marc and
Lady McKentrie.

"You see," Lady McKentrie had been inspired to say,
"we take no chances when we go abroad, we bring our
own cook from Gloucestershire."

"*Tiens*," Marc had answered, looking at the food on
his plate. "And your wine, too, I can taste, was grown
in Gloucestershire." She could hear from his voice that
he was savagely angry, far angrier than she had ever
seen him before. It amazed her that he should have so
little sense of proportion, for in the worst attack that
she had ever seen made on his pride and dignity, when
Monsieur Campofiore had come to him full of insolence
and malignity and had inflicted on him a humiliation

threatening his life-work, he had kept his temper and
had been able to talk with sweetness of his tormentor.
But now, simply because this imbecile woman had made
a remark so comically stupid that had they been malicious
they could have dined out on it for a fortnight, his face
was dark with rage, his hand was playing so nervously
with the stem of his glass that in an effort to regain his
self-control he lifted it to his lips and drained in one
draught the wine he had condemned. His mouth twitched
in distaste, and she expected him to laugh at having
inflicted on himself this unnecessary punishment, but he
continued to stare in front of him, stiffly solemn in fury.
She realized that the remark had offended his national-
ism, that he was feeling in little over the implied insult
to French cooking what he must have felt in large over
the bombing of Rheims Cathedral by the Germans, but
she still could not understand how anybody who had
usually such a strong sense of humour could let himself
feel like that. An exclamation of wonder fell from her,
and when the painter asked her its cause, she was not
sufficiently organized to invent an evasive reply, so that
she found herself murmuring, "It is strange that one
cannot understand anybody else completely, even if one
is married to them, that there is always a mystery . . ."
But she immediately perceived that she was interesting
him too much, and she recovered herself by asking
whether he did not as an artist think Luba immensely
beautiful. He gave her pleasure by agreeing, but Isabelle
did not enjoy contemplating Luba as she sat with her
eyes on her plate, between her two silent neighbours.
Poots was having a better time. She was still not eating,
she was pushing her food about with a fork, or thrusting

away her plate, but she was looking up under drooping
lids into Mr. Pillans's face, and talking to him in a gabbling undertone. He looked like a country boy who for
the first time has had a spare penny to spend on a peep-
show. It was incredible that he should now be so inferior to
himself as he had been at lunchtime.

Isabelle was glad when the time came for the women
to leave the table, though it was not very pleasant in the
drawing-room. Nobody took any notice of her and Luba.
Poots and Bridget and Lettice sat down on the sofa again,
putting their heads together and whispering like ill-
mannered schoolgirls. It was evident that Poots felt so
confident in her new triumph that she could not be both-
ered keeping up appearances with people who were simply friends of her husband's family. Lady Barron and
Lady McKentrie and the third plain woman gathered
together in front of the hearth, where a wood fire was
smoking, and talked among themselves, each putting one
boat-shaped foot in a low-heeled slipper on the fender and
wagging it backwards and forwards. Luba strolled over
to a seat by the window, and pulled apart the curtains so
that she could look on the garden, which was frosted by
the light from the full moon that rode among the tree-
tops of the wood beyond. All the others paused while
she did this, and stared, as if she were showing signs of
eccentricity. Isabelle sat down by the group at the fireside, because she wanted to know what such women as
these talked about, and as she did not intend to see them
again this would be her last opportunity; and they
seemed so completely unaware of her that she could
hardly be considered to be intruding. They were talking,
she learned, about members of their own family. One

had had a note from Guy, another had heard from, Stephen, the third had had a line from Janet. The famous names of great houses were mentioned as being moved from or into by these and many other of their tribe, as being opened or shut by them, inherited or sold. There were reported also comings and goings between the Embassies of the earth, of visits, always agreeable, to the Colonies and Protectorates, of a constant kind and wise attention to both by the home Legislatures, but Isabelle noticed that these reports were made modestly, as indeed was logical, for it was evidently felt that such contacts did not add lustre to the family, but were specimens of the rays which, taken in mass, composed that lustre. There was, in fact, an astonishing vanity implicit in this conversation, very quietly and moderately expressed. A listening simpleton would have seen England as a vinery where there was being fostered only one bunch of grapes, and that the Lauriston family, but where this paucity of production was never regretted, since each Lauriston grape was so enormous, so velvety with bloom, so bursting with sweetness, that the single bunch far exceeded in value what could have been hoped for from letting the vine bear its full crop; and he would have believed that he was hearing this from sober and reliable vine-growers, repeating the common talk of their trade.

Isabelle had not come to this dinner-party to give her lower nature an opportunity to rejoice in the oddity of her fellow-creatures; but now she was there it seemed ridiculous not to listen. So she heard that Lionel was head of Pop and promised to be as fine a classical scholar as his grandfather, and that Clare had profited by her visit to her aunt's villa at Settignano to do some really remarkable water-colours, and she greatly enjoyed the overtones of the conversation, which implied that, if scholarship should pass beyond the limits accessible to Lionel and his grandfather, it became pedantry, and incompatible with the ready response to the call for action which was required of the great, and that, if the art of painting followed more ambitious ends than Clare's water-colours, it had forgotten its place. She heard, too, the third plain woman, who always spoke with an air of pleasure at her own downrightness, ask why Jack had got into this tiresome habit of saying everything three times over and, on receiving the hushed answer that he had been like that ever since he had had a stroke last Christmas, express a fear that that must have meant his leaving the service, only to be reassured. For the two others owned that this had been suggested by tiresome people, who had somehow intruded into positions of importance while remaining spiritually outside, but that of course he had been begged to remain.

"After all," said Lady Barron, "he still has the Lauriston charm."

"Yes, indeed," said the third plain woman. "And it's a very wonderful thing, the Lauriston charm."

They all uttered deep, assenting sounds, and looked reflectively into the fire, waggling their broad, low-heeled black satin shoes on the fender.

"I've often wondered how one could analyse the Lauriston charm," said Lady Barron.

"I remember we talked that over once, one Sunday at Harthing, in the old days when Gilbert was still alive," said Lady McKentrie. "Eva said something that got very close to it, I thought."

"Yes?" said the other two.

"She said that we were always true to our principles and our sense of duty, but at the same time we never ceased to be gay and carefree and unaffected, and the combination was irresistible."

Lady Barron shook her head. "There's more in it than that," she said.

"Yes," said the third plain woman, "that isn't all there is to it."

They looked down again into the fire and waggled their shoes. Isabelle, while still hoping not to be ill-natured, wished that the conversation might continue, and when Luba rose from her seat at the window and came towards her, she raised a finger to her lips. But Luba's movement had already reminded the three women that they had guests, and they turned about, smiling graciously.

"We were talking," said Lady McKentrie, "of the Lauriston charm. We were trying to define it."

"You should talk that over with my husband," said Isabelle, "he has sometimes a very nice sense of language."

"Who is this that has charm?" asked Luba.

"The Lauristons," answered Lady Barron.

"Who are the Lauristons?" asked Luba.

"We are the Lauristons," answered the third plain woman.

"Ah," said Luba, her face filling with kind laughter, "you are the Lauristons and you are asking yourselves why you have charm? Why, you have given yourselves the answer. You have charm because you are like little children, because only little children would be simple enough to ask themselves that question. But come to the window, I have something important to show you." She linked one arm about Isabelle's shoulders and the other about the waist of the third plain woman, who assumed an unamused expression of amused indulgence. "Look, look!" she said.

The lawn was sanded over with moonlight, and in this strong, diffused brightness the trees that pressed in on the garden seemed to be covered with a bloom like the velvet on a young stag's antlers. A clearing within the wood caught the full force of the downpouring light and shone silver between the black trunks, suddenly definite among the vagueness.

"Ah, beautiful!" sighed Isabelle. She remembered Roy, who had been young and strong, who was now dead; she was aware of the warmth and tenderness of Marc; she admitted to herself that childbirth had its dangers; it appeared possible to her that her child might live, and be adorable, while she lay cheated and forgotten in her grave. Tears stood in her eyes because things were so sweet, and so unguaranteed by fate. The moment ached, as if music were being played somewhere on an instrument whose strings had some connexion with her heart.

"How I would like to walk in that wood," said Luba, "if only one could be sure that the path led nowhere! Would it not be enchanting?"

"Oh, no," said the plain woman. "One might meet a man."

They stood looking out into the moonlight, until a

telephone whirred at a table beside them. Lady Barron
went to it, beaming at them and saying, with an air of
one promising the people good news, "It might be
George, to tell us that Violet's baby has come." But Isabelle, feeling no pleasure, expressed none; and Lady Barron gave her a sharp look, that to anyone who had been
socially dependent on her would have carried an alarming rebuke. Isabelle understood how it was that Virgil,
writing of the expected birth of a child to some Roman
Lauristons, had been thought by later generations to
have prophesied the birth of a Messiah. It was, however,
not George who was on the telephone, but Bonzo, ring-
ing up from Frinton-on-Sea. Poots hurried up, with an
air of solving an emergency by her common sense which
would hardly have been justified if she had come to stop
a gas escape, and Bonzo and she had a jabbered conversation such as monkeys might have on the telephone, could
monkeys telephone.

Isabelle went and sat apart, her melancholy deepening.
These women were fatuous with a fatuity which had
threatened her all her life, as it threatened all people of
means, and which was of mournful significance for humanity in general, since it proved the emptiness of one
of man's most reasonable expectations. No more sensible
form of government could be imagined than aristocracy.
If certain able stocks in the community were able to
amass enough wealth to give their descendants beautiful
houses to grow up in, the widest opportunities of education, complete economic security, so that they need never
be influenced by mercenary considerations, and easy access to any form of public work they chose to undertake
—why, then, the community had a race of perfect gov-

ernors ready made. Only, as the Lauristons showed, the process worked out wholly different in practice. There came to these selected stocks a deadly, ungrateful complacence, which made them count these opportunities as their achievements, and belittle everybody else's achievements unless these were similarly confused with opportunities; and which did worse than this, by abolishing all standards from their minds except what they themselves were and did. That these women were plain was of no importance; she knew many very pleasing women who were that. But the lack of bashfulness with which they carried their plainness, and their failure to mitigate it in any way by the cultivation of grace or the niceties of dress, showed that they had dismissed the ideal of beauty from their world. They were conscious that the female appearance sometimes offered gratifications that theirs did not, but this recognition did not make them humble or put them under any obligation to admire people outside their clan. Simply they identified the appearance which offered these gratifications with that presented by female Lauristons under thirty. When Janet and Clare and the pregnant Violet had been mentioned, time had been spared to comment on their attractiveness, which was so great that it even recalled the attractiveness which their mothers, aunts, and elder female cousins had possessed at the same age. Indeed, beauty was to them merely a photograph in a family album, just as scholarship in their language was not an abstract noun, but the name of something won, with almost unfair ease, by Lionel and his grandfather. There could be no end to the things which to them seemed far less complicated than they were. A prolonged sojourn with them would make one see England itself as a wormcast of the Lauristons.

They might, of course, be living a simple and sincere life in the midst of these misconceptions. That was what Isabelle had heard their friends say of them, and in the course of the family gossip by the fireside the three women had constantly remarked of their relatives that they were so natural, so unaffected, so unspoiled. But she knew well, because her own circumstances had often tempted her very near their mode of living, that nothing could be more fatal to singleness of heart than wealth. At that very moment she could hear Lady Barron, while she explained to Luba how she longed to be back in her home in England, saying, "You know, I am never so happy as when I put on my old rush hat and go out to potter in my garden." It could be heard in her tone that she had no clear vision of the delight of wearing easy clothes and moving in loved surroundings, but was in part standing outside herself, rapt in admiration of her own simplicity, which could find satisfaction in a pleasure so much less pompous than the special recreations within the reach of the Lauristons. Such a disposition reduced every thought and action to a gesticulation made in a mirror; it made life an incoherent succession of self-gratulatory moments, in which no real moral habit could be formed. One lived solely according to the dictates of vanity, without the discipline of obedience to fixed external standards. One was kind, out of a bounty that could hardly be exhausted, to old governesses and gardeners, who could be relied upon to give thanks with proper abjection; one performed public duties, for which one was paid in full by deference; one was chaste, re-

fusing to run away from one's husband with other men
who for the most part did not ask one to do so, and who
in any case had nothing to offer better than one's own
home. Knowing no difficulties one was without fortitude;
knowing no criteria but one's own achievements one was
without taste. So, if one's economic support was ripped
away, and one was left with no inexhaustible bounty, nor
governesses, nor gardeners, nor the same inducements
to chastity, one was disclosed as Poots.

Isabelle felt intolerably constrained and indeed
guilty, sitting in this room full of fatuous women,
of doggedly perverse girls, who exhaled an infection to which she had recently felt susceptible. Only
the other day she had congratulated herself on the
promptitude with which she paid her bills, although it
could only have been by the most perversely extravagant
purchase of commodities for which one has but a limited
appetite, such as furs and jewels, that she could have
come near to straining the ample funds of her own income and Marc's allowance. She could see how even
Marc's sweetness could degenerate, through the influences of their money state, into dangerous smugness, for
his unconsciousness that people were influenced in their
attitude towards him by the thought of his great wealth
necessarily meant that he thought people liked him more
than they did most people, and it would be hardly natural for a popular person not to ascribe his popularity to
deep and self-flattering causes. The same situation meant
that he had been exempt from criticism nearly all his
adult life, and though this had not made him morally
null like the Lauristons, thanks to his sounder instincts,
it had made him undisciplined and uncontrolled. But

since Marc was certainly superior to herself in every
way, she knew that she must possess these faults or worse.
She was aware that she had a tendency to be priggish and
censorious, and now she wondered in panic just how far
it had gone. She looked round at the clutch of painted
girls whispering together on the sofa, the frieze of ex-
planatory women who had separated Luba from the
moonlight and were telling her about their family with
an air of doing mission work among foreigners, and she
detested them all because they had nothing sensible and
comminatory to say against her. It would have pleased
her to be rebuked caustically for some grave fault till
the tears ran down her cheeks, so that a regenerative
process could begin at once.

Hastily she rose and went to the mantelpiece and
looked in the mirror while she powdered herself. "There
is a lot in what you are saying," she told her image in
the glass, "but the way you are taking it is due to the
fact that you are going to have a baby quite soon."

She was confounded at realizing for the first time as
a matter of experience that her body and her mind were
not welded together into immutable amity, that her
body could wage a war on her mind and overpower it
into acting in a mode altogether out of its taste. She
paused as she was lifting the puff to her face and stared
at the blue veins on her wrist. They were her, they were
not her, they were part of a system that might develop a
profound hostility to her, that might even abolish her
altogether. Regret possessed her that she had not been
born on some other planet where the arrangements were
less paradoxical, and she would have liked to run out of
this room, where the paradoxical quality of this earth

seemed to exist in a highly concentrated form. At that very moment she saw in the mirror the men coming through the door behind her, and turned about to go to Marc, in a flutter of relief that a tender, older woman in herself marked as girlish. For a second she was distressed because the purplish shadows of Marc's face showed that to drag himself through the evening he had taken more than might have been expected of the wine he had recognized as from Gloucestershire. But he turned a kind eye on her, he held his fingers crooked against his trouser-braid as he did when he wanted to give her a sign that if she stood close beside him she could hold his hand without people noticing.

"Darling," she murmured to him, "I feel so miserable. Take me home."

"At once, at once," he said. "We will make our apologies as soon as these ordures of the second rank have taken their departure."

For Ferdy Monck had gone to his aunts and was saying, with a large, proconsular gesture, directed towards the moonlight, "Sorry, I've got to get back. Got to see. A man." His tone suggested there were thousands of sexes from which might have been drawn suitable subjects for this stately conference; but he happened to have chosen a man. Nothing could, however, have been clearer than that it was not a man he was going to meet. And, indeed, behind him, Bridget jumped up from the sofa and said, "Ferdy, dear, could you give me a lift? I have to be back to see a tiresome woman," with a weary detachment that would have been unnatural between casual acquaintances, much less friends and relatives, though not more so than the weary detachment of his answer.

A desert, cold and broad as the face of the moon, seemed to divide them. It could not be doubted by any person of experience that presently they would be divided by nothing at all.

"Look, how the girls on the sofa give her a little business-like nod, and go on talking," said Marc. "I tell you, it is just what you will see in a very low café, at two or three in the morning, when one of the girls has a bit of luck and goes on, leaving the others sitting round an iron table. Come now, we ought to be able to get away in a minute."

But just then the door was thrown open, and a woman like an eagle came in, crying, "Would you believe it, those other Americans didn't shoot either."

"More and more ordures," said Marc.

"Hush," said Isabelle.

"We are only their guests, they are not listening," said Marc.

In accents of adoration Lady McKentrie said to them, "This is my sister, Lady Barnaclouth. For some reason her dinner seems to have broken up early. Come, you must meet her. Eva, my dear."

"Charmed to·meet you," said the aquiline woman to Marc and Isabelle. "So sorry I couldn't be here for dinner. But who did you say you were?"

Lady McKentrie said, "This is Monsieur and Madame Sallafranque."

"Yes, yes," said the aquiline woman. "But why are you talking such nonsense, Katherine? I don't know why you call them Monsieur and Madame. They are Americans. These are the first Americans who didn't shoot.

Now, let's talk this thing out, Mr. Sallafranque. I'm a great believer in talking things out. That's how I've gone through life, and learned what I have learned. By talking things out, straight from the shoulder. I've always found that if you talk to really great men they don't mind how straight you are, and I know, I've talked to all the greatest men in Europe ever since I was a girl. I'm paying you a compliment by treating you as I treated them. Now, Mr. Sallafranque, why don't you shoot?"

"I do shoot," said Marc. "For four years I did nothing but shoot. But I shot only Germans. How foolish it seems now that I shot only Germans."

"Oh, I don't mean that kind of shooting," said the aquiline woman. "Though of course I feel as you do about the war. It was a great mistake. If people had listened to my husband, it never would have happened. But we always pamper the French, who are the meanest, most imperialist people on earth. I am a Liberal. But to get back to the point, why don't you shoot? As a sport, I mean. It trains eye and hand, and it takes one into the healthy open air. You Americans need more of that sort of thing. You sit in those great ugly skyscrapers all day, thinking of nothing but making money, and drink ice water and get baked by that horrid central heating. It's no wonder you all get ill and quarrel with your wives."

"How perfectly you know my life," said Marc.

Isabelle turned away, for she had remembered the existence of Luba. If they were leaving, and it seemed advisable that they should do so as soon as possible, they must take her with them, and Mr. Pillans also, if that could be done. She caught Luba's eye at once, but Mr. Pillans had seated himself in the moonlight by the window and was gazing at Poots. To reach him she had to make an apologetic gesture to the painter, Alan Fielding, who was coming towards her with that gay, dark fire of eye that she knew would be all she would recall of him when they left the room. He evidently meant to talk, and she had to excuse herself for evading him by giving a glance which, she knew immediately, suggested too emphatically that she would like to talk to him some other time. That was a pity, for she wanted not one more person in her life. But she forgot the annoyance at this mistake in the pleasure of executing an ingenious idea that had occurred to her.

"Come," she murmured into Mr. Pillans's ear, "it is time that we were going."

He lifted his head in surprise. "What, already?" he exclaimed.

She affected a blank stare, which after a moment she allowed to be brightened by pity and comprehension. "Did you not know," she asked kindly, "when one dines with the English aristocracy one leaves immediately after the meal? It is the rule. Did you not see that Mr. Monck and his young cousins have left already?"

"Why, so they have," said Mr. Pillans.

"And watch Lady Barnaclouth. Does she not show signs of irritation as she talks to my husband?"

"She sure does," said Mr. Pillans.

"It is because she thinks we ought already to be making our farewells," said Isabelle. "Come, let us go."

As Mr. Pillans followed her across the room, he said, "I see how lucky I am in having friends like you to pilot me round. We have no such rule as this in St. Louis, and I would just have stayed awn and awn, getting myself in wrong. I am very grateful to you."

"Do not thank me," said Isabelle. But her amusement waned when she brought Luba and Mr. Pillans up to the group of their hostesses, for Marc did not turn to her at once, but preferred to remain under the spell of his fury with Lady Barnaclouth.

"No exercise, that's what's wrong with you Americans," she was saying. "Not enough fresh air. Did you ever read what St. Francis said about the air? My girl Clare, who's going to be a great artist, copied it out when she was only fifteen in India ink on vellum and we had it framed and hung in the gunroom at Harthing. Everybody's moved by it, even Prime Ministers. Everybody except Lord Curzon. But he had no heart. Well, that's what you need. It's for lack of fresh air and sport that you Americans have no virility. That, and being taught by women teachers."

"Madame, you are making an extraordinary complaint against me," said Marc.

Isabelle jerked his arm. She thought he was being silly in getting so angry with this woman, in not seeing that she was in her way a prodigy. She looked like an eagle, she had an air of soaring like an eagle; and though the name of the empyrean in which she soared was stupidity, there was power in the spread wings, beating higher and higher from folly to folly. Moreover, Isabelle thought, Marc was being unkind. He was not taking her away when she wanted to go. There rushed upon her a sense of desolation that would have been extreme if he had driven off in his automobile and left her to find her own way back to the hotel. Remembering her state, she held up her hand and looked at the blue veins in her wrist.

VIII

"'SHALL WE leave this infected place and go home?" Marc had asked Isabelle as he was dressing next morning. But she had shaken her head. She felt too tired to face the drive back at once; indeed she found herself more ill at ease in her body than ever before, and she had had bad dreams. Even if they did go, they would only let themselves in for two days of discomfort, as she had sent both the chef and the maître d'hôtel off on a holiday. Still, she was sorry for her decision several times that day, and on the afternoon of the next day it seemed to her that she had been monstrously imprudent. They were sitting in the lounge of the Guillaume-le-Conquérant while lashes of rain striped the great windows almost horizontally, and they were obliged to converse about unpleasant subjects, since so many unpleasant things, and those vitally affecting their friends, had happened to them during the last forty-eight hours.

"I suppose you will insist on our child being taught English," said Marc.

"Do not be absurd, my love," said Isabelle. "Poots is not the entire English-speaking world."

"No, but with the Lauristons she makes up the majority," said Marc. "My God, my God, how I pray that

227

she has got separated from the party, and that the rain
will drench her to the skin, and that she will catch pneu-
monia, and die like an animal."

"She has perfect health," said Isabelle, "she will outlive us all."

"There you are both right and wrong," said Marc.
"She has superb health, I know. When I prayed that she
should be stricken with sudden death, I had no real hope
that this would occur, I was merely expressing a desire
that for once destiny might act exquisitely and directly
instead of clumsily and circuitously, as is its habit. But
though she is so marvellously healthy, she will not outlive us. One day she will be found dead in a small hotel
near the Gare du Nord, either strangled or with her
throat cut from ear to ear. Later it will be proved that a
garçon de café left the hotel between three and four that
morning, carrying a suitcase. That will happen a long
time before we are dead, in ten or twelve years. Though,
my God, my God, that is a long time to wait."

"You attach far too much importance to Poots," said
Isabelle. "If it were not that she is trying to take from
Luba the husband we hoped for her, we need never think
of her."

"You are an optimist," said Marc. "You show it by
saying, 'trying to take.' She has taken him. Yesterday
and this morning have showed that. The idiot is infatuated. He is plucking up his courage to kiss her. I could
see that this morning on the golf-course."

"It cannot be!" exclaimed Isabelle.

"You mean, 'it should not be,' " said Marc. "The two
things are not the same." She shuddered, and was displeased to realize that she was now so changed that she

required words not of truth but of comfort. "You will see, she will leave Philippe and she will marry Pillans, though not for longer than is necessary to make a profitable divorce."

"It is hard on everyone," said Isabelle, "even on Philippe."

"For him, no," said Marc. "There are men who do not mind suffering from the most disagreeable diseases provided that they have contracted them from duchesses. He wants to be talked of as being on the most intimate terms with the grandest families of Great Britain. Well, he has caused a lot of talk by being married to a member of one of them, and he will cause a lot more when he is *cocu* by her."

"He is very different from his father and mother," said Isabelle.

"Ah, yes! They are serious," said Marc.

"Does it not strike you that we have strayed into a difficult and detestable world?" asked Isabelle.

"Not as a rule," said Marc. "You have made me a corner that is almost wholly free from *cochonneries*, my dear. But here I most certainly feel it. I drank too much again yesterday. What else was there to do, sitting in that golf house while it rained, and listening to all that stale rubbish? Oh God, oh God, here is Ferdy Monck."

"Control yourself," said Isabelle. "Some day you will ruin us all because of this inability to accept creation."

"He is much taller than me, and far inferior," said Marc. "That is not to be borne."

Ferdy hovered over them, making benedictory noises, and sat down, heavily, splendidly, the Viceroy about to spend a few friendly moments with the native princes.

The consent of the native princes is taken for granted on these occasions. "Light, Marc? . . ." he murmured, and, "Good kit you've got on today, Madame Sallafranque . . . Chanel?" and fell into a brooding, amiable silence, his eyes picking and stealing among the people in the room, his handsome, impassive head sunk on its broad shoulders, making its claim to men, "You know I am a cadger and a wastrel, but you know too I am a good soldier; if we had to fight together I would never let you down," making its claim to women, "I will cheat you and humiliate you, but I will give you moments of utter blackness and refreshment and rebirth such as you have never had before." Behind his monumental profile the vast windows were striped with grey running weals of water, from the blows that were being dealt them by a universe of which nothing could be seen save that it was hostile, monotonous, desolate.

"Mmm," said Ferdy, his lips leaving a glass that had, since he had sat down at the table, somehow come to his hand. "Mmm." He laughed suddenly, happily. "Laura and Annette have had another quarrel."

"They quarrel at Antibes, they quarrel at St. Moritz, it is all arranged by the Syndicat d'Initiative, there is nothing spontaneous or amusing about it," said Marc.

"Oh, it amuses me," said Ferdy. He laughed again, richly, deeply.

"They are the kind of women who ought to die at forty," said Marc.

"Oh, well, that's true of all women," said Ferdy.

A girl passed the table, raising her eyebrows and stretching her mouth without opening it, as if it were elastic, in a smile of fervent and insincere greeting to

Marc and Isabelle. She turned on Ferdy a look of hostile
and estranging recognition; they might perhaps have
known and hated each other as children. It was Bridget,
the girl he had taken home from Lady Barnaclouth's
party. He looked at his wrist-watch and after five minutes went out by the same swing door through which
she had gone. The human race had spent an enormous
proportion of its time in devising a system of restrictions
which would prevent·Ferdy and Bridget getting at each
other, and all those labours had come to nothing. Women
who had property, or were in touch with property, were
inalienably free. Isabelle reflected that the greater part
of the women in the room, including herself, would
have been in danger of spending their lives doing laun-
dry-work under strict religious supervision, had they
been born in less fortunate circumstances. But though
there had been defeat for moralists, there would be no
victory for lovers. Ferdy and Bridget would perform the
greatest miracle possible to the human body, they would
break the universe to pieces and remake it, and afterwards they would be precisely the same as they had been
before, Ferdy brooding strongly, darkly like a god, but
not saying, "Let there be light," saying simply, "Ferdy
golfin' today?" or "Ferdy not golfin' today?" and
Bridget slapping her face with floured swansdown, re-
pairing an imagined loss of the bloom which was actually
one of her few positive possessions, and gabbling, "Darling, I simply must telephone." The law and the breach
of it were equally futile. There was nothing to do in this
world except to love, but that had to be done with prudence carried to a degree that amounted to agony. There
was certainly Marc, but then there had also been André

de Verviers and Laurence. Absently she laid her hand on the belt of her gown and reflected with satisfaction that, so far as she could see, the relationship of parents and children gave no opportunity to decent people for any dramas of humiliation.

"There is Luba, standing at the door over there," said Marc, "but unfortunately the carcass of the dead camel has attached itself to her."

"I thought it would be so," said Isabelle. "I manœuvred it that she and Mr. Pillans should be invited together to Sally Bourges's lunch, because I know Gustave Bourges was in love with Luba when she was a girl, and he treats her like a great lady and an irresistible beauty. I was as clever as I could be. But I knew all the time that it would end as everything has that we have tried to do for them during the last two days, with Poots separating them, and coming back with one or other of them, her meagreness gorged with her mean little triumphs."

"But how does she do it?"

"Oh, quite simply. There is a technique of leaving people out. Horrible little girls master it for life at their first kindergarten. Today probably she made some excuse to call at Sally Bourges's house after lunch and then she saw that Mr. Pillans was falling under Luba's rich, warm, autumn-afternoonish spell, and that they would probably have spent some exquisite hours walking slowly about the streets here, eating bad ices at a little pâtisserie, and looking at the rubbish in the shops, and that something might happen which she would not be able to break. It would have seemed too crude if she had stepped forward and taken Mr. Pillans from Luba, so

she took Luba from Mr. Pillans. I expect she suggested
that they should go and do something peculiarly feminine, to which he could not accompany them. But you
will see."

"Well, so here you are," said Poots.

"Yes," said Marc. "Will you have a cocktail, you
two?"

"No, thank you, Marc, darling," said Luba. She
seemed tired. She put her elbows on the glass table and
rested her chin on her cupped hands.

"I will not ask you what cocktail you are going to
have, Madame Renart," said Marc, "because always you
ask for cocktails they have not got, for the speciality of
the bar, the name of which you unfortunately cannot
remember, on the other side of the town. If you do not
mind, you will have a side-car. So it will be much simpler. Now, tell me how it is that you two are together."

"Oh, that!" said Poots. "Well, it was like this. She
was at lunch with Sally Bourges, and I'd promised Con-
nie Bridger to give her a Paul Robeson record Dugey
gave me and I heard she was having lunch at Sally
Bourges's, and I had to go to the villa next door, so I
just went in and left the record."

"Oh, she is a funny woman, that Lady Bridger,"
said Luba, laughing. "Isabelle, she is worse than I am.
You say I forget everything, but she forgot things and
did not remember when she was told about them, which
I always do. She told Madame Renart she did not know
anything about this record, she got quite cross about it,
it was too ridiculous."

"And then?" said Marc.

"Then I noticed the varnish was all splittin' on the

Princess's nails," said Poots, "so we went off to a little woman who does manicures that somebody told me about."

"Was she good?" said Isabelle.

"She was very nice," said Luba. "You need not have been frightened to go alone, Madame Renart. She was so nice, and she had the sweetest fat black cat."

There was a silence. A fresh gale spattered the plateglass with bullets of water.

"Ever want a cat?" said Poots to Isabelle in a burst of hopefulness. "I got a cousin, married to a man in the Air Force; they haven't got a bean, she breeds Siamese."

Isabelle shook her head.

"Funny how nobody's talkin'," said Poots. "Ruins anything, I always think, this devastating sort of weather." She appeared to be visited by a suspicion that the silence at the table where she sat was perhaps specially intense, and they could see her wondering whether she had betrayed too grossly her indifference towards them, and determining to disguise it. "Good shade of varnish you got on your nails," she said to Isabelle, with a sudden, jerky smile. "But then I think you're terribly well turned out, I really do."

"There is no reason why I should not be," said Isabelle.

"Well, I know it's easier if you got a flair for it, but it's hard to get good clothes," said Poots. "Who dresses you?"

"All sorts of people," said Isabelle.

"Funny, you look as if you had got somebody who understood you and you stuck to them," said Poots. "But I suppose living in Paris you go to see all the collections." Her eye was ranging over Isabelle's clothes with an admiration that was without generosity, that announced nothing but an eagerness to steal a secret and use it.

"No," said Isabelle.

"Then how do you get your clothes?" said Poots.

"By telephone," said Isabelle.

Suddenly Luba clapped her hands. "Ah, I had forgotten!"

"What have you forgotten?" asked Isabelle.

"Oh, it is terrible of me to have forgotten! Today it used to be one of our greatest feasts in Russia. We used to kiss each other on both cheeks and say, 'Christ is risen.'"

"No, you did not!" cried Isabelle. "This is Easter Monday, not Easter Sunday! Oh, Luba, there really had to be a revolution!"

"Ah, Isabelle, you must not be cross with our Luba," said Marc. "If you come to think of it, how little it matters whether they said it on a Sunday or a Monday."

"No, no," said Luba. "Isabelle is quite right. I am an idiot, and usually people are too kind to tell me, and so I just go on getting stupider and stupider. It is quite right, it is very kind of you to pull me up, when I am getting too dreadful."

"No, Luba, it is you who are right, you are far righter than any of us," said Isabelle. "You only make mistakes about things that do not matter. Forgive me, Luba."

"But I tell you it was nothing at all," said Luba. Their hands met on the table.

Poots pushed away her glass and said, "Don't like

the cocktails here, I believe they put something in them. Foul stuff." She tried to light a cigarette with a lighter that was out of order, so that it rasped again and again without achieving the climax, till Marc took it away and held his in front of her face. "Here's Serge," she said, peering along her immense cigarette-holder. "Divine looks." She said it in curious thick accents, suggestive of incurable laryngitis and immediately curable lust, but it sounded insincere, as if she were merely obeying a sexual convention of her kind.

Serge bent on the aliens the tired springtime of his boyish charm, which he had exploited among them for so many years. After he had kissed the women's hands, he asked Marc, "Have you any news from the Ukraine?" but he made the inquiry from habit, his eyes did not lighten, he did not wait for an answer. Then he turned to Luba and said, with something of a realler springtime in his eyes, "Luba, do you remember the quince jelly Aunt Tania always brought us when she came back from France?"

Luba smiled down between her hands at the table. "I can taste it now," she said. "There was never any jelly like it."

"It was called cotignac," said Serge. "I do not know why."

"It was poured into little round boxes made of bast, and one ate it out of the box with a teaspoon," said Luba. "But one will never eat it again. It is only made at Orleans, that is where Aunt Tania's husband's château was, and there is no reason why one should go to Orleans."

"You are wrong about that," said Serge, "for I have

found a pâtisserie here where they have it. It is no distance, it is not far from L'Atlantique. I found it today when I was taking out Gladys's dogs."

"Ah, no!" cried Luba. "It cannot be the same!"

"It is," said Serge. "Let us take a taxi and go there, and eat cotignac and talk about Aunt Tania and the girls, until it stops raining."

"You will excuse me," said Luba to Marc and Isabelle, standing up. She threw back her head and laughed. "Oh, it is not to be believed that there is cotignac here! Perhaps it is an omen, and we will all go home again and be happy. Though I am very happy here," she told them politely. "Good-bye, Madame Renart. Ah, be careful! You will lose that pretty scarf, it is slipping right off your shoulders."

"I know, the damn thing keeps on doing that," said Poots. "It ought to button on to the dress, but the buttonhole is too big. It's disgustin'."

"But you must not lose that scarf," said Luba. "It is so pretty, and the dress would not be the same without it." She put her hand to her breast and unfastened a brooch. "Here, fix it with this. You need not give it back to me."

Marc and Isabelle exchanged a long look. They were sure now that at last Luba understood where her fate had led her and in what desert it was about to abandon her. For though they found it impossible to foresee what she would do on any ordinary occasion, they knew with complete certainty that, if she ever suffered a deadly injury, she would feel compelled to offer the enemy who inflicted it the most cherished possession she had about her at the moment. It was not her folly but her wisdom that made her do this. She was laying down a principle, she was mildly affirming that she would prefer life not to be conducted so harshly, even if she had to suffer by it. They looked at the jewel in her hand and were glad she did not draw it back.

Poots looked down her cigarette-holder at the brooch, and up it at Luba. She said, crinkling up her eyes, baring her teeth, "Couldn't think of it, no, really not, doesn't matter a bit, thanks awfully." A greedy acceptance would have been better, for it would have deprived Luba of the jewel and nothing else. But this refusal deprived her of everything by implying that not possibly could anything Luba owned be new or valuable enough for Poots, and that she was a funny woman not to know it was so.

"The cotignac," said Serge, "the cotignac."

"A moment," said Luba, pinning back the brooch. Her hands fell to her sides. "I am so clumsy, I am pricking myself," she said.

"Let me do it," said Serge.

She smiled at Marc and Isabelle over his fingers. "Good-bye, and tonight I will try to be in time for dinner."

When they had gone, Poots said, "It's too awful about Russians, isn't it? I mean, it's all gone on so long that one can't still be sorry for them."

"There is no reason that I know why one should be sorry for the Princess Couranoff," said Isabelle.

"Oh, well," said Poots. She showed that she knew Isabelle was lying. Her eyes ranged slowly about the lounge, she rolled her cigarette-holder backwards and forwards in her mouth, the pace of her breathing deliberate and contented and voluptuous. "Talking of tonight," she began, but was slapped on the back by a young man in a dove-coloured pullover who was, it appeared, an English earl who wrote the gossip column for a certain Sunday paper. On hearing his occupation Isabelle felt more intensely than she had done during the last forty-eight hours as if she had been forced to take up her residence in a house riddled with rat holes. But the young man was civil enough and had, indeed, come to take Poots away to play poker with someone called Froggie. Marc and Isabelle gazed up at him with an amiability that they felt to be fatuous, as soon as what Poots was telling them had penetrated to their understanding. She had reminded them that they had said she and Philippe and Bridget might bring Johnny Durham with them to dinner tonight, since they had invited him to dine with them before there was the question of this joint farewell dinner with them and Mr. Pillans and the Princess; and for a minute Marc and Isabelle had both been lost in speculation as to how far it was stupidity, how far it was brassy impudence, which enabled her to speak in such terms of the invitation that she had tricked and cadged out of their reluctance. They hardly realized till they were staring at her retreating back, how handsomely she had owned that, not having the brains of a flea, she had made a mistake in the identity of the permitted extra guest. They would, she had begged, remember that she had been alone when she asked their permission. When she got back to Philippe, he had told her that it was not Johnny Durham but Benny d'Alperoussa with whom they had been going to dinner, who would therefore be Marc and Isabelle's guest. And there would be his wife, too, of course.

"But this is too much," said Marc. "This is not to be borne."

Isabelle saw that his face had become purple, and braced herself to teach him to exercise more self-control. "It is impossible that anything so little serious cannot be borne," she told him crisply.

"So little serious?" repeated Marc.

"So little serious," she echoed him confidently. "He is a vulgar and detestable man, we must admit. But it will not hurt us to dine with him tonight, for tonight will pass, and from tomorrow morning we need never see him again. So just let us make up our minds to see the business through, and the less fuss we make the better we will feel."

"Oh, you are clever," said Marc. "You are always cleverer than anybody else." His face was suffused with a dark flush, and he spoke almost as roughly as he did sometimes when he was rebuking a servant. She had always felt ashamed that he should use that tone on those occasions, and she found it intolerable that he should use it to her now. A pang of pure hatred against him passed through her body. "So it is not serious, that I should have to dine with Benny d'Alperoussa? you really think that? Well, listen carefully and you will learn something. Benny d'Alperoussa is the last word in the filth of great international affairs. All over the world that dirty Greek has cheated good people into thinking that they were guaranteeing themselves a hearth in their old age, and bad people into thinking that at last roguery was going to draw a profit; and good and bad alike have found themselves out in the streets. And the cheats who worked with him to put them there have found themselves out in the streets too, but with knives in their backs. I am telling you, several men who have worked with Benny have been found dead just about the time when there should have been a sharing of the spoils. He is in the armament traffic, and he would supply arms to the enemies of France as well as to France, the dirty beast. And more than that he has corrupted our political system. Half our Cabinet is in his pay, and countless deputies, and countless journalists. To be involved with him, so that he should be able to make me a request which I might have to refuse, may put me into every sort of trouble you can imagine. If I am pleasant to him, I make an enemy of every honest man whom he has not been able to bribe, of every friend in high places that his dead enemies have left behind them. And you know how I am placed in regard to the government." He broke off, looked away, and then lifted the eyes of a beaten dog to hers. "You see, I lose my temper with you because I am in a tight place, and I am in a tight place only because of my own fault. If I had not been a gambler and a waster, I would not have to fear anyone on earth. And because I feel fear. I have been rude to you, my love, my angel."

"Oh, but I deserve it!" breathed Isabelle. Tears stood in her eyes. She had learned nothing. Had he not taught her this lesson long before, that there was an immense territory of which he knew every detail and of which she was almost entirely ignorant, when at Cap d'Antibes she had made so gross an error about the status and mission oi Monsieur Campofiore? "Forgive me, forgive me," she murmured.

"No, it is my fault, it is I that have to be forgiven," he said.

"No, no," she said. His hands found hers under the table, and their fingers played together, interlacing and returning pressures.

"I love you so," he said.

"I love you so," she answered, "but apart from that, you were right. You knew all about these things. I am an ignorant fool, you were right to shut me up."

"No, in any case I must not talk to you like that," he muttered. "Because—because"—he could not speak the words, and their hands twisted and turned together again.

At their elbows Lady McKentrie said, "Well, you're both looking very glum for two such fortunate young people. May my sister and I sit down for a minute?" They settled themselves comfortably, opening their wet mackintoshes, which exhaled a smell of rubber. "Well, what was the trouble?" she continued. "The bad weather, I expect. Well, it's a pity the new generation isn't as hardy as ours."

"We've been a long, healthy walk," said Lady Barron. "The whole length of the esplanade and back."

"All we Lauristons are great walkers," said Lady McKentrie.

"The promenade and back is, however, not a very great distance," said Marc.

"Oh, Marc, Marc," said Isabelle under her breath.

"But then the way we were brought up made us sturdier than other people," said Lady Barron. "The plainest of food, the plainest of clothes, early to bed, early to rise."

"Well, why not?" asked Marc. "Why not?"

"It would do you two good," said Lady Barron benevolently, "to see how simply people of our sort live in England. There is a lot of fast living and extravagance in London, but it's only there, and among the new people who have come up. If you come to the country, you will find people like us living just as they have always lived, quietly and soberly."

"But very happily," said Lady McKentrie. "We have our pleasures, Mr. Sallafranque, our own quiet pleasures."

She and her sister sat nodding their heads rhythmically for a minute or two, and then Lady Barron said, in that tone of pure welcome, untainted by any anxieties about rooms and dates and compatibility with other guests, which is used by hostesses when issuing invitations in general terms that will never become more specific. "You must come and spend Christmas with us."

"Yes, indeed," said Lady Barron. "It would be lovely for them."

"It would be charming," said Isabelle.

"Plain good fare," said Lady McKentrie, "and the house full of young people, and old and young join in the children's games."

"Ah, if only Harthing wasn't let!" said Lady Barron. "That was my sister-in-law's place. Ah, do you remember the Christmas before poor Gilbert died?"

"Yes, indeed!" said Lady McKentrie. "Such a houseparty. They were all there. There was Lord Liddington —he was Prime Minister—and poor Eddie Charles-

worth——he was Viceroy the next year——and Sir Henry
Flaxman, who was at the Admiralty, a most brilliant
man. Constantly you'll find him reading things in the
original, just for his own amusement. And there were
twenty of us Lauristons. We began the morning so beau-
tifully with such a happy breakfast, and then we all
went to the schoolroom and gave the children their presents, and they played and sang and recited to us; I remember Clare——that's Lady Barnaclouth's wonderful
daughter, a genius if ever there was one——reciting a
long, long piece from Racine. And then we all went and
skated on the lake till churchtime——"

"But stop a minute," said Marc. "Why did Lady
Barnaclouth's daughter recite a piece from Racine on
Christmas morning?"

"She had been taught it by her governess," said Lady
Barron. "Do you French people not learn your classics
when you are children?"

"We learn them to an altogether excessive degree,"
said Marc. "It is precisely because I was so forcibly acquainted with the works of Racine at school that I am
astonished by this anecdote of life among the English
aristocracy. I cannot think why your niece should have
chosen this material to recite on that occasion, or why
all these famous men should have listened to it. Did they
really find that Racine was sympathetic to the Christmas
spirit?"

"The better the day, the better the deed," said Lady
McKentrie.

"It is really a most peculiar picture," mused Marc.
"All these famous men sitting round and listening to
your niece——how old was she, by the way?"

"Thirteen," said Lady Barron.

"To a child of thirteen reciting Racine on Christmas morning. It is a consequence that could hardly have crossed the mind of Jehovah when he offered up His son as an atonement for the sins of the world. It is a consequence that would certainly have astonished Racine when he wrote, *'Quel est l'étrange acceuil qu'on fait à votre père, mon fils.'* " He paused, struck by a thought. "I still know that scene by heart," he said; and he began again, " *'Phèdre peut seule expliquer ce mystère, Mais si mes vœux ardents vous peuvent émouvoir, Permettez-moi, seigneur, de ne la plus revoir, Souffrez que pour jamais le tremblant Hippolyte Disparaisse des lieux que votre épouse habite.'* " He continued for some time and then paused. "The scene is about eighty or ninety lines long. I know them all. This is a magnificent speech which is coming now, *'Que vois-je? Quelle horreur dans ces lieux répandue Fait fuir devant mes yeux ma famille éperdue?'* " When he paused for breath, Lady Barron and Lady McKentrie said they thought they must be going, and he rose at once. "Good-bye, good-bye," he said. "Some day I must give myself the pleasure of asking you many questions. I would like to know for one thing whether those famous men were offered any alternative amusement to gathering round your little niece while she recited the verses of my glorious compatriot. And in the meantime I assure you, along the promenade and back is not a very long walk."

Isabelle said softly, "Marc, you are absurd." A vein on his forehead was raised and blackberry-coloured, and he was tapping with his clenched fist on the table.

"I cannot bear those imbeciles with their vast, flat

feet, their coats that smell like the corridors of a lycée in
wintertime, and their perpetual pose of being honest
women who know how to bring up a family, when what
they have done is to let loose on the world a pack of
decaying cranes like that Bridget and that Poots, that
Poots who has let us in for dining with Benny d'Alperoussa. Ah, I must have another drink."

"But, Marc," said Isabelle, "can we not cancel this
dinner? Can you not say that I am ill and that you are
frightened to leave me, and then we could dine in our
rooms?"

"He would not believe it," said Marc. "Even if it
were true, he would not believe it. Men who are in-
famous like that are as sensitive as young girls making
their entrance into society. The suspicion of a rebuff
lacerates them. But Benny is no young girl; disagreeable
things may happen to those whom he suspects. Oh, we
must see it through."

"My poor Marc," murmured Isabelle.

"It is a greater humiliation than you can imagine,"
Marc grumbled, "because I should not let you meet
Madame d'Alperoussa. She is the lowest of women. She
was born in some Balkan town where all the females become courtesans at the age of twelve years unless prevented by some relevant deformity, and even there her
lack of virtue struck people as remarkable. After some
years of intensive cultivation of the vices she became the
mistress of the Minister of War, who, when at last his
digestion revolted, insisted on d'Alperoussa taking her
over as the price for getting a new army clothing con-
tract. I tell you, it is not pleasant for me that, owing to

my own folly, I must see my wife sit at the same table
with such a woman."

"Come now," said Isabelle, "it is exceedingly unlikely
that at a distance of several feet, and under the restrictions of a restaurant dinner, she should be able to con-
taminate me. It will be very entertaining to watch her
and try to guess whether Benny gave the poor Balkan
soldiers better or worse boots because of her."

"It is all very well for you to talk like that," said
Marc gloomily, "you do not know such people. If the
talk gets too disgusting, you must pretend to feel ill and
go." He drummed on the table, and stood up with an
exclamation of impatience. "This will never do! I was
about to order another drink, and I have already drunk
too much today. I must be good. You will see, I will be
very good. See, I will put you in the elevator and you
will go up and rest. I must go out, it has nearly stopped
raining now." As they walked along the lounge, he suddenly exclaimed with violence, "I will go and prove that
those vain and hideous old women lied. I am sure it is
not more than half an hour, along the promenade and
back."

She pressed his arm and laughed, saying, "You are
taking all these people much too seriously," but as the
elevator shot up, she knew that her complaint was not
correctly worded. They were surrounded by every element in life which must be taken seriously if they
wanted to continue to live, and none was under their
control; but they were neither of them making any motion that would bring the situation into their power.
Marc had gone out to prove that it took not more than

half an hour to walk up and down the promenade of Le Touquet, and from a congested quality in his appearance and movements, and the grumbled roughness of the French he was talking, she knew that for all his sincere protestations of good behaviour he would behave worse before the day was done, just as one may sometimes tell by a person's swollen features that he has been attacked by a cold of which he himself is as yet unconscious. She would, of course, be able to cope with him, but the rest of life was running through her fingers like water. It was a measure of her present incompetence, she reflected as she stepped out of the elevator and confronted Mr. Pillans, that she could not even control him. He looked as if he were abashed by the width and length of these vast corridors, and had never considered that, if they had been built wide and high and vast, it was only because the builder had aimed at pleasing him; and he made an anxious gesture of apology to the elevator boy because he wished to stay awhile and talk to her, as if his obligation to go down in the elevator were of a more servile and binding nature than the boy's obligation to take him. Surely she should have found some trick by which she could persuade this malleable material to submit to the stamp she had chosen for it.

"I hope you enjoyed your lunch with Monsieur and Madame Bourges," she said, after the first greetings. "They are charming people. I did not come myself because I did not feel very well, and after all I do not know them very well. I knew that if you went as Luba's friend they would treat you as an honoured guest, for they adore her."

"Well, who wouldn't do that?" assented Mr. Pillans. "The Princess is just as lovely as she is beautiful."

She had to listen to the echo of the words before she remembered that the Middle West, wiser than other parts, used two different words to express harmony of body and harmony of mind; and in listening she realized how tamely he had spoken, how like he sounded to a little boy assenting politely to a visitor's praise of his kind mother or nurse, when he is bursting to talk about some fascinating little girl newly come to his school. "Yes, Luba is lucky," she said obstinately, "she has everything the world admires." But she was prepared for his next words.

"The person I'm crazy about, though," he said, beginning to laugh and shake his head from side to side, "is that Madame Renart. I'm just mad about her. I think she's the grandest girl I've met in years. She just doesn't give a darn, does she? Not for anything in the world?"

"No," said Isabelle. "I do not think she does."

"And isn't it funny," he continued, "that though she's Madame Renart, she isn't French, because she's just an ideal Frenchwoman, isn't she? Carefree and light-hearted, ready to walk out on the President himself, if she felt like it, without a thought for tomorrow. . . ."

Isabelle would have liked to say coldly, "You are an imbecile," and leave him. All that part of her which was French and allied with France was humourlessly offended by his words, but the immense naïveté disclosed by them made her feel again that she should have been able to do what she willed with this simpleton. She lingered, raising her eyes to his face in an exasperated

scrutiny, trying to make out what particular kind of
trick it was she should have used on his simplicity. Immediately she was abashed; for though he was looking like
a fool whose sensuality was weakened but not excused
by his fatuity, though he was screwing up his eyes and
shaking his head and rocking with suppressed amusement at the thought of Poots's delicious antics, that was
not the essence of his expression. However he might
crumple up his muscles into laughter, there still stared
from his face a paralysed submission to martyrdom and
the most tranquil and hopeless recognition of its nature.
She was reminded of a little boy she had once seen mis-
behaving at a children's party, shouting and snatching
toys out of their owners' hands, waving his arms and
kicking the furniture, while his eyes grew dark and
fixed, his mouth became a heavy drooping line, in antici-
pation and fear of the punishment he was bringing on
himself. She had been monstrously stupid in thinking
that it was a trick which the situation required. What
was called for was a flash of poetic genius which would
find the words to make the dark thing in this poor creature declare why it forced him to mount this idiot cross.
But her body and mind alike were empty of the vitality
which was the first condition of such genius.

When she got to her room, she sat for quite a long
time on her bed, holding her head in her hands. "It is a
more serious matter than I supposed to have a child,"
she thought. "I knew I was getting clumsier in my body,
but I did not realize that I was also getting clumsy in
my mind."

She lay down and tried to go to sleep, but her mind
wandered through the halls and antechambers, the crazy

toppling towers and the cellars, lighted to look as if they
were above ground, but very dark, of the palace where
the rich must live. There was the closely matching imbecility of herself and the Lauristons. There was the
knavery, bred of this imbecility which could acquire no
standards, of Poots. Actually she was poor, of course,
but an enormous number of persons succeeded in remaining rich when without means; they continued by
reason of charm or associations of one or another sort,
to frequent buildings, eat food, and use means of transport, that were financed by a first and never explicitly
defended charge on the world's wealth. They might even
continue thus against their will. Luba had made countless touching and modest attempts to earn her bread,
and each time the world of poverty, terrified into keeping a strict rule of industry and discipline, had roughly
rejected her and sent her spinning back to the rich, who
because of their lack of values, of their imbecility and
consequent knavery, could not respect her genius for
love, and sent her spinning back to the poor again. The
fate of Luba was not to be borne. Isabelle felt that, if she
herself had been harried along the roads and forbidden
to rest all the time she was carrying her child, it would
have been no crueller than the world's refusal to let this
woman live quietly and use her gift for tenderness.

But even if wealth was loyal to its possessor, it might
destroy him. Isabelle saw again Mr. Pillans, who so
needed Luba's love and was compelled to reject it, who
had looked at her through the twilight of the corridor
as if he were looking up through water, saying that his
fate was accomplished, his destruction complete. She
liked him, she saw in his perverse abandonment to a

sought misery an obscure but saintly gesture, an attempt to offer up an atonement for the sin and folly of the world, which pretended that he (whose weakness he knew so well) should be paid great honour because he had great possessions. It was true that Mr. Pillans's destiny might not have been so spectacularly tragic if he had not been quite such a fool; but on the other hand wealth might malform a man's destiny even if he were not a fool. Marc was wise in his head and his body, but because of this exemption from criticism, this ability to evade the consequences of any action, he was without discipline, he was without appropriate reverence for reality. He might get a little drunk tonight, he might say foolish and dangerous things. There was no safety where there were riches. Isabelle rolled over on her face and threw her pillows about, wishing she were altering the structure of the world.

She reminded herself that the poor probably suffered as many spiritual inconveniences as the rich, but found that no consolation. If one is tuberculous it helps one's case not at all that certain other people are diabetic. Indeed, it added to her apprehension, by proving how grossly mistaken most human beings are regarding the cardinal facts of their existence, that she knew perfectly well how vast a proportion of the public would have asked nothing better than to be one of the very same group of rich people which were convincing her of the unwholesomeness of possessions. They would think it must be heaven on earth to be at Le Touquet for Easter, with the famous Lauristons, the Madame Renart whose photograph was always in the papers, the great lover Ferdy Monck, the beautiful Princess Couranoff,

the fabulously wealthy Alexander Pillans. Some of them
would think this with an excess of passion that would be
formidable. They would resemble Monsieur Campofiore,
of whom she found herself thinking with a nightmare intensity. She remembered the first night she had met him
at the minister's ball, of how she had seen him, after they
had parted, leaning against the wall and jerking his head
about as he scornfully recapitulated their conversation to
himself; she remembered him as he had sat on the edge
of the marble conduit in the garden on the Cap d'Antibes,
crushing his newspaper against his chest, his teeth bared,
his head thrown back, in an orgasm of hate. The intensity with which this extraordinary man envied the rich
amounted to the degree of genius; and since the life for
which he envied them existed only in his imagination,
as was proved by his inability to enter into it and gratify
his thirst for it as he himself rose in the world, the quality of this genius could justly be termed really poetic,
really creative.

He was one among those innumerable children of the
poor, both male and female, who spend their whole lives
in the composition of a poem about the wealthy, which,
though it cannot be a true poem because it is not the
symbol of any reality, must nevertheless be engendered
in them by some authentic though deflected ray of inspiration, since there is nothing in their environment,
or at least nothing that could be logically expected, to
suggest to them their subject matter. They sit at the
doors of their dark hovels, with the carcass of the dead
dog drawing flies to itself a few yards away on the cob-
bles, waiting till the wrinkled women with hanging bel-
lies who are their mothers shall tell them that the offal

which is stinking on the stove has reached the point at which it is arbitrarily supposed to be fit to eat; and from the most trifling intimations, from half a page of an illustrated paper found inside a packing case, from a glimpse of tourists waiting outside a garage while their car is being repaired, from intimations so trifling that they convey nothing whatsoever to those clairvoyant children's playmates, they derive the knowledge that somewhere there are palaces full of air and light, shapely and shining lovers, delicate food and drink. This knowledge excites the female children to become beautiful, the male children to pass examinations and to install themselves in offices which have no desire to receive them; it empowers them to travel vast distances over the earth, to make huge disturbances in the distribution of property, to meet astonishing dooms far from the places where they were born. There is absolutely nothing easy or miraculous in this process. Their knowledge acts on them by injecting them with frenzy, so that the world whispers of the savage temper of these beautiful women, the harshness of these invincible men, of the rapacity in both. She thought of Monsieur Campofiore as he must have been when he entered upon his agony, a dark and ugly and prophetic child, sitting at a back garlic-breathing doorway among the stones of Origno, glaring at imagined fortunate people as years later he was to glare at herself and Marc. Distressed, she wandered about the stony village in her dreams; and there, and in other desolate places, saw him constantly and always with fear.

So, when Isabelle woke up and found Marc bending over her, she cried, "What, is he really here?"

"Is who really here?" he asked, smiling.

"Oh, who, indeed?" she wailed. "Monsieur Campofiore, of course."

He straightened himself and walked some paces from her bed. "Need you speak of him, this night of all nights?" he burst out.

She sat up and rubbed her head, and remembered her dreams. "But, Marc," she said, almost weeping, "you cannot be cross with me for something I said when I was still asleep."

In an instant he was back beside her, and his arms were round her. "It is extraordinary, the way I am speaking to you today," he said sadly.

"It does not matter at all," she answered, "but do let us be careful. I feel so frightened of everything."

"You will not believe how well I will look after you," he said, and they kissed. "I am a clumsy fool to have awakened you," he confessed. "You might have slept for nearly half an hour more. But I came to ask you if I had done right. You see, when I was out, I realized that, since our party was to include the charming Madame d'Alperoussa tonight, we were a man short, since that Bridget is coming, so as I ran into Alan Fielding I asked him to come along, and I wanted to know if you thought he would be all right."

"Who is Alan Fielding?" she asked, lying back on the pillows and letting drowsiness submerge her again.

• "That painter we met when we dined with the ordure's aunts. Dark, handsome——"

"Oh, yes, quite a nice man," she murmured, yawning. "But he smiles at one too much, I think."

"What do you mean, he smiles at one too much?" demanded Marc. "Tell me, what do you mean? Has he been impertinent to you? Tell me! You know, I am the least jealous of men, and I am sure that you can look after yourself, but I will not have you annoyed."

She felt for his fingers and laid them across her lips, and laughed through them, murmuring as she fell deeper into sleep, "The old fool I have married, the old fool . . ."

IX

S H E   H A D said to Marc as they went down in the
elevator, "I wish you had not had that cocktail sent up
to our room, it is so necessary that you should keep your
head," and he had answered in the words which are
never used by a completely sober man, "Nonsense, you
know that it is impossible for me to get really drunk. I
always know what I am doing." When they had seated
themselves in the lounge to wait for their abominable
party, he said mildly, as if hoping to repair the brusque-
ness of this reply, to allay the fears which it was bound
to awaken in her, "Yes, my dear, it will be all right.
You know, you were really quite sensible in what you
said about tonight. I am exaggerating its importance, it
can pass over quite quietly if only we are discreet." As
he spoke, he looked about him with a glance far more
intelligent and apprehensive than his words, but the
pouted thickness of his lips and the blotched flush on
his cheeks and even his brow suggested that part of
him was obstinately stupid and reckless. For a second she
compressed her lips and repudiated him with a total
bigotry, wishing she had never married him. But while
he was ordering cocktails for his party, Annette came
and stood beside them, greeting Isabelle briefly and

257

then waiting for his attention with the air of one who
bears news so important that out of respect for reality
the audience must be collected and hushed before it is
delivered; and as soon as he had dismissed the waiter, he
lifted his head and looked up at Annette with a kind
of clumsy, blindish vigour, which Isabelle had noticed
about him at moments when he had suddenly reversed
some narrow judgment she had passed on him and re-
established himself as her superior.

She watched him hopefully. He bade Annette sit down
but she refused. For the moment, it was apparent, she felt
herself purely a messenger. They had seen her moving
from group to group before she came to them, and she
had evidently taken no time to dress, for her hennaed
hair hung in uncombed wisps round her ears, and her
gown was neither new enough nor elaborate enough for
the night. She bent forward, fixing them with fine eyes
dilated by earnestness, and said in a hushed voice, "Did
you hear what I said to Laura at the Golf House this
morning?" Isabelle uttered an exclamation of dismay.
The sense of waste she had had in the afternoon, when
Ferdy Monck had laughed at the quarrel between the
two fading women as if he had been legitimately amused
by some interplay of wit, was now intensified. These
fine eyes should have rolled only under the stimulus of
some grandiose antagonism, arising from the love of
children or country. Isabelle was aware that the point at
issue probably concerned backgammon. The degree of
incredulity which she would have felt, had she been informed that their quarrel related to anything so important as the love of children or country, made her admit that Ferdy had spoken part of the truth when he had

said that women ought to die at forty. There was an immense number of her sex whose relationship with importance ceased absolutely some years even before their menstrual functions. Annette bent lower and continued in this solemn, self-impressed voice, "Well, let me tell you. I thought it was time somebody told her the truth, so I just let her have it." She was taking breath, in order to start on some proliferating story, when Marc interrupted her. "But are you not Laura?" he asked, sleepily but not stupidly. Annette drew back her head sharply. "What are you talking about, Marc?" she asked. Her voice dragged into a whine. "I'm Annette Lexington. You know me!" Her expression became charged with an infantile meanness. "You've been to my house often enough. At Antibes." "Was it your house?" asked Marc, still speaking in the same drowsy yet penetrating tone, "I thought it was Laura's." "Well, you have been to Laura's house as well," said Annette with a grudging air; "she has a house at Antibes too." "That is what I am complaining about," Marc continued. "You both have houses at Antibes, you both have the same colour of hair, you have both had several husbands. There are really not sufficient points of difference between you. Naturally I cannot tell you apart. I met Laura and Annette, how was I to tell which was which? If you disagree with her, you should be silent about it. It is in the nature of a personal business within yourself, like the engenderment of gas in one's intestines, which should not be shared with the rest of the world." Annette stared at him, looked at Isabelle, and shrugged her shoulders. "Well, Marc, you've begun early this evening," she said, with an acid air of good sense refraining from rebuke only because it would certainly be wasted.

"Did you really make that mistake?" asked Isabelle, though she knew he had not. As Marc continued to stare in front of him, she laid her hand on his arm and persisted, "Did you really think Annette was Laura?" She wanted to be certain that Annette was wrong and that he was at least more sober than drunk, though she was not really anxious or displeased at what had passed. She knew that she was glad again that she had married him, that what he had felt about the quarrelling women was sane and just, even before he turned on her his veiled and sulky gaze and said, "This damned life, it makes us all the same. There is no difference between us all. It wipes out the gifts God gave us. They are all pooled, like the pourboires one gives to the waiters in a restaurant. Only it is not a question of pourboires, it is a question of all that one is ever going to have. . . ." He stared at the ground and repeated softly and bitterly, "D'Alperoussa, d'Alperoussa." She saw that he treasured within himself, as a woman who has been ceaselessly tempted to sexual union on undignified terms has a right to treasure the virginity she has defended, an obstinate honesty, an untarnished financial fastidiousness; and to him this dinner meant that the society of which he was a part was about to steal that treasure and waste it. He had not followed up his resentment at his personal misadventures by such deductions from the situation as had filled her day, but he had derived a sudden poetic vision of the nullity with which it threatened the human race, from the spectacle of these two women, between whom there could be no differences, since there was no differ-

ence. She had noticed often before that he knew no
intermediate process between the passing of common-
sense judgment on practical problems and this profound,
intuitive poetic vision, which was now making his face
darker than his slight drunkenness, his eyes more desperate than his knowledge of his plight. Hardly ever did
he move in the sphere of logic and analysis which was
her natural home; and she looked with infatuation at
him, recognizing that in all this long lighted room of
well-made and glittering men and women, he alone had
the dark bloom of romantic and passionate things. She
marvelled at the dynamic power, far beyond the reach
of her own type, emanated by those who think without
the use of thought, and she asked herself what critic of
social conditions, moved by an intellectual conviction
that the capitalist system was a source of suffering,
burned with such visible fires as Monsieur Campofiore,
to whom the rich and the poor were simply persons in
an intuitively apprehended poem. The reflection had not
passed from her mind when she laid her hand on her
waist, in agony. She was uncertain whether the bearded
man who was standing, awkwardly alone, against the
wall at the very end of the lounge, almost at the entrance
to the restaurant, was or was not Monsieur Campofiore.
She did not know if the idea that it might be Monsieur
Campofiore had occurred to her because she had just
been thinking of him, or if she had thought of him because she had already recognized him.

"Isabelle," said Marc, to tell her that one of their
guests had come; and her attention was free, for she had
seen that it was not Monsieur Campofiore. It was an
older man, much less provincial in appearance. She

turned and greeted Alan Fielding with a happy, ab-
stracted smile, and found that his answering smile was
not less dazzling than her own, but was not at all ab-
stracted. It would have been fatuous for her to ignore
that he was smiling because he was about to spend an
evening with her, and it had already begun. She felt the
complacency which every woman feels when, perfectly
contented with the path she is following through the
universe, she finds that a new acquaintance is anxious
to indicate an alternative route, on which he is anxious to
accompany her. "Does he not notice that I am going to
have a child?" she asked herself; but plainly he was so
determined to be content in his meeting with her that he
would either refuse to notice it or pretend that it was a
circumstance of no particular importance. "Yes, you are
right, Madame Sallafranque is expecting a baby," she
could hear him saying, in the same tender, admiring tone
in which he would have said, "Yes, she was wearing
emeralds last night at dinner, and carrying a small gold
tissue bag." Isabelle recognized that she had made one
of those instantaneous killings which are, alas, most
often involuntary. Of course it was all of no consequence,
but it gave her an agreeable assurance that she had preserved her elegance in the most inelegant situation to
which the body can be subjected. There were, after all,
many advantages in the life of luxury. She was aware,
as Poots and Bridget and Philippe and Luba and Mr.
Pillans gathered around her, that they were not only
her guests but excellent raw material for a masque repre-
senting the more horrible and tragic elements in human
nature; but their carefully cleansed skins glowed, their
seemly bodies were straight inside good clothes and silks,

they extended to her hands that were delicate beyond
any possible intention of nature. It all made for a certain degree of ceremonious pleasantness which usually
engendered good humour. Already the need to respond
to it civilly had driven the prophetic sullenness from
Marc's face, and he was behaving like any other good
host in the world of appearances, the safe world that in
spite of all its incidents persisted and survived. Everything would go well tonight, particularly when they had
eaten the good dinner Marc and she had ordered. She
threw back her head and laughed, prolonged her laughter when she perceived that Alan Fielding was watching
her with delight.

"Isabelle," said Marc again; and she found that Poots
was presenting their unwelcome guests to them. But
they were nothing to be afraid of, an old man like a
grey tortoise, and a cliff of a woman such as short, rich
men are apt to marry. Indeed, as soon as the introduc-
tions had all been made, she heard Marc saying, "Not at
all, we are charmed that you and Madame could dine
with us tonight," while she herself said, "Oh, but we
were delighted that you and your husband could honour
us at such short notice." They found themselves actually
inclining protectively, like adults in charge of a children's party who have found two little ones too shy to
play, towards these beings whom they had loathed and
dreaded.

But the face of Monsieur d'Alperoussa suddenly
clouded again. "Pardon me, Monsieur Sallafranque,"
he said, "and you, Madame. But . . ." Keeping his eyes
on Marc's shirt front he shifted his position so that he
faced only the wall of the lounge.

"What is happening?" asked Marc apprehensively, for Monsieur d'Alperoussa had the air of one of those old men who suffer from the more audible type of digestive malady.

"It is only Michelaides," muttered the other. "He wants me to recognize him, and I will not. The man is not honest, and I will have nothing to do with him, and he knows it. So always when there is a public occasion like this, he hangs about. But I have my principles. I will not let my hand be forced. No, no."

"It is very tiresome when such things happen," said Marc.

"Are you neither of you having cocktails?" asked Isabelle.

"No, thank you, we do not drink cocktails!" exclaimed the d'Alperoussas in unison and very quickly, as if combining to rebut some proposal as monstrous as that they should sniff cocaine.

"Shall we go in to dinner, then?" said Marc.

"A minute, a minute," said Benny urgently. "Let us give Michelaides time to lose hope and go away. You do not know how important this is for me." He shook his head gravely, and maintained the strict chastity of his glance by staring under contracted brows at the wall.

To break what was beginning to resemble the two minutes' silence in solemnity and duration Isabelle murmured to Madame d'Alperoussa, "That is the great drawback about staying at hotels; one is exposed to these disagreeable encounters that offend one's business principles."

Madame d'Alperoussa's magnificent eyes rolled under her arched eyebrows. "And if those were the only disagreeable encounters to which one was exposed!" she said darkly.

Isabelle gazed at her in question. It was impossible to imagine what she could mean, save that in a hotel one was more liable to meet one's former lovers than anywhere else. This was indeed the case, and on this woman it might draw down certain humiliations, even certain perils. She might recognize in some bartender a companion with whom in her early days she had wrestled in some Balkan brothel; and, far worse, one of the rogues who hang about any resort of the wealthy might recognize her as a companion not in a vice but in a crime. That this woman should choose to confide to a stranger the nature of the disgrace overshadowing her life could only be because there had been vouchsafed to them one of those strange Pentecostal moments when mouths use the unknown tongue of confession to acknowledge their true experience of reality. "Yes?" Isabelle said tenderly.

"These women," said Madame d'Alperoussa. "These cocottes. Everywhere." She shuddered.

"Ah, yes, yes! Everywhere," cried Isabelle. "Even," she added to herself, for she was well aware that her past life did not satisfy the immensely exigent standards implied in the shudder, "inside your dress and mine." She looked round sharply to see what Poots was doing, hoping that she was leaving Mr. Pillans alone, now that she had had her own way over Benny d'Alperoussa, but though she was relieved to see that Mr. Pillans was talking to Luba, she was puzzled because Poots was talking to a young man who bowed to her, and whom she thought she remembered having seen before, but who was staring about him at her other guests with a curious,

professional, ungentlemanly air. He might have been
the man from the wigmaker who comes to make up the
players before an amateur dramatic performance.

"Who is that young man?" she murmured to Marc.

"It is the friend who took Poots to play poker this
afternoon," he answered quietly. "The English earl who
writes gossip notes for a Sunday paper."

As they watched the young man, they saw him turn
to Poots with a question and heard her answer, "The
Benny d'Alperoussas, of course."

Isabelle felt for Marc's hand and pressed it. "Do you
think we can get them in to dinner now?"

"I will try."

On the way to the restaurant Isabelle overheard the
man whom she had thought to be Monsieur Campofiore
speaking savagely to a waiter. He was beside himself
with anger, it appeared, because he had mistaken either
the time or the place of a rendezvous with some friends.
She trembled to think of the intensity of the rage that
burned in Monsieur Campofiore, which was so absolute
that any exhibition of lost temper seen even from a long
way off evoked his presence. There was too much hatred
in the world; it was manifestly as dangerous as gun-
powder, yet people let it lie about, in the way of ignition.
At the table next to theirs there sat a party which she
judged from the long, yellowish, and petulantly fastid-
ious faces of the men, and the dull hair and rusty clothes
of all the women save one, who was voluntarily blonde
and sleekly clad, to be a decayed aristocratic family bid-
den to Le Touquet by an American heiress who had recently married one of their titles. They looked at Marc
and his party with an impertinent and officious hostility

which, had he been in certain moods she knew, would
have provoked him to some outburst of fury, to the over-
turning of chairs, to a blow on the face and a challenge.
As it was, he averted his darkened face, moving with the
slowness and resignation of a punished dog, and set himself to cope with the torpid failure of his dinner-party.
For that it was a failure for everybody except Alan
Fielding was evident before the middle of the meal; and
what he was enjoying was so plainly a fiction private to
himself that his enjoyment was almost a condemnation
of the reality. Out of Isabelle's disciplined smiles and
pack-drill remarks he was creating such a masterpiece
of gaiety and wit and intelligence that, when she turned
from him to talk to Monsieur d'Alperoussa, he could not
get on with the business of eating and drinking, but had
from time to time to lay down his knife and fork and
push away his glass so that he could smile at the empty
air in front of him. He made no effort to talk to Bridget,
who was on his other side; and she spent most of her
time communicating by raised eyebrows and shrugged
shoulders with Poots, whose dissatisfaction with the party
was manifest.

She had been too stupid to realize that an ordinary
pretty woman has hardly more chance of impressing a
gross and enormously rich elderly man than one particular Brussels sprout has of being remembered by an epi-
cure, and that to attract Monsieur d'Alperoussa's attention she would have been obliged either to be the mistress
of somebody he desired to humiliate, or to perform some
spectacular feat that appealed to his sense of improper
fun, such as changing her drawers on a flying trapeze
at one of the classic circuses. It was affecting her almost

to tears that he did not speak to her, and she had just sufficient self-control left to jerk an occasional word and glance at Mr. Pillans. But for him that was enough. His glasses were twinkling archly, and he had the expression of one who, if not actually using baby talk, was thinking it. Only his natural sweetness and good manners made him sometimes turn to Luba; but nothing good came of that. When she was strained beyond bearing, she lapsed into coherence as other people lapse into incoherence. The child in her gave up its struggle to make the grown-ups understand, and she fell back on the conventional phrases she had been taught by her governess when they were preparing her for life at Court. Nothing passed her lips which could be of the slightest service to her or the man beside her. She was no longer in communication with her own genius, and there was something dead in her aspect, as if she had severed connexion with her external beauty also.

It might have been possible for Marc and Isabelle to organize their guests into some semblance of festivity, had it not been for the d'Alperoussas' desperate need to explain the rigidity of their moral attitudes. This wrecked the normal development of the dinner-party, the more so because Monsieur d'Alperoussa wished to make his explanation to Marc, and Madame d'Alperoussa wished to make hers to Isabelle, and as Monsieur d'Alperoussa was on Isabelle's left and Madame d'Alperoussa on Marc's right, this meant that they were hurling their declarations of integrity diagonally across the table. Madame d'Alperoussa alone would have wrecked the occasion. She was so large and so spectacular in her gestures that by contrast Philippe Renart's efforts to make small talk with her acquired the touching quality of futile activity carried on by some miniscule animal, say the turning of a wheel by a white mouse in a cage. Her shoulders were as broad as Alan Fielding's, and she had such a profile, classical and collapsed, yet fine in ruin, as one of the Roman Emperors that Suetonius thought worst of, in his later days. The crenellations of her superbly dyed hair were immensely deep and formidably regular, and it would have been impudence to attempt to evade the majestic glance she bent on Isabelle's face as she pointed out that they were being obliged to eat their dinner only two tables away from that woman, Noémie Aveline. When Isabelle inquired who Mademoiselle Aveline might be, Madame d'Alperoussa threw her eyes to the ceiling, held up an immense and trembling hand, palm forwards, and said, *"C'est la dernière des . . ."* Her emotion was so great that it forbade her to articulate the last word. Only the airy feather of an *f*, quivering between her lips, revealed that it must have been *"filles."* Having swallowed, she was able to tell Isabelle that only last winter this creature had committed the most incredible series of infamies, taking a young man of good birth from his beautiful young wife, who was now dying in a sanatorium in Switzerland, and plundering him with such rapacity that his father and mother had had to part with their last penny before they went down to the grave in grief.

It appeared during the rest of the meal that there were several other women in the restaurant whose presence was felt by Madame d'Alperoussa as a monstrous insult. Wearing a noble and mournful expression which gave her the contours of a bloodhound, she related story after story closely resembling the pious tracts and novels of the early nineteenth century, since they represented every illicit love-affair as designed by the seducer with the intention of treachery, and every victim of cruelty as dying in body as well as soul. A deserted wife's heart or lungs never stood by her, a well-brought-up child inevitably developed meningitis on being orphaned by its father's misconduct. At the end of each of these recitals Madame d'Alperoussa returned to the food on her plate and the wine in her glass with the slow avidity of one seeking to be restored after a severe emotional strain; and indeed she might well have been exhausted, for she was digging deep, she was revealing her innermost process, she was showing herself as an immensely powerful human soul repudiating itself. This woman might quite well have claimed that she feared nothing. She was in essence Madame Léonie, the lion-tamer, to be seen on the posters of the travelling menagerie, in tights and hessians, with her six maned monarchs of the darkest continent standing cowed on their barrels behind her. Nothing could kill her. If she had been involved in some historical disaster of the first magnitude, some supreme breakdown of the masculine system, some triumph of disorder, she would somehow have reintroduced the principle of order. One could imagine an ancestress of hers, so like her as to be practically herself, following an army in retreat. No matter how deep the snow, how loud the cannon, she would have marched on with long undismayed strides, dropping out only to perform brusquely and efficiently the characteristically feminine functions, to brew fortifying soup out of horsemeat over the chopped boards of an abandoned carriage, to console with

her body some comrade who in his delirium and despair
had remembered the delights of sex, to give birth to a
child and to sling it on her shoulders as she rose. In her
large, widely dilating nostrils, in her long, deeply fluted
upper lip, could be read that faith in discipline and en-
durance as the solution of all problems which is to be
found, not among generals, for leadership in itself en-
tails a certain degree of softer fantasy, but among
sergeant-majors. Yet she insisted on denying that faith,
in twisting the countenance on which it was so bluffly
inscribed into the lachrymose grimace of a plaster saint,
and in ending her request that Isabelle should join her
Committee for the Assistance of Unmarried Mothers
with the phrase, incongruously uttered in a voice hoarse
as from the parade-ground, "Some of their stories are
too terrible to be heard." She knew perfectly well that no
stories are too terrible to be heard, but she was determined to offer treachery to all her knowledge and experience. She had cast out fear, and for stupid and trivial
reasons she was letting it in again. After having made
a magnificent recovery from early rape, innumerable
abortions, and progressive infamy, she was humbling
herself before a standard which she must have known to
be fatuous and cruel in its imposition of artificial penal-
ties under the pretence they were natural consequences.
Something in society was nullifying this woman as it
had nullified Annette and Laura, as it was threatening to
nullify Marc.

"How necessary it is," said Madame d'Alperoussa
deeply, "to guard well the young girls." She shook her
head at her plate, on which there was still some foie gras
mousse, and a waiter bent down to take it away, thinking

she had made a sign of dismissal. But she clapped both
her hands on the rim of her plate and cried, "Hé quoi!"
with such a hearty, good-humoured determination to be
done out of not one single mouthful of what she liked
that it could easily be seen what would have happened to
anyone who had tried to guard her well when she was a
young girl. She would have meant no real harm, but
there would have been a certain number of black eyes
and broken bones. Isabelle looked up at Marc to see if he
was enjoying the peculiar savour of this woman, but as
at all times during the meal, his eyes and ears were held
by the grappling-hooks of Monsieur d'Alperoussa's words
and gestures. These words came with extreme fluency in
a French as grubbily international as a sleeping-car; and
his gestures not only illustrated the stories he was telling
but particularized that he had been born in some country
where it is necessary to bargain in the bazaars, where
marriages are arranged by professional intermediaries
and performed during the childhood of the contracting
parties, where the administration of the law is corrupt,
and where it is not safe to drink the water unboiled. The
actual stories he was telling were pitifully thin compared
with these rich implications, being mere cartoons illus-
trating his own financial integrity. "There he comes
every day for six weeks to my office, and he sends his
name in to me, and I say, 'No, I won't see him. He may
be the sixth richest man in France, but I won't see him.
He's not honest.'" They were incredibly naïve stories;
one could not imagine anybody believing them. It was
impossible to credit that he was a very clever man. He
looked, indeed, like the kind of misshapen little creature
who sleeps under railway arches or on embankments in

great cities; and Isabelle wondered if it could not be that a man could fall into grandeur, as he can fall into misery, simply because he cannot satisfy the demands that society makes on those who petition it for a modest living.

But when Monsieur d'Alperoussa was looking furtively at Marc to see if he had made his point, or when a waiter brushed against him and he swung round suddenly, it could be seen that he had his peculiar gift. He had a talent for crime. It was as detached from intellectual ability as a naturally well-placed voice. Simply he would know by instinct, always and everywhere, how to slip the false coin across the counter so that it would be taken, how to grip the detective round the knees without losing one's balance so that the minute he goes down one can be off and away. This trait at first seemed comic, because of the vast difference between what he and his wife were and what they hoped to appear. It was evident that they were full of social ambition. Isabelle had watched them bow deeply to an ageing man and woman who scarcely responded, and she had watched them scarcely respond to a young man and woman who had bowed deeply to them. But in fact they were so firmly imprinted with the mark of what they were that it would not have seemed surprising if at any moment Madame d'Alperoussa, on catching sight of some individual connected with the law, should have put her thumbs in the corners of her mouth and emitted a piercing whistle, on which Monsieur d'Alperoussa would leap to his feet and, hastening to some spot on the restaurant floor marked with a chalk sign such as tramps leave on barns, would pull up a trap-door, down which a stream of accomplices would disappear. So inherently disreputable were they that their own funerals would be the only public functions which they would ever be able to attend without raising expectation of a police-raid. But Isabelle began to imagine what these people were like when they ceased to play at being respectable, and did not laugh. To follow the expressions on the little man's cold grey face, that was at once cringing and menacing, was like feeling vermin move between one's body and one's clothes. She could believe that he paid men to commit murder. She asked herself how it was possible that she should be sitting at table with him, and she had to remind herself that she had put to sea in a very comfortable ship that took on only passengers of certain means, and that he had been well able to pay his fare. There was no help for it. Society, which was merciless to so many, which persecuted the weak and the trustful with flails, would not lift its hand against this man. It came into her mind that Monsieur Campofiore was a state official, and with a shudder she wished that she had been born on a different planet. She looked for help to Marc, but he had just swung round towards the table of jaundiced men and dowdy women who had been regarding him satirically all the evening and were now breaking into bitter laughter, and when he turned his head again, he stared down at the tablecloth, contracting his lips and nodding wearily in pretended attention to Monsieur d'Alperoussa's current story of tremendous financial gain rejected on account of fine moral scruples.

It was of those people at the next table that he spoke when they found themselves side by side in the lobby, waiting while their guests got ready to cross the road with them to the Casino. She was beginning to tell him that she felt quite ill when he said, "Did you see those salt cods at the next table? They are the Delaveries. They would be here this night of all nights, they who never move out of their fourteenth-century fish-basket in the Pas de Calais. I tell you, God hates me."

"But who are the Delaveries?" asked Isabelle.

"They are reactionaries who hate me because I am not far enough to the Right," he answered. "It is an old story. The Delaveries own property all round the town where my father's factories were, and they are very active politically. There has been a war between our families for years. They have said the most frightful things about us." He was silent for an instant, then spoke of what was never spoken of among the Sallafranques. "They have even stated that we have Jewish blood in us." He twitched and went on. "They have been aching to find out something against me, and of course the gambling business was meat and drink to them. But this is far better."

She pressed his hand. But he said disagreeably, "Please do not begin to tell me that all this does not matter."

"No, no," she murmured; and to distract his attention she went on, "But after all the d'Alperoussas are funny. You can't deny that they are funny. Do you remember how you told me that if the talk was too improper I was to pretend to be ill and leave the table? Well, there's been no need for that. I don't think we've either of us heard such edifying conversation since we left school."

But he did not laugh. They stood side by side in silence till their guests gathered about them, and they all moved towards the door, to go over to the Casino.

In her ear Alan Fielding said, "You know, when

somebody who swears they've never studied painting
can say such penetrating and fundamental things as you
were saying about Masaccio, it makes people like me who
have done nothing else all our lives but stew over pictures just sit down and despair."

She could have said nothing about Masaccio, a painter
with whose work she was imperfectly acquainted, except
"Yes" or "No." But he had to take the cigarette out of
his mouth, he was smiling so happily over her wisdom.

Luba was crossing the road ahead of them, alone. Nobody had wanted to walk with her. "What is she doing?"
asked Poots in a mean, amused tone; and Mr. Pillans
laughed in a shame-faced way, but taking care that she
should see he was following her lead like the child who
has been raised to favour by the school bully and jeers
at its humbler playmate of yesterday. The road was lit
by the double glare of the moon and the electric standards to the brightness of a stage in some cheap and artless theatre. The budding trees, flooded with light from
above and sideways, had the insubstantial look of painted
canvas scenery, while the clothes and demeanour of the
people passing into the Casino gardens, being adapted
to a dimmer atmosphere, gave them the air of an unsuitably clad and ill-rehearsed troupe. As Luba advanced
across this unfavourable area, she was inspired to swing
her arms up and over her head and down again in a
wide circle, while she stared up into the sky. Actually
she was following the beam cast by the lighthouse which
stands in the middle of Le Touquet, which had been
standing there long before one brick of the Casino and
the hotels and the villas was laid; and Isabelle knew she
had passed into contemplation of a life determined by

necessity, of men tending a lamp so that boats should reach port in safety, of men on these boats hauling ropes with bleeding hands so that there should be food for the women and children, of women bearing children as fields grow corn, because it is their season, and the sowers have passed that way. A world so firmly welded together by natural processes would easily find some room for a loving slattern, while this horrible world they inhabited demanded such artificial activities from all its creatures that they had to cultivate the concentration and suppleness of acrobats. It was unfortunate that the place should make her look like an artless prima ballerina, swayed by some absurdly private and provincial conception of the romantic.

"Isn't the Princess beautiful?" asked Isabelle coldly. Poots slewed her head round and looked at her through the darkness, plainly reminding herself that hostesses often had dreary hobbies—they liked one to go to church on Sunday morning, or insisted on breaking up the dinner-party to be in time for a performance of cheap opera at a working-man's theatre—and that because they were hostesses they had to be humoured. "Gorgeous," she agreed, "gorgeous," and at the same time Mr. Pillans said with authentic fervour, "Yes, indeed," although a minute before he had been echoing her mockery. Nothing had happened to change his attitude except the authority of Isabelle's tone. She noted that he was still malleable to a certain degree.

As they entered the hall of the Casino, Madame d'Alperoussa came smartly to a halt and faced Isabelle and Alan, lifting a massive forefinger. They felt small and alarmed, but she slowly engaged them in a smile full of roguish reference and began to beat time with the band, which was playing the "Habanera" from *Carmen*. "*L'amour, l'amour est enfant de Bohème,*" she hummed. "*Il n'a jamais, jamais connu de loi, Si tu ne m'aimes pas, je t'aime, Si je t'aime, prends garde à toi.*" For a second they saw her young and adorned with cotton poppies, tenderly self-divested of her strength. But that had been only an episode in her inflexible career. Immediately she reassumed her grand manner, like a veteran putting on his shako and his top-boots after a moment snatched for pleasure, and looked about her with dilating nostrils to see where her duty lay.

Isabelle turned to Marc to see if he had seen this little performance, and murmured to him, smiling, "Do you know, she is so absurd that sometimes I find myself liking her." But Marc stared out of hot eyes and said, "I object to you feeling that you like her. You are my wife. It is an infamy that you should have had to sit at the same table with her. You are my wife." He made a sweeping, pompous gesture, wholly devoid of his own personal quality. "Such women," he pronounced, "are perils to France, a temptation to its manhood and an insult to its womanhood."

Isabelle saw that he was now completely drunk. His good humour and his wit had gone from him. He was therefore infinitely dangerous. She said, "Oh, Marc, Marc, be careful."

"I know what you mean," he grumbled. "Oh, I will not gamble. I will be a good child. You will like that. All women like making children out of men."

"No, no," she said, and smiled at him. "Well, it will be all right again soon." But there was no good in staying with him. She followed the rest of the party through the crowd to the baccara-room, and immediately she was surrounded by people she felt exceedingly ill. She suspected that she must have passed into some new phase of pregnancy which was going to be sufficiently disagreeable to make her understand at last why women consider childbearing a hardship. Though her child was not so restless as it had usually been of late at this hour, it seemed suddenly to have become much heavier. This was not marked enough to cause her pain. She was already so fond of her child that no direct contact with it struck her as anything but pleasant, and she interpreted this heaviness as a sign that it was going to be specially fine and large. Her eyes flashed in pride. But she was filled with alarm by the indirect effects of her state. For some reason the life she had been leading all her adult life seemed wholly new to her. For years she had been visiting places like this Casino, but all at once it had become completely strange to her, and she felt like a child who has been brought to some school or hospital, and finds herself unable to believe all the assurances which are made to her regarding its benevolence because of the unfamiliarity and the sheer incomprehensibility of the routine. She looked about her, trying to take refuge in the surface of the scene, in the bright lights, in the brilliant flesh of these well-nourished people. But something had happened to her eyes; the scene seemed tinselled and palpitating, the deeper colours seemed to glow as if they were under water, people's faces seemed like stretched silk visors. And everything seemed to have slowed down to crawling pace. She had been wondering why Alan Fielding was talking so tediously, but when Gladys and

Serge spoke to her, she felt the same impatient anxiety
that they should get to the end of what they were saying,
and she realized that the fault was in herself; and everybody seemed to her to be moving sluggishly through a
hot and throbbing atmosphere. None of these errors in
impression amounted to a delusion, but she found herself
thinking with a silliness that appalled her. She caught
her eyes staring in strained attention at an elderly woman
with witch-locks falling on her shoulders and a Fortuny
dress of pleated silk, the kind of woman who would
probably claim to be an early interpreter of Debussy and
to have bravely sung Mélisande to whistling audiences,
and who was now talking to a cluster of friends with an
outmoded vivacity which made her bring down a large
ostrich feather fan alternately on the arms of the man
on her right and the man on her left with a coquettish
rap. Isabelle recognized she was watching this to see
whether the man on the right or the man on the left received the last blow delivered before the party moved
away, because she had formed the imbecile idea that if
it were the man on the left the evening would be unlucky
for her.

"I am quite ill," she thought, "quite ill." A fine sweat
came out on her forehead and under her armpits. "I
cannot stay here any longer. I must go home and lie
down." She turned to Madame d'Alperoussa, feeling
childishly eager to cast her weakness down before the
strength of this old soldier, who would no doubt slip a
hand like a trestle under her elbow and steer her out of
the crowd, muttering heartening and comradely oaths in
her ear. But just at that moment she was tapped on the
spine by a pair of peculiarly hard knuckles, and when

she swung round she saw Lady Barnaclouth, looking
more like an eagle than ever, in a very smart, clear-cut
sequined dress such as a female bird of prey would certainly have chosen, and followed by her sisters as by two
ravens.

"I say, your husband's French," said Lady Barnaclouth.

"I know," said Isabelle.

"Then why did you say you were Americans?"

"I did not, and I am," said Isabelle.

"You don't express yourself very clearly," said Lady
Barnaclouth, "but then very few women do. What I was
thinking was that, as you're French, you'd be able to
tell me how I could get my grandnephew Toby Lauriston
into the wine trade over here without any nonsense about
a premium."

"Oh, God! Oh, God!" exclaimed Isabelle. Just then
Lady Barron and Lady McKentrie began to call to their
sister. "Eva! Eva! Here's Lord Stavenham," and she
found herself alone. She turned again to Madame d'Alperoussa, more eager for the support of her strength
than ever, her face flaming with exasperation, tears of
self-pity standing in her eyes. "I feel so ill!" she began,
"I feel so awfully ill!"

But Madame d'Alperoussa stared at the mask of her
distress as if she were a wardress in charge of a prisoner
who was affecting to be hysterical in order to evade
search. "Is that not the great English Lady Barnaclouth?" she asked gruffly.

"It is, it is," said Isabelle, "and, Madame d'Alperoussa,
I am so sorry, I am afraid I will have to go back to
the hotel—" But she stopped, because Madame d'Al-

peroussa's face did not soften. On the contrary, it hard-
ened.

"I understand perfectly," she said sullenly.

"But what is this?" Isabelle asked herself in amazement. "She isn't sorry for me! But I have said I am ill.
How can she not be sorry for me?" Her eyes sought
Marc, but he was standing by the entrance of the
baccara-room waiting till Monsieur d'Alperoussa had
finished greeting some friends. He was looking at the
floor, the very set of his neck on his shoulders showed
that he was drunk, nothing was further from his mind
than any thought of her. Feeling alone, she trembled
and wondered, "Why have I made this woman so angry?
My God, the lines running from her nose to her mouth!
She will try to punish us for this, and her idea of punishment will be something as subtle as a sandbagging on a
dark night. Marc was right, these are really dangerous
people. But what can I have done to her? What can I
have done to her?"

She stared in perplexity at Madame d'Alperoussa, and
immediately perceived the answer to her question; for
the woman was looking at Lady Barnaclouth as a dog
might look at a bone through a shut window. This was
evidently an example of the peculiarity in the social universe which is similar to interstellar time in the physical
universe. People at a sufficient distance from conspicuous
personages do not see them as they are, but as they were
long ago, perhaps ten or twenty years before, and these
remote observers may be dazzled by fires which, at the
moment of dazzlement, are the coldest of ashes. Madame
d'Alperoussa had so grossly misinterpreted the incidents
of the last few moments as to suppose that Isabelle was

in awe of Lady Barnaclouth as a social superior, that she had been embarrassed at being seen by her in such company, and that her plea of illness had been an excuse to bring the situation to an end. This tough old sergeant-major had the same waking nightmares as the stupidest little schoolgirls who sob on their pillows because the Latin mistress did not smile at them on the stairs, and she must have seen one of them now. "Madame d'Alperoussa," she said, "would you like to meet Lady Barnaclouth?"

Madame d'Alperoussa ran her tongue over her dry lips. "She is a very famous great lady," she replied.

"Then I will introduce her to you in a moment," said Isabelle. "But I did not think you would want to meet her, she is not very interesting. It is a great name, but she is *assez chose*." She tried to make her point clear, though the stale air was beating in her ears like a drum. "She is always begging favours and trying to sell things."

"Well, one can buy," said Madame d'Alperoussa.

Isabelle turned away and passed her handkerchief over her forehead and her lips. In her ear Alan Fielding murmured, "I say, you do look wild."

"Do you mean I am untidy?" she asked in consternation.

"Oh, no!" he answered. "I don't suppose you have ever been untidy in your life."

"I do not think I have," she said.

"I only meant that your eyes are blazing and your colour is brighter than I've ever seen it, and you look as if at any moment you might cry out some tremendous tragic secret." He gave one of those rich, contented laughs which any new aspect of her drew up from the depths of his big, handsome body. "You look superb. Queenly but Bacchic."

She thought wearily, "My good young man, how I wish the conventions of society were such that I could frankly own to you that the tragic secret which chiefly worries me is that the baby I am going to have in four months has suddenly begun to weigh a ton. Also my husband is drunk, we have a couple of gangsters hung round our neck, to say nothing of Poots and Lady Barnaclouth. I am forced to stay in this detestable place because I do not wish to be sandbagged by the gangsters, when my one desire is to be lying on my bed in my room at the hotel, in the darkness, feeling my child grow." She cried out urgently, seeing an unfavourable movement of the crowd, "Lady Barnaclouth! Lady Barnaclouth!"

Lady Barnaclouth at first believed that Isabelle was recalling her for the purpose of discussing the prospects of her grandnephew in the wine trade, but the introduction was at last effected, although not until Isabelle had mentioned several times, the last time very loudly, that Madame d'Alperoussa's husband was a most interesting man and exceedingly rich. Then they were able to go into the baccara-room, and there she could at least sit down on one of the benches against the wall, but she narrowed her eyes because she did not want to see the scene. This was the core of the life of pleasure in a town built for pleasure; it was thronged with people who would have been embarrassed had it been put to them that they pursued any other end than pleasure. But it reminded her of a waiting-room in a railway junction at which she had once spent an hour in the course of a journey across England. The walls were monotonously panelled and painted an unpleasant greenish neutral tint, and the carpets, the electric-light brackets, the benches, the official desks, the chairs round the gaming-tables, were solid and well made but of the dreariest design, as if they had been purchased out of public funds by depressed functionaries. Not only did the room offer nothing beautiful to the eyes of its frequenters, it destroyed their own beauty, which was the principal asset of many of them. Against this harsh background delicacy and youth were devoured, and coarseness and age were magnified, particularly near the gaming-tables, which were hideous in themselves, which radiated hideousness. With their green baize and mahogany they recalled the heavy fittings of a Victorian household, the billiard-table, the butler's tray, the wood-framed bath; and they were made sinister as operating-tables by the lamps which poured on them cones of brutal light.

It was impossible to see what satisfaction the scene offered to either the higher or the lower nature of man, yet the room was crowded, simply because there was here the exploitation by powerful and professional minds of that resort to number by people pledged to break down life to nothingness, which she had first noticed among Marc's friends on the Riviera. These master intelligences had banished beauty from the Casino because the lust of the eye may lead either to love or to thought, to coherent processes, ultimately to civilization, to the preservation of life. Within these walls those who hated life should be able to take refuge from it in number, pure number, its intricate and insignificant whims. They could bend heavy brows over the game which, with its circulation of the shoe, the drawing of the cards, the sharp, spasmodic cries of the players, the rattling pounce and withdrawal of the croupier's rake, the sudden dropping of the cards through the trap in the table, and the solemnity of all the spectators, had the air of an elaborate ritual of divination. So indeed it was, for all gambling is the telling of a fortune, but of a monstrously depleted fortune, empty of everything save one numerical circumstance, shorn of all such richness as a voyage across the water, a fair man that loves you, a dark woman that means you harm. So the present was wiped out and the future robbed of its content, moment by moment; and since there were no clocks in the room, these nihilists could enjoy the delusion that this harshly lit night of complete and stately waste would continue for ever, as if they were safe and underground, where there is no time.

Isabelle began to laugh because, though she was talking to Alan Fielding, she was also listening to Lady Barnaclouth and Madame d'Alperoussa, and the budding friendship between the two ladies had just been threatened by a profound misunderstanding. A young woman passed by who seemed to be exhausted by the weight of her diamonds, and Lady Barnaclouth had asked who she might be. Madame d'Alperoussa had replied that it was the celebrated Noémie Aveline, whose name she found herself able to pronounce much more easily now than during dinner when she imagined herself to be addressing a French bourgeois family, and further, having been brought up in the Continental belief that the unsensuous appearance of English ladies was a cloak to cover every kind of natural and unnatural vice, and

having heard stories that Lady Barnaclouth had had several children by a chauffeur and was given to Lesbian
practices, she permitted herself knowing and facetious
references to Mademoiselle Aveline's means of liveli-
hood and distractions. These stories of Lady Barnaclouth's
vices were, however, grotesquely false. She had in all
her life never stopped talking long enough to give anyone time to approach her with any proposition regarding
sexual irregularity; and the general tendency to be censorious of the vices to which one has not been tempted
was present in her in a specially rank form. As her conceit was far too great to be restrained by her self-interest,
she scolded Madame d'Alperoussa for mentioning such a
person and such distractions in her presence, very much
as if she would have scolded an impertinent housemaid.
To listen to the tirade was not amusing for more than a
moment, for it showed a real lack of consideration for
the feelings of the person to whom it was addressed; but
it was impossible to be sorry for Madame d'Alperoussa,
for as she sat watching her castigator with her eyes rolling slowly round and round and her hands plucking at
her diamond bracelets, she recalled a hurt cobra rather
than a hurt child. In search of some more pleasant sight
Isabelle looked away, and saw Poots take up her stand
beside Mr. Pillans, catch his attention with a remark,
open her handbag, affect astonishment at its emptiness,
and accept with reluctance the thousand-franc notes he
pressed upon her. Isabelle could not complain of her ill-
luck in witnessing this scene, for she knew that these
were fair samples of the type of human transaction to be
observed in a Casino.

"How quickly you change," said Alan Fielding. "Now you look as if you were going to cry, and a minute ago you looked as if you were going to burst out laughing."

"It was because those women are so stupid," she said.

"I do not expect they are any more stupid than you are," he said.

It would have seemed too rude not to ask, "Why do you say that?"

"Because you look anxious and alarmed, and you must be very stupid not to recognize that you are too triumphant a person to need fear anything in the world."

It was not of the slightest importance what he meant, and she was feeling very ill. "I wonder what Marc is doing?" she said. "Let us go and look for him."

"Will he be playing?" he asked.

"No."

They crossed the room slowly towards the tables where the stakes were highest. At one they saw Ferdy Monck and Bridget and Poots sitting in a row bending heavy brows over the game, grave as Buddhas in the earth-touching position, with Mr. Pillans at their side, adoring them as if he were a child and they were glorious grown-ups. At the next table, where the stakes were highest of all, Monsieur d'Alperoussa had fallen in with a few friends, grey and close-clipped and bodily ignoble like himself, who although they were all bound to be rich and were manifestly gross, had a curiously negative air of enjoyment, as if no indulgence they could buy compared with the luxury of no longer being wanted by the police. They looked extremely insipid compared with the relatively innocent people who were gambling beside them, the English duke who, doubtless enacting some symbolic drama of self-repudiation, hunted the wild boar all over France, and smelt even here of fresh air, and the party of soaped and flushed Americans. Yet Monsieur d'Alperoussa and his friends looked more potent, and had the air of principals. It seemed fitting that the table should be hedged off by rails to prevent the crowd from pressing in to watch them; and it seemed fitting too that leaning on these rails should be Philippe and Luba, standing with bowed shoulders side by side, but not speaking, as if they knew both alike were supers and could be of no help to each other. Everything that happened in this room arranged itself according to a consistent and sordid scale of values, which could not be dismissed as merely objectionable, since it could not have been able to impose itself so successfully unless it appealed to something fundamental in human nature. The place had its power.

"But I was sure that Marc would be with Luba!" exclaimed Isabelle.

"So that is what is worrying you," said Alan. "I told you you were stupid." She met the adoring impertinence in his eyes with the despair a mother feels when she comes in after some hours' absence and finds her little boy still playing with his tin trumpet. But he continued, "If by some miracle of bad taste your husband were to prefer the loosely picturesque to the austerely beautiful, it couldn't last twenty-four hours."

"What's that?" asked Isabelle. "What's that?"

"The first-rate spoils the palate for the second-rate," said Alan, and jerked his head at Luba.

"But no!" exclaimed Isabelle, and she would have explained to him that what he was imagining did not happen between well-bred women of today, had her eyes not been caught by a movement she recognized, in the distance behind his shoulder. Marc was standing just inside the bar with a glass in his hand, talking to Gustave and Sarah Bourges. It was impossible that he should drink one drop more alcohol without becoming noticeably drunk, and the mean amusement expressed in the poses of Gustave and Sarah showed that this had happened. She took a step forward. But she could see that she was running near a classic risk of making herself ridiculous, and indeed she was possibly alarming herself without reason. For Marc was huddled into a shape which told of complete surrender to self-dramatization, which recalled the favourite pose, never convincing to women, of Napoleon; and that must mean that the kind of drunkenness into which he had fallen was pompous and opinionative. He was less likely to misbehave than to inform people who did not want to listen that the next time Germany invaded France it would be victorious because of the moral decay of the French.

"Let us go back and see how Madame d'Alperoussa and Lady Barnaclouth are getting on," she said, blinking back her tears.

"Anything you say," said Alan Fielding. "I wish I could help."

The two ladies were not getting on very well. Lady Barnaclouth had continued her tirade against immorality, simply because no other subject had come up into her mind and she was under a necessity to keep on talking; but to Madame d'Alperoussa it appeared that she was not only being rebuked, and that as an inferior, but at inordinate length. Plainly she would have liked to start one of the grand, satisfying rows she used to enjoy in the old days, usually conducted with a colleague on a staircase, and attaining a climax when all the doors on the landings above and below were thrown open and her other colleagues rushed out in pink chemises ready to take sides. Finally her jaws opened and shut in silence several times, while all the stories she had heard about Lady Barnaclouth seethed in her mind; and suddenly the words spurted between her teeth, "At least no one has ever said that she has had children by her chauffeur." "What's that?" asked Lady Barnaclouth. Her large body trembling violently, Madame d'Alperoussa repeated the words. Lady Barnaclouth, in honest perplexity, demanded, "What, are times so degraded that a woman's reckoned decent till she's done that?" To this Madame d'Alperoussa could find no reply, for she interpreted it as magnificent bravado, of a sort that she would not herself have been able to command, had she been taunted with her early Balkan days. She sat with bowed head, meekly acknowledging herself to be an inferior; and in order to fall in with Lady Barnaclouth's mood, she began to speak in a peculiar muted voice, resembling the tone of a cornet-player who is aware that he is performing sacred music, describing the work of her Committee for the Assistance of Unmarried Mothers.

Again she suffered a reverse, for Lady Barnaclouth bluffly announced that she saw no sense in helping such disgustingly weak-minded creatures. "What I always ask," she said, "is why they didn't think of all that at the time?" But that reverse was soon over, for before Lady Barnaclouth had finished this inquiry, her voice had become inspissated with speculation. Did Madame d'Alperoussa not think that the best thing for such women was to be wholly cut off from all their former surroundings? Because her sister owned a house with fifty bedrooms, built in the nineteenth-century Gothic style on the banks of the Thames, which would be the very thing for such women, "and," she added with belated and insincere benevolence, "their babies." Madame d'Alperoussa paused before she said tentatively, "I would have to see the place," and Lady Barnaclouth hardly paused at all before she said desperately, "Come and stay with me for a week and we can go over and have a look at it." The two ladies exchanged a glance solid with the sense of possible barter of favours. It appeared extremely probable that because of this meeting between a Balkan criminal and an English clown a large number of young women, already bitterly disappointed with the results of unlicensed revelry at Lille and Nantes and Rouen, would know a new and lower level of despair in staring out through misted windows at Thames floods. These women, unreal in everything, had through their position the faculty of creating real pain.

"Let us go back and see what Monsieur d'Alperoussa is doing," said Isabelle.

"Yes, but steady on, steady on," said Alan Fielding.

"Why do you say that?" she asked angrily.

"Your eyes are blazing," he answered.

"It must be something to do with my . . ." Her voice died as she remembered that she must not speak to him of her pregnancy, that he was a man, although he meant so little to her that he might as well have been a woman. "Let us go back to Monsieur d'Alperoussa's table. Look how the people are gathering round, somebody must be winning a lot."

Monsieur d'Alperoussa had, indeed, won about four
hundred and fifty thousand francs. The croupier was shov-
elling piles of chips over to him, and he was gathering
them to him with the grey, limited geniality of a gratified tortoise. His wrist became rigid in mid-air, it wav-
ered, it flicked some chips back to the croupier with a
fluency that was neither casual nor enthusiastic; the
gesture revealed that he was without the instinct for
generosity, that it had been as difficult for him to learn
to give as it is for a bear to walk the tight-rope. The
game went on, the shoe began to circulate. Alan made
comments on the play, which she was careful not to answer, lest he should find out she knew nothing about the
game, and should begin to explain to her whether they
were playing baccara or chemin de fer, and what the
differences between the two were, which were complicated items of knowledge she passionately did not want
to acquire. People about them began to breathe as if
there were fireworks, the shoe at last came to a stop, it
appeared that Monsieur d'Alperoussa had done it again.
This time he seemed to be irked by his own inexpressive-
ness. As he stroked the chips towards him, he turned his
head from side to side, smiling towards the excited crowd,
while drooping his lids so that he could not see it, and it
could be guessed from a strained and creaking quality
about his smile that he would have liked to gain the
crowd's favour as well as its interest, that he would have
liked to find the word or gesture to establish himself in
the popular mind as a "character." The game began
again, and the shoe travelled round to him; and it was
apparent that inspiration had visited him.

His face softened and even exalted by satisfaction at

what he was doing, he turned and held out some chips to
a woman who was leaning on the rail immediately behind him, crying in a howling, grinning, wolf-like ex-
aggeration of his usual barbaric accent, "Twenty thousand
francs for you, Madame, if you'll stop breathing on my
neck and go away." There was a moment's silence. The
woman straightened herself. She was middle-aged and
vulgar in physique, with a freckled skin, prominent
eyes, and heavy hips, but there were many signs in her
appearance that she was aware of the necessities of elegance, though she had not the means to procure them.
She could safely be put down as one of those unhappy
women who by some only temporarily fortunate circumstance, such as the possession of a beautiful complexion
in youth, or the awakening of an unreasonable passion
in some rich man, are committed to a mode of existence
for which they have inadequate physical capital, and
spend all their years in a desperate struggle to live beyond their looks. At first she smiled foolishly, then she
looked at the chips with a growing earnestness. Monsieur
d'Alperoussa did not give them to her, he held them some
distance away, so that she would have to make a positive
and grasping movement to get them. Continuing to
watch them, she ran her tongue over her lips. Suddenly
she put her hand out to take them. Monsieur d'Alperoussa, made vivacious by the titters of the crowd,
affected to withdraw them just as her fingers closed on
them, but at that she became pale and her eyes closed,
and he gaped at her in fear that she was about to fall
forward in a faint. Then she recovered herself, took the
chips, and walked away, looking very vulgar, smiling
foolishly again, and flushed like a cook who has been

bending over her range. She stopped at the desk as if she were going to change her chips into francs, but then drew her shoulder blades together sharply and went out. Monsieur d'Alperoussa, relaxed and warmed, continued the game.

"What has been happening over here?" asked Mr. Pillans.

"Nothing very good," said Alan Fielding.

"So I guessed from Monsieur Sallafranque's expression," said Mr. Pillans. "He seemed to be getting pretty mad at something."

"What, was he here?" exclaimed Isabelle.

"Standing right behind you," said Mr. Pillans. "He left just as I came up." He paused, and then added with a certain luxury of self-abasement, "I guess that's how people seem to be feeling about me tonight."

"What has made you feel that?" asked Isabelle.

"I'm not bright enough to amuse your friend, Madame Renart," he explained in laborious lightness. "A boy friend of hers came along, name of Barnard, and she asked me to give him my place at the table."

"Is that Barnard the South African millionaire?" asked Alan Fielding.

"Yes, that would be him," said Mr. Pillans. He repeated with a full sense of the implications in his statement. "Yes, that would certainly be him." But there was still luxury in his tone. It was apparent that nobody could cure him of his infatuation for Poots by giving him proofs that she was mercenary and treacherous, since these emetic qualities affected his perverse soul as aphrodisiacs.

"I believe," thought Isabelle, "he would think more

of Luba if that ridiculous idea of this young man Fielding were true." She began to laugh.

"Am I being very funny?" asked Mr. Pillans.

"No, not funny, but simple," said Isabelle. "Do not be
offended. I am an American too, so I have the right to
say that all Americans are simple." She had not meant to
say that any more than she had meant to laugh, but the
place and the heat and the horrible people and her own
physical misery were acting on her like the kind of
drunkenness which dictates intricate speeches and actions to its astonished subjects. She found herself continuing, "You think Madame Renart very chic, don't
you?"

"Why, yes," said Mr. Pillans timidly. "Don't you
think that she is?"

"Oh, yes, she is very chic indeed," answered Isabelle,
"so chic that anyone could see it across the road. And
she's wicked too, isn't she?"

"Why, no," protested Mr. Pillans. "I think she's
lovely. She may be a little playful, and apt to walk out
on people if they aren't giving her a good time, but that's
only natural. She's young, and so very attractive that
she's used to having things her way."

"But you think she's wicked, don't you?" Isabelle
pressed him. "Wicked, I mean, in little exciting ways,
like being unfaithful to her lovers, and getting what she
can out of them, and throwing them over before they
have stopped caring for her. You see she's full of that,
don't you?"

His eyes glistened, he smiled bashfully, as if he were
a boy owning to some precocious appetite. "I guess all
the most attractive women are like that," he said. "They

get spoiled with all of us men running after them."

"But she's wicked in such a simple way," said Isabelle. "There is no subtlety about it, no grandeur. You know, although these English put it over on us Americans, their roots are not so very deep. Their aristocrats don't go back and back into the past, the way the good French families do, the ones that aren't Bonapartist. There are very few English titles that go back to the Tudors, and many of them date from the eighteenth century. There are even a lot that came up in the nineteenth century, just like our families in the Middle West. They stand not for tradition, or romance, or anything beautiful at all, but just for money, just as they say of us in the Middle West."

"Is that so?" asked Mr. Pillans. "Is that so?"

"It is indeed," said Isabelle. "I believe the Lauristons made their money out of iron. It is no wonder that, when the daughters of such families go wrong, they cannot be distinguished from young women in Chicago or Milwaukee or Cedar Rapids who find themselves obliged to supplement their incomes by prostitution. God found it necessary to bring Madame Renart into the world three thousand miles from the Atlantic seaboard in order to prevent her using the term 'sugar-daddy,' and I am not sure that He is going to be successful."

"You are very sarcastic," said Mr. Pillans.

"But Luba," said Isabelle, and stopped and watched his face. For a second it cleared, as if he were a small boy who remembers in the middle of trouble at school that at lunchtime he will be back with his mother. Then it clouded again, as if the small boy remembered that this kind of trouble would shock and grieve his mother, and she might be angry with him. But though such small boys think of running away, it is their mothers they really want. "Luba," she said again, and her whole body shook with exasperation because the emotion on his face would not precipitate, he remained idiotically incapable of seizing the satisfaction offered to his deepest need. In a voice harsh with contempt, she began to demonstrate his idiocy. "Luba, however," she said. "does it in the grand manner."

"Does what in the grand manner?" asked Mr. Pillans.

"Why, what you consider so romantic and interesting," said Isabelle. "Breaks faith, is exigent, cruel, and lascivious. Takes men away from women for other reasons than that she cares for them, leaves those men for other reasons than that she wants to give them back to the women from whom she stole them. Just sweeps on, triumphant and pitiless."

"Now, that's what I used to think she must be like when I first saw her," said Mr. Pillans. "She carries her head very high, and all that golden hair's like a crown."

"And what made you change your mind?" asked Isabelle.

"Why, she seems such a home-body when you get to know her," said Mr. Pillans.

"My dear Mr. Pillans!" exclaimed Isabelle. "How easily you are taken in, simply because, being a great lady, she doesn't wear her duplicity on her sleeve. Ah, there's race, there's race."

"But are you sure she really is like that?" doubted Mr. Pillans.

"Do you not remember how you first saw her in a theatre with a man who was besotted with her?" asked

Isabelle. "I think you know from your own experience that that is not done by kindness."

"True enough," he agreed, and for a moment looked old.

"But if you find Madame Renart more attractive," she continued cruelly, "you are at liberty to do so. Many people"—she made her laughter more offensive with pity—"particularly among us poor Americans, would consider Madame Renart far more fascinating than Princess Couranoff."

"Oh, no, no, I saw the difference between them at once," murmured Mr. Pillans.

"But I thought better of you," said Isabelle. "I thought you were one of those rare Americans who have a taste for magnificence, who are not afraid of life when it becomes dramatic. And even I must admit that Luba is magnificent, that she is making my life a drama that would hold a theatre enthralled."

"Even you must admit . . . ?" repeated Mr. Pillans. "But why do you say, even you?"

"Well, consider my part in the drama," said Isabelle darkly; and after he had remained gaping for a moment or two, she added with affected sharpness and impatience, "Have you noticed nothing, Mr. Pillans? Has everything that has happened during the last few days gone clear past you?"

"Well, I'm not sure that I've got everything quite straight in my mind," he owned.

"Good heavens!" exclaimed Isabelle tragically. "Can it be that you have not noticed that my husband is madly in love with Luba?"

His mouth opened and did not shut.

"Oh, I treat her as if she were my friend, I cover it all over, because that is how women are expected to behave in Europe," she continued. "And of course you would never guess it from her. She is superb. And it is not only a question of self-possession. She is not aware that she has any guilt to betray, for she has no heart and no conscience, nothing but pride and acquisitiveness."

There came to him again that look of a boy giving way to some shameful appetite. "Ah, she can't help it," he said. "Women like that can't help it."

"And women like that own the world, don't they?" she asked. "You would give women like that everything, wouldn't you? You feel they have an innate right of precedence over the women who are simple and faithful and loving, don't you?"

He looked at her with dazed and honest eyes. "I know just how badly you must be feeling about all this business," he said. "But still I guess it may help if you face the truth and realize your husband isn't himself over this. There are women men feel about just the way you say. They aren't good, but you have to give them everything they want. There are men that way too, like Napoleon. I don't suppose anybody would call him a good man, but his soldiers didn't ask anything better than to follow him. The great thing to remember is that they get tired, that sort of people. That's what you've got to remember now about your husband and the Princess. They get tired and then they quit, they don't give a darn, that kind of woman." His face shone as if he had newly washed it with soap, so radiant was he in his enjoyment of his past experience of being robbed,

cuckolded, and deserted, and in his sure and certain hope
of being so again.

Isabelle could have struck him; yet she felt also generous and exalted. Perhaps because she was now feeling
as ill as if she were sunstruck, the drunkenness which
was dictating her speeches and her actions had mounted
to inspiration. Usually, even when she knew, she could
not share her knowledge. That was not true, of course,
when she was speaking to Marc, and she was certain she
would always be able to say what she wanted to her baby,
as soon as it was old enough; but that was because they
were parts of her, as she was a part of them. To everybody else she could present only her intellectual findings
in almost diagrammatic form, without persuasiveness,
without fidelity to a hundred observed details: a brittle
and transparent model of the warm and living truth in
her mind. Now, suddenly, she found her mouth un-
stopped. The same kind of poetic power that dazzled her
when it proceeded from Marc, flashing out of the night
of his sullenness, was now flashing out of her numbness.
She knew she had at her command an amplitude of
images by which she would be able to convince Mr.
Pillans that he was pursuing death, and not life, and
that he was near reaching his goal. She would be able to
shame him for the complaisance with which he had received her lie about Luba's treachery, and point out that
in his lickerishness after that treachery he was more
perverse than many a poor soul in jail on account of
preference for his own sex. She would be able to preach
to him the security of such love as she enjoyed with
Marc, the defence it provided against instability and
tragedy and disorder.

But she was interrupted by Alan Fielding, who said, "I see your husband is going to teach Monsieur d'Alperoussa how to do it." She fixed her eyes on his face and felt them grow enormous. She looked away from him, down on the floor, and murmured, "To do what?"

"Gamble, of course," said Alan Fielding.

"Of course," she said. Not to betray Marc, she gave a sweet, insipid smile. "Where is he?" she asked.

"Just over there, by Lady Barnaclouth and Madame d'Alperoussa. He is talking to Princess Couranoff," he added awkwardly, as if preparing her for a sight which might displease her.

She groaned aloud at his innocence. If Marc could have been distracted at this moment by the body of another woman, she would have made their bed with her own hands. When she had pressed her way to his side, she looked first at the chips in his hands. Like such rich men as are not mean, it was his habit to carry a great deal of money on him, sometimes as much as sixty thousand francs; he must have bought at least that amount of chips, counting those he had already given to Luba. Then she looked at Marc's face; he managed to have the appearance at once of a pompous elderly man and a vicious boy. Then she looked round the room. The universe would be quite simple and enjoyable if this room and its contents could be lifted out of it on a fishing-line and dropped into nothingness. For a second she amused herself with that inept thought, playing that she was pulling up the fishing-line.

"But take more than that, Luba," she heard Marc say. "Take all you want."

"But I do not want so many," said Luba. "Please do

not give me any more. They will be all wasted; you know I have no luck."

"Marc," said Isabelle. "You know you must not gamble."

He answered insolently, "Why must I not gamble?"

"Because you gave an undertaking that you would not," she said. "They will take the business away from you. Remember Monsieur Campofiore." It seemed to her possible after all that the man raging in the restaurant had been Monsieur Campofiore, and she looked wildly round the room to see if he was there.

The minute she took her eyes off Marc's face, she lost her power over him. He said, "They will not take away my business. Let them take away my business. Then they will see. That is why I am going to play tonight. It is a challenge, a challenge to the government. Which persecutes me, a loyal son of my country. Which treats me like a child. Which says I may not do what I like with my own money." He threw some of the chips into the air, and though they fell widely he caught them all with a delicate turn of his gross wrist. People about them stopped talking and began to watch. He raised his voice. "While it permits these aliens, these criminals, these métèques, these men without a country, to throw about the millions they have leeched from the veins of France."

She shuddered, recognizing what a fool and a bore Marc would be if he were not continually subjected to the discipline of his business, if idleness were to begin its work on him. She murmured, "Marc, Marc," and pressed close against him, trying to remind him who she was.

"Let us go along and take our seats," he said to Luba. "The duke and his friends are going."

"But, Marc!" said Isabelle. "You must listen. You must not do this thing. I am ill."

He was an infinity of distance away from her. He sneered, "You are trying to make a child of me."

"No, no," she said. "I am really ill."

"You were feeling perfectly well at dinner," he said. "You are trying to prevent me from making my protest. You are a woman, and women do not understand impersonal matters. Besides," he added with malice, "you are not French."

"But, Marc," she said, "I am ill now. I think I am going to faint."

"Nonsense," he said, "you are not the sort of woman who faints. I do not believe you have ever fainted in your life."

Knowing herself, she muttered, "How could you say that? I shall never be able to forget it. You ought to know I will never be able to forget it. I will never say anything about it, of course, but it will always be there." She laid her hand on his forearm and smiled, turning her face about so that the people round them could see it and think them enjoying some small family joke.

"If you please, Marc," said Luba, "I do not want to play. I have no luck, you see."

"You are afraid of Isabelle," said Marc, roughly. "Come on, come on. Let us take our seats."

Isabelle knew that in a second he would throw off her hand. Thoughtfully she looked round the hateful room. She and Luba stood for life, but they were in a minority in this place where life itself lay stretched on the tables as on mortuary slabs. Yet, though they were in a minority, they were not helpless, for she still possessed this new poetic power, to which the nature of all problems was immediately apparent, which plotted out their solutions in points bright as stars where there had been blankness before. It had not left her, though she had not been conscious of it while she had been pleading with Marc. She stood swaying, leaning on his arm, and let the power have its way with her, working through the painful darkness of her mind like a great iridescent snake, strong and flexible and strange.

"Ah!" she breathed. She perceived a plan by which she might save Marc, and save Luba too. It had presented itself to her instantaneously achieved and intricate, like one of those complex knots a snake can form with a single turn of its coils. By using the very same lie she had been telling Mr. Pillans, she could save them all.

"Let go," said Marc. "Let go. I do not want to lose my place at the table."

She shuddered, but not at his unkindness. She had realized that the plan demanded from her the kind of behaviour she found most repellent. Her body must become an instrument of violence and disorder.

"Let go," said Marc.

She opened her mouth and listened to the high scream that came out of it. It passed like a wind through the room, turning towards her all the people who had specially acute senses, or who had not been specially interested in what they were doing. The others remained, huddled over the cards or staring into the faces of those whom they loved, like bushes or trees too sturdy to be moved by a breeze.

"But, Isabelle!" said Marc.

It did not seem possible that she was sufficiently dis-

ciplined to carry out this undisciplined action. She felt
as she had when she was grinding the roses into the mud
outside André de Verviers's door, but this time the
brutality she was doing to her own nature amounted to
torture. But the power within her had its strength, it
lifted her arm and made her strike Luba loudly on the
cheek.

She cried in a mad, clear voice, "Do you think I do
not know, Luba? Do you think I do not know that you
are my husband's mistress?"

Her heart leapt up in her for she saw Marc's face
darken and change from the loose-fitting mask of a
stupid, sodden man to the twitching muzzle of an
anxious, faithful dog; and she also saw Mr. Pillans move
to Luba's side and slip his arm through hers.

"Look at her!" she cried. "Look at her innocent face!
She will never admit it, never in her life. But it is true!"
Her voice was almost a shriek.

"You are mad, Isabelle, you are mad!" breathed Marc.

"This is your own damn fault, Sallafranque," said
Alan Fielding. "I'll take her home. I can look after her
if you can't."

"That you will not do," said Marc. "Will you let go
of my wife's arm? Come, Isabelle."

"I will take care of the Princess," announced Mr.
Pillans.

The whole room had fallen silent. The people at the
tables had all stopped playing and were standing up.
Isabelle's power had left her, she had let it go out of her
like an exhaled breath after her last monstrous shrilling.
She had now to manage the situation with her ordinary
wits, and this she felt unable to do, because some new

factor developed which she could not identify, though she knew it was appalling. There was something happening in this room worse than the awful action she had just been forced to commit, and it was outside her control. While Marc and Alan Fielding put their arms about her, urging her to move, she stood stock-still, wondering what it was. She imagined it might be her recognition that the turning of all these faces towards her meant that for the rest of her life she would be pointed out as a hysteric, if not an actual madwoman. Many people would be sure to say she had been drunk. Those who hated her in this vile world would despise her as she despised them, which she felt to be insolence, and those who liked her would extend her a greasy leering tolerance, such as Hell would show to one who had arrived there after being counted on earth as a saint. But she had no real hope that this was what appalled her, and a moment's waiting made it plain that it was not. She was suffering from pain of the body as well as that of the mind. A dull grinding of the muscles in her back was sharpening to agony.

"I am destroyed," she said, and her chin fell forward on her chest.

"Only come home, Isabelle," said Marc, "I will do anything you want, always."

"You'll feel much better when you get back to the hotel," said Alan.

But she could not go. They pulled her by the arms, but she only jerked a little way and then swung back again, with a thickset motion absurd for her fineness. Even as it had seemed to her when she first heard of Marc's gambling that the room could be lifted up on a fishing-line and dropped into nothingness, so now it seemed to her that if she thought hard enough a trap-door would open in the floor beneath her and she would drop straight down into death.

She whispered to herself, "Down, down, down."

Marc dropped her arm and groaned to the nearest woman, "My God, what am I to do with her?"

Without being aware of it he was addressing Madame d'Alperoussa, who had been compelled to remain beside him by the appetite for life which made her invariably lean forward whenever her automobile passed any sort of commotion in the street and tell her chauffeur to find out what was happening. But when Marc made what she believed to be an appeal for her personal help, she turned her back and fled, recognizing the approach of her im-placable enemy, scandal, which she rightly conceived as perpetually pursuing her, which she falsely imagined she had always, till then, escaped. As she ran, she caught her heel in the hem of her dress and fell full-length on the ground. She sat up immediately, but her jewels were awry, her sinewy legs stuck out in front of her at an obtuse angle, covered only at the vertex by her crumpled dress and the rose-coloured chiffon frills of her drawers, which looked as incongruous as if they had been decorat-ing a mule or a pylon; and an unspoken oath was clearly visible between her firm, fluted lips. The people round her broke into nervous laughter, which spread all through the crowd behind, becoming fainter and yet more harsh and spiteful as it travelled. Isabelle, feeling the place as an insult to her unhappy child, at last was able to move and went to the door. Outside, even in the hot room with the glaring showcases, it was as if the air were fresh,

because the people out there did not yet know what she
had been doing. She grasped Marc's sleeve with her right
hand and Alan's with her left, and stood still and rested,
but it was no rest because the pain leaned more heavily
on her than she on them. She had now no doubt of what
was happening to her.

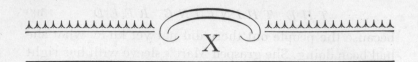

N O T H I N G   P L E A S E D Isabelle for a long time
afterwards. She found her greatest satisfaction in the
company of Luba, who had failed to notice anything
whatsoever unusual about the evening in the Casino,
and who constantly took time off from the buying of her
trousseau to come to Isabelle's bedside, bringing presents which were so useless as to be almost unidentifiable,
but which looked very pretty when she scattered them
on the eiderdown and the carpet. It did not occur to
Luba that Isabelle should be asked to furnish any explanation for the scene she had made, and this handsomeness was not due to any lack of self-respect. But having
been able to forgive God for the miseries He had brought
on her through the medium of history, she could scarcely
be hard on her fellow-creatures, who had so many more
excuses for their misbehaviour. She wept bitterly when
she came to say good-bye, the day before she sailed for
New York with her husband; and Isabelle wept too, and
passed into a phase of dejection. There had been two days
when she had hoped to die; then there had been three
days when she had feared she was dying; then there had
been some weeks when she had lain in bed wishing to
die, praying that she might sink through the mattress

into the dark. The beam from the lighthouse, passing through her bedroom, reminded her that, had she been a sailor's wife, rough nursing and an over-worked doctor might by now have lowered her into the black earth; and then she used to whimper into her pillow, as if she had thought of a withheld pleasure.

But now that Luba had gone, she wanted to get out of her bed and struggle to some place where she had never been before. This did not mean that she was content to live. It meant simply that even death, if it came to her here, would seem stale. She felt that most keenly when Marc came down from Paris to see her. He would sit huddled in an arm-chair, and presently talk would die down between them. Then she would roll over and stare at the other side of the room, though the light from the window tired her eyes; because she knew that before long tears would roll down his flushed and swollen cheeks, and follow the channels round his broad, flattened nostrils. His tears were too big, like the grapes he brought her. She realized that he was suffering, but that was not enough. Or rather it was too much, for she felt that by his sufferings he was piling up a claim on her and it seemed to her that there could never be anything but fatigue in any relationship between them. As she lay in bed, the suspicion frequently crossed her mind that the relationship between men and women could never be very satisfactory; she thought with exasperation of Roy's excessive mechanical curiosity, which led him to prefer falling five thousand feet from the air to staying safely with her on earth, and of André's lapidary fatuity. Then she would find herself living over again that imbecile and murderous evening at the Casino, and she would roll about in bed to break the direction of her thought, and ask in a harsh and desperate voice for something she did not want. "Marc, give me some water!" "Marc, fetch Nurse!"

She had begun to be irritated by Marc the first time she saw him after the surgeons had finished with her. He had knelt trembling by her bedside and had said, "But you know now, don't you, my darling, that there was nothing in what you thought?"

Isabelle asked in weak amazement, "What, do you mean that you weren't going to gamble?"

"Oh, yes, God forgive me," he sobbed, "that was what I was going to do all right. But I mean, about me and Luba."

"But I never thought that really," she murmured.

"But you did, my darling," he assured her. "Really, you did, in the Casino. You are sure you did not think it?"

"Of course I did not," she said.

"I am so glad, you must have been quite out of yourself," he said.

"No, no," she protested.

"You were, indeed, my darling," he told her. "But in the midst of your delirium you were inspired to make the unique gesture and speak the unique words that saved me."

With an immense effort of impatience she opened her eyes, and she saw that his attitude and expression so closely resembled the abjection of the faithful on their knees at a shrine that she would have been a fool to interfere with it. She reflected that it would be better for a wife to be regarded by her husband as humanity regards St. Catherine, or any female saint, even including those

who most certainly did not exist, rather than as it regards Queen Elizabeth, or any other female genius, even
including those who have been of most practical service
to it. It seemed to her, the more she thought of it, that
she must never try to convince Marc that she had deliberately decided to make the scene in the baccara-room
in order to stop him gambling, and that the loss of her
child had been, not the cause of that decision, but its
consequence. If she did, criticism would set in, it would
go on nibbling through the years. First Marc would begin to complain to himself that a more tactful woman
would have found another way of getting him to stop
gambling; and in the end it would seem to him that by
abandonment to shrewishness she had killed his child. It
was entirely necessary that she should let him go on believing she had been demented and blind instead of cunning and far-sighted. Nevertheless, she disliked having
to lie continuously about a matter so important to her.
Often she asked herself furiously how Marc would have
liked it, had he found himself obliged to pretend to
everybody, even his board of directors, that the Sallafranque automobile was made, not from the designs of
engineers he had employed for the purpose, but according to the revelations of a nun living in a cave, to whom
he had been directed in a dream. Enraged, she would
close her eyes and pretend to sleep; and she would not
open them even when she felt Marc bending over her,
though she knew it would distress him to go back to
Paris without having said good-bye and hearing once
more that she had forgiven him.

Fortunately, it seemed to be understood by the doctors that it would be best for her to go somewhere else

than her home when she could leave her bed and walk.
She went first to a clinic thirty miles from Paris, but in
the opposite direction from her home in the valley of
the Chevreuse. For a short time she was pleased by the
change. The clinic was situated in one of those parts of
France which, without possessing any distinctive features, are infinitely pleasing to the eye, simply because
they are both water-logged and light-logged. The garden was divided from pastures juicy with broad-bladed
grass; all day and all night the blue-grey leaves of the
poplars rustled by her windows, murmuring of cool
springs at their roots, as a shell murmurs of the sea
whence it came; and she could walk no distance without
coming on scattered ponds and intersecting canals on
which patterns of yellow and white water-lilies were
superimposed on the reflected skies. But the lens of the
air was undimmed, nothing was merged by dampness,
every object was chastely and brilliantly distinct. She
would have enjoyed it greatly, had she enjoyed anything.

Here, too, she found Marc's visits irritating. He would
say, "Why are you touching that tree-trunk as if it
were something extraordinary?" And she would realize
that she had been standing in a trance by a felled oak
beside the path in the woods, marvelling that the mas-
siveness of things should mean nothing, that the three-
dimensional world should, in fact, not be solid at all,
should be only the flimsiest membrane over a void. He
would say, "What interests you about that angler?" And
she would realize that she had been watching the man
fishing on the edge of the canal for some moments, astonished that he could stand there so calmly, when his

doom was in front of him and behind him, and might even take what he loved before it took him. She was obsessed with the immanence of death, and her only safety lay in ignoring her obsession. It was fatuous. What had happened to her at Le Touquet had brought no new fact before her attention. She had always known that everybody must die, and that she, and the people belonging to her, were not exempt from this rule. Since there was no life known which was free from these conditions, every reasonable person must take them for granted.

This despairing preoccupation with death must therefore, Isabelle supposed, be due to some such state of hypersensitiveness as she had passed through after the only attack of influenza she had ever suffered, when the ticking of a clock seemed a perverse assault on the senses. Then they had cured her quite quickly with tonics and massage, which showed that such distress had a physical basis. They were giving her tonics and massage now, but evidently not enough, nor of the right kind. She therefore mentioned her depression to the doctor in charge, a short, sensible-looking man with a beard, in the hope that he might suggest a change in her regime. But he answered her chiefly in abstract nouns, of which she had often noticed there were more in general circulation in France than in any other country, and she saw that she had fallen into the hands of one of those modern doctors who have strayed too far from aperients in the direction of the soul. He gave her no helpful prescription, but spent every day a longer period in her room, using more and more abstract nouns, until his conversation seemed to have broken all links with reality. But she grasped that this was not the case the afternoon he led her to the window and pointed out that, even as in the garden below the delicate blossoms of spring had given place to the roses of summer, so youth and its illusions gave place to maturity and its deeper, richer, and, he could swear, more delicious experiences. His voice throbbed, and she recalled with embarrassment that, whereas in England and America a beard usually means that its owner would rather be considered venerable than virile, on the continent of Europe it often means that its owner makes a special claim to virility.

"Do not be dismayed," he continued, "by the malignity of fate, but step forward into the smiling garden of life and pluck with those beautiful white hands the roses of love. Bend over them with all that abandonment of which I saw at the first glance that you are capable, inhale deeply those perfumes of sensuality which nature has designed as an inspiration for such superb women as yourself."

"Ah, how you understand me!" sighed Isabelle. "It is for precisely these reasons that I desire to return to Paris."

The doctor's beard fell. "No one can admire Monsieur Sallafranque more than I do," he said. "It is to be seen at once that he is a king of industry, full of force, full of geniality. But I wonder if he can treat you as you ought to be treated at this crisis of your existence, with delicacy and consideration as well as masterfulness?"

"I must confess," said Isabelle, to bring the encounter to an end, "that it would not be only my husband whom I should hope to see in Paris." She cast down her eyes.

As she had anticipated, the doctor felt there were certain plans which no right-minded man could oppose. He sighed and left her shortly afterwards, showing no sign of malice, but warning her sadly that Englishmen knew nothing of the arts of love. This puzzled her until she remembered that he had been in her room a few days before when Alan Fielding had called to see her. She was immensely amused by this man who knew everything about life and made such gross errors in his observations of it. When Marc's automobile stopped outside the house half an hour later, she had an impulse to run downstairs, put her arm through his, and walk him round the garden, sharing her amusement with him. But she gave up the idea, it had become fatiguing for her to tell him anything long or involved.

She did not go home yet. She went to another clinic which her specialist recommended to her, some two hours before Grenoble, so far away that Marc could come to see her only at week-ends. Here she was at first happier. The countryside had a jolly quality which prevented it assuming the bleakness characteristic of mountains, in spite of its elevation. The heights lifted shoulders as full-fleshed as a young peasant woman's, and the slope falling from a cliff that caught the very first light of dawn was as green as the grass in a valley orchard, and the red roofs of the villages were the very colour of comfort. Most of the flowers that grew in the district she had never seen before, and when she came to a crossroad, the names on the sign-posts were all unfamiliar. It was as if she were starting in a world that was new but not in the least strange. Here she slept and ate better than she had done since Easter, but she was still melancholy, so she asked the doctor in charge if he could not give her a stronger tonic. But nothing he gave her did what she required, though he was of a more modern school than the doctor with the beard. He had the manner of a believing priest when he spoke about fresh air; he prescribed sun-bathing as if it were a step towards some audaciously selected goal; it was his pleasure to go about dressed in flannel trousers and a sailor's singlet, some sizes too small for him; and he rolled about the grounds stretched taut across an exercise wheel. As the weather grew warmer, he presented himself without the singlet, nude to the waist. He was agreeably tanned by the sun, but was disfigured by over-developed muscles, which came and went under his skin like small peripatetic tortoises; also he carried his chest as if it were a highly inflated football hung round his neck. Isabelle liked him for the sparrow-like cheerfulness he derived from his hygienic obsession, and his visits to her grew daily longer.

But one day it happened that they met in the village and halted together to watch a young farmer leading his bride from church; and with the manner of one demonstrating to a class of students he turned to her and said, "In the presence of such happy children of the soil as those, one realizes what is so often forgotten in the devitalizing atmosphere of great cities, that nature has given men and women the power to re-create themselves through the enjoyment of their bodies, provided only that those bodies are healthy." As he concluded, he struck himself a sharp blow on the strained singlet.

"I have never been in a great city which seemed to have forgotten that truth," said Isabelle.

"Come," he said, "let us go back to the clinic." As

they walked along, he said in a vibrant undertone, "It is
not good, Madame Sallafranque, for a woman young and
vigorous as yourself to live in a solitude that is contrary
to the laws of nature."

For a second Isabelle contended with that sensation
which, so oddly, spreads over the skin alike when a chalk
is drawn down a blackboard or when an advance is made
by an undesired person; and then she replied, "I agree
with you entirely. It was for that reason I wished to
return home almost immediately."

Tensing his biceps, he objected angrily, "Monsieur
Sallafranque is too much a man of the metropolis to give
you the revitalization of your forces which you require
just now."

She murmured, "It is not Monsieur Sallafranque
whom I desire to see in Paris."

The doctor was silent for a moment. Then, expanding
his ribs and caressing his hollow stomach, he asked her if
her lover was a real man, if he could play tennis, if he
did winter sports, if he could climb mountains.

"I wish to return to Paris at this particular moment,"
said Isabelle, "in order that I may say good-bye to him
before he leaves to lead an expedition up Mount Ever-
est."

The little doctor's arms dropped limp by his sides, he
let his ribs and his stomach fall, and he looked so woebe-
gone as they walked in silence to the clinic that she
wished she could confess to her lie. But when she told
Alan Fielding, who looked in at the clinic on his way to
inspect a picture that had just been left to the museum
at Grenoble, his amusement revived her brutality. They
laughed over it until their laughter lost connexion with

its cause, and became amusing and satisfying in itself, like the laughter of children. She was sitting on the window-ledge, and she was so shaken that she looked behind her to make sure that the window was closed and she could lean back. Her eye travelled through the glass to the plain below, which, when she had last looked at it, had been enamelled to an intense green by the glow of a cloudless sunset. It was now a bowl of chilly shadow. She shuddered, and the thought of death returned to her.

Again she did not go home. She went to a clinic in Switzerland kept by a famous German doctor, who had helped to restore some relative of Marc's after a bereavement. It appeared to her, as soon as she saw him, that it was unlikely he would do the same for her, and that she would feel offended and outwitted if he did. He was tall and bent and moved very slowly; he had long, thick white hair, and his eyes always seemed to be looking into the distance; and though these characteristics delighted his other patients, she found in them only ground for mistrust. From his reminiscences she deduced that he had been a child at the time of the Franco-Prussian War and must therefore be under or just seventy; had he taken reasonable care of himself, he should have been still upright and alert. Hair so long was out of place in a hospital, and eyes which were always looking into the distance might have been admirable in a sailor or a shepherd, but were plainly not the sort most useful to a competent doctor. She felt increased suspicion of him when he closed their first interview by laying his large and prematurely tremulous hand on her head and saying gutturally, "Ah, my child, you will see how small your troubles will seem to you, up here in the mountains." It did not seem to her that it could ever seem to her a trifling matter that her husband had got drunk and forced her into making a scene which had brought on a miscarriage, and she saw no reason why she should be likely to take this curious view of the affair more among mountains than in flat country.

One night he came to her room when she was standing on her veranda, which looked across the valley at a snow-covered peak, now ghost-coloured in the starlight, rising above the crumpled darkness of the lower mountains. He joined her, and after a moment's silence, which was not so silent as he supposed owing to his stertorous breathing, he extended a trembling finger towards the peak and said in a strangled tone, as if a piece of wisdom were fighting its way up from the bottom of some accumulated store within him, "Ah, our wise old brother, the Hüpfenstrudelalp. On how much suffering has he not looked down . . . on how much sorrow . . . and on how much joy. Ah, he will soon cure you, my child." He then took her hand and recited Heine's "Du bist wie eine Blume," and left with florid gestures of farewell, greatly coarsened by his own sense of their picturesqueness. She found herself quivering with rage. What right had he to feel that he was doing anything that ought to be done, taking notice of anything that ought to be noticed, when he was merely indicating that, in the same world where she and a great many unhappy people found themselves, there was also a mountain? In point of fact, the Hüpfenstrudelalp had probably not looked down on any great amount of human emotion, for the valley beneath, being infertile and poor in timber, had hardly been settled till the English began mountaineering in the middle of the nineteenth century. It had probably been witnessing joy and sorrow for about as long as the local railway station. But in any case, even if it had seen as much human passion as the whole of the Occidental civilization put together, that would still not have given it any power to cure her. She was not at all sure that these mountains were not definitely the worst place for her mental malady, for the sudden evenings, which flooded the valleys with cold darkness at an instant's warning, always brought back the idea of death into her mind. After every sundown it was with her. She had been on the balcony when the doctor came because she wished to isolate this thought and argue it into its proper place, which she could not do in her lighted room. There her attention was distracted by innumerable objects, the pictures on the walls, the books on the table, the brushes and combs and manicure-set on her dressing-table, so that the obsession was able to insinuate itself into the background of her mind, and all at once she would find herself in the power of her insanity.

It was not that she was afraid of dying herself. She had faced that many times in her imagination during her flying days with Roy, and she knew that it would probably mean a painful convulsion and a moment of great terror followed by relaxation into nothingness, no worse than fainting to the person who suffered it, though falsely considered so by those who witnessed it, for the purely subjective reason that they perceived it to come at the end of the victim's life and not at some point during it. It was the general aspect of it that appalled her. She was not resentful because it took everything. Nobody would want to live for ever, and the variety of life depended on the occupation of the stage by successive generations. She hated death because it took its victims in a disorderly and violent way, without regard for their value, at the wrong time, with disgusting physical results. It had taken her child, who might have become anything, whom she had known from its movements to have some special glorious and endearing quality. But even if it had been an ordinary child, Death should not have taken it, for it was absolutely necessary, if the universe was not to be a chaos of pain, that parents should die before their children. Anyway it should not have taken the child at such a stage and in such a way that sensible human opinion denied it a grave. She was not able to think of it as being in any particular place.

When Isabelle found herself possessed once again by that particular thought, she went back into the lighted room and began to manicure her nails. Then, laying down the orange-stick, she looked at herself in the mirror and said, "This is absurd. At that stage it has no more consciousness than a sea anemone or a limpet. It is absurd to feel about it as if it were a person whom I had known." She rose and took off her clothes very quickly, as if she were stripping herself of her destiny, and got into bed, and turned out the light. After some time she turned on the light again, and opened a book. She was reading only German books now, though her French blood made her feel that German was not a rational growth like any Latin language, but was an arbitrary invention like Esperanto or Ido; and indeed their writers struck her as working under a handicap, since their tongue made the most perfunctory remark sound like a considered judgment. It was impossible to listen to the bloodhound solemnity of the German vowels without believing that they clothed a philosophical revelation proceeding from profound experience, to regard the massive span of a German sentence without believing that it had been constructed to meet the strain of the heaviest conceivable intellectual traffic. French writers laboured under a handicap of the contrary kind, for their language made a considered judgment sound like a perfunctory remark; and this worked to their advantage, because they were therefore under the continual need to justify their claims to seriousness by the exhibition of their subtlest and most valid intellectual processes.

But for all that, she knew quite well that the French were not perfect. Her own life had come to ruin in France, and that was natural enough, for there was in French life a contentment with the petty which was enough to prevent it from forming any noble and continuous pattern. She recalled contemptuously how the two doctors in the other clinics had made love to her. If she had acceded to their desires, the encounters must have produced so little pleasure, owing to her manifest preoccupation, and the complete lack of physical or mental sympathy between them, that it would have been as disgusting for them to have gone to any trouble to procure it as it would have been if they had greedily put themselves about to obtain a small sugar cake. All that could be said for them was that they had a greater sense of reality than the German doctor. When they perceived that she was suffering from a malady too insidious to cure, they offered to have sexual intercourse with her, which they could in fact have done. In the same situation the German doctor had attempted to distract her by pretending that a mountain understood her complaint and could remove it, which was not the case. Her heart went out in rage against the two peoples: the French, who had their eyes always set on the mean little satisfactions well within their grasp, on over-complicated food and over-simplified sex, on the steady pay of the civil servant, on the ribbon of the Legion of Honour, on a glass of syrup taken on the terrace of a café with a group of friends, and who never looked up to wonder at the strangeness of the forces of which these were only the superficial manifestations; and the Germans, who are so absorbed in recognizing the existence of these forces that they entirely ignore their superficial manifestations, which after all are valued preliminary points of contact with them, who talk about food and sit at table during hours of ritual consumption, yet have invented only a few dishes, who are infatuated with the idea of music and the large rhythms on which it rolled among the spheres, yet go to concerts and play musical instruments with the most promiscuously invariable enthusiasm and the starkest insensibility to the quality of the actual sounds produced.

She rebuked herself for her irritability. These people were doing their best, they were carrying on. Though these doctors were useless in regard to herself, they did other work well. The doctor with the beard was an impassioned neurologist, and had talked to her with fire of a disease which made its victims fling their bodies about as if in unremitting fanaticism, and of a fantastic but successful treatment which mitigated their sufferings by adjustment of a nerve in the nose. She had seen the doctor with the inflated chest tenderly intelligent over a child with weak lungs; and this German doctor was without doubt being of service to those of his patients who were accustomed to eat and drink too much. All over France, and all over Germany too, there were men milking cows and getting the churns to the railway stations on time, and women nursing sick children so that they got better instead of worse. There were, in fact, in both these countries, and indeed in all countries, innumerable people living lives which made her revolt in shame against the kind of night she was probably going to spend. She would rise from her bed, hour by hour she would walk from the window to the door and from the door to the window, leaning her hand on the dressing-table as she passed so that she could know the reassurance of contact with solidity, while her heart raged uselessly against death and grieved after a child that had been irrevocably destroyed. Then all the next day she would be drugged by lack of sleep. She could imagine no more completely wasteful manner of spending the twenty-four hours, and suddenly she thought with nostalgia of her house in Paris, of the pigeon-hole in her desk where she kept her housekeeping books, of the clear morning light that shone through the muslin curtains in her dressing-room and irradiated the bowed white head of her cook, who stood waiting for the day's orders on flat-heeled shoes thrust wide apart under bunched black skirts, acting the part of a poor old widow woman, simple and patient and honest, whereas she was in fact a thief and a miser, a tyrant to her subordinates, the depraved and jealous mistress of the twenty-year-old second chauffeur, a sublime artist, better than any chef, and a devoted servant so long as she was ridden on the curb.

Isabelle hungered to be back wrestling with this woman,
or fortifying the maître d'hôtel, who was a strayed intellectual and apt to become melancholy at dinner-parties,
and to betray written on his face a doubt whether there
was any real justification for that or any other festivity
in this universe, but who was perfect in staging their
everyday life, or making any of those personal adjust-
ments which made her populous household endure from
day to day, and to the next.

She started up, kneeling on her bed, and said aloud,
"I ought to be at home! I am not leading a normal life.
They have got me again." She had miscarried her child
because she formed part of a society that was itself a
miscarriage, that had not cohered into a culture or a
civilization, that could not cohere into even the simplest
sort of pattern. There came back to her that disgusting
night on the Riviera, where innumerable gorged people,
scattered over a garden, had failed to be born into a
party, though the voice of a great singer hung in the air
above them, calling them to voluptuousness as to prayer,
though fireworks multiplied and exceeded the beauty of
the stars above them. It was the same night that Marc
had for the first time revealed before her his passion for
gambling, that destiny had for an instant lifted its hand
from the map of the future and had clapped it back
again before she could comprehend what she saw. It
seemed to her that the tale begun on that evening had
been accomplished at Le Touquet. But suddenly she saw
that it was continuing here and now in the clinic. She
stared about her at the hygienic surfaces of her room as
if it were a dungeon, and she remembered how the beam
of the lighthouse at Le Touquet, passing over her walls,

had made her think that if she had been a sailor's wife she might have been dead by then. Now she felt that if she had been a sailor's wife she might have been much more alive than she was, since she would have had neither the freedom nor the money to wander from one useless regime to another, among people who meant nothing to her.

She said aloud, "Marc, I must come home." Then she looked at herself anxiously in the pierglass of the wardrobe opposite her bed, for she was aware that she was undertaking an immensely difficult task. She was not sure if she could possibly stop thinking about Le Touquet, and her reflection made her doubt it. There was a darkness about her face which was not of her skin. But her eyes travelled down the glass to her body, which was naked, since she had thrown herself between the sheets without a nightdress in her precipitate flight from her obsession, and she was astonished and amused. Her body knew nothing of what had happened to her. Her skin was lustred by the sun just as it had been during any other summer, even the most fortunate. Neither it, nor the high medallions of her breasts, nor the arch of her ribs, nor the hollow of her stomach, gave any intimation that she had of late been utterly worsted by humiliation and grief. Serene in its muscular and venous wisdom, idyllic in its smoothness as a land where the art of writing has not yet been discovered, her body confronted her without memory. She stood up on the bed, watching in the mirror how her knees pressed out and straightened, perfectly accomplishing what her will designed. She said, "I am young, I am strong," and she put her hand to her head, tilting it backwards so that she could

look distastefully at its dark and sullen gravity, as hypo-
chondriacal in its resolve to be the reverse of a sundial
and mark only the shadowed hours. "The thing is not
to think so much!" she cried. "I will go back to Paris
and live, just live. I will run the house, and be busy all
the time, and never remember Le Touquet." She lay
down and turned out the light, and slept till morning.

Isabelle went early to the doctor's room, to tell him
that she was leaving that night, and when he objected,
she reminded him that he had promised her that the
mountains would give her peace, and firmly assured him
that they had. She perceived at once that she had been
right in supposing this to be a proposition which he
would not find in his heart to dispute, any more than
the French doctors had found themselves able to frus-
trate her intention of returning to a lover; but he was
unable to disguise a certain amount of regret that the
mountains had acted quite so promptly on one of his
wealthiest patients. He controlled himself, however, and
gave her a long address on health and happiness and
courage and simplicity, looking immensely wise and
speaking with sibylline deliberation, but achieving nothing but a loose association of ideas, while she fixed her
eyes on the photographs of his nine sons and daughters
which were ranged along the mantelpiece. As his dis-
course continued, it appeared likely that these children,
though differing widely in age, were all the result of a
single intolerably long and discursive sexual act. She
found herself longing for the clarity and sharpness of
speech that she heard from Marc and his relatives; and
she found herself thinking of the man before her with
fear and hostility, as if he must be dangerous because he

was not lucid, which was not logical but was exactly what Marc and his relatives would have felt about him. "I have become a Sallafranque," she said to herself; "I must go home to the Sallafranques." She smiled to think of herself acquiring ideas through family alliances, through habit and the frequentation of the herd, instead of through the use of the mind.

She wired to Marc telling him that she would arrive some time next morning, and that he must not meet her, because she was not sure that she might not break her journey for an hour or two, and might even take an aeroplane from Geneva. This was not true, but she wanted to arrive in Paris alone, as if she were a young person with her life still to make, as if she were going to Marc not because she was committed to return to him, but because he represented the most favourable opportunity in a world full of alternatives. And, indeed, the sight of Paris filled her with delight. The drive from the Gare de Lyon intoxicated her with a sense of possible distractions because it took her through parts of the town which she never visited and which she looked on with the fresh eye of the stranger. The morning sun was shining on the quays in the Bercy quarter, stencilling on the amber water the oily yellow image of the chestnut leaves, already half consumed by summer, and setting long, shallow shadows beside the hills of barrels, which were far less familiar to her and far more astonishing than the Taj Mahal. "I must drive out here one day," she said to herself, "and see if this extraordinary district really exists. Miles and miles of nothing but barrels, it is really not credible." Suddenly a woodfire sent its country smell to her nostrils, and she remembered that this was the only great city which is also a village, where countless metropolitans follow unaltered village ways. It showed its bucolic quality in the little shops on the river, which, in the very face of Notre Dame and the Law Courts, and at the elbow of the Hôtel de Ville, offered seeds and plants, birds and fishes, on so modest a scale that they might have been functioning in the most inglorious provincial town; and on the stalls by the river-parapet which exposed for sale all sorts of printed rubbish that in any other capital would have been hawked in the suburbs or left in the attics, so obviously could most of it appeal to nothing but the simpletonish desire to turn over the page just to see what was on the next. But the Parisians who were hurrying along the streets to their work had remained villagers, not because they were unsophisticated or unadaptable, but because they were fierce. They defended the customs that suited them as savagely as they would attack anyone who tried to take from them lovers that suited them. Many of them were ugly, a certain number of them looked cruel, they wore dark clothes with an air of murderous thrift and contempt for lightness. But they were all splendidly themselves, having been compelled by the extreme degree of their aggressiveness to throw aside everything that was not real and necessary to them and worth the trouble, which in their case was apt to be furiously inordinate, of defending. "What an amusing people to live among!" Isabelle thought affectionately; and she added, "What an amusing family!" For it was from these people that the Sallafranques had risen unperturbed by their good fortune; it was to these people that the Sallafranques would return unperturbed by poverty if their fortune changed.

"What I have to do will be quite easy," she told herself, as the taxi passed the sky-broad spaces of the Place de la Concorde, and she looked up the wide trench of the Champs-Élysées to the Arc de Triomphe. This was her own Paris, where she lived, where she walked every day, and her memory was charmed by a thousand recollections of morning freshness and the harmless extravagance of early sunshine spilt over pavements, of prodigal purchases of flowers in the name of housewifely duty, of unplanned, unfatiguing encounters with acquaintances and their dogs.

When she arrived at her house, she was inordinately amused at its ugly handsomeness. She ran into it and found Marc having breakfast in the little sitting-room at the back of the house, and since the door was wide open, she was able to pass round it and look at him unobserved. He was lying on his back in a deep arm-chair, his stout rubbery legs crossed on a level with his head; and he was munching a brioche and reading a newspaper, which he held crumpled under his eyes, as if he were short-sighted or illiterate, though he was neither. She had forgotten how grotesque he was, with his compact and springy build, his mobile muzzle, his bright black hair, and his look of being sluiced down with vitality. It was noticeable that during her absence he had gone back to the vivid shirts and ties and socks she had discouraged, and he was again wearing those brown shoes which were almost yellow. As he read, he kept up a soft animal murmur and shook his head from side to side. Presently he grumbled, "The dirty pigs!" It was the political article he was reading. Looking very shocked and keeping his eye on the paper, he stretched out his hand and soaked his brioche in the cup of coffee which was standing on the table at his elbow. As he slowly brought it back to his mouth, drops fell from it on to his trousers. She moved forward, laughing. "You disgusting child!" she cried.

Marc looked up and saw her. "Isabelle! Isabelle!" He threw the brioche into his cup of coffee and took her in his arms, which always seemed to contain her so completely, though they were so short. "Oh, my darling, you should have let me meet you!"

She said, "No, I wanted to walk in just like this, as though I needn't have come if I hadn't chosen!"

"Ah, there aren't half a dozen women in France I'd rather have seen coming through the door," said Marc, and kissed her firmly and noisily on the mouth.

"What great vulgar kisses, you grocer," she said. His hands were warm and dry, she lifted them and laid them against her throat. "He is enchanting," she thought, and smiled at her reflection in the mirror over the mantelpiece, the chin tiptilted over the collar of his spread fingers. Even though she was sunburned, she looked anæmic and frangible beside him. "I wonder where his stock came from originally," her mind continued. "I am sure that a thousand years ago they were Berbers or Arabs. He is the kind of barbarian that Rome could absorb; that was what made all the greatness of Rome."

"But now we must get you some breakfast," he said.

"No, let us think of ourselves for a little," she begged.

"I don't mind doing that," he said, and kissed her again.

"I have never known anything as coarse as your kisses," she said, "except that dish of pork, goose, and beans they gave us at that inn near Le Puy."

"And how you liked it!" he said. "My God, how you liked it! I have never seen a woman eat so much at one time." But he stopped to exclaim, "No, really, you must have some breakfast, you frighten me because you are still so fragile. You are so small in my arms. You have come home like a little plucked dog from the vet's."

"Well, if you will go on about it," she said, "I should adore some coffee, though I had some on the train."

"Perhaps," said Marc, "you ought to have an egg. Or some of those extraordinary things they have in America for breakfast. Yes, I think that would be a very good idea." He spoke very seriously, as if it might be possible that all their troubles might have been avoided had Isabelle only eaten buckwheat cakes every morning, a practice which had previously struck him as disgusting, but which, it occurred to him now, might have a medicinal or even magical value.

She took his wrist and began twisting it about, as if he were weak and she were brutally strong. "An egg," she said, mocking his gravity and pouting her lips so that her voice came out gruff like his, and as loaded with a wistful hope that the solution of a troubling problem had been found. She mocked him with it again when they had brought her the coffee and she was lying on the chaise-longue. They talked for a while about such things as their house in the valley of the Chevreuse and when they should go down to it again, and the way that Yolande's Madeleine was suddenly showing signs of becoming a beauty, and Madame Sallafranque's success at the races this season; and then a happy silence fell, and she put down her cup and folded her arms behind her head, and looked at him, and laughed. "An egg," she mimicked.

"Very well, then, an egg," he grumbled. "But you see, I want to do something for you and it is so difficult. It is summer, so I cannot fetch you a rug, and you are as flexible as a cat, you fit exactly into whatever basket you find yourself, there is no use bringing you any more cushions. But seriously, darling, you must eat simple things that do you good."

"I do, I do," said Isabelle. "Besides, my dear, I am perfectly well."

"That may be, my dear," he said, "but you wouldn't go down with the army, you know, the way you are now."

"Enough of that," said Isabelle, "enough of that." She closed her eyes and began to smooth her eyebrows, thinking, "If he takes hold of me roughly as he used to do when I did this, it will all be as it was. I am so fond of him."

But he took hold of her very gently and, after he had kissed her hair, he said, "Now you must rest this morning."

"I suppose so," she answered, asking herself, "Why is he not like a bear as he used to be?"

"I have arranged not to go to the works at all today," Marc went on.

"That is lovely," she said mechanically, and she told herself, "but of course I understand why he is not being rough and hurting me. All that was play, it was done on the understanding that it could never happen in earnest.

Now he has really hurt me, we will never be able to make a game of it again."

"I thought you'd rest all the morning, and I would sit by you and lick your hand and wag my tail," Marc went on, "and then I had certain plans for the afternoon, but I really don't think we ought to carry them out, because you've begun to look tired again."

"Nonsense," said Isabelle. "Do tell me what they were. You don't understand, I've been buried in the country so long that I'm yearning to be amused again."

"Well," he said, "I thought we might go down into the town and choose a present for you, just to mark your homecoming. Something from Cartier's, I thought."

"Oh, my darling, how lovely!" cried Isabelle. "You know how greedy I am, and it is so pleasant to come back to all those town-things after all that milk and white enamel in the clinics." She said to herself, "It is not going to be quite so easy to forget, after all." Then she cried out, alarmed in case she had betrayed her thought, "But why are you looking so miserable, Marc? What has suddenly come into your head?"

"Only that I have done my best, and it is not good enough," he said.

"What do you mean? It is a charming idea, and I am delighted."

"No, that is not the point," he said. "The point is that what I am offering you costs only money, and I have plenty of that. Whatever you choose, I will hardly feel it: I wish I could give you something that meant I must scrape and save and go without sleep to pay for it. That would be a real present. But that's the one thing I can't afford to give you."

"Ah, Marc," said Isabelle, "sometimes when I was ill I forgot what you were like. I cannot tell you what a loss that was."

XI

A L A N F I E L D I N G and Isabelle leant out of her boudoir window as far as they could.

"It's all very well," he said, "but no cat would make that noise unless it had fallen down a grating, or got treed by a dog."

"Yes, possibly something has happened to that cat at last," she said.

"It is funny we can't see it anywhere," he said, "because that miawling is terrific. It must be somewhere quite near. Well, I'll be damned! There it is."

"Where?" she asked.

"Standing on the other side of that tree. It poked out its head on the one side for a minute, and then I saw the tip of its tail waving on the other. It doesn't seem to be in any trouble, it's just standing there. What an extraordinary thing. I wonder why on earth it's raising that din."

"To torment our humanitarian feelings," said Isabelle. "It probably recognized that you were an Englishman—that cat has all the experience of hell behind it—and knows that the English are inordinately sentimental about animals. I tell you that cat is a fiend."

"How did you get it?" asked Alan. "Have you had it long?"

"The day I came home. Marc took me down to Cartier's to buy me this bracelet, and we walked part of the way home, and we passed an animal shop with three Siamese cats. I stopped and admired them—I think they're the loveliest of beasts, don't you?—and Marc said, 'Let's take home a living present as well as a dead one,' and he went in and bought this child of sin."

"I expect he loves buying you presents," said Alan. "It must be fun."

"Marc is the most generous soul in the world," said Isabelle. "Since that day we have never had a civil word from the beast. It is not a bit softened by the knowledge that we paid an enormous price for it, or that we have provided it with every possible luxury. On the contrary, that has helped it to decide that we are rich vulgar people. The only sign of recognizing our existence is that it sometimes spits at us, and it continually tears the upholstery of our chairs and sofas to ribbons. But that I do not believe it does from spite. I think it merely finds the action of drawing the claws slowly down through silk æsthetically pleasurable. But still I think it might refrain, considering all we have done for it."

"I suppose you like your other present better," said Alan.

"Don't you?" she asked.

"I don't know anything about this jewel business," he said. "It's just something I haven't got any feeling for. It's a bit heavy, isn't it?"

"It is a little," she said. "The trouble is, Marc had been down to the shop the day before and fallen in love with this, and I couldn't find it in my heart not to choose it. But you're right, it is too heavy." She looked up at

him and caught him smiling down at the funnel of diamonds and emeralds. "I do not mean in design," she said
coldly. "Marc has exquisite taste, and the French like
their jewellery massive."

"I know, I know," he hastily agreed.

"I meant heavy in weight," she went on to explain.
"It tires my wrist."

"That I can well believe," he said. "You have the
loveliest wrists in the world, Isabelle. I have never seen
anything so delicate and yet so strong. There isn't a hint
of weakness about them, yet they're as finely made as
part of a flower."

She burst out laughing. "What bad manners men
have!" she said.

"Why, what have I said?" he asked. "I was only telling the truth."

"That is what is such bad manners," she said. "Oh, it
isn't you specially that I am complaining against, it's
your whole sex, with their habit of paying compliments.
It is quite rude, you know. It puts me in such an embarrassing position. You see, I don't know what to say.
Would you, if I suddenly said to you, 'Alan, you've got
the longest eyelashes I have ever seen on a man'?"

"Well, I wouldn't," he smiled. "But that is different."

"No, it is not," she told him. "It would be easy enough,
of course, if you went on to make love to me. Then we
would both have a very good idea of how the conversation should develop. But nothing is more impossible than
that you should ever think of making love to me, since
you know that I am devoted to Marc, and I am sure you
have your own rose-garden somewhere."

"No," he said.

"You make your gentlemanly denial, of course, but I shan't believe you. Anyway, you know my state of mind, so we cannot go on to a love-scene. So here I am, hung up, with nothing to say, and it's all your fault."

"That never happens between us, really," said Alan. "We always have something to say to each other. It's extraordinary how the time passes when we're together. It must be quite late, it's time I left you to rest."

"No—don't go for a minute," said Isabelle. "Stay and say how do you do to my husband. He has just come in."

"How do you know?"

"I hear the doors slamming."

"I suppose the thing is that he amuses you," said Alan thoughtfully.

"He does much more than that!" said Isabelle. "Look here, my good friend, just give me your attention for a moment. Stop staring at the floor and look at me."

"I am delighted to do that," said Alan. "Really, you must come to my suburban studio some day, and let me paint you."

"If you should be falling into the error of the Siamese cat about this family, I shall be very sorry," she said.

"What do you mean?" he asked.

"If you are conceiving the idea that either Marc or I is rich and vulgar, I shall be very sorry," she said, "because I shall have to turn you out. You see you have none of the advantages that make me keep the Siamese cat in spite of its errors. You aren't a smudged soot-and-dove colour; you have not those marvellous blue eyes which show what can be done with blue eyes, provided they aren't in Nordic heads. You have merely very long eyelashes."

They exchanged a smile, and he stood up. "Well, I'd better go back to Louveciennes before worse happens to me," he said.

"No, stay a moment and meet Marc," said Isabelle. "He was saying only the other day how much he wanted to meet you again. See, Marc, here is Mr. Fielding."

"How do you do?" said Marc, who, on seeing the visitor, had not closed the door behind him. "My dear, ought you not to be resting if we are going to the theatre?"

When Alan had gone, Isabelle said, "That wasn't very nice of you, Marc. Also it made me look a fool. I had just told him that you had said you wanted to see him again."

"Well, it is not my fault you said that," Marc told her.

"But you did say it," Isabelle reminded him; "you said it only last night."

"Yes, but only to please you, and in front of the butler," said Marc.

"Well, how was I to know that, and what has the butler to do with it?" exclaimed Isabelle.

"Oh, my God, my God, have it your own way," said Marc, "I suppose I was rude to that young man. But let me tell you that it was disconcerting to come in and find you tiring yourself out."

"Mr. Fielding was not here for very long, and I rested all the time from lunch till he came for tea."

"That is as it may be," said Marc, "but you look exceedingly tired."

"Very well," said Isabelle, "I am tired, I need rest, it is six o'clock, and we are not going out until nearly nine. Go away then, and let me rest until half-past eight."

She lay down on her chaise-longue and closed her eyes.

"I am glad to see that under pressure you can become sensible," he said, and went to the door. But from there he turned back and knelt down beside her. "Forgive me, but I am so anxious about you."

For a minute she did not answer, and then she put out her hand. When he laid his face against it, she felt that his features were crumpled together. At that she sat up and drew his head to her breast, as if he were her child, but cried out, as if she were his child, "Oh, do not be angry with me any more! Do you realize, we are quarrelling because we love each other? You are cross with me because you are anxious about me; I am cross because you are cross on the day that was to be our fête, and so it goes on, and we act like enemies."

"But we love each other, it is quite certain that we love each other," he said.

"That is just what I cannot bear," she told him, "that we should love each other and should act as enemies."

"That is just the funny way it often happens," said Marc placidly.

"But I do not like it," she said. He rubbed his face in her hand, and she murmured, "Not that it is worth while labouring that point when I like you so much."

"You do?" he asked, and laid his lips to her throat.

She reflected that soon she must let him make love to her again; that perhaps it would be good to begin that night. But she found herself thinking of it less as a surrender to her affection for him than as a performance she had to give, and she asked, "Is this a very long play we're going to?"

He said, "No, and we needn't stay after the second

act. It isn't the play I want you to see, it's Mardrelle.
She wouldn't be playing at all at this time of the summer if she wasn't the mistress of Duroc, who can't leave
Paris because of the work he's doing for the government, and it won't be put on again in the autumn, so I
wanted you to take the chance of seeing her. She's really
got something, she reminds me of what Ève Lavallière
was like when I was a little boy." Like most Parisians of
his class, he had been reared from childhood to be a
pedantic and grudging but impassioned dramatic critic.
"And it's precisely in the second act that she's so good.
We could come out before the third act."

"Then I can manage it," said Isabelle drowsily.

Isabelle was indeed glad that she attended the play. It
had seemed to her a nervous and exhausting business to
be a woman, unsustained by public opinion, when she
left her house. She had turned round enviously as they
drove down the Champs-Élysées, to look back at the sunset which was blazing through and about the Arc de
Triomphe with a scarlet, militarist romanticism that
was superbly appropriate, triumphantly harmonious with
the French idea of glory; and it had occurred to her that,
while participation in the least important battle of any
campaign brings a man the support of a whole nation,
the most tremendous sexual victory, ending in the cap-
ture of a position vitally important from the highest
biological standards, brings a woman nothing but the
approval, which may be momentary, of her actual partner. But at the theatre she realized that she had been
thinking as a member of the English-speaking races.
The whole of the play was the character played by Mardrelle, a charming woman; but here it was given an hon-

ourable treatment which it would not have received among her own people. An English play about a charming woman would have had to allay the audience's anxiety as to whether she was not costing men too much and whether she was fulfilling her moral obligations; its last scene would inevitably have been a disclosure that she was really a good sort and comparatively inexpensive. An American play on the same subject would have been dictated by an interest in regionalism; the woman would have been not of the earth but of Park Avenue or Broadway or the Middle West. But this play was simply written to exhibit an actress who was neither beautiful nor very young, but who had the gift of remembering exactly what it had been like to pass through the characteristic stages of a woman's life in a society dominated by Christian ideas of sex, to be a virgin and to be taken by a man, to be pursued and to be abandoned, to be deceived and to deceive, to be happy and to outlive the conception of happiness. Neither the audience nor the playwright nor the actress doubted for a moment that this material was interesting for its own sake, and that the interest it aroused was of a respectable kind; and it was significant that the actress also must have been sustained by this faith, for it was known that she had come from the slums of Toulon by a road which must again and again have exposed her to brutality and desertion. The flesh across her cheekbones was infinitely tired, and it could be imagined that she had often learned what it is to be buffeted across the mouth, to be thrown about by unguaranteed strangers in transports, divided only by a hairbreadth from the murderous, to face the police without the weapon of prosperity. But from the pride of her stance, from the serenity of her high-pitched, miaow-like voice, and the perfect assurance with which she rehearsed her feminine experience, she showed that at no time during the frightful ordeal had it been suggested to her that women were not important, or that what she was doing was unadmirable apart from the displeasing circumstances in which it was done. There was more here than the integrity of a healthy body and a uniquely sturdy will. Over the actress and the spectators arched a consolidating national ideal. Had an indiscreet angel breathed over the auditorium that Marc and Isabelle were that night to be united after a long severance, Mardrelle herself would have waved her handkerchief and led the audience in the expression of an enthusiasm that would have had something in common with the sunset round the Arc de Triomphe and the idea of glory.

"Do you want to wait for the next act?" asked Marc as the curtain fell.

"Do I? Do I?" asked Isabelle hesitantly. She was about to answer that she did not when she caught sight of André de Verviers standing in a box opposite them. He had a companion, an Englishwoman or an American, in travelling clothes, and he was holding the door open for her while she picked up her gloves and bag. It was evidently an affair. He was looking down on her in an absorbed silence, which he would probably break by saying very thoughtfully, if she did not wear ear-rings, "I would like to see how you look with ear-rings," or, if she wore them, "Some day you must let me see how you look without those ear-rings."

"Yes, Marc," said Isabelle. "This woman is so delightful that I would like to see the play to the end." She

could not endure to think of meeting André, she was not
clear why.

"You see, I begin to know a little what you like," said
Marc. "But, indeed, you have quite French taste now.
That is quite natural, however, since you have so much
French blood in you. I need not talk as if I had been a
missionary."

"You French do not worry yourselves lest French
taste should be the worst in the world," she teased him;
and they sat hand in hand looking at the ill-drawn cartoons, spotted news photographs, and naïvely unattractive
advertisements which were flashed on the curtain, offering yet another proof that Paris is a village as well as a
capital, since they were of an order to be expected in a
parish hall rather than in a fashionable theatre. She was
warm with thankfulness because she was with Marc and
not with André; and she wondered what complication
was behind his presence there that night. His entrance
into the box was probably the climax of several concur-
rent dramas, all painful to everyone but himself, all
completely gratuitous. He would not be in Paris at this
time of the year had it not thereby bought some perverse
pleasure. Either he had extracted from his companion,
whose good looks were slightly disordered by unhappiness, that she should break her plans for a reasonable
summer and disappoint the friends who had hoped for
her society, and should endure the heat and dust for the
sake of being solitary with him; or he had compelled
her presence without asking for it by leading her to
suspect that he was remaining in Paris in order to be
with another woman, so that she felt forced to stay on
and on, exciting him to embraces so that she might prove

that there was nothing in her suspicions, which, however, he would always carefully renew immediately afterwards. Isabelle pressed close to Marc, who was a good animal with direct reactions, who ate when he was hungry, who roared when he was enraged, who howled when he was hurt,· who guffawed when he saw a joke; and when most of the people who had left their seats had returned from the foyer, she said, "Do you know, now that the people are coming back and sitting down for the next act, I do not believe I want to stay for it after all. I believe it will be too much for me."

"Well, well," grumbled Marc happily. "I suppose it was God who made you a little windmill."

She took some time to put on her gloves, so that the three blows which raise the curtain had already sounded before they left their seats, and then she moved briskly, since it was certain that there could be no further risk of running into André. She had foreseen that she and Marc would go out into a calm warm darkness which, in the wide and empty streets of a Paris midsummer night, would be private to themselves. But a sudden storm had broken, heavy rains were beating back from the pavements. Marc ran out in search of their car, and Isabelle stood watching him from the door for a moment, smiling at the way he shook himself like a sturdy little dog under the onslaught of the falling waters; and when he was out of sight, she turned back into the lobby, meaning to look at a frame full of photographs of Mardrelle. But she checked herself at once, for there were two other people beside herself in the lobby, and these were André de Verviers and his companion. Isabelle had forgotten to reckon with one of André's most persistent whims in the

conduct of a love-affair, which was to go to a place only
visited for the purpose of witnessing a certain spectacle,
and probably extremely difficult of access because of the
large number of people who desired to witness this spectacle, and then to ignore it totally in a show of absorption
in his beloved. He would secure front-row seats for the
Davis Cup or a ringside table for the most fashionable
night club, and then never look at the players or the
cabaret, but only at the woman he had brought with
him. He would turn on her a dark and drowning stare so
fixed, so completely not to be affected by a rally between
Tilden and Cochet, or the worst that a Negress wearing
a peacock's feather in her behind could do for sight
and sound, that before long it successfully competed
with the spectacle for public attention. This technical
trick served two purposes. It enhanced his reputation
as a romantic lover, and it afforded the basis for many
exciting quarrels with his mistresses, who could be ac-
cused of coldness when they writhed under this adoring
gaze, which made them only a little less conspicuous than
Tilden or Cochet or Josephine Baker, and that in richly
compromising circumstances.

It was to this second purpose that he was turning it
now. Isabelle could hear the woman begging him to remember the other occupants of the loge, who, from what
she said, were certainly their friends and had probably
even accompanied them to the theatre, and what they
were bound to think if he and she left before the end of
the performance. And as Isabelle turned round to hide
her face from them and stood looking out into the rain,
tapping her heel with impatience because Marc did not
come back, she heard André, in a voice sad as the falling

of leaves, ask her companion if it could possibly be that
such trifles seemed important to her. He began another
sentence, on a slightly higher pitch, as if he intended it
to be longer and more poignant; but he did not complete
it. A silence fell. When he spoke again, it was very
softly, and his companion answered by an exclamation
of surprise. Isabelle was so certain he had seen her that
she pulled open the swing door and tried to go out; but
the rain was too violent, she had to step back, and she
found him beside her, holding out his hand. She realized
as soon as she met his eyes why she had feared meeting
him. It was not, of course, simply because they had had
a love-affair and she was now married. That had happened, but so had the battle of Sadowa; neither event
touched any nerve in her mind, her life would have gone
on in the same way had all her knowledge of them been
excised. It was because she had known exactly how he
would smile at her when they met.

Aloud, André said with perfect good manners, with a
touch of brotherly affection that was even more than
correct, that was a charming offering to a woman who
had been in social difficulties from a man whose position
had never been disturbed, "But, my dear Isabelle, what
a pleasure to meet you! One never sees you anywhere
nowadays. How are you? How are you?" But his narrowed knowing eyes and his twitching lips conveyed,
"So you surprised them all, did you not, by the extraordinary scene you made in the Casino at Le Touquet?
But you did not surprise me, my dear, who remembered
how you flung down the roses outside my door, that
insane day not so very long ago! And I admire you none
the less for it, because I know that such excesses are part

of your temperament, your really delicious temperament."

Isabelle replied, "Ah, André, you have such a good heart that you will be hardly disappointed at all to learn that I am far better than you hoped."

As he broke into nervous laughter and felt for words, she looked over her shoulder, anxious to leave this man who had forced her to counter his folly by a greater one, and saw through the glass door that Marc had found the car and was hurrying back under an open umbrella; and the excessively energetic movements of his squat body. bent low under the storm, and the excessively concerned expression on his rain-wet face, reminded her that she was turning her back on André only to go to a man who had been even more foolish and had thereby forced her to a still greater folly. She looked away from these two men who were her enemies, to André's companion, who, she felt, ought to be to some extent her friend, or at least drawn to her by a common belief in moderation, since she was a woman. But it unfortunately happened that the Englishwoman or American, whichever she was, was turning on her a grey-blue stare coarsened by that claim to complete understanding, that abandonment to unreserved condemnation, which human beings will never permit themselves regarding those of whom they know much and rarely regarding those of whom they know little, but which they indulge in without hesitation regarding those of whom they know nothing. It was evident that she had heard about the scene at Le Touquet and was finding an acute pleasure, such as nasty people find in seeing someone extremely drunk, in thinking of Isabelle as a brawling virago.

Isabelle asked herself, "Why should I mind this? I am not a brawling virago. This woman is almost certainly inferior to me. She is more in love with André de Verviers than I ever was, and her clothes are stupid. Why should I care if she thinks me a brawling virago?" But she was obliged to answer herself, "You care because on the facts she is right. You struck a woman in the baccara-room at Le Touquet and screamed accusations at her and your husband. That was an ugly thing to do. If she has not done that, or anything as ugly as that, she has a perfect right to despise you. Most of the hundreds, or it might be thousands, of people who saw or heard of what you did are well within their rights in despising you. The only person who was not within his rights was your husband, who, out of pure idiocy, forced you to make that scene." Pride failed in her like a physical nerve; it was as if humiliation were a kind of stroke. The farewell words she spoke to André were muddled, the movement with which she pushed open the swing door was clumsy.

Marc halted and stared up at her from his umbrella. "But, my God!" he muttered.

"It is only that I am tired," she said. "I am so tired that I feel faint. After all I should not have come out so soon."

"Come, come, my love," he said, and hurried her to the car. When it had started, he put his arms round her, and she did not try to evade them. She had need for shelter, and if she had so arranged her life that the only arms which offered it to her were those which had brought on the calamity from which she required to be shielded, there was no help for it. In resignation she stared into the darkness of his sleeve, and presently felt she might be in a worse place. Marc was very kind. She must not let herself think of what had happened at Le Touquet. It could be done. She had hardly ever let it cross her mind since she had returned to Paris. But she kept on saying again and again, "I am so tired. I am so tired. I want to go to bed. I want to sleep." And Marc answered, "Yes, yes, you need a great deal more rest. I shall go on sleeping in the dressing-room so as not to disturb you."

One evening about a week later she said to Marc, looking up at him from her chaise-longue, "I am sick of cook's cooking, aren't you?"

"It is indeed a little Comédie Française when there are just two of us," agreed Marc.

"Then let us go out for dinner," said Isabelle.

"Nothing would please me more," said Marc. "Is there any particular place you are thinking of?"

"Laurent's," said Isabelle. "It is a place I regard with some affection, since something of importance happened to me there, though at this moment I cannot remember exactly what it was."

"You are the most charming woman in the world," said Marc, "and I will hope to find some way of assisting your memory."

At Laurent's they dined in the open under an orange awning, beside the trellis-wall which hid the sooted tree-trunks and the parched public gardens where they grew, and showed only the eternally, undiscourageably sylvan tree-tops. The distant traffic sounded as rhythmic and as soothing as the waters that fell back into some little pond near by. They ate beef in jelly, flavoured strongly with some country herb, and drank a Rhone wine that tasted

of blackberries. Dusk fell, and a green light flowed out
of the trees and suffused the air and became darkness.
Marc lit a cigar and began one of those conversations
with the wine-waiter which Frenchmen enjoy as Englishmen enjoy talking about cricket. Nothing is learned
thereby. Both parties know before they begin that 1914
and 1917 were good for red bordeaux and nothing remarkable for white, but 1920 was good for both, and
that the last time Harrow beat Eton was in 1908. It is a
refined and allusive way of satisfying the same need that
is met by chewing gum, and it does no harm. Isabelle
rested her elbows on the table and cupped her chin in
her hands, affecting to listen, but actually smiling into
her fingers at the thought that here, on this spot, she
had believed her heart was broken because Laurence
Vernon did not wish to marry her.

"I wonder," said Marc, when he had dismissed the
wine-waiter, "how your friend Laurence Vernon is getting on?"

Her fingers crisped on the table-cloth, and she answered with an indifferent laugh, remembering his mis-
conception of her relations with Laurence, "I wonder."

"You never hear from him?" he asked.

"No, never," she answered. "But then, I wouldn't."

"No, and in any case he would write terrible letters,
full of news, full of information about the health of
aunts, the condition of the canaries. Yes, I am not a vain
man, but I must own I am not surprised that I got you
for myself under his nose."

She made an affectionate murmur.

"Though I have to remember that you have an odd
liking for men who have no marked characteristics," he

went on. "Wasn't Alan Fielding to tea with you again
yesterday?"

"He was," she said, "but do you mind? If you did, I
would never have him to the house again."

"No, no!" he assured her. "Of course, I do not mind.
But it is a little odd that you should care to have him
about you so much. It is like finding bottles all over a
house, to an extent that would justify you in concluding
that the owner was a drunkard, were it not that all the
bottles were of mineral water."

"Superb, superb!" cried Isabelle.

"You mean not so bad," said Marc. "Yes, I feel like
stretching myself and being the possessive male tonight,
I could enjoy fighting somebody for your sake. But a man
like myself, not like Alan Fielding."

"It is a shame that I know nothing of your women,"
she said. "I could say things about them too."

"I am such a gentleman," said Marc. "You will never
know them. Also I should find considerable difficulty in
telling you about them even if I were not, because you
have made them all very vague in my mind."

She said, "Crack me a green almond."

He pressed it between his finger and thumb and
dropped it open on her plate.

"Oh, I don't want to eat it," she said. "I only wanted
to see you do it."

"You will eat it," he said. "You can't do that sort of
thing with me. And you will drink up that cherry
brandy. If you make me order that sort of thing instead
of a decent *fine* or Armagnac, you will stand by the
consequences."

She ate and drank, grumbling a little, while Marc

went on with his cigar. It would be all right now, she
felt, to be his wife again. She would not be afraid of those
embraces which had so often reminded her, as she lay
submerged in their tossing darkness, of the backgrounds
of Delacroix's vaster pictures, of crimson curtains hanging from huge marble pillars whose capitals were lost in
rich opacity, of stacked lances and jewelled and hieratic
helmets, of immense fruits and iridescent serpents.

He said, "How does it go?"

"Very well," she said, sitting back. "I have never felt
more contented than I am here. I feel like a cat in its
basket. I could stay here all night."

"Hein," said Marc.

The dusk became night, and the world became blacker
but less vague. The trees, which by day had been soft
and inarticulated masses of foliage, were now defined by
the starry radiance behind them as far more osseous in
proportion than human beings, possessing a whole system
of skeleton upon skeleton in trunks and branches and
twigs. Fairy-lamps and floodlights put out their beams,
and the restaurant building, which had been bland and
featureless, projected into the electric glare jutting balconies and porches of an unsuspected architectural posi-
tiveness. Everything seen was raised to preternatural
visibility by the surrounding frame of the unseen. The
chestnut leaves that penetrated between the orange awning and the trellis-wall into the sphere of the brightness
cast by the lamp on their table, had apparently no support other than themselves, and they were green with
the bright pigment, not of chlorophyll, but of wet paint,
and looked not like anything calm and vegetable, but like

the petitioning tongues of animals. A blackness and a whiteness that had been inclined towards each other at one of the tables deepest in shadow pushed back their chairs, stood up, and became a man and a woman, and stepped into the light, which illuminated the joy on their faces before their prudence had time to expunge it.

"They are lovers all right," said Marc after the pair had gone past the table.

"And did you see?" said Isabelle. "They were quite old, they were middle-aged."

"Yes, that was good," said Marc.

They lifted their glasses and looked at each other gravely while they drank. "We will go now," he said. "If you wish, that is. Tonight everything happens as you wish it. Tomorrow it will probably be all quite different. But that is how it goes tonight."

"And if I said I wanted to sit here another hour or two, watching you cracking green almonds which I did not want to eat, and then to motor to Chartres to see it by moonlight?" asked Isabelle.

"I should smack your behind," he said and clicked his fingers towards the light for the bill. "And some day you must tell me who it was that told the Americans about Chartres. I suppose it was Pierpont Morgan."

When they were in the automobile, he brought down his mouth on hers, sharply, masterfully, as he had not done since she had come back to Paris, as she had longed for him to do. When he let her go, she sat quite still, steadying her head with her hand, astounded that she could be feeling sick. He brought down his mouth again, lower, on her throat; and she found herself on her knees on the floor of the car. A convulsion had passed through her body that was more violent than any opinion she could have conceived herself holding in regard to Marc, that was like a judgment passed on him by some person inside herself who had no affection for him, who condemned him utterly, who was wiser than she was.

He lifted her tenderly, saying, "What happened then, my dear?"

She stammered, "I hate it when you do that in here. I feel everybody can see us, there is so much glass."

"No one can see in," he said; "you are nervous."

He did not touch her again until he followed her into the little library and found her reading a cable which had awaited her on the Canton enamel dish by the lamp on her desk. Then he put his hands on each side of her waist and asked, "Well, have they fixed the day when the world is coming to an end?"

"Uncle Honoré says that he is quite certain to be coming in September," said Isabelle.

"I am so glad," said Marc. "It will do you so much good to have one of your own people with you. Alas, you poor slaves, you women, who have to settle down in the countries of your masters! I would have gone mad if the way of the world had been the other way round and I had had to move myself to the United States when we were married. Now see what is in that telegram, and then we can go to bed."

She told him, "It is from Blanche Yates. She wants me to go and stay with her in Scotland."

"Why do you not go," he said, "while I am tied here in Paris?"

"I do not want to," she answered shortly.

"My dear, I am not sure that you are well yet," he said. "It might do you good."

"If I go away at all," she said, "I would like to go to Provence, to some quiet place, and swim." She covered her eyes and saw blue-green purifying waters.

"Sit down and we will smoke a cigarette, so that you can grow calmer," he said, kindly. He led her to the biggest chair, stacked up the cushions for her, and sat himself down on the arm. "I know the kind of place you want. A farmhouse coloured red, with lots of grasshoppers, and lots of frogs croaking in the cisterns, and lots of garlic in the aubergines. I am so glad you love the simple things in France. I am so glad I did not marry the kind of American woman who likes only the big things of France, Versailles and Chartres, the châteaux on the Loire. Thank God, I married you, who are exquisite in everything but who like the good simple things. Ah, but I forgot to give you a cigarette."

She said, closing her eyes and trying to smile, "No, I don't want to smoke."

"No, that is not what we want," he said, and bent down and kissed her on the lips: and again that involuntary convulsion ran through her body, utterly rejecting him.

Marc jumped quickly to his feet, and went to sit on the other side of the room. He said, "Do you mind if I have one of those coarse cigarettes I smoke at the works? I know they smell."

She shook her head.

After he had smoked for some moments, he said at

last, "This is not what I had hoped earlier in the evening. I had thought from the way you looked that we were going to be close together again."

He waited for an answer, but Isabelle found she could only shake her head.

"But, yes," he persisted gently, "but, yes. You said nothing, you made no gesture, but you looked soft as a flower, and as if you were waiting. By this time I know a little what you look like at certain times. Pardon me for reminding you, but we used to know each other very well."

The force that had convulsed her body with its rage against him said silently all through her blood, "Before you got drunk and shamed me before the world and killed my child." But she could say none of these things aloud because they were violent.

He asked mildly, "Then you are not going to let me be your lover tonight?"

She muttered, "I am tired."

It seemed as if he were listening to some sound outside the room. "What was that you said?" he asked.

"I am tired," she repeated.

"Ah, forgive me," he said. "I am nòt a fool, and I know that excuse is never true. A woman who loves a man does not refuse herself to him when she is tired. It is then, when there can be no pleasure for her body, that she finds a particular pleasure for her soul in submitting." He watched her face for a long time, as if he longed to see something there which would disprove what she had said; but she now found herself as incapable of moving as she had been of speaking.

He went on, "When a woman says, 'I am tired,' she

means, 'I hate you, the whole thing is finished.' In fact, Isabelle, you find that after all you cannot forgive me."

Isabelle whispered, "That is so."

"I suppose it is the child," he said.

"Yes, my womb hates you," she said. Tears began to flow down her cheeks, but after a moment's effort she found that this did not prevent her from going on talking. "Forgive me for saying that, but it is true."

"You must say whatever is true," he assured her. "We must know how things stand."

The lines on his face reminded her that he had known long and atrocious sufferings from wounds in the war. She murmured, her tears flowing faster, "I would never have come back if I had known, but I thought it was going to be all right."

"Of course you could not tell, you did everything for the best; in the circumstances everything that has happened is most natural," he told her. Suddenly an expression of concern crossed his face, he looked as she had seen him when he had forgotten to leave some necessary instruction to his secretary. He rose, letting his packet of cigarettes fall on the floor, and, without picking them up, went to the door, saying, "I will be back in a minute."

But he did not return for some time. She went to the mirror and looked at her ravaged face. It was no use powdering it, for she could not stop weeping. She went to the window and flung it open, leaning out into the night, and stopped weeping to wonder, because she saw that on the high wall at the end of their garden was reflected not only the small oblong of the window where she stood, but the three broad windows of the drawing-

room on the story above. He must be standing there
with all the lights burning in those chandeliers which
she had thought of as a symbol of domesticity, with the
four eaglets springing away to the four corners of the
globe but held back by gold bands in beauty greater
than free flight. As she looked, the lights went on in
their bedroom, on the story above. He was walking about
the house, filling it with brightness, remembering it as
it had been when they were lovers, pretending that it
was not soon to be deserted. Incredulously she asked herself how she could make another human creature so unhappy. But she knew that it was not in her power to
cancel her repudiation of him. Her body and soul were
closed against him. If she lay in his arms now, she would
not think of curtains and lances, of helmets and serpents;
she would simply say to herself, "By the same violence
my child was killed," and if she saw him commit one of
his great swinging acts of generosity, it would simply
seem to her, "He threw away my child's life just as
easily." For the rest of her life she would stay among
the kind and mild, like Alan Fielding.

When Marc came back, he was quite composed. He
picked up the cigarettes from the floor and said, "It is
strange, the things that come into one's mind at such a
time. I keep on thinking of an Englishwoman I met on
the boat coming over from New York. She was very
attractive, but she was very unhappy on account of some
love-affair that had gone wrong, and for some reason
connected with that, though she gave me the ultimate
privileges quite freely, she would not let me kiss her on
the mouth."

"I can understand a woman doing that," said Isabelle.

"One's body, that might be a matter of money, or pleasure. But one's mouth, that is love."

"Yes, I can understand it now," said Marc, "but what horrifies me is that I made no attempt to understand it then. I was alternately amused and irritated by it. Well, well. You are looking very pale, you know, my dear. I see they have put out a bottle of Chablis for us along with the whisky and soda, you always like that. Won't you have a glass now?"

"Yes, thank you," she said. "You are very kind to me, Marc."

He said, "I am not being kind. I realize I did something frightful to you that cannot be atoned for. Anything I can do for you . . ." He stopped talking and poured out the wine with an agonized exactitude, as if much depended on his not spilling a drop. She rose to take her glass from him, and they sat side by side on the edge of the table, looking down as they sipped.

"It is funny," said Marc. "I keep on thinking of that Englishwoman. You do not mind me speaking of such things at this time, do you?"

"No, no," said Isabelle. "It is right that we should remember that many other people have been unhappy as well as ourselves."

"Yes," he said. "The poor woman was very unhappy." After a long silence, he asked, "Do you want a divorce?"

She whispered, "Yes."

For a long time he continued to take his wine in little painful sips. "But will you not now go to stay with Blanche Yates?" he asked abruptly. "After all, she is your oldest friend!"

"No, no!" she exclaimed. "I could not bear it. I will go South."

"Listen," he said, "a storm has begun."

They sat for some moments, thoughtfully drinking the wine they did not taste, while the rain lashed the panes. He asked her again, "You are sure you want a divorce?"

"What else is there to do?" she answered. She was astonished to find how profusely she wept, considering she was not thinking of the child, but only of him and her. As soon as she could speak again, she repeated firmly, "What else is there to do?"

XII

AT HALF-PAST two in the morning Isabelle had not slept, so she took three of the tablets the German doctor had given her, and in consequence she did not wake until after ten. She sat up in bed and cried out to her maid, "But, Adrienne, you let me sleep so late! Monsieur must have gone to the works long ago!" Yet she had no idea why she wished she had seen him before he went, and when the maid brought a note which Marc had left to be given to her with her coffee, she did not want to read it. She held open the envelope and peered inside trying to see a phrase which would indicate the quality of the whole, before she dared to take out the letter. It was, however, only to say that he would return earlier than usual in the evening, so that they might settle the ways and means of their parting, and that she could rely on him to consider her convenience in everything. At the thought of how many tedious discussions of this sort there would have to be before they were free, she burst into tears. She believed that under the Code Napoléon she had rights over Marc's property which she would have to take a great deal of trouble to renounce, but it was not that which had broken her nerves, it was the amount of time and energy she would have to expend in detaching her personal possessions from Marc's, both here in Paris and out at the house in the valley of the Chevreuse. She would have liked simply to abandon them, and refit herself in America, or England, or wherever it was she would make her new home; but that would not have been fair to Marc, who would then have to clear them out himself. And there would be so much to clear up. The marriage with Roy had left hardly any debris: only their furniture, which she had sold without regret since it had all been chosen for them by an interior decorator as they were too busy travelling from airport to airport to do it themselves, and his flying equipment and library, which she had distributed among his friends. But while she was with Marc, she had bought an infinity of things, books, pictures, silly little bibelots that might amuse children, contemporary records that would be amusing to look over forty years hence. She would never have the strength or the fortitude to winnow what she had designed to be the setting for her whole lifetime.

Adrienne came back into the room, leaving the door half open and saying doubtfully, "Madame Élise is here to fit those new chemises. Shall I tell her to go away?"

"Why should you tell her to go away?" asked Isabelle, blowing her nose.

"I thought you were not very well, Madame," said Adrienne.

"I have a slight cold," said Isabelle, "but, as the room is warm, that need not prevent me trying on chemises. Are you there, Madame Élise? Come in, come in."

"Good morning, Madame," said Madame Élise, whipping in through the doorway with the sinister little black

box, resembling a child's coffin, in which the makers of
women's underclothing always carry their wares, as if
they were trying to cheat some supernal eye into believing that they were hurrying about the streets of Paris
on one of the gloomier kinds of good work. "How beautiful you are looking this morning, Madame! And what
an exquisite bedroom this is! None of my other clients
has such a chic bedroom."

"You are a humbug," said Isabelle, stepping out of
bed. "I am sure you say that to every single client you
visit. But you are very nice, and you are so pretty that
it is extraordinary you should be going about selling
underclothes to other women not so pretty as yourself,
and I hope the children are well. Now we will try on the
chemises, and find out that, as usual, you have made the
shoulder-straps too long."

"They will be perfect," said Madame Élise. "These
will be perfect. It's a good thing I saw you in this nightdress, Madame, I see the tucks at the neck need redoing.
She wasn't good, the girl I had that did these night
dresses. What, are my fingers cold?"

"Not at all," said Isabelle.

"But you are shuddering, Madame," said Élise.

"Madame is not quite herself yet," said Adrienne.

"She is certainly thinner," said Élise. "Madame
should go to Bad Garbrück in the Tirol, the season's not
over yet. All my clients who go there come back feeling
marvellous."

"What do you have to do there?" asked Adrienne.

"Oh, it's the mildest cure you can think of," said
Élise. "You don't drink any waters, or eat any filthy
rusks, or walk up any hills. You just take a bath in the

radium springs for ten minutes every morning and that rejuvenates you."

"Ah, in France we are more matter of fact," said Adrienne. "Our spas set out to do good in any ordinary way for particular organs. You go to Vichy to clean out your kidneys, and to Aix to clean out your liver. But an Austrian spa, that would be bound to be a little bit like a fairy-tale."

"But there's some sense in it," said Élise. "You should see Madame Justin de Bonétat when she's come back from there. You'd think she was thirty, and she'll never see forty-five again."

"Ah, but that's a special case," said Adrienne. "Nothing's ever happened to her, as we all know. That leaves a woman always like a young girl."

"I don't believe that has anything to do with the case," said Élise. "Look at Madame de Saint-Bernasche, she's another one of the same sort, you'd think her twenty years younger than her age, and she's got several children, though, as the whole world can tell, not so many as she might have had. Madame, it's too mortifying, but about these last two chemises, you are perfectly right. The first two were perfect, they couldn't have been better, but these two, it's no use trying to hide the truth, they need just the breath of a centimetre over the shoulder-straps."

"Madame Élise, you are the most tiresome of creatures," said Isabelle.

"That I am not," said Élise, "for I can sit down and alter them in a couple of minutes, and it's your fault because you have too beautiful a figure. I haven't another client whose bosom is so high."

"You lie, Madame Élise," said Isabelle. "You make for Madame Emil Sarrach, and she has a figure exactly like mine, we could go to each other's fittings. Anyway I am going to get back into bed till you are ready. But don't bother about me, I am feeling perfectly well."

"How's your husband?" Adrienne asked Élise.

"Not so good, not so bad," said Élise.

"Is he still so insane about politics?"

"Ah, no, he's beginning to see through the leaders," said Élise. "He sees that the workers are being betrayed all right. You should have heard him going on after Achille Clairon's speech in the Chamber last Thursday."

"I didn't read it," said Adrienne. "They were quarrelling about it downstairs on Friday, but some said one thing and some said another, I couldn't make out what it was all about."

"Well, it shouldn't have been made at all," said Élise. "He's a fine one to speak for the people."

"Why, he's of the people, isn't he?" said Adrienne. "I was at a place once where one of the footmen said he was related to him. They came from the Dordogne, I think it was."

"It isn't where you come from, it's what you do afterwards," said Élise. "You know that rez-de-chaussée flat, the Duchesse de Campierre's house in the Avenue Montaigne? It's supposed to be let, you know, and that's what the Duke thinks, but I've had two of my clients go after it, and each time they've been told that somebody's just about to take it, and that they can't even see over it. Well, that's where Monsieur Achille Clairon has his hideaway. He doesn't waste much time in that humble little apartment at Ménilmontant we've all heard so much about. He's been the Duchess's lover for a year. So, you see, that's a fine one to speak for the people."

"Madame Élise! Madame Élise!" exclaimed Isabelle, who had suddenly caught a name which was familiar to her and had begun to listen to what they were saying. She pulled down the sheet with which she had been covering her face, and leaned up on her elbows. "You must not tell such stories! I know the Duchesse de Campierre very well, and she is the most serious of women. There cannot be a word of truth in what you say. They may be friends, that is all."

"Ah, but I know it as if I had seen it with my own eyes," said Élise. "Lovers have to have their washing done like anybody else, and I know the laundress who works for the house, and she takes a full set of household linen from the rez-de-chaussée, which shows that somebody's living there, and she is always finding among the sheets and table-cloths, shirts marked with Monsieur Clairon's name. That may be friendship, but it's of an extreme form."

"But it is not possible," said Isabelle, "you cannot think how good a woman the Duchess is. You really must not spread such a story."

"But I have said nothing to suggest that she is not good," said Élise. "After all the Duke is twenty-five years older than she is, and Monsieur Clairon is a very distinguished man, and quite passable to look at. There would be nothing perverse about such an affair. But really, Madame, I'm certain of what I say. For just consider, Madame! All her life the Duchess has had her hair done at home, by a very old maid that she inherited from her mother, that's why she always looked

like a friend of King Edward the Seventh. Why does she
now have her hair set three times a week by one of the
best assistants of Monsieur Padoue?"

"But how can you possibly know all this?" protested
Isabelle.

"Because the assistant told me himself," said Élise.
"He is a charming young man, called Claude Issot, not
at all the same as most of Monsieur Padoue's assistants, I
can assure you; his tastes are not at all of that sort."

"Oh, Madame Élise, you are formidable!" sighed Isabelle.

"Shall I try on this chemise before I alter the other,"
asked Élise, "or shall I go on with the other and shall we
try them both on together at the end?"

"Go on with the other," said Isabelle. "There is
something I want to do. Adrienne, give me my dressing-
gown."

She went into Marc's room and sat down on his bed.
She was aware that in Paris one could do anything one
liked in complete secrecy, provided only that one did not
mind everybody in the world knowing what one was doing; that it was impossible for any amorous or political
or financial association between important people, however carefully they might conceal it from their own kind,
not to come at some point under the observation of
some member of a vast confraternity of concierges, laun-
dresses, hairdressers, florists, telephone operators, mes-
sengers, and servants, which was here far more united
and powerful than such confraternities in other capitals,
because it read the papers intelligently, was less divided
by a sense of social differences among itself, and found
satire its natural means of expression. This meant that

only rarely did a scandal break with a shock on **Paris,**
however much it might startle the husbands, wives,
fellow-ministers, or business partners of the intriguers.
It gradually emerged into the common consciousness, as
a coral reef is lifted above the waters by the efforts of
individually insignificant but innumerable and tireless
workers. His friends would not be surprised when Marc
and she separated. They would have learned it long ago,
through Adrienne, through Élise, through the Duchesse
de Campierre's laundress, through Monsieur Claude Issot. Their attitudes, whether they were approving or
disapproving, would have been so long considered that
they would present no element of shock. The trouble in
every such affair came later, when it was sufficiently established in fact to become the subject of journalistic
comment. There then broke out those satanic intellectual
exercises which proved that the French genius was too
universal, since coprophilists, who in other countries
timidly attempt to smear the world with small portions
of filth and are hustled into lunatic asylums, here use
their vice as an artistic medium and turn the whole
world into filth by the magic of superb prose. She shuddered to think of the atrocious verbal martyrdom to
which Angèle de Campierre and Achille Clairon, Marc
and she, alike were doomed.

Isabelle knew she would be jeered at as yet another
American heiress who had forced her way into
a French home and had proved unable to maintain its
standards of decorum; and all Marc's enemies who hated
him because he was not sufficiently to the Right would
join with those who hated him because he was not
sufficiently to the Left, in order to revive the charges of

dangerous publicity which had been brought against him first over his gambling. Only because their divorce was entirely necessary for the well-being of both of them could she endure to bring such an ordeal on either Marc or herself; and she had felt the most acute anguish as she lay on her bed, trying to prefigure at what point her story would be betrayed to Adrienne and Élise, to the laundress and Monsieur Claude Issot, and it occurred to her that their acute intelligences would probably begin to work when Marc removed her photographs from his room. He had an inordinate number of them, because he liked to take snapshots of her and have them enlarged, usually to an excessive size. It was unthinkable that he should want to go on sleeping in a room with twelve or fourteen large representations of her. Sooner or later he would throw them into a drawer, and Adrienne and Élise, the laundress and Monsieur Claude Issot, would set in motion the spoken words that would in course of time rot into the vile printed words which even the bravest must fear. Her heart began to beat very fast. She could not bear to think of this moment of betrayal although, if it did not come in this form, it would certainly come in another; and it occurred to her that she might collect them now under the pretext of having them put into new frames of a kind which she had lately heard him admire.

She went about the room, taking them from the walls and the tables: the one of her when she was still at Miss Pence's school; the one of her when she came to Paris for the first time to go to the Sorbonne—she had never been able to think why he liked them so, for in both she was a starched and leggy child, with the pasteurized look

of a wealthy orphan; the one they got from a newspaper, at the garden-party at Rambouillet, bending down
over a group of short and plump official wives like a
civilly condescending giraffe—it was perhaps a sign how
little they were really suited to one another that he
should be without any sense whether a photograph
showed her at her best or at her worst. On his dressing-
table stood the one which showed her in her wedding-
gown; but that her outstretched hand did not reach.
There lay in front of it, on a sheet of foolscap, a heap of
crystal and metal fragments. They were large enough
for her to recognize them as the ruins of Marc's favourite clock, which always stood on the table beside his
bed. She drew the tip of her forefinger along her lips.
She did not believe this had happened by accident. Marc's
bedside table had to be exceptionally broad and deep to
carry the mass of papers and technical books he brought
back from the office, the bottles of mineral water he liked
to drink in great gorging draughts when he woke for a
minute, the cigarettes, the many small objects—such as
wooden dogs, a pocket adding-machine, or a tiny cactus
—which he collected during the course of the day; and
she was aware of his tendency to express rage and misery
by throwing things on the floor, though he was careful
not to give way to it in her presence. She put down the
photographs and began to pick up and lay down again
the metal wheels and springs, the small bright jewels,
the broken arcs of thick crystal. Marc must have stayed
awake longer than she did, for the breaking of the clock
must have made a considerable noise, and she had heard
nothing.

The door flew open and Marc's valet came in, whistling and carrying a tray of clean linen. "Ah, pardon, Madame," he said, and by something too kind in his greeting, too concentrated in the attention with which he laid his tray on a chair and began sorting out the shirts from the vests, Isabelle knew that she must be looking agitated.

Steadying her voice, she said, "It isn't like you, Marcel, to leave this rubbish about. Yes, what's left of the clock. It looks untidy."

"It does indeed, Madame," answered the valet. He was a great rogue, with an unctuous manner of agreement. "But what am I to do? Monsieur forgot to telephone to me about it. He said it was given to him by Monsieur Dompeyre at the works, and that he would inquire of him whether he got it here in Paris or in Switzerland, and that he would ring me up as soon as he knew, so that I could send the firm the pieces, for them to identify it and send him one just like it. But he forgot, and I'm just leaving them here, hoping he'll remember it today, for though this is a big house and nothing is lacking, Madame, there is no sense in my packing those pieces as I would had they to go to Switzerland, if all I have to do is to take them round the corner. String and cardboard and sealing-wax are cheap, I know, but there's no sense in waste."

"You are admirable, Marcel," said Isabelle, understanding him perfectly. Actually he meant that he would not be deflected by his duties from his prosecution of intricate personal relationship among the female members of the staff till the last possible moment. But the ring of

one of his phrases echoed in her ear and puzzled her.
"What do you mean : you hope Monsieur will remember
today?" she asked.

"Well, he forgot yesterday," said the valet. "But then
we all know how busy Monsieur is. If he wasn't another
Napoleon, he'd never be able to remember anything."

"But wasn't this clock broken last night?" asked Isabelle.

"Oh, no, Madame," answered the valet. "You know
what Monsieur is, how quite like Napoleon. He had arranged to ring up Monsieur Delnomdedieu, who always
leaves home at nine, and he left it till ten to, by this
clock, and then he found Monsieur Delnomdedieu had
gone and that the clock was a quarter of an hour slow,
so he threw it on the floor. Ah, these great men, they're
all alike, they all have their little ways."

Isabelle picked up the photographs from the dressing-
table and the others from the writing-table, the mantelpiece, the wall between the windows, and went out of the
room. In the passage she stood still for a minute, murmuring to herself, "What insupportable behaviour! Of
course I am right to go. As we got older, it would become too degrading. Nothing would ever be safe." At
the door of her room she came to an abrupt halt, aware
that Adrienne and Élise had turned on her faces which
ominously indicated that they found her appearance
even more interesting than their conversation; and she
realized that she had almost certainly precipitated the
moment she had hoped to delay by entering with her
face drawn in disgust and her arms full of her own
photographs, which she had removed from her husband's room. For an instant she felt abandoned by the

whole world, including destiny. She would have liked to throw the photographs on the floor and sit down among the shattered glass with her head on her knees and cry. Nobody cared for her, the only person who could ever have really belonged to her had been taken from her by a violent and uncalled-for act of cruelty, she was somebody who was doomed to blunder and be watched by people who were without tenderness for her.

She put down the photographs neatly on her writing-table and said, "Adrienne, we must send these photographs to be reframed. Monsieur has suddenly got a craze to have them all set in shagreen."

"In shagreen?" said Adrienne. "That seems not quite the right material for Monsieur's room, which could not be more masculine."

"In shagreen," said Isabelle firmly. "He saw some photographs at Monsieur Delnomdedieu's that had been framed in shagreen, and they pleased him enormously. You must send them off to Cartier's this afternoon." She would pay the bill and order them to be destroyed before she left the country. The desolation of that voyage, even if it were only over to Dover, brought tears to her eyes, and she walked past the two women into her bathroom.

"Madame, wait a moment, the telephone," said Adrienne.

"I do not want to speak to anybody," said Isabelle, keeping straight on towards the bathroom. But the wing-sleeve of her dressing-gown caught on the back of a chair and ripped from hem to shoulder, and she cried out, "Oh, God! Oh, God!" She leaned over the chair and began to weep in harsh and painful sobs.

"Oh, Madame, lie down on your bed! Allo! Allo!"

said Adrienne. "Madame, you are not yourself yet! Mademoiselle, j'écoute, j'écoute!"

"Oh, Madame, you must sit down!" said Élise, putting her arms about Isabelle and drawing her into the chair. "And you should go back to the country. One doesn't get over a bad illness in a day, you know."

"Give her a glass of water," said Adrienne. "Allo! Allo!" Her face expressed the kindliest concern for her mistress, but her hands were crooked avidly round the telephone, and it could be seen that she could not bear to detach herself from the instrument, lest the identity of the caller should give her a clue to the situation. She was physically agitated from side to side by this conflict between her heart and her head. Isabelle, seeing this, burst into laughter, and Adrienne, swaying even more violently, cried out, "Quick, quick! A glass of water, I said! And some eau de carmes!"

"No, no," said Isabelle, "I may be ill, but I am not hysterical. I am only being amused."

"Yes, yes," said Élise, "but we have each our own way of being hysterical. Madame, I beg you to go back to your bed."

"It is Mr. Fielding," said Adrienne triumphantly. "It is Mr. Fielding," she repeated mournfully. It was evident that she was gratified to find that certain suspicions she had formed were correct, but doubted whether she ought to feel such gratification while her mistress was so troubled.

"Oh, what does it all matter? What is the good?" exclaimed Isabelle. "Yes, I will speak to him." His voice came to her from the distance with its peculiar and pleasant quality, like a freshet of clear water, and she cried gaily, before the women had time to leave the room, "Ah, yes, what a good idea! I should like nothing better than to come out and see your house today! Yes, come and call for me in your car, I prefer little cars, and I can eat anything for lunch. Yes, I will be ready in half an hour—no, three-quarters."

When Isabelle looked over the banisters and saw Alan Fielding walking up and down the hall, she felt as if he had come to let her out of prison. The flash of his smile was like the brightness of a key that could unlock the heavy doors which shut her in with waste and violence and uncertainty. When they crossed the pavement to his automobile, she wished that they were living in a ballet, so that she could dance and spread out her skirts against the wind which, having driven plump golden clouds across the sky all morning, had suddenly dropped to the level of the town and was romping through the streets like a boisterous country visitor. It was not credible that she should feel so well and happy so soon after she had been despairing and hysterical; and her content ment endured, it was evidently not merely the effect of getting out of the house. In the Bois de Boulogne it would not have surprised her if the people rowing on the lakes and walking on their shores had all known each other and assembled with some common festive purpose which they would all at once declare by waving across the fretted silver waters and bursting into song; and the couples sitting under the trees, although their attitudes expressed fatigue at least as often as affection, and the leaves and grass were grey with dust, and the sun had gone behind a cloud, made pictures of the eternal harmlessness of the human race, which co-exists with

the eternal harmfulness, and may be sought everywhere in vain during the working hours of man, but
discloses itself in all its inefficacious innocence and gaiety
whenever a holiday has been granted. Isabelle was about
to ask Alan if he did not notice a special cheerfulness
about the day, when she reflected that that might perhaps not be wise.

As they raced along by the river, Alan Fielding said,
"My luck's been rather good. I got you to come out here
and have lunch with me because the day looked fine, and
now it isn't going to be fine at all, it just stayed clear
long enough to give me my chance."

It was pleasant to sit beside this easy-tempered man
while he spun the speed out of his automobile like a silk
thread. She began to sing softly to herself. A lorry held
them up, and they waited a few moments outside an
absurd house, built perhaps seventy or eighty years ago,
when a Swiss chalet was considered a romantic object.
Its garden was precise yet rank, too thickly crowded with
trees and bushes and plants, though well tended. The
wistaria which covered the balconies had been neatly
pruned, but by somebody who liked it to grow in a thick
mat, even though it kept the light from the windows it
overhung; and the front door and jalousies had been
painted a dark malachite green, a colour too portentous
for such domestic use. On the steps leading up to the
house a woman stood, dressed in a full-skirted grey silk
dress, older than her age, and carrying an old-fashioned
parasol, and gave orders with a slightly pompous gesture
of her ringed hand to a gardener who looked excessively
rural, like a servant one might expect to find in some
ancient but poverty-stricken château in the Auvergne,

who really might have been asked to smarten up considering he was so near Paris. If some chance led one to live in that house as it was, with the same people inhabiting it, one's whole destiny would be changed, so established was its presiding spirit of stately, voluntary stupidity, of proud self-confinement within minute picturesque limits. She laughed to think what a romantic idiot one would be. But one would have an entirely different destiny if one crossed the road and went to live in the small pink house opposite, which the house agents would have described as *villa coquette*. There a pretty housemaid stood on a balcony crowded with geraniums, the wind blowing through her fair hair, and struck a birdcage with her forefinger to make the canaries sing. That was all that any woman would ever be able to do in that house, to stand on the balcony and let the wind blow through her hair and make the canaries sing. In fact a different destiny waited for one in every house in the world. One had only to seize one's opportunity to leave the wrong house. One had only to wait for the opportunity that would lead to the right house. Life could not be as simple as that, but the charming quality of the morning made her believe that it was.

But she felt that she was neglecting Alan in her private satisfactions and must make conversation with him. She found herself asking, "What is your house like?"

"You will see in a minute," he answered, "though it won't be looking its best as it is going to rain any minute now. That's a pity because I want you to like it, since I hope to live there all my life."

"All your life!" she exclaimed. "I had no idea this

was such a serious enterprise, I thought it was probably some place you had taken for the summer."

"No," he said. "It's more than that." His voice grew grave, and that slight sickness came over her which she always felt when a doctor said he must give her a hypodermic injection, or when a friend announced an intention to admit her to some special intimacy. But that passed immediately; she liked him very much. She listened attentively as he told her that he had bought this house three years before, when he had quarrelled with his family in England and decided to live in France, and that he had chosen this particular house for reasons which he would explain when they arrived there.

"But what other reason need you have had for buying this house," she asked, as she stepped out of the automobile, "than that it is one of the nicest houses in the world?"

"If I were a Spaniard or a Chinee," he said, "I would just be being polite and would not really mean it when I said that it was yours if you wanted it."

She took off her hat and walked up and down in front of the house, looking at the good weathered stone, the wide windows, the broad-browed gables. The place had been built in the late seventeenth century, to be a little grander than a farm; but it had still the essential character of a farm, the hardy roughness of sacking, the useful simplicity of a preserving-pan, the tested adaptability to human needs of the handles to a plough. The grandeur lay in nothing material, but was an emanation from the minds of the builders, who had worked in a calm that had permitted them to choose out of all possible proportions those which would make a house

built on this plot of ground, of these materials, most
spacious and most lasting, and would show its qualities
to the eye, so that those within it would feel uncongested
and unhurried and would begin at leisure plans not to
be accomplished under a generation or two. She stood
smoothing her hair and smiling through narrowed eyes
at the façade, but she was infinitely and unreasonably
troubled by the perfection of the place, by its exact correspondence to her ideal. She wished that this had been
a house belonging to strangers which they had chanced
to see as they drove by on their way to lunch at an inn
that would mean nothing to them. For so long as she
could, she lingered in the garden, exclaiming at the
beauty of the rich and sober stonework, of the solid
walnut door, of the old tamarisk trees which half-hid the
mossed stone tiles of the outhouses with the dry green
foam of their foliage, the dry flushed foam of their
flowers. But she saw a servant watching her from a
kitchen window, a plain woman with a face as hardy and
simple and serviceable as the house, whose tired yet clear
eyes gave the visitor the benign range of her attention
while her hands continued tensely with the more important business of scraping some carrots. Suddenly Isabelle
felt ashamed of all her evasions, her curvettings, her
runnings to and fro and up and down, her freedom from
any determination by necessity.

She said timidly to Alan, "Yes, now I want to go in."
But when they were inside, she felt again troubled and
embarrassed, as if there was a threat in the exact correspondence between what she had always wanted her
house to be like, and these well-shaped rooms, full of
sound and not costly provincial French furniture. When

Alan bade her come to the window of the living-room
and look out at his orchard and its boughs burdened
with apples, and feel the thickness of the walls, which
kept the house warm in winter and cool in summer, she
felt a little sick, as if presently she would be called into
a court of law to give testimony before a great audience
on some vital matter. She murmured an expression of
interest, and turned away as if to look at the room again.
On the two walls where there were no windows there
hung two Louis Quatorze mirrors giving back the green
light of France which filtered through the orchard
boughs, and on a table beneath them stood crystal beakers
holding tree anemones, pale pink, like sugar almonds;
and on a tray there were two wine-glasses and a decanter
etched with the bees of Empire. She covered her eyes
with her hand, not before it occurred to her how appropriate this gentle brilliance of old glass was to Alan, to
his smile, which was without reservations, like a child's,
to his fresh voice, to the unclouded translucence of his
pleasantness. Her conviction of his extreme worth affected her most disagreeably. She sat down on a sofa,
her head aching a little at the temples, and gooseflesh
running over her body.

"Are you cold?" asked Alan. "You're shivering.
Would you like a fire?"

She answered, "No, no. It is lovely in here. But you
are a curious person. You came into the house, and the
post had come since you left, so there were several letters lying on the table by the door. And you did not stop
to look at one of them. That seems to me an inhuman
lack of curiosity."

She had hoped this would make him go out and look

at the letters, so that she would have time to control this
disorder of her nerves, which was idiotic since she was no
longer sixteen. But he answered, "Why should I look at
my letters? The only letter which could interest me
would be one from you. And I conclude you haven't
written to me, as you haven't said so." Again a shiver
ran through her; she realized that, like Marc, he belonged to the class of men who feel an obligation to
speak the truth to women. At this moment she would
have preferred him to belong to the same class as André
de Verviers, who regarded a lie to a woman as having a
value quite apart from the purpose it served in persuading her to any particular act, as being in itself a
sexual triumph and even a mystically rejuvenating rite.
For if he had been like that, it would have been good
sense to leave him and go on her way.

Alan said, "Anyway have some sherry. You look pale.
Maybe I should not have asked you to come here when
you're not properly well yet."

Isabelle drank, and felt instantly a little drunk. The
light in the room appeared to have become greener, and
to gleam like old glass. As a patient going under an
anæsthetic feels an urgent impatience that the doctors
should get on with the operation, however much it has
been feared till then, so she longed for him to fulfil his
threat of telling her what he was really like and get it
over. She looked up at him and said, "You were going to
explain why you bought this house."

As she listened to him, she kept on raising her glass to
her lips, so that he should think there were still a few
drops for her to drink. For if he offered her any more
sherry, she would not be able to refuse, since all her

instinct at this moment was to comply. What she wanted was someone to tell her what to do; if she could have chosen a miracle to clarify her life, it would have taken the form of a series of orders which, when she had obeyed them all implicitly, would have turned out to be a rule imposing rightness on all departments of her being, so that no blunder, like her marriage to Marc, like the loss of her child, could ever shame her again. So much did she want this that she feared to make any gesture of resistance, lest she not be ready to submit when the word of command came. But if she drank any more sherry, she would put down her head on the sofa and weep, because every word Alan Fielding spoke made it plainer that she ought to make a certain decision, for which she was not yet prepared, which made her feel excited and exhausted. For he was telling her that he was the same sort of person as herself, and that he had come to live in this house because he wanted to detach himself from the life of his rich family, which seemed to him vulgar and brutal. She had often heard him utter expressions of disgust regarding certain persons and places, but she had taken them as examples of the trick of denigration characteristic of his class, which made all young men like him complain of whatever party they had attended on the previous night, as if it had been some sort of tedious accident, like being imprisoned in a lift. Now he was making her understand that they proceeded from a hungry fastidiousness like her own. He wanted, he was saying, life to have a moral beginning and middle and end. He wanted to form part of a pattern. The confidence with which he was telling her this, plainly a slow agony to his natural reserve, proved all the assurances he had made her that his feelings for her were of the utmost seriousness. If she indeed wanted a husband with whom she could live in dignity and peace while she brought into the world children who would be heirs to honour, she had no need to travel further. It was true, what she had thought as she drove here, that a different destiny waited for one in every house; and in this house waited the destiny she desired.

She said to herself, "There is no hurry." But she had to bend her lips again to the empty glass, so that Alan should not see her shiver. That was of course not true. There was every reason for hurry. She could not believe that Marc would let her leave him as quietly as he had promised last night. A tingling of her nerves warned her that the violence and disorder which had killed her child was certain to break out again and that she might at any moment be the victim of some humiliating attempt to constrain her freedom of movement. But, as soon as she thought that, she realized that she did not believe it. She was afraid of something like that, but slightly different. It occurred to her that perhaps what she feared was that any such attack might appeal to something violent and disorderly in herself such as had made her weep that morning, which might make her want to go back to Marc. She put her hand to her head, amazed that she should be vexed by any such wild imagination; nothing was more impossible than that she should ever want to go back to Marc. But in any case, whether she had Marc or herself to fear, she would be immensely safer if she could declare that she intended to marry Alan.

"Nevertheless, this is a little too much," she thought,

"I am not yet twenty-eight, and this man will be my third husband and my fourth lover." She was aware, however, that in making this objection she was insincerely subscribing to the fiction that sexual relations, while obviously offering certain satisfactions, are so inherently disagreeable that persons of fine taste, especially women, are obliged to treat them with that remote precaution which they apply to garlic, which they will never suffer to appear undisguised on their tables, but which they will rub on a crust of bread, which they will rub round a salad-bowl, out of which they will eventually eat a salad. But Isabelle knew quite well that she did not find sexual relations disagreeable. They might be so, of course, if they took place between persons of poor physique and character, who were not united by affection, but she had no intention of attempting them in those conditions. Alan was splendidly made, he was full of tenderness, she had grown very fond of him during the summer; if there would be no ecstasy at her bridal, there would be ecstasy at the birth of her children. She saw no reason to ward off such an experience. It was absurd that she should be filled with such a strong desire to run out of the house; but she was feeling better. She put down her glass and smiled at Alan.

"That silly little bell meant that lunch is ready," he told her. In the dining-room too, the light came green through the apple-boughs and shone back from good glass. "I don't know that the food's very good," he said as they sat down at the table. "I've only three servants to run the whole place, a man and his wife and this girl who's waiting on us, their daughter. I don't want more servants than I can really get friendly with and feel responsible for. I do hate that rabble of servants we had at home, half of whom you didn't know, and half of whom you knew too well, so that, as they haven't the live-and-let-live of equals, they laugh at you behind your back and cringe to your face."

She said, "I know," and thought of Adrienne and Élise, of the laundress and Monsieur Claude Issot. Her face became convulsed as she thought how badly Marc would fare at the hands of the caricaturists if the tide of scandal flowed so far. She asked quickly, "How did you first start thinking of things like this? How did you first get discontented with the way you lived?"

"It was living in the shadow of my grandmother, I think," said Alan. "She was the famous Marchioness of Nunchester. I can't tell you how horrible she was."

"I've seen portraits of her," said Isabelle.

"I bet you have," said Alan. "Thousands, and all vilely flattering."

"So are mine," said Isabelle.

"No, they're not," said Alan. "They make you infinitely less beautiful than you are. But you're right. They did fake you in an attempt to do you proud. They try to make you the maximum achievement of the prevailing fashion."

"I hate it," she said. "I hate it. It would be such bad training for me if that were what I wanted. I'd be told I had succeeded where I hadn't."

"Don't I know it," said Alan. "Over in England the most exclusive galleries gave me shows when I didn't know the first thing about painting, just because all my own lot could be depended on to turn up and behave as if I were a real painter."

"By the way, are any of these pictures yours?" asked Isabelle.

"I say, that is nice of you," said Alan. "You're a polite child. No, they're not. That's a Derain, and that's a Picasso, and that's a Dufresne. My own efforts I keep up in the studio, on the top floor, I'll show them to you afterwards. But to go on about my grandmother. She was utterly awful just for this very reason that we've been talking about. She'd been flattered all her life, not only by painters, but by everybody. She was revoltingly rich in her own right, and all her life she'd never had the smallest discipline. I don't think she did drink, but she looked exactly as if she did. Her face was swollen and bloated with getting her own way and never exercising any self-control."

"It stands to reason that that is what would happen to one if one went on till one was old," said Isabelle. "It makes life one long debauch of vanity. But didn't having children do her any good?"

"Why should it?" said Alan. "She had the physique of a Guard's sergeant-major, and the minute they were born they were handed over to Nannies. After that she judged them on their points. If the girls married well, they scored, and if they didn't, they were out; and if the sons did well in politics or the services they scored, and none of them dared do anything else. My own father was a huge success, he's a general and he's always being terribly worried about India in the very best company. No really first-class publisher would accept a diary unless it had at least one entry running, 'Met Fitz Fielding, he thinks the news from India very grave.' No, I don't think the mere physical act of maternity could have done anything to her. Why should it? It's not having children that's good for people, it's the way they live with them."

"Yes," said Isabelle.

"But I've theories about that," he went on. "I think it is a disgrace and not a merit to have children unless you bring them up not to grab and lose their tempers and smash things."

"Yes, yes," said Isabelle.

"Well, to get back to old Agatha. She was the nightmare of my life when I was a child. We had to spend at least three months down at Gormont House every year, and I hated it from the time I could notice things. She bullied the servants, she bullied her family, she bullied her guests. I shall never forget how one June Sunday at luncheon she carefully waited till there was a hush in the conversation, and then leaned forward and very coldly and clearly insulted a girl of seventeen about the way she was eating some strawberries. 'You will either stop eating those strawberries in that disgusting manner or leave the table.' God, I can hear her saying it, and see the tears rolling down the girl's cheeks. There was nothing in it of course, the girl was eating her strawberries in some perfectly normal way. It was just the old elephant trumpeting."

"One can fight that sort of woman," said Isabelle. "But it is so bad for one to do it. One learns her kind of technique, and there's no sort of external discipline working on one to make one use it for civilized purposes. The victory is simply to the strong. It's an overwhelming temptation to become a brute oneself."

"Yes, you could be pretty fierce," said Alan.

"I know," said Isabelle. "But why do you say that? Does it show?"

"No, not at all," said Alan. "I only know it because once or twice at Le Touquet I saw that Poots woman limping away held together with bandages. But that was holy work, of course. You were superb."

"Go on telling me about your grandmother," said Isabelle.

"Well, she was horrible," said Alan, "and it wasn't any delusion of mine, due to family feeling, though she was foul to my mother, simply because she wasn't strong. I proved she really was horrible by looking into her public record, after I grew up. God, that woman! She owned some mines in the North and she fought several strikes there thirty and forty years ago. I read the reports of them, and you wouldn't believe the cruelty and callousness and above all the greed of the woman. You'd have thought she was fighting for her last crust, not the miners', from the way she carried on."

"If the poor ever feel poor as the rich do," said Isabelle, "we will have a most bloody revolution."

"But there was a kind of spiritual edge, a kind of sharpened vileness superadded to the blunt brutality. She was an anti-suffragist, of course, but she got elected to everything she could, just so that she could have more people to bully, and, by God, the worms elected her, though she had no sort of claim to competence."

"Wasn't she able?" asked Isabelle. "There's always a pretence that that sort of woman is."

"Not a bit. She kept the estate solvent, but only by meanness," said Alan. "She shot expenses down by gypping everybody. But I don't think there's any record of

her ever having to make a decision and making it right.
Well, once she got elected to some Council or other that
had to appoint nurses who had to go round and look
after children in the slums, and there was some talk of
raising the wages of these women, who must have a dog's
life anyway, and give them ninety pounds a year instead
of eighty. Do you know that that old ghoul had the ice
to get up and say that if they raised the wages they
would no longer get women with the missionary spirit!"

"I tell you, money is a poison," said Isabelle. "Only
wealth or some toxic condition like alcoholism could degenerate the brain to that degree. But, tell me, did you
ever have a quarrel with this gorgon?"

"No, I didn't," said Alan, "because all the time she
was alive I wasn't sure. Everybody said, 'Isn't old Agatha
marvellous?' and carried on as if they liked it. I had a
queer divided sort of feeling about her. She always had
a morbid fascination for me. I used to stare at her for
hours; she was gorgeous in a way, rather like Turner's
picture of the Fighting Temeraire being towed to its last
home. As a matter of fact, since I've grown up, I've
always liked the *femme maîtresse* kind of women, so I
suppose she was really rather my type. Anyway I never
wanted to believe in my own hatred of her, I half hoped
it was something silly about me, like the feeling I had
when I was small that the cupboard on the nursery landing was inhabited by cannibals. And really everybody
else seemed to worship her. All the greatest men in England came down and stayed at Gormont House, and
looked as if they liked it. Do you know, I've seen a Prime
Minister and a Lord Chancellor and the head of an Ox-
ford College sit round on the grass terrace at Gormont

and listen for hours while the old hag talked blood-
thirsty nonsense about Ireland, that would have been
recognizably nonsense whatever your views on Ireland
were, even if you thought Ulster Loyalists ought to be
allowed to eat Catholic babies on Friday as a double insult to the Pope."

"I think English society is perhaps particularly susceptible to the charm of insufferable old women," said
Isabelle.

"Well put," said Alan.

"No," said Isabelle. "It had too much the ring of
something an insufferable old lady might say in youth.
Your grandmother is terribly like what I might be in
my old age, if I do not alter my way of living."

"Rubbish," said Alan. "But I know what you feel
like, I've had just the same fear that I might end as a
replica of my father. I've got the right shoulders for
uniform, I did quite well in the army, and with my
serious, Vandyke sort of face I would look terribly im-
pressive if I worried about some British possession, particularly as I got older and went silver at the temples.
Only I'd choose to be worried about some possession
nearer England and with a better climate than India:
say Malta." He broke off. "I say, isn't this pretty tedious
for you, all this life and times of Alan Fielding stuff?"

"No, no," said Isabelle. "And I love being here. It is
so quiet."

"I know, we're getting that quietness which is better
than silence," he said. "It's the slight, steady rain. The
minute silvery sort of noise it makes kills all the other
noises. Well, to get back to my grandmother. She got
worse as she grew older. All my life she'd had a lover, a

man with a face like a boat who took a strong line in
foreign politics—if the Great War hadn't happened,
he'd have found another one for us—but she got terribly moral as she got too old for it, and she ran round
the country treeing poor wretches of schoolmistresses or
clergymen or district nurses if there'd ever been the
slightest whisper about whether they had or hadn't."

"One might do that," said Isabelle. "Any humiliation like age would be changed by this sort of destiny
into avenging cruelty."

"At last, thank God, she died," said Alan. "She was
fond, and if one wanted to regard the matter in a carp-
ing spirit, one might say over-fond, of grouse; fonder,
anyway, than one dare be at seventy-four. There was a
terrific flow of saliva from all sides. Admirals and judges
and clergymen peers all sent in recollections of her to
The Times and called her a *grande dame*, as if that were
the French for old bitch, and said how wonderfully she
had upheld the traditions of English aristocracy, which
simply couldn't be true, unless it is also true that that
tradition of English aristocracy consisted of unbridled
selfishness and stupidity and greed. They actually mentioned dignity in connexion with her, which was the
last quality she could claim, either physically or men-
tally. I was staggered. But everybody said it, so I just
went round thinking I had a blind spot and had missed
seeing something rather good. Then the crash came,
which knocked me out."

"I can't think what it was," said Isabelle. "It can't
have been anything you found out about Agatha, because you already knew everything about her."

"It was what I found out about everybody but

Agatha," said Alan. "You see, once she was gone, and
the requiem chorus had died down, they all blossomed
like the rose. My mother was a new being now that
Agatha didn't scowl at her as if she had sold the pass
to the Socialists, just because she sometimes had to lie
on a sofa. The butler looked twenty years younger,
Agatha's maid jumped at her legacy and rapidly went
twice round the world, with the air of a soul let loose
out of hell. The committees remained standing for two
minutes in homage to the departed and then sat down
and drenched the minutes in tears of joy. And the Prime
Minister and the Lord Chancellor and the Master of
Ballodham, all accepted invitations to Gormont Hall just
as often as they got invitations, and they used to sit on
the grass terrace almost visibly not regretting Agatha's
absence. In fact, every man jack of them had hated her
just as much as I had. They'd known everything I knew
about her, but they hadn't given it away."

"Because she was rich," said Isabelle.

"Exactly; and because they were swabs and cowards
and cadgers and spongers," said Alan. "I didn't like that,
since after all they were my own kind. I suddenly woke
up and realized that what are called nice people aren't
nice at all. They're very nasty. They've got an unfair
proportion of the world's goods, and only a few wipe
out that unfairness by what they do with their good
luck. The rest of them want more, and they don't care
how they get it. They'll close their eyes to any vice on
the part of anybody who's rich and who has a comfortable house they can go and stay in, or who can give
them tips on the Stock Exchange. They are complete
parasites, who can't earn their keep. My father doesn't

know anything about India, really. Not a thing that
would help to keep it or to make it more prosperous. All
he knows is that the inhabitants are coloured, a fact that
he interprets exactly as any old woman who has been
no nearer India than a Gloucestershire rectory. His
mind's amœbic, because the world's never demanded that
he organize it into efficiency. He's an old dear and so's
my mother, but they haven't put anything into life.
They've stood by while that old devil Agatha made girls
of seventeen cry and tortured her maid and prevented
slum nurses having decent meals and clothes and kept
miners' children on skim milk. I don't like it, since this
is the only life we've got."

"I know, I know," said Isabelle.

"And I can't stand my own generation," he said. "It
isn't their fault, of course. People like Agatha and my
father and mother haven't handed them on any principles, and they just barge about like a pack of monkeys.
I hate the ones who still have money, even if they do
their jobs, because they don't see that the system doesn't
work as a whole and has got to be stopped. And I hate the
ones who haven't got money and run about trying to
make a living and showing at every turn that they
haven't got as much fastidiousness as if they'd been born
in a slum. I hate the men who sell silly shiny cars to
silly men who haven't got anything to do but dash
about in them. I hate the women who sell silly clothes
to silly women who have no plans except to take them
off as often as possible."

"Poots was horrible," said Isabelle.

"Wasn't she?" said Alan. "It seemed such an offense
that she should be about when we first met. Yes, Poots

is foul. Well, it was to get away from all the Pootses that
I chucked the whole thing up and came over here and
bought this house, and settled down to live on a little
income I have, and what I made out of commercial stuff,
posters and textile designing, and so on. And I've never
regretted it."

"And you are perfectly happy?" said Isabelle, looking about her.

"Well, I would be," said Alan, "if I hadn't gone to
Le Touquet and met you."

She covered her lips with her fingers and looked piteously at him, but she could not herself tell whether she
was imploring him to advance or retreat.

Her hand was resting on the table; he put his over it.
"Don't take that away," he said. "I want to touch it, if
only out of friendship. I knew at any rate that we'd be
great friends from that very first night we met in that
pond of old trout at Lady Barnaclouth's. I saw at once
that I mightn't get everything I wanted from you, as
you were married and trying to make a go of it. But I
did think we'd quite possibly know each other awfully
well all the time till we died."

"I hope we will," she murmured.

"I was sure you would like the right things," he went
on, "because you so hated the wrong things. God, how
you hated that party! You loathed the whole lot of them,
the bawdy, skimpy girls, those tailor's dummies who
looked as if they wouldn't talk although the truth was
that they couldn't talk, those pretentious women gabbling about their spawn. You loathed them and loathed
them and loathed them, and I loved you for it. A train
of emotion started then that hasn't stopped."

His fingers closed on hers and loosened. She smiled blindly at him, dropping her lids, and said faintly, "I must have behaved terribly at that dinner-party if you could see how I felt about it. My manners must be very bad."

"No, they are perfect," he said. "But you have a little pulse in your throat that beats. I noticed it in the first five minutes after we met. It is beating now."

She took her hand away from him and covered her throat. She still could not look at him.

"You are the most nervous and fragile human being I've ever known," said Alan. "It frightens me, I wish to God you'd let me look after you."

She whispered, "But, Alan, you forget . . ." She paused because she did not know what she was trying to say. She could not be wanting to remind him that she was married, since she was going to leave Marc. Probably she was only satisfying that instinct for flight from all profound relationships which is the sincere basis of insincere maidenly bashfulness.

"If you're going to tell me that someone else looks after you, you needn't bother," said Alan. "I saw how that worked out at Le Touquet."

She cried out, and he said, "Am I a brute to remind you of that? But, my dearest, it's very relevant."

"You are perfectly right," she told him. Her voice was hoarse, as if she were very ill. "Of course that is relevant. It is more than relevant, it is supremely important. Of course I must think of that. Alan, you are charming, and you are so kind. You are so much better than I deserve."

"That I am not," he said, and raised her hand to his

lips, but set it down as the servant came into the room. "Ah, Mariette," he said heartily, "it's very kind of your mother to send us in some of that special jelly. Madame Sallafranque, this is one of my cook's greatest triumphs. . . . Oh God," he said, as she left the room, "I'll take a whack of this with both our spoons and she'll think we've both solemnly consumed some. It's revolting stuff, made of mistletoe or parsnips or something else that human opinion has long ago and most wisely decided is totally unfitted for making jelly. If you don't mind, I think we'd better go upstairs to the studio and have coffee up there, for if we hang about here, the meal is apt to be prolonged and to become distressingly regional. It's only by God's mercy we haven't already been sent in some cheese which, thank Heaven, is only made in the Franche-Comté."

Up in the studio Alan put his arm round Isabelle's shoulders very kindly, while she looked round her, murmuring at the pleasantness of the place. She liked the blue-grey paint on the walls, the sound the rain made running down the sloping skylights. For a little they sat on the floor beside the bookshelves, which were full of the pearly roughness of paper-covered volumes, the smaller ones brownish and dishevelled, the large ones smoother and paler, while he showed her a book he was fond of, about the Summer Palace at Peking. Then they leaned over his work-bench and looked at some drawing-boards, on which there were the beginnings of some textile designs, but they were only whorls and cubes as yet, she could learn nothing about him from them. She was about to ask him to uncover the veiled picture on the easel or turn round any of the canvases that were

propped against the wall, but with a sudden gentle roar
of enjoyment he took her to admire two pages he had
torn that morning out of an art magazine and pinned up
on a screen. In one a wing fetched an angel's shoulder
right up through the paper, according to the will of an
unknown sixteenth-century Italian painter, in the other
Dufy evoked the raffish expatriate palm trees on the
Promenade des Anglais at Nice.

She thought, "He is full of intelligent interests, there
will be no narrow and perverted passions suddenly breaking out and running away with life, everything will be
easy and fluid." When the servant had brought them
coffee, and they had drunk it and put down their cups,
a silence fell, and she lowered her eyelids and waited,
expecting him to touch her. But she heard him draw in
his breath and utter an exclamation of distress at her
intense pallor. She opened her eyes and covered her
mouth with her hands, ashamed because of the concern
in his face, which was more than she could ever deserve.

He said, "You must lie down on the divan, you really
must," and when she had settled herself, he threw over
her a coverlet of very soft chestnut-velvet. "I won't talk
to you for a bit," he told her, "I've overtired you terribly, you've got to rest." He tiptoed to the other side of
the room and sat down on a couch, while she lay still
and held the velvet over her face, delighting in the bloom
of its softness against her lips. Over and over again she
said to herself that at last she had found peace, until she
was no longer conscious of his tense self-effacement, and
she fell asleep. But there came a scratching at the door
and she cried out and started to her knees, thinking that
someone had come for her. But Alan said, "I'm so sorry,

it's the dogs, they usually drift up here about this time,"
and he went and let in two collies. They crossed the room
making a sound as if knitting needles were rattling out
of their paws, and lurched up on the sofa, and were
bade to be quiet; and she drew the velvet over her face
and tried to sleep again. But the time for that had passed.
She rolled over to speak to Alan, meaning to ask him
how he had begun to paint, but remained silent because
she was disconcerted by his appearance. The dogs were
sitting on each side of him, importuning him for sugar,
and with their long well-shaped heads, their strong flashing teeth, and their shining eyes, clear brown like peat
streams, they looked too like him. She felt as if she were
contemplating marrying into the Kennel Club. She rolled
back to face the wall, and stared at its blue-grey paint,
and listened to the rain pouring down the skylights, telling herself how fortunate she was to have been received
into this peace. Seeing her move, he said, "I don't wonder
you can't rest, with that infernal racket. I do love sunshine and hate the rain." His words made her remember
how Marc loved rain. She saw him as he had been one
day in that summer in the garden of her first clinic, as
pleased with a cloudburst as if it had been a firework
display, crying out with pleasure as the heavy peony-
buds, gashed with red, bobbed up and down under the
gross drops and the mud bounced up brown and liquid
from the flower-beds. The recollection nauseated her.

She sat up and took a comb from her hand-bag, and
began to set her hair in order. Alan whispered across
the room, "Isabelle, marry me, marry me." She smiled
and blew him a kiss, and tried to whisper, "Yes." But no
sound at all came from her lips, and suddenly she found

herself becoming exasperated at the sight of Alan and
the dogs sitting in a row on the sofa, all looking at her
with their shining, good-tempered eyes. As an excuse to
look away she took out her mirror and powdered her
face, and then was able to say, "Alan, show me your
pictures."

"Why now?" he grumbled.

"Please, please," she said.

He said reluctantly, "I will if you like. But they're no
good really, you know."

"I want so much to see them," she said.

"Well, if you must, you must," he said reluctantly.
"There's one on the easel that I've just finished." He
rose, and the dogs dropped off the sofa after him. "It's
nothing really, just a corner of the garden," he said,
twitching off the cloth and looking down on the picture
pensively. The dogs stood at his knees, gazing up at it
and slowly wagging their tails. From their attitude every
one of the three might have painted it. "Perhaps I have
got something in that light on the wall beyond the gate,"
he decided with modest complacency. "Yes, I think you
may see it," he said, standing back.

She stood up and swayed for a minute. He came over
to her and held her up in his kind arms. "You had better
lie down again," he said. "I am going to look after
you."

"No, I want to see your picture," she said.

He did not let go of her, so she felt his heart beating
while she asked herself, "What is wrong with it exactly?" and said aloud, "But it is charming, Alan, it is
really charming." She freed herself and put her hands
on each side of the frame, and felt as she had done when

she put her hands on her hips after she had lost her child, as if barrenness itself lay between her palms. Her skin was smooth, her bones were delicate, her muscles kept their cunning, but her womb, which should have been full, was empty and a type of ruin. She had only the memory of fertility. This picture recalled many pleasures, it remembered grass and trees and flowers and the quality of light, but it was a memory of life, it did not live. It was a part of death. She tried to put a name to what it lacked, and knew instantly that it was something which would have been present in any picture that Marc had painted.

"Do you really like it?" asked Alan.

She looked up into his delightful face and marvelled how she could ever have thought that his gentleness could fight the violence and disorder that she hated. That could only be worsted by a force greater than itself, such as made Marc so strong a man. She found herself glowing as she said, "Alan, I adore it," and continued to think of Marc.

"Great guns, how lovely you are looking!" said Alan. "Do you know that you have completely changed in the last ten seconds? You look awfully well now, well to the point of hockey-playing. I don't believe that I care very much whether you like my picture or not."

"But I do, I do," she murmured, moving away from the easel.

"I'm telling you that I don't care whether you do or don't," said Alan. He was fiddling with some paint on the canvas and spoke without looking round at her. "What I want is an assurance that you're going to be sensible and leave Marc and marry me."

Isabelle stood silent, wringing her hands and looking at his back.

"Speak up," he said, with easy lazy confidence.

"No, I'm not," she said.

He swung round and looked at her incredulously. "Here, what's all this?" he asked.

"I love Marc," she said. She added, "I know I have behaved disgracefully," but she was so happy that she gave the words the wrong intonation and broke off.

"My good girl, you're lying," said Alan. "I just don't believe a word of this. Marc treated you vilely at Le Touquet and you know it, and you've been very unhappy ever since."

"We are neither of us lying," said Isabelle. "He treated me atrociously at Le Touquet, and I knew it, and I have been very unhappy ever since. Nevertheless I love him."

"Look here, are you sure I haven't rushed you and that you aren't stalling for time?" asked Alan. "I can't believe a word of what you're saying. You aren't a doormat and you aren't perverse. I refuse to believe that you can love a man who got drunk and gave way to an idiot passion for gambling while you damn well nearly died at his feet."

"Ah, ah!" said Isabelle. "Now you have hurt me."

"Hurt you?" said Alan. "I've only pointed out to you what Marc did to you. I can assure you I've always wished I had the chance to hurt Marc."

"No, no," she said, a painful eloquence rushing out of her like tears. "You have pointed out to me what I did to Marc. Listen, listen. I have been feeling guilty all the time at the back of my mind as if I had done something to Marc, but I could not think what offence I could have committed against him, since all the offences in the situation seemed to have been committed by him against me. But now I understand. You have just explained it to me."

"That's clever of me," said Alan, "because it must be a tricky point, from what I've seen."

"I will not be able to tell you exactly what it is," said Isabelle, "because it is a part of our marriage, it is something private to ourselves. I do not mean that it is anything physically intimate, I mean that it is hard to explain except to people who are married themselves."

"I believe you are talking about something that is real to you," said Alan, regretfully.

"I am, I am," said Isabelle, "and I must tell you about it, partly so that you will understand that nothing is less thinkable than that I should leave Marc, and partly because it will be a help to you when you get married, for you certainly must get married, and partly so that I shall not forget it myself. For one forgets the best things in life, the other things press in on one so. Listen, listen. You said that Marc got drunk at Le Touquet and gave way to an idiot passion for gambling while I damn well nearly died at his feet."

"Well, that's the cold truth," said Alan.

"No, it is not," said Isabelle. "It is not the truth at all. That is just how much a stranger would make out of the facts when he looked at them from outside. But I am Marc's wife. I was in a position to look at the facts from the inside, to know the real truth."

"Do you mind telling me what that was, in your opinion?" asked Alan.

"Ah," she said, "it is such a long story. He was so

tired with the strain of running that great business, you
cannot believe how tired he was. Why, the morning after
we got there we went and sat on the sands, and he fell
asleep with his head on my skirt. I had forgotten that.
Oh, God, what has happened to me that I could ever
have forgotten it! Then the whole system you hate, of
luxury and parasitism, closed in on him. He hated Poots
because she was vile and because he was sorry for Luba.
He was so nice to Luba, you cannot think how much
nicer to her he was than any other man would have been.
And then Lady Barnaclouth settled down on his nerves,
as she has settled down on everything good and rich she
has ever come across in her life, and saw what she could
peck out of them. And there were the d'Alperoussas, who
threatened his work, his life. Then he got drunk, and
once he was drunk he did not know what he was doing,
and what he did struck him as it struck me, for it was
his child as well as mine that died. My God, my God,
how could I have forgotten that?" She was weeping, and
had to swallow her tears to say, "It is an extraordinary
thing, and I do not approve of it, that I am much more
excited than I usually let myself be, and yet I believe I
am talking much more sensibly than I usually do. But
let me go on. I have been making this hideous fuss because I was hurt by the loss of my baby, and I felt a
mean impulse to take it out of life by hurting someone
else, and of course I got the maximum sensation out of
hurting Marc, because he is nearest to me. I gave way
to that impulse without restraint, because I am a rich
woman and have never been disciplined. So I committed
this horrible offence of treating my husband as if what
strangers saw counted, which destroys the whole purpose

of marriage, which betrays the trust which is the real
point of marriage. It is a cad's trick, but of course I am
a cad because I am a privileged person, and the two
things are bound to be the same. In fact I am Agatha."

"You are not," said Alan, as she dried her eyes, "you
are just what I thought. I might have known I couldn't
get you."

She put away her handkerchief and wound her arms
round his neck and said, "Oh, Alan, forgive me for coming here to see what I could get out of you. I saw I could
get heaven from you, you are so nice. But I ought to
have known that I loved Marc. How did I come to forget it? That is what I cannot understand." Laying her
face against his cheek she begged, "But don't cast me off
altogether, I am so fond of you." To herself she said,
"You are touching him in such a way that he will remember you as more beautiful than you are, you are
etching yourself on his memory as deeply as you can.
Can you not leave him alone if you don't want him?"
She was obliged to answer, "No." Nor, she reflected, was
this the sole way in which she was an exceedingly unpleasant woman. "I am like Monsieur Campofiore, only
I crave moral and not material riches. Heiress as I am
to ethical squalor, and exposed throughout my childhood to every disadvantageous influence, I am driven on
through life by an insatiable craving for goodness. But
even as Monsieur Campofiore hates those who are born
to the kind of wealth he covets, so I hate Marc, who is
naturally good. How I detest myself! But I must struggle on under the burden of what I am."

The dogs, aware that distress had entered the room,
uttered faint well-bred whimpers against her skirts; and

Alan turned from her a face that was wooden with misery. "Oh, my dear!" she whispered. "Please do not mind so much! You should be sorry for Marc, I am so dreadful a creature! You will be so much happier with someone nicer than I am!" But there rushed through her veins the hope that she would not have to stay comforting him too long and could return to Marc. She listened with delight to the sound of the rain running abundantly down the skylights.

XIII

WHEN ISABELLE entered the little library, she found Marc sitting in an arm-chair, looking at his shoes, while the maître d'hôtel moved about the room, picking up the newspapers and journals which covered the floor, and addressing his master with pointedly casual remarks of a stoical tendency. "At the end of life, they say," Isabelle heard him pronouncing, "one usually finds that life has been neither so good nor so bad as one thought it." As he perceived her, he became silent; and her ears were immediately caught by a certain risping sound with which she was already familiar. She looked about and found the Siamese cat drawing its claws down the back of Marc's chair.

Whipping it up, she said to the maître d'hôtel, "Could you find any use for this cat if we gave it to you?"

He was, as she had often noticed before, particularly at her dinner-parties, a contemplative. He said, "Madame is extremely kind, but I am not sure . . ." Across his face there could be seen rolling, like slow ideological cyclones, complicated doubts as to the morality of keeping animals with untamed instincts in the confinement of a home, of providing them with delicate food for which many a human being might have been glad, of lavishing affection on them when their response was bound to be partly mechanical and partly mercenary. Isabelle said, "Ah, well, I think I saw Marcel outside." She opened the door and called to her husband's valet, who was lingering in the hall with an air of eagerly awaiting an opportunity to serve his master's interests, if necessary by an act of self-sacrifice; although his actual purpose was probably to collect the commission on some clothes returned from the dry cleaners'. "Marcel, could you take this cat if we gave it to you?"

He looked at her sharply to make quite sure that she meant it before he asked, "Oh, Madame, do you really mean it?"

"Most definitely," said Isabelle.

"Then, Madame, I'll take the little darling with pleasure," he said. "I know the very home for it, where they're aching for a cat, their own, which they worshipped like their own child, having just died and they not having the money to buy another one. Ah, it will be pleasant to see the bright faces round that hearth when they find what Madame's kindness has brought them."

"He is going to sell it, of course," said Isabelle, when he had gone. "But we would only have talked about it, and never have done it. Marc, Marc, what is the matter?"

Marc said, "That is not like you, Isabelle. That is like some quite other kind of woman. To give a present I had given you to a servant, because it is all over."

"But, Marc," she said, "you do not understand. I gave the cat away because we cannot possibly keep it when there are children about the house, so we might as well get rid of it now, before it does any more damage."

"But of what children are you speaking?" said Marc.

"Why, of ours," said Isabelle. "Whose else?"

"My God, my God," said Marc. "Are we not going to be divorced?"

"Certainly not," said Isabelle. "But of course, I have not told you. I realize now that it was an absurd idea. Do you not think so yourself?"

He did not answer but sank back into his arm-chair. Panic filled her, the room became black, she flung herself down between his knees and cried, "Marc, you have not begun to like the idea during the day? Marc, I cannot bear it, I could not live without you. Tell me that you do not want to leave me!"

He muttered, "No, I do not want to leave you," and put his hands under her armpits and raised her until their mouths were level.

When her lips were free, she said, weeping, "I did not know," and he answered, "Neither did I."

"One knows nothing," she said.

"Nothing," he repeated.

They clung together, and forces within them, which they could not have identified by any name, which were harsher and more pitiable and more august than love is supposed to be, used their two bodies, as if in an effort to wrestle clear of the flesh and fuse.

At last Marc said, "We will live quite differently. I will look after you so well. I will never make a fool of myself again."

"Hush, hush!" she said. "You must not talk of that any more."

"Why not?" he asked. "I was a fool, a murderous fool."

"But we must not think of that any more!" she murmured. "We are going back to the beginning. The thing that happened was only a mistake, it was an accident, now I want to forget it, I want to think of you as being better than I am in every way. But what am I saying?" She started to her feet and stood in confusion. "That sounds abject, but it is not. I want to feel like that about you not because you are a man and I am a woman, but because you are you and I am I. If we were different people and I were really better than you, I should be quite content to think it, it should be possible for a wife to feel that her husband is not superior to her and for the marriage to be all right." But she stopped and covered her eyes. With reluctance, because Roy was still dear to her, she saw her first marriage as splendid but relatively insipid. Thinking of it was like watching an aeroplane speed glittering through high blue space with the monotony characteristic of successful flights, and it appeared to her the secret cause of this insipidity, this monotony, was that she had never felt Roy to be better than herself. They had been equals and comrades, as she approved. She cried, shuddering, "Marc, I cannot understand it, I feel we ought to be equals, and yet I know you to be my superior, and I like it. Tell me, is everything I have thought about men and women wrong, or am I being swayed by my emotions?"

"How soon after all this you are able to talk," said Marc.

"But if we do not talk about it, we will not understand it," said Isabelle, "and we must understand everything about ourselves or we may go wrong again."

"Oh, I am not blaming you," said Marc. "No, I do

not think you need worry about your feeling that I am superior to you. For I too feel quite sure that you are superior to me, and I too like it. So, you see, that makes a kind of equality between us."

"Nonsense, that will not do," said Isabelle. "You could not have two people running a department in your works, each thinking the other was the head. It would have to be definitely settled which was first and which was second."

"My works," said Marc, "though doubtless among the most important objects in the universe, are not a pattern for all departments of it. I think the process is a little different. You see, none of us can see our own faces. The faces we see in mirrors are not our own, the left is turned to the right, and as soon as we know that we are regarding our own images we falsify our experiences." He rested his brow on his hand and became silent.

"Go on, go on," she said.

He lifted his head with an effort and continued, "You see in my face a self which I do not know, which must amount to far more than myself as I know it, since it is the sum of all that has happened to me, and I only know what is happening to myself from minute to minute. You think the self you see in my face is superior to yourself, just because you can't see your own face, because you too judge yourself by the minute to minute specimens, which are only parts of the whole."

She deliberated gravely on what he said, cupping her chin in her fingers. "Perhaps you are right," she said, "but still I think that people who look on both our faces would like your self better than mine."

"Do not be stupid," he said. "You know that you are talking of what never happens. Neither of us ever shows a true face except to the other. That is why we are important to each other." He dropped his head on his hand again, and his muffled voice went on, "It is a mystery, it is all a mystery. I have often thought that in loving you I love a woman of whom you have never heard, of whom you have not the slightest idea, who is nevertheless entirely real."

Isabelle said nervously, crossing her hands on her breast, "You are making too much of the mystery, I do not think there are many women to be made out of me. I am as clear as glass, you know everything about me. . . ."

She paused. A number of things that he did not know about her, or knew falsely, raced through her mind. He believed that she had loved André de Verviers in proud, dumb misery, like a sculptured woman on a sarcophagus, folding her marble draperies across her marble lips; whereas she had known with him first a cheerful delight, almost wholly without implications, like swimming or riding a good horse, and then a nightmare vexation as of clearing up the litter of a picnic-party in a high wind. He believed that she had smiled kindly at a door closing on Laurence Vernon, and gone back to her book with relief; whereas, in the infatuation of that time, she had longed for his pithlessness as if he were more than even the flawless man she imagined, as if he were a way of living that led to peace. And Marc did not suspect that at the moment she had promised to marry him she had indeed been a sculptured woman, folding her marble draperies across her marble lips, her eyes as sightless with humiliation as if they were chiselled circles. In

astonishment she recalled the flash of Marc's yellow shoe
as it flew up to kick the waiter's behind in the vestibule
at Laurent's. She stared at him as he crouched in his
chair, so obviously and pre-eminently the most valuable
object that the world could offer her, and realized that,
when she had actually taken the first steps towards marriage with him, she had believed it to be a farce into
which she had been compelled by a tragedy. In fact,
though in a sense Marc knew everything about her, he
was grossly mistaken about her relations with the most
important people in her life, including himself; and
though her mind lay open before him, vowed to a perpetual extremity of candour, there was in fact nothing
less possible than that she could correct these errors.

Marc looked up at her and laughed. "You look so like
a little girl when you suck your thumb like that," he
said, and again let his head fall forward on his hand.

Isabelle stood still in perplexed silence. The motives
that had brought her to this marriage, she reflected, were
a secret not only from Marc; should she make them public, the whole world would disbelieve either in them or in
her present emotions regarding him. That was not how
love was supposed to begin. In fact, this was an uncharted
universe. But Marc was saying something, speaking very
indistinctly, his lips against the palm of his hand. "What
is it?" she asked, kneeling at his feet.

He said, "All day there was just one thing I thought
of over and over again."

"Oh, darling, was it something good?" she asked. "I
do so hope I left about some piece of evidence which
showed my real mind, which showed I would not lose
you for the world."

"It was the telegram," he said. He narrowed his eyes and nodded at her, sly, like a peasant. "The telegram from your friend Blanche. I figured out to myself that, if it were all finished between us, you would not be able to bear being alone, you would want to run back to somebody you had known in the old days when you were a little girl in America. But you did not think for one moment of going to stay with Blanche. But then . . ."

She cried out and put up her hand to smooth away the lines on his face.

"But then I had to remember that you are stiff-lipped, you have grand manners, you will not break. Other women who had left their husbands might run about to their friends, telling them all about it, but you would not, you would go white and precise and would see no one. I could see you, like a cold day. I became sure that the very reason you had refused to go and stay with Blanche was that you meant to divorce me. Ah, don't do that, don't pity me, for then I became atrocious." He pounded on the arm of his chair and began to shout. "I pretended to myself that your grand manners were a lie, that underneath them you were just like all other women, that when you seemed to differ from them it was just a woman of the world's trick, and so all that argument didn't apply. I went about saying to myself, 'Ah, she's just like the rest of them, if she'd really done with me she'd be with her gossips!' And then I couldn't keep that up, to pretend you were not proud is like pretending that a cart that goes on four wheels goes on two. Do you know what I did then? I dwelt on what I'd done to you. I said to myself, 'Yes, she is proud, but think what agony she has been through, I made her lose her child, that would break down anybody's reserve, if she were going to leave me she would have to talk, so my argument about the telegram holds.' I said that to myself. Isabelle."

"Will you be quiet?" she sobbed. "It is not only I who talk too much. Kiss me."

They clung together, and again the forces within them wrestled and nearly met.

"But one knows nothing, nothing at all," she breathed, when they had come to the end of their strength.

"Nothing," he murmured.

"Why are we so important to each other?" she asked. "Why does it matter as much as food and drink that we should be close like this? Why is it so necessary that we should make love? It is not merely a question of pleasure."

"No," he answered, "pleasure one can get anywhere."

They both covered their mouths with their hands and were silent, thinking of people outside the room.

After a little Isabelle said, "I wish I were not a woman."

"You had better leave things as they are," said Marc. "It is your only chance of being where you are, as my morals are not what they call special."

"No, I am speaking seriously," said Isabelle, "I detest being a woman." A sudden flame of anger passed through her and she slipped from his arms and went to the window and stood looking out on the paved garden and the trellis-work on the blank wall beyond, tapping her lip with her finger very slowly, in order to regain her self-control. She had never been able to live according to her own soul, to describe her own course through

life as her intellect would have been able to plan it. She
had progressed erratically, dizzily, often losing sight of
her goal, by repercussion after repercussion with men
travelling at violent rates of speed on paths chosen for
no other motive than the opportunities they gave for
violence. She had desired to make an ordered life with
Roy, her body and her mind had worked to accommodate
themselves to his; and all her adaptations had been made
futile and changed into jangling nerves of grief by his
rejection of all other activities in favour of the pleasures
of describing vast trajectories through space, no matter
what might happen at the point of impact. It had, of
course, been Roy's own fault that he had crashed. She
had never admitted it before, it had been too painful;
but Roy had taken a chance in letting the new and un-
tried mechanic test his engine that morning, just as he
had taken chances again and again before, with the
weather, with the fall of dusk, with uncharted country.
It was a wonder that he had escaped so long. She shook
with rage against him. Then she had ricocheted from
that shock to the arms of André de Verviers, where she
should have found the rest and harmony that comes of
matching beauty with beauty, had not his violent frivol-
ity sent her staggering to the violent act of destroying
the roses at his door, which sent her into collision with
the violent coldness of Laurence, which sent her into the
orbit of the violent heat of Marc. She shuddered, hearing her thin voice scream through the sudden hush in
the baccara-room at Le Touquet, feeling the pain sweep
in waves through her pelvis and slowly in the following
months change into a pain of the mind, but still keep
a physical lodgement in her breast.

In terror she thought, "All men are my enemies, what am I doing with any of them?" But then it flashed into her mind, "That is why making love is important, it is a reconciliation between all such enemies, and there are degrees in such reconciliations. My reconciliation with Marc is absolute." She turned and went back to him with outstretched arms. But as he drew her to him, she thought, "All the same, it is terrible what men do to women. Even if we annihilate the emotions it sets up, we cannot pretend it has no consequences. I may forget what Marc has done to me, but it has shattered me. I shall not be the same again." A voice advised her coldly from the remote recesses of her mind. Had you not better learn to put up with men, since there is no third sex here on earth? Or have you made arrangements for travelling to some other planet where there is a greater variety? But it would be as well at this moment if you did not think, but felt. Pressing her mouth against his, she tried to preserve a sort of fairness in life. "It is probably that I do something to men as dreadful as they do to me, without knowing it. Perhaps I trip them up just as they beat me down." But she knew that she was only softening the harsh lines of the picture her mind had taken of the world.

She said into his sleeve, "Also I do not like being rich."

"What, my silly one, do you wish to be poor?" asked Marc.

"Not in the least," she said. "That is a false alternative. If I dislike being lame, it is not because I desire to be hunchbacked. But do you not think that we live in some ways a detestable life? With Poots, and Lady Barnaclouth, and Laura and Annette, and all the pack of

them?" She had changed her sentence abruptly in order
not to name the d'Alperoussas, but she knew at once
that he had noticed it, and was aware of her line of
thought.

"Yes, our life sometimes forces us into surroundings
that are not sufficiently unlike a drain," he said soberly.
"But what would you have us do? Go Bolshevik?"

"Why not?" she asked, as soberly. But his brows came
together and he bent on her a kind, teasing smile, as if
she had said something endearingly, femininely foolish.
She thought, "How queer men are, they cannot detach
themselves from their surroundings and criticize them;
it is as if they were joined to the earth where they stand
by the soles of their feet." It occurred to her that Alan
Fielding had not been like that, but again a cold voice
spoke from the back of her mind and said, "But you
know he was not quite a man." She gripped Marc's
shoulders, enjoying their squareness, and with closed
eyes she cried out in his defence, trying to identify what
was necessary to her with what was right and subtle and
penetrating, "It is comprehensible enough that you should
not want to change society, because you have your work;
that gives you discipline, that keeps you in touch with
reality, when you do wrong you fail, when you do right
you succeed. But a rich woman, she is nothing, she lives
in a vacuum, insulated from life by flattery. One has
complete freedom of choice, and no experience of reality to tell one what to choose. That is why I so terribly
want a child, it is partly because I love you, but it is
partly because, when I am having it, it will be the only
time when my life is determined by necessity."

"Stop talking and get up," said Marc, rising to his feet.

"But if we do not talk things out, we will never know where we are," said Isabelle.

"Yes, I know all that, but at this particular moment it is not quite true," said Marc. "You see at the moment your lips are talking of one thing but your eyes are talking of another, and I think your eyes are talking the better sense. I would not dream of letting you have a child for at least another six months, but you are coming upstairs with me now. There is, after all, something between you and me which has nothing to do with children, which would exist if we were both sterile. Get up."

"Oh, not just now, not just now," murmured Isabelle.

"You are as heavy as lead to lift," said Marc.

When she awoke, the room was nearly dark, and Marc was standing at the end of the bed in his dressing-gown, looking down on her. They exchanged a smile; and she turned aside, drawing up the sheet to cover her breast, and pressed her still smiling face into the pillow and sank back into sleep. But Marc said, "Hé there! Wake up, there's something I want explained. Where are all the photographs of you that were in my room?"

"Oh, that," she murmured. "Ah." She rubbed her face into the pillows, and affected complete repose.

"No, I really want to know," he said. "You'll have to wake up in a few minutes anyhow. It's nearly dinner-time. Pull yourself together and tell me what you have done with them."

"It is of no consequence," she muttered, keeping her eyes shut. "I assure you they are all right."

"And where exactly are they?"

She opened her eyes. "At Cartier's," she said. "They

are having something done to them. I tell you it is all right."

"But what is being done to them?"

She closed her eyes. "They are being reframed in shagreen," she said, and drew the deep, regular breaths of a sleeping child.

"In shagreen! For the love of God, why? It will make my room look as if I were a tapette!" exclaimed Marc. "Now, it would interest me enormously to hear why you did that."

"Nothing seemed more reasonable at the time," she said. "I thought that the servants would all know at once what had happened if I left the house and then you suddenly put away all my photographs, so I sent them away to be reframed, as an excuse. It appears fantastic that only this morning I should have been so wicked. Oh, darling, how horrible it was. But, darling, why are you laughing?"

"Because the idea is so like you," he said. "It is so ingenious, and so subtle, and it would have made so little difference in the end." He blew a kiss over his shoulder as he left the room.

"Oh, darling, you are cruel!" she grumbled. Then she started up in bed, and called after him, "Marc, Marc! Come back! There is something I want to ask you."

He came back, still laughing, and sat on the bed. "Well, what is it? Upon my soul, though I have no further use for you at the moment, I must admit that you are a well-made woman."

"Why," asked Isabelle, "do you have those ugly photographs of me in your room? You know, the one of

me when I was at Miss Pence's school, looking a frosty
little prig, and that other dreadful one where I am looking like a giraffe at Rambouillet."

"Oh, I don't know," he answered, composing his features. "Somehow or other I like them." But he burst into
uncontrollable laughter again.

"I see what it is!" cried Isabelle, putting her arms
round his neck and shaking him. "You like them because they make me look funny, and you think that I
am funny! You think I do look like a frosty prig quite
often, and that I do look like a giraffe when I am trying
to be polite to people whom I do not much like, and you
like laughing at me!"

"Oh, no! Oh, no!" said Marc, but his laughter shook
him as he put away her arms and rose to leave her.

"Ah, you are cruel, you are mean, you are wicked!"
she complained, throwing herself back on the bed. She
remembered with what perfect taste André de Verviers
had chosen the three most beautiful photographs she
had ever had taken, and she cried out, in rapture, "Ah,
this is real love."

"One cannot have such good lust as we have had,"
said Marc, "without real love."

Isabelle did not think that she had better say that she
agreed with him; she covered herself up and returned
to sleep. When she woke again, the room was quite dark,
and she clasped her hands behind her head and lay
smiling at the vague summer stars behind the window-
panes. Then Marc's squat shape appeared in the lighted
oblong of the door, he turned on the switches, and the
windows became like mirrors. She leaned towards them

on her elbow, delighted by the reflection of her happiness.

"See how good a little man I am in my dinner-jacket," said Marc. "Madame will please make herself look more like the head of a household. Yes, that is better. I have told them to send up some dinner on a tray, since Madame is so recently returned from the clinic and is not yet very robust. And it appears that the American mail has come in. Here is the famous letter from Uncle Honoré. It is to me. But here is one for you."

"It is from Luba," said Isabelle. They were silent for some minutes, bending over their letters with that rapt attention which people find it easier to give their friends' written than their spoken words. Then Isabelle asked, "Why should wild geese fly north at the beginning of the winter? It seems excessively imprudent."

"I do not believe that wild geese would do any such thing, in spite of their reputation," said Marc. "Who says they do?"

"Luba," said Isabelle. "She says that the state of Missouri is exactly like Russia, and she has found a spot on the edge of her husband's estate where there is rough grass and some birch trees and a long view over the prairies, and it resembles the spot on her father's estate where she used to stand with her sisters and watch the wild geese flying north at the beginning of the winter."

"Well, it may have been so in White Russia," said Marc. "But how is she?"

"She does not say," answered Isabelle. "She says only that there are many wild geese in America, so she will be able to stand there in the fall, watching them fly overhead, and that she will feel then just as if she were back in Russia."

"One might have hoped for more precise news of her," said Marc.

"Yes, indeed," said Isabelle. "She is really the most provoking of creatures. There is hardly a line in the whole letter that is not about wild geese. Wait a minute, here is something written on the back of the envelope. But I cannot read it. Can you?"

"No, because it is in Russian," said Marc. "Really, this is very tiresome. We must get it translated at once, for if the poor girl's husband had died and she was left stranded without any money, this is precisely the manner in which she would choose to inform us. I shall take it down to the works tomorrow and find a correspondence clerk who can tell us what it means."

"We need not wait so long," said Isabelle. "The new footman is Russian, even to the extent of being called Ivan."

"I will give it at once to Marcel and tell him to get Ivan to translate it."

When Marc came back into the room, she asked him, "What is the matter? Has anything in Uncle Honoré's letter worried you?"

He answered, "It is perhaps a pity that I should have made it up with a wife who can see through me so clearly. I did not think I had given anything away. Yes, Isabelle, the news in this letter is not altogether good."

"Uncle Honoré is not ill?" she asked.

"No, he says he is in very good health," said Marc. "But he is not coming to Europe this autumn after all."

"Oh, Marc!" cried Isabelle. "What a shame! Oh,

Marc, I am so childishly disappointed! Much more than I would have thought I could be!"

"I knew you would be," said Marc. "I have thought lately that any woman who has endured as much as you have during the past few months must feel a natural desire to see some of her own people. But, darling, you must not cry. And surely you will not have so strong a need for him now that we are together again and are going to be happy."

"No, that is not so," said Isabelle. "Indeed I want him more now than before, to bless us, and to make me feel that I have people behind me as you have. And he is so sweet, he has such lovely clean white hair; he is always clean like a little white dog that has just been washed. And he is so kind, and so delicate. When my father and mother died, he did not stop me crying, but he conveyed to me that I ought not to cry too much, that it was an offence against peace and order if I did not cry less and less every day. I have always been able to rely on him to tell me what behaviour would hurt everyone least. That is partly why I wanted to see him now, he is so wise; there were a great many things I wanted to ask him. Tell me, does he not even suggest that we should go and see him?"

"No, but you must not be surprised at that, he is preoccupied with other things," Marc told her. "His letter is almost entirely about business."

"But is it not the case that business is going superbly?" asked Isabelle.

"Well, that is just the point," said Marc. "Your uncle has suddenly become afraid that it is going a little too superbly. An Englishman, who is greatly respected in the London world of affairs, has been visiting New York, and has frightened your uncle by prophesying a collapse. He says that American finance has become insane, and if prices rise any higher the whole structure will come tumbling down; and of course there have been some signs lately that the market is cracking. He has been going round among his banker friends and it seems that they too are feeling alarmed. So he thinks it will be wiser if he stays at home, and keeps an eye on your affairs and his own. He is acting out of affection for you all the time, really."

"Do you think he has any reason to feel frightened?" asked Isabelle.

"Well, I do not know," said Marc. "I am an industrialist, not a financier. But one has heard rumours. The stock market in America is really grotesque, you know. The increase in the capital value of your fortune during the last few years is so enormous that it must be pure fantasy, it can have no correspondence with reality."

"But what are you afraid will happen?"

"The people who are buying stock will suddenly realize that they are being asked too much for it and will calculate a proper price for it, and will pay no more than that. Then the people who hold it will hurry to get rid of it in the fear that the value will sink still lower, and they will throw masses of it on the market at the same time, and its price will fall and fall. Your fortune, which has been doubled for no reason, will be halved for as little reason. Then, since everybody has lost a lot of capital, they refuse to buy things. There is a slump. Then nobody buys my automobiles. Oh, you and I could get much poorer in no time, once that started."

"I hope we will," said Isabelle. He smiled at her indulgently, and she assured him, "I really mean that."

"I do not think you would like it so much if it really happened," he said.

"Of course I would flinch," she said. "I do not think that I have much courage. But I know that it ought to happen." She regarded him with curiosity. "Is it possible that you do not feel that the mould in which our lives have been cast is horrible, and ought to be broken?"

He shook his head, still smiling. "It is not so bad."

Yet she remembered quite well that she had seen him at certain moments when his vision burned dark, hating their circumstances as much as she did. But on his face, as on the faces of all the men she knew who had power over the immediate world, there lay an expression of acquiescence in what was going on around him, which was dissociated from the findings of the critical brain behind, yet was not exactly insincere. It was as if vigorous personalities found they could get their own way better by pretending that they had none other than the common will. So animals, who must go about the jungle unnoticed if they are to survive, assume protective colouring, and stand among the dappled leaves, dappled leaves themselves. "There is no compromise men cannot make," thought Isabelle; "they have no sense of objective reality. They feel that they can make it anew every five minutes if it suits them. The fact is that they do not belong to the same race as women."

The door opened and disclosed the butler handing over the dinner tray to Marcel. Marcel came in, set down the tray on the table by the bed, straightened himself, and handed Isabelle Luba's envelope.

"Ivan says that the lady who wrote that says she is going to have a baby, but she is not sure exactly when," he said.

"Indeed," said Isabelle.

"Ivan says, too, that in Russia women are very, very fond of babies," continued Marcel.

"Indeed," said Isabelle. "Thank you, Marcel." She dipped her spoon into her soup, and when he had left the room, she said, "Well, that is news which one might have preferred to hear more privately. Still, I am more glad than I can say, to hear that everything is settled and Luba is happy. But really Marcel is very impudent. He should not have let us see so clearly that he thinks Ivan a fool. One's servants are terrifying. By the way, how is it that that snob of a cook has given us this glorious onion soup?"

"It is my doing," said Marc. "She was going to give us something with a lot of that pond-weed parsley floating about in it, but Marcel let out to me that they were having this downstairs, so I told them to keep the other for themselves and to send this up to us. By God, I am hungry."

They were silent for a time, bringing up the spoonfuls of good brown gravy to their mouths. Isabelle thought, "It is not because Uncle Honoré is heartless that he does not want to see me, it is because he is growing old. When one gets old, the hands get thin, the voice gets thin, the affections get thin. And indeed he could not have helped me if he had come, if he feels the most important thing in the world is to keep our money, for if I have learned anything, it is that the most important thing in the world is to lose it. Yet he was wise in his day. What a frightening world this is, if the wisdom of one day is the folly of the next! It makes being wise seem not worth while, yet I am sure that there is nothing else worth doing." She said aloud, "Why are you laughing at me again?"

"Because you are so sweet," said Marc. "You think everything ought to be unsettled, and then when you hear that a woman is going to have a baby, you say that now everything is settled."

"And what is funny about that?" she asked.

"It is just a little bit of a contradiction, that is all," he said.

"Well, there are many things in life that seem to be contradictions, and we will be able to reconcile them only when we know more," said Isabelle pedantically. She put out her left hand and he caught it in his, and at the same time he looked past her, with a concerned expression of his mouth, a triumphant lifting of the brows. She had not the least idea what he was thinking. It struck her that the difference between men and women is the rock on which civilization will split before it can reach any goal that could justify its expenditure of effort. She knew also that her life would not be tolerable if he were not always there to crush gently her smooth hands with his strong short fingers.

THE END